THE TWELFTH ENCHANTMENT

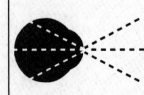

This Large Print Book carries the
Seal of Approval of N.A.V.H.

THE TWELFTH ENCHANTMENT

DAVID LISS

WHEELER PUBLISHING
A part of Gale, Cengage Learning

GALE
CENGAGE Learning®

Detroit • New York • San Francisco • New Haven, Conn • Waterville, Maine • London

LIBRARY OF CONGRESS CATALOGING-IN-PUBLICATION DATA

Liss, David, 1966–
　　The twelfth enchantment / by David Liss.
　　　p. cm.
　　ISBN-13: 978-1-4104-4517-9 (hardcover)
　　ISBN-10: 1-4104-4517-8 (hardcover)
　　1. Young women—England—Fiction. 2. England—Social conditions—19th century—Fiction. 3. Byron, George Gordon Byron, Baron, 1788-1824—Fiction. 4. Blake, William, 1757-1827—Fiction. 5. Large type books. I. Title.
　　PS3562.I7814D37 2012
　　813'.54—dc23　　　　　　　　　　　　　　　　　2011042969

Published in 2012 by arrangement with Random House, Inc.

Printed in the United States of America
1 2 3 4 5 6 7 16 15 14 13 12

For Eleanor and Simon

1

The house was astir with activity, which was something most unusual, for its owner, Mr. Richard Lowell, preferred his home to remain a very dour and torpid place. Accordingly, what transpired was activity without delight — that of a graveyard in which the sexton erects a particularly large or novel tombstone. Metaphors of this sort came easily to Miss Lucy Derrick, on whose behalf this commotion centered, for it was her intended husband whom the house prepared to receive. Lucy had no wish to entertain that gentleman. None at all. It was not that Lucy did not wish to marry Mr. Olson, for she had no doubt that marrying him was the most practical thing to do. Nevertheless, she would very much rather avoid the necessity of making conversation with him.

Marriage, as Lucy understood it, involved only infrequent dialogue upon the most essential of subjects, but today her role would be to think of all sorts of engaging things to say, which would not be easy, for Mr. Olson was no great talker. She had not yet discovered how to hold his interest, for their previous exchanges had been at gatherings and assemblies, where dancing or the consumption of punch could stand in for anything resembling an actual exchange of ideas and sentiments.

Mr. Olson's social charms, such as they were, had no bearing on her decision to marry him. More than anything else, Lucy wished to be free of her uncle's house on Pepper Street — near, if not exactly in, the most desirable neighborhoods of Nottingham. She wanted sufficient money that she could feed and clothe herself without reminders of the burden presented by these encumbrances. She wanted to be free of prying and critical eyes, free of the perpetual fear of making an error for which she would be punished like a child. She wanted to feel as though her life were her own, that it was a life in which she belonged, in which she had choices, purpose, even some pleasure.

There had been a time when Lucy had hoped for the things all young ladies desire. She had been the sort of girl — which is to say a very ordinary sort of girl of the middle ranks, though perhaps more that sort of girl than most — who took it upon faith that she was destined for a great and adventurous love. She had two older sisters, and surely at least one of them would marry with the family's security in mind. Their practical unions would free Lucy to follow her heart, and she had longed to do just that.

Lucy no longer believed herself destined for anything in particular. Her life had come to feel alien, as though her soul itself were not hers, but a copy so clever in its construction that it very nearly deceived her own body. She had been thrust into a strange existence, and her real life had been lost in the misty past, like a favorite childhood toy whose features she could not recall even while her longing for it remained painful and vivid.

In preparation for Mr. Olson's arrival, Lucy thought it advisable to make herself as presentable as her limited circumstances would permit, so she had no choice but to depend upon her uncle's serving woman for aid. Mrs. Quince was near forty, and once handsome herself, but was now faded in both beauty and color. In the three years since Lucy had traveled the near two hundred miles from Kent to Nottingham, she'd seen Mrs. Quince's hair turn from bright orange to the dull russet of an overripe peach. Her complexion, previously creamy in its pallor, had turned the befreckled sallow of old linen. Lucy did not take actual pleasure in watching the woman's last charms vanish, but she did experience a sort of grim satisfaction.

The only advantage she had over Mrs. Quince, over anyone, was her youth.

Lucy owned little enough that was presentable, and what she had was purchased of her small annuity, resentfully provided by her sister's husband. Today she wore her best afternoon frock with a bodice *en cœur,* pale blue with white filigree — charming if one but overlooked the fact that it was suited to fashions popular three or four years past. This was Nottingham, however, and Mr. Olson would be disinclined to notice even if she presented herself in a costume of the second Charles's reign. Or the first's. Lucy doubted he would notice much at all, despite her looking quite well that afternoon. She was of slightly below-average stature, somewhat dark of complexion, and, if no striking beauty, she was, in the view of most men, certainly pretty with her long nose, arched brows over large eyes, and moderately, if not excessively, full lips. Mrs. Quince, who was very tall and slender, often called Lucy fat, but Lucy considered herself — in contrast to Mrs. Quince — to be shaped like a woman rather than, let us say, a boy.

It was no comfortable thing to put her appearance in such ungenerous hands, but Lucy thought it wisest to submit herself to the older woman's grim ministrations. Mrs. Quince had ever been solicitous of Mr. Olson's connection with Lucy, and had shown cheerless satisfaction with the proposal. Now she helped arrange Lucy's hair, pulling on it, Lucy suspected, harder than necessary. Still, she was dexterous at such matters, and Mrs. Quince arranged her charge's hair — just shy of black in its darkness — so that it appeared contained, and yet a few strands wantonly escaped from her bonnet to frame Lucy's round face. When she was finished, Mrs. Quince paraded her before her sepia-toned mirror, and Lucy flattered herself that Mr. Olson would be getting no frump for his pains. Perhaps if he would flirt, she might like him better.

Mrs. Quince made one last adjustment. "I've done what I can," she said. "Your hair is almost negro in its coarseness, and it clings to your head as though wetted by the rain."

"Thank you, Mrs. Quince," Lucy said in a fair approximation of gratitude.

"Thank you, Mrs. Quince," she repeated, imitating Lucy's slightly nasal voice. "You might attempt to be polite given that I am making an effort to present you to the world as something respectable." This she punctuated with a derisive snort.

When she was sixteen, Lucy had briefly run off with a gentleman nearly ten years her senior, but the scheme had been disrupted soon after their departure. Lucy marked this moment as the end of her childhood, the end of her happiness, for during her brief absence,

11

Emily, her beloved elder sister, died from a sudden illness. A year later, Lucy's father died, and then Martha, the middle sister, entered into an unhappy marriage. One disaster after another, leaving the fabric of Lucy's life an unrecognizable tangle of thread, and all beginning with her own act of foolish defiance.

Then and now, Lucy could not help but wonder what role her elopement had played in the unmaking of her family. Had she not been so reckless as to run off with Jonas Morrison, would Emily have fallen so suddenly and devastatingly ill? Would her dear sister Emily today be alive? Would her father have died if Emily yet lived? Would Martha have still married their cousin, that horrid clergyman Mr. Buckles? Lucy had sacrificed more hours to merciless speculation upon this subject than could be reckoned. Four years earlier, Lucy had nearly run off with a man, and that remained the most significant thing that could be said about her.

She had believed she truly loved Jonas Morrison, the young gentleman who had once enchanted her, but he had now become the worst of men in her mind. Jonas Morrison, with his easy conversation and his good humor and wit, with his endless card tricks and parlor illusions — pulling brightly colored scarves out of seemingly empty cups or making coins vanish, only to reappear across

12

the room. He had seemed to Lucy the most delightful of men, but his charm had all been a trick, like one of his clever artifices, an act of sleight of hand and misdirection. He was a monster who had encouraged a youthful Lucy to believe his wanton urgings were right and just and dignified, and all these years later, the mere thought of him set her to clenching her teeth and muttering under her breath. All of Lucy's life had been a game then, with her fine home, and many friends, and loving sisters, and her distantly protective father. She'd been safe and free to indulge her fancies and think nothing at all of consequences. Perhaps she had not truly believed in consequences at all.

She believed in them now. The exposure of her scheme had taught her all about consequences and humiliation and regret though, thankfully, not full-fledged scandal. She had been spared that at least, for while word of running off with Mr. Morrison soon became general knowledge, so too did the fact that Lucy was safely brought home without having given up her virtue. She may have been widely regarded as a foolish, impulsive girl, but at least she was not thought a whore. Perhaps her actions would have had more damaging consequences at the time had her family not been torn asunder by her sister's death, and so the wagging tongues of gossips made little impression upon Lucy or her father at the time. But Mrs. Quince would not permit her to forget what she had done. Early on, she had divined Lucy's antipathy to the name *Jonas Morrison,* and so she loved to use it freely. When Mr. Olson had begun to show an interest in Lucy, Mrs. Quince delighted in comparing him to the great *Jonas Morrison.* The teasing had abated somewhat once it became clear that Mr. Olson's attentions were serious, for she wanted Lucy gone from the house as much as Lucy wished to depart.

Mrs. Quince now adjusted Lucy's posture in the mirror and took a step back and examined what she saw, placing a finger to the corner of her mouth in a pose of thoughtful scrutiny. "I feared you would look the whore, as can often happen in these cases. Happily, I was, in the main, mistaken."

Being the sort of man who held punctuality as a cardinal virtue, Mr. Olson arrived at the appointed hour and, upon entering the parlor, bowed stiffly to Lucy. He then turned to Mrs. Quince, as if to say something, and then decided against it. He could make no sense of Mrs. Quince's standing within the household and so found it convenient to ignore her entirely. During this awkward moment, his eyes lingered for a second or two on Lucy, particularly, she believed, in the area of her neckline. Once he had taken note of her, his eyes did not return to take pleasure in what must soon be his. There was little to be gained in reevaluating merchandise whose quality he had already established.

Like his manners, his dress was plain and without affect. He wore a brown jacket of a somewhat antiquated cut, though he showed his fashion sense by wearing trousers rather than breeches, and a fine blue ascot hung clumsily round his neck. His limp brown hair hung slightly long and had been brushed forward in the front, as was the fashion. There was something intense in his sunken eyes that some women found arresting, but Lucy was inclined to find unnerving.

Upon invitation, Mr. Olson sat down in a chair across from her, his posture exceedingly upright. Lucy found her attention to be unusually sharp. It was as though she were seeing Mr. Olson clearly for the very first time. His rigid manner, his mechanical gait, his hooded, appraising gaze, and — at five-and-thirty — his extreme age. There was a faint, and not entirely unpleasant, scent of sawdust and tobacco about him. She had many times told herself that being married to him would not be so very bad, but though she recalled believing this, she could not take hold of the belief now.

To distract herself, Lucy did her best to make amiable conversation. She inquired how he did, and Mr. Olson assured her that he did well. She asked how the work at his mill proceeded, and so discovered that it proceeded apace. She asked after the health of his mother, and he reminded Lucy that his mother had been dead for several years. Perhaps, he speculated, she thought of his Aunt Olson. Lucy, who had not been aware that Mr. Olson had an aunt, conceded that he was quite right.

Theirs had been a cool courtship, with more awkward silences than bright exchanges, so it was perhaps unsurprising that there was so little to discuss now. They had traded a few stiff words and danced at various social events about town over the preceding year. After asking her to dance three times at the assembly last month, Mr. Olson had contacted Lucy's Uncle Lowell and proposed the marriage to him. Uncle Lowell accepted on her behalf, and, in turn, passed the intelligence along to Mrs. Quince, who related to Lucy the happy news. So it was that without ever having been asked, or having accepted, Lucy was now engaged to marry a man to whom she had little to say. It was therefore much to Lucy's relief when Uncle Lowell made his entrance into the room, and in her current mood, the irony of these feelings were not lost on her. What wisdom could there be in marrying a man whose conversation was so awkward that the arrival of her uncle must be regarded as an improvement?

Uncle Lowell was a relation by marriage, not blood — the widower of Lucy's mother's sister — and demonstrated perhaps more than the inevitable resentment toward an orphaned niece come to live with him. In his middle fifties, Uncle Lowell was a lean man, tall with an unyielding posture. He had some, though by no means much, of his hair, and that which remained was very white and cut short so that it rose up in a comical way at odds with his dour affect. The long, bulbous shape of his nose made his dark eyes appear deeper than their already considerable natural depth. His suit was of the same brown color as Mr. Olson's, but of a more antiquated cut, with breeches and stockings, and its heavy material gave the impression that any jostling might well liberate a voluminous cloud of dust. Lucy thought that if one but disregarded his quintessentially English attire, her uncle looked remarkably like a picture of a mummified corpse from the Americas she had seen drawn in one of the monthly magazines.

"Yes, yes, you are come, Olson. I've kept you waiting, but what of it?" Uncle Lowell demanded, daring Mr. Olson to object. "These affairs of mine could not be put off. A man of business like you will understand."

What these pressing affairs could be Lucy could not guess, for her uncle had been long disengaged from all serious business. If there was one thing Uncle Lowell prized above

17

money it was quiet, and so having made a fine fortune in the Levant trade, he had retired ten years earlier to his ancestral home in Nottingham. The house on Pepper Street was then in a state of disrepair, the Lowell family having not the means it once possessed. Mr. Lowell had altered the family means, but not the family home, and the building remained much decayed from neglect. The very room they sat in testified to that with its uncomfortable chairs, its scratched tables, its dusty, faded pictures, and a Turkey rug so stained, torn, and bleached with sun and age that the original pattern could scarce be divined.

Mr. Olson rose to take Uncle Lowell's hand with the brave determination of a schoolboy who knows his master's critical eye is upon him. "A pleasure, sir," said Mr. Olson, who appeared to derive no pleasure at all.

"The pleasure is mine," said Uncle Lowell, whose puckered mouth suggested that he derived even less.

"You know Quince, my woman," he continued, with a blunt jab of his middle finger. "She is my niece's companion, and will act here in the capacity of my late brother's wife."

Her mother had died when Lucy was little more than an infant, and she remembered nothing of her, but she nevertheless resented the comparison. Whatever her mother had been like, she had surely borne no similarity

18

to Mrs. Quince.

Once they were all seated, Mrs. Quince wasted no time in cutting to the heart of the matter. "Mr. Olson, have you discussed with Lucy a date for your wedding?" This was a disingenuous question, as she knew he had not raised the question at all. He had not so much as sent Lucy a note expressing joy at their upcoming union. "I cannot but think the sooner a date is set, the greater will be your happiness," Mrs. Quince added.

Mr. Olson turned to the serving woman as though the effort strained his neck, but then addressed his answer to Uncle Lowell. "It is not convenient to set a date. The establishment of my mill consumes my time. The machines are new and the workers unaccustomed to their use."

"Quite right," said Uncle Lowell. "A man who does not put his business first is a buffoon. And yet," added he who so wished his niece gone from his home, "I wonder if your efforts would not be aided by the acquisition of a wife to manage your household. You might then freely fix your mind upon matters of business."

"You and I think very much alike," said Mr. Olson. "I should be surprised to find you had considered an option that had eluded me entirely. I conclude the disadvantages of the scheme you suggest most certainly outweigh the benefits. A new wife must bring with her demands and distractions and difficulties to be resolved."

"Yes, yes, and I suppose you have your hands full with these" — Uncle Lowell waved his hand about the air, a gesture he often reserved for discussions of people he thought contemptible — "*Luddites,* as they style themselves. You must worry that they will set themselves against your mill."

"The Luddites are malcontents and brutes," said Mr. Olson, who now smiled for the first time since his arrival. "They are like children who complain a game is unfair because they have lost. I make twenty pieces of hose at a labor cost that would previously have produced but one, but they say that I take away their employment. It is their own fault for not being so efficient as I."

Lucy knew of these debates. Everyone in Nottingham did, for Nottinghamshire was the heart of this uprising of laboring men who set out to destroy the machines that had deprived them of their work and, as a result, beggared them. Now the army was in town to stop the Luddites, but everyone said there had been no abatement in the destruction. Not a week went by without a hosiery mill burned or fired upon or broken open and its machinery smashed.

Lucy's father had always been against these mills, had spoken of them as a curse upon both nature and labor. Once she had stood with him looking upon a pottery mill not far from their home, and he had shaken his head with disgust. "Behold one possible future, Lucy, and a terrible one. These mills strip their laborers of their humanity, and soon enough they may strip it from the rest of us." Lucy felt herself inclined to side with her late father over her future husband. Indeed, the growing poverty in the county over the past few years only made her more inclined to sympathize with the Luddites. Their wild rhetoric — with talk of their fictional General Ludd — and certainly their violent acts disquieted her, but given the shortages of food that had struck Nottingham, the weakened trade caused by the ongoing war with France, and the general decline in opportunities to earn wages, perhaps wild rhetoric was appropriate.

Though used to keeping such opinions to herself, Lucy now thought she ought to voice what had been her father's opinions in these matters. "But men lose their livelihood to machines like yours, and the wages you pay can hardly support a family. It is what I read in the newspaper." Both the man who currently paid her way in the world, as well as the one who proposed to take upon himself that responsibility, stared at her. In response to this silence, Lucy pressed on, affecting a light cheer in her voice. "Do not their grievances have some merit?"

Mr. Olson cleared his throat, perhaps to signal that he would bear the burden of addressing this question, but then paused for many agonizing seconds. At last, after indulging in a leisurely gaze upon his intended bride with an expression of something like surprise, or perhaps with a pinch of distaste, he offered his response to her inquiry. "It is a silly question."

All her life she had been dismissed as foolish. Emily had ever been the clever one, and Martha the bookish. She, the youngest, was but a silly girl, and her great mistake when she was sixteen had only confirmed to the world that she was an empty-headed thing, incapable of making sound decisions. Perhaps she had been silly once, but are not all children? She was now twenty years of age and did not like for her opinion to be of so little account.

"I find it distressing," said Uncle Lowell, "that you sympathize with these layabouts over your future husband. Let them open their own mills if they like. Mr. Olson cannot refuse to profit because doing so might cost another man his income."

Mr. Olson turned to Lucy, his expression an awkward attempt at softness. "I am certain Miss Derrick is only showing the goodness of spirit for which we hold her sex in such esteem. It is, however, my belief that one comment such as hers, while charming, is sufficient. Such a refrain soon becomes shrill."

"Just so," said Uncle Lowell. "My late wife always stayed away from my affairs. Lucy, I trust you will do the same."

Lucy knew her part. It ought to have been the easiest thing in the world for her to say that of course they were correct, that she could not hope to understand the complexities of Mr. Olson's business. In truth she did not, and though she felt compassion for the men she daily saw in want of food, she did not believe she comprehended either the cause or the solution to the changes that affected the hosiery trade. Yet that she was now being asked to rebuke herself, to promise never again to offer an opinion, infuriated her.

The heavy silence dragged on while the clock ticked and Uncle Lowell attempted to clear something from his throat and Mrs. Quince shot daggers from her eyes.

Lucy was saved from having to speak further by a violent pounding upon the door and the muffled sound of shouting from without. This noise continued for some time, for, other than Mrs. Quince and the cook, Uncle Lowell employed a single servant, the same he had employed for near forty years. This was a stooped old fellow called Ungston who was distressingly slow in his movement, owing to arthritic joints. Lucy, who had grown accustomed to the sounds of the house, noted the distinctive shuffling noise as the aged serving man approached the front door.

"Rather a ruckus," said Uncle Lowell.

It seemed to Lucy someone ought to have gone to help the old man, but all remained seated, with ears cocked, better to hear whatever there was to be heard — which consisted of Ungston muttering while he unbolted the lock and then the creak of the heavy door.

After that came more shouting, which encouraged them to rise.

"Lucy Derrick!" an unknown man called. His voice was hoarse and ragged, but frighteningly powerful, and yet shrill, like a dog's howl. "I will speak to Lucy Derrick!"

The voice sent through Lucy a wave of confusion and guilt. She must have done *something* to cause a man to come to her uncle's home and cry out her name, but she could not think what that might have been nor to whom she might have done it. Like any young lady, she indulged in mild flirtations, and she enjoyed dancing at the monthly assemblies, but she had made no secretive connections. No one made love to her with serious intent, and she had neither teased nor spurned any man since her arrival in Nottinghamshire. She might be a gentleman's daughter with some personal charms, but her situation made her an uncertain match.

"What is this?" Her uncle pushed himself up from his chair. His was the sharp tone of a man who suddenly realized he had been cheated. As the burden of his niece was about to be lifted, here came some unexpected trouble to ruin the enterprise. His scalp turned red, and the fringes of his hair appeared to puff out, as a cat's fur when the creature is agitated.

Lucy did not trust herself to speak, fearing her confusion must be mistaken for culpability, so she only shook her head.

"Stay here," said Mr. Olson. He no doubt believed there was some other love come to claim his prize, and it would serve him right for his coolness, Lucy thought. Once Mr. Olson had left the room, with Uncle Lowell close behind him, Lucy managed to get to her feet.

"What have you done?" said Mrs. Quince in a low and dangerous voice. She gripped Lucy hard by the wrist and did not let go, though she did no more. On occasion Mrs. Quince would pinch or kick, and once she had even scalded Lucy with hot water, which had left a pale scar on the back of her hand. But Lucy's engagement to Mr. Olson had changed all that. The balance of power had begun to shift, and Mrs. Quince had been content to abuse Lucy when she was powerless, but it was another thing to take liberties with a young lady on the verge of independence. Still, she gripped hard and made no sign of letting go. "Is this some new Jonas Morrison with whom you play the whore?"

Lucy tried to pull away, but Mrs. Quince would not let go. "I've done nothing. I have no notion of who it is. But I wish to see."

Perhaps Mrs. Quince also wished to see, for she shoved Lucy before her and followed her to the front of the house.

As they approached the door, Lucy saw the intruder standing upon the steps. He no longer cried out, but he spoke loudly and with a great deal of animation. Out in the narrow street, a small gathering of pedestrians, and a single cart man, paused to observe the confusion.

The man on the steps was startling handsome, possessed of an almost feminine beauty. His face was sculpted and even and flawless beneath a wild tangle of black hair. His eyes were wide and dark and moist, even as they appeared red-rimmed and slightly crazed. He wore fashionable clothes — the close-cut jacket, a once-white shirt open at the collar, and buff trousers that were now all the fashion in London. These looked expertly tailored, but they were tattered below the knees and filthy. When she approached as near as she dared, Lucy saw that the man's boots were torn open upon their soles, and one of his feet appeared oversized and misshapen.

"I must speak to her," he said. "The leaves are scattered, and I must speak to her."

Lucy started, as though she'd stumbled into an invisible wall. Scattered leaves? It was as though she'd heard these words before, but she could not remember when, like something she'd dreamed, but long ago, lost in both confusion and time.

"Who are you?" demanded Mr. Olson. "You'll speak to no one without telling me your name and your business, and perhaps not even then." His tone was angry but also restrained. Something about the stranger suggested that he was not appearing at his best, and that a certain deference was advised.

"I must speak —" The stranger paused and looked up, meeting Lucy's eye. Something shifted and softened in his gaze. His eyes went wide, and his posture shifted. He took a deep breath and, for an instant so brief she might have missed it, he smiled, wide and brilliant. "You," he said. "Are you the lady I seek? Are you Lucy Derrick?"

Lucy found she could not speak, but she managed a slow nod.

The stranger lowered his head for a moment and then looked again at Lucy. "I've been sent . . . been made to tell you, that you . . . you must not marry him. You must gather the leaves, but you must not marry him!" He arched his back, threw his head toward the sky, and took a step backwards, missing the step and falling upon his side to the street. With his head down, as if in a posture of religious subjugation, he raised one hand and pointed at Mr. Olson.

Lucy turned away, which was very well, for she heard the ranting man begin to retch like a drunkard, and she took a step back in disgust. She might have retreated into the house entirely, afraid of she knew not what except that this — all of this — was about her. Somehow it was about her, and Lucy felt shame and humiliation afresh. She wanted only to run away, but she then heard gasps, then a woman shrieked, and Mr. Olson cried out in surprise. "It cannot be!" he said in a hushed voice. Upon the street one of the gathered crowd — a woman — called to Jesus to save her.

Unable to contain her curiosity, Lucy crept forward. Peering out into the street, she saw the man bent over, upon all fours like a dog. This strange and disordered and beautiful man was upon the ground. His body convulsed, undulating like a wave, and then he vomited again, emitting a long string of shining, nearly dry, silver pins. They fell from his mouth in a slow and steady stream, tinkling a thin music as they fell upon the steps.

When he looked up, the man locked his eyes with Lucy's, his expression full of yearning and a desperation so deep that tears came to her eyes. Somehow this astonishing man, this impossible event was about poor, penniless, friendless Lucy Derrick. She wanted to ask him how, to make him explain himself so she and the world would understand, but she could make herself say nothing. Then it was too late, for he wiped his mouth with the back of his hand and fell over, utterly insensible to the world.

2

Mr. Olson, with some marginal assistance from Ungston, managed to carry the stranger to one of the long-unused guest rooms on the second floor, where they set him upon a dusty counterpane and left him, mumbling incoherently, seemingly unaware of his sur- roundings. Having done his duty as the youn- gest and fittest man present, Mr. Olson departed without further comment.

The moment he was gone, Uncle Lowell, with Mrs. Quince at his side, turned to confront Lucy. Anger had scalded his scalp purple, and his thin mouth twisted with consternation. "He will withdraw his offer of marriage, and I cannot say I blame him. Can't blame him at all." He looked upstairs, in the vague direction of the stranger.

Mrs. Quince nodded gravely while he spoke. Unless solicited, she knew better than to venture an opinion when her master was in such a temper.

"He'll need a doctor, I suppose," Uncle

Lowell said. "You tease a man into swallowing pins, and I will have to pay for his care out of my own pocket. My own pocket! It is as though you've sent a thief to my home to rob me in the night."

Lucy had a great deal of difficulty composing herself, for she had no way of making sense of the events she had only just witnessed. She felt the tears welling up, but she knew her uncle and Mrs. Quince would choose to interpret tears as a sign of guilt rather than confusion.

Lucy found herself desperately missing her father. He would know what to do. He would know what these strange events meant. With a withering glance or a stern aside he would have silenced Uncle Lowell, but her father was dead, and she would have to manage on her own.

With a great effort, she took a deep breath and spoke the words she had been rehearsing from the moment she had recovered from the initial shock. "I have never before looked upon that man. I have no idea who he is or what connection he could have to me — and as for the physician's bill, perhaps the stranger will pay it himself."

"Pay it himself! Quince, the girl says he will pay it himself."

Mrs. Quince shook her head. "I heard the words, but I can hardly credit them."

"Hardly credit them!" cried Uncle Lowell.

"He will pay for a medical man when he cannot pay for shoes. Quince, send for Snyder, if you please. You may tell him to give the *gentleman* above the bill. Perhaps he will vomit forth shillings to settle matters."

He strode from the room and slammed the door to his study, but Mrs. Quince remained, her mouth pinched tight and bloodless. "Miss Lucy Derrick," she said, her high, almost girlish voice now a sort of singsong. "It was only a matter of time until you found some new Jonas Morrison with whom to play the slut. Shall you destroy your uncle's health with your scandals as you did your late sister's?"

Lucy stepped back, fearful that Mrs. Quince would punctuate her words with a slap. When no such violence came, and it became clear that the serving woman awaited a reply, Lucy managed, "You must fetch Mr. Snyder."

Mrs. Quince walked about the room, adjusting a painting and removing a line of dust from atop a sconce. "I shall indeed, for if that man dies, he cannot tell us what you have been about. What is he, Lucy? A merchant's son? An innkeeper? A dissolute gentleman? I know you have a fondness for *those*. And what shall happen now? Mr. Olson will never marry a girl so scandalized as you, and your uncle will expel you for your crimes." She nodded at her own wisdom and strode from the room with her chin up, like an actress upon the boards.

32

Lucy remained in the parlor, close to the fire, though she could not banish the chill that left her teeth chattering. She hated life in her uncle's house, hated it beyond anything she had ever known, but to be cast out with no prospects was unthinkable. She was twenty years old, and Uncle Lowell had no legal obligation to care for her. He was also a man singularly immune to reflection and therefore capable of sending Lucy away and giving no thought to what suffering and horrors would become her fate. When Lucy, newly orphaned, had first come to live with her uncle, she would sit for hours dwelling upon the staggering injustice of her life. In those first few months, Mrs. Quince had been her friend and had comforted her and confided in her. Then everything changed, and Mrs. Quince became cold and cruel and hateful, and Lucy imagined herself the most put-upon young lady in the world. Her miseries had been real enough, but she had known them to have finite boundaries. Now she faced a bottomless abyss of suffering, a life in which there truly were no limits to the pain, humiliation, and want she might know. The threat of ruin was real, and it was true, and it could be upon her as soon as tomorrow.

When Mr. Snyder arrived, he went upstairs at once, and Uncle Lowell and Mrs. Quince joined Lucy in the parlor. Uncle Lowell demanded that Lucy vacate the seat nearest

the fire so he might be warm while he brooded in reptilian silence. Mrs. Quince sat near him with her needlework, her fingers quick and dexterous. Now and then she would let out a breathy laugh at some unspoken thought. The tall case clock, off in its timekeeping by at least fifteen minutes, ticked as erratically as a dying man's heart.

After no more than half an hour, the medical man entered the room, bowed, and stood with his hands behind his back, like an officer awaiting orders. Snyder was a serious sort of man, the type many would choose for their physician. He was of about Uncle Lowell's age, though he wore his years with more dignity, and dressed in black so that he was often mistaken for a man of the church. Not tall, he possessed a thin frame and narrow, humorless eyes the color of mud. Lucy had seen him often in the years she'd lived in her uncle's house, and had never observed him to smile. He made a habit of presenting his findings with absolute confidence, but today he looked about the room with a great deal of uncertainty. He began speaking three or four times before he could find his words.

"I am afraid, sir, that I can do nothing for your guest," he said at last.

Lucy heard herself gasp, and though she put a regretful hand to her lips, the damage was done. Mrs. Quince turned to sneer at her.

Uncle Lowell leapt from his chair with the vigor of the genuinely wronged. "You mean he is to die here? I'll not pay for his burial, I can assure you."

Mr. Snyder prodded the fraying fringe of the rug with the toe of his shoe. "What I mean, sir, is that if there is anything to be done, I cannot do it. His suffering is not of a medical nature." He placed his hands behind his back and stood erect, as though preparing to say something momentous. "I believe the man suffers from what is . . . is commonly called a curse."

A silence, heavy and vibrating, filled the room. Lucy had seen the man vomit pins, but even so, she could not have been more astonished if the doctor had said he suffered from the ill effects of a voyage to the moon.

Uncle Lowell stomped his foot like an angry child. A cloud of dust rose up in reply. "A *curse*, Snyder? Are you an old woman to say so? My opinion of you is no longer what it was."

Mr. Snyder bowed. "You have in the past done me the honor of heeding my advice, and I urge you to do so in this case."

"I thought you a natural philosopher, not a superstitious fool," Uncle Lowell barked.

"Natural philosophy, above all things, concerns itself with what can be observed," said the doctor in the sort of calming voice medical men use to convince others that they know of what they speak. "If I were to presume I possessed the skill to cure that man simply because I have trained as a physician, then I would be guilty of irrational belief in what no evidence has demonstrated. I would, in point of fact, be guilty of clinging to superstition."

During this exchange, Lucy sat pressing her hands together hard enough to make her knuckles ache. It all seemed so unreal, and yet it concerned her as nearly as anything ever had. She looked over to Mrs. Quince, who was now turned away from Snyder. *She* might know something of curses if anyone did, but she volunteered nothing.

Lucy ventured to speak her mind. "Sir, we have all heard tales in which the vomiting of pins signifies bewitchment, but perhaps he simply swallowed them?"

"No," said Snyder. "I — I saw things during my examination. I will not discuss the particulars — I will never speak of what I saw to anyone. Suffice to say I have no doubt in my mind that this gentleman suffers from an affliction medicine cannot remedy."

"And so you plan to desert me?" asked Uncle Lowell. "You cannot cure him, so you walk away and leave this man in my care?"

"Not quite," Mr. Snyder said. "In my youth there were several cunning women with excellent reputations in the county, but they have since died. However, I know of a lady recently come to town — not a cunning woman, but a respectable gentlewoman learned in such matters."

"You tell me to invite a witch into my home?" Uncle Lowell cried incredulously.

"She is no witch, but a lady of means."

With great reluctance, Uncle Lowell listened to the information about the woman and suffered Mr. Snyder to depart. He then turned to Mrs. Quince and commanded her to go fetch this woman at once. "Tell her I will brook no delay," he said, apparently forgetting or disregarding Mr. Snyder's comments about the lady's status.

"It is dark, and I am quite disordered by these events," Mrs. Quince said. "I should like to take Miss Derrick with me."

Lucy never wished to go anywhere with Mrs. Quince, but under these circumstances, she wished it less than any time she could recall. It was extremely uncharacteristic for Mrs. Quince to request Lucy's presence unless there was some difficult or unpleasant work to be done, but Lucy was not now surprised to be summoned. Given the unusual circumstances, they would now have to speak of private things, of the one secret they shared. There was no helping it. Best to get it out of the way, for though there was nothing but bitterness between them, fate had conspired to place them in a position in which they must protect each other.

3

With the dull motions of a somnambulist, Lucy put on her gloves, a warm bonnet, and a plain muslin pelisse. She stepped out of the house with Mrs. Quince, and they both walked in silence for a brief while. It was cool and crisp, and the Nottingham streets were lightly trafficked. Lucy believed it unlikely the rough men who caused so much trouble in the country would dare molest two such as they, walking upon the fashionable lanes in the shadow of the castle, but in the spring of the year 1812, it was difficult not to be frightened. These once-placid streets were now haunted by luckless men, hulking and impoverished and starving, skulking about with their shovels and hammers and spades. They sought to destroy, to beat back into its proper shape a world that had betrayed them with war and famine and rising prices. Twice before Lucy had seen bands of these Luddites, though only at a distance, and they had shocked her with their sunken eyes and animal desperation.

After several minutes of silence, Mrs. Quince finally spoke without bothering to turn to Lucy. "Shall I presume you are the cause of that man's difficulties?"

Lucy could not help but laugh. "You know far more of these matters than I."

"Now you would call me a witch?" snapped Mrs. Quince.

"I only suggest that what little I know I have learned from you."

"I hardly know anything myself. Perhaps you have studied elsewhere," said Mrs. Quince.

"Of course not," answered Lucy, and this was mostly true — certainly true for all practical effect. Lucy had once secretly purchased a book, *The Magus* by Francis Barrett, with money from her meager annuity, but this volume had proved utterly unilluminating. In any case, she could not quite make herself believe in the seriousness of these things. Did Mrs. Quince truly suspect Lucy cooked up hexes and spells like a witch in a fairy tale? What they had done together those years before now seemed silly, no more than a girls' game, and they had not attempted anything so implausible as a *curse*. Yet Lucy knew learned men had believed in such things for millennia. Her father had directed her to read about the lives of Paracelsus and Cornelius Agrippa and Isaac Newton

— great thinkers and natural philosophers who also delved into magic and alchemy and the summoning of spirits. Only in the modern world had the educated begun to reject such beliefs. Yet, here she was, walking the streets of Nottingham at night to find a mysterious woman who might help lift the curse off a handsome stranger.

Three years ago, it was Mrs. Quince, then her friend, who wished to explore such matters, who said it would be fun, who laughed with her about the secrets they might discover. Now that business was being thrown in her face, as though Lucy were to blame.

The doctor had informed them that the woman they sought, Miss Mary Crawford, lived on High Pavement, which was among the most desirable streets in Nottingham, but her house was modest, very narrow and lower in height than those surrounding it. They walked up the steps, and Mrs. Quince turned to Lucy. "I shall speak. Pray do not trouble the lady."

Within moments of their knocking, the door opened, and a curious sort of woman greeted them. She grinned widely and absurdly, showing a mouth of perfectly white and even teeth. She was plump and of indeterminate age, with a dingy complexion, narrow eyes, and a round face that would conceal many wrinkles, assuming she was old enough to possess them. This woman might have been thirty or she might have been fifty. She wore a shapeless, mouse-colored frock, and her bonnet was so low upon her forehead that it rested just above her eyebrows, and its odd placement gave the woman the look of a simpleton.

"It is Miss Lucy Derrick!" the woman cried out with evident joy, and grabbed Lucy by the hand. "Oh, you must come in. Miss Crawford will be so happy to hear of your arrival."

Lucy did not try to escape the woman's firm grip, but her mind raced in confusion. She did not often forget faces, and she believed she must recognize the woman if they had previously met. Now, with her accusation only minutes old, Mrs. Quince stared at Lucy with cold fury.

"I am very sorry," Lucy said, "but I do not believe I know you."

The woman waved a plump hand dismissively. "Do not trouble your mind, my dear. We've not met, but how could I not know a young lady as sweet as Lucy Derrick?"

Lucy had no answer to this question, and for entirely different reasons, neither did Mrs. Quince, but they allowed the peculiar woman to lead them into the sitting room, which was a small but comfortable space.

"I am Mrs. Emmett," the woman said to Lucy, ignoring Mrs. Quince entirely. She reached out and took Lucy's hand in both of

41

hers. Her skin was warm, almost hot, and as soft as a baby's. *"Mrs. Emmett."* She pronounced each syllable with much exaggeration. "You'll recollect it, I hope, Miss Derrick. You'll not forget me now."

"Indeed, I shall not," said Lucy.

"I am so happy." She released Lucy's hand. "I shall fetch Miss Crawford at once."

She then hurried out of the room, muttering to herself and waving her hands excitedly.

Mrs. Quince, who did not love to be slighted, turned hard to Lucy. "You claim to have no knowledge of curses, and yet the cunning woman's servant knows you."

"She does appear to, but you heard that she did not expect me to know her. Perhaps she foresaw my arrival in the cards," Lucy said, enjoying the moment of sauciness.

Mrs. Quince snorted and turned to examine the gilt wallpaper, which she said she thought rather shabby for a gentlewoman's.

After a few moments, they heard the approach of feminine footsteps, and in walked a strikingly pretty woman of perhaps five-and-twenty, tall and graceful, with fair skin, hair so blond it was nearly white, and extraordinarily pale green eyes. She wore a fine tunic of green and gold, cut square in the front, and cut low, as was also the London fashion, and it showed her shape to great advantage. She dressed as though she were entertaining or prepared to go out, though Lucy could see no signs that either case was true.

She did not hesitate to take Lucy's hand. "Miss Derrick, I am Mary Crawford. I hope my woman's excitement did not trouble you. She has seen you about town and admired you. Mrs. Emmett has her peculiarities, but she is a good woman and means no harm." There was something about her — not her appearance certainly, but some elusive quality — that made Lucy think at once of her late sister, Emily. It may have been the way she tilted her head when she spoke, or in the kindness of her words. Perhaps it was the hint of cleverness that revealed itself in even the most banal statements.

That had been the essence of Emily — not merely her remarkable, if unusual, beauty, with her nose slightly too large, her lips too thin, her chin too long — not merely her wit or charm or winning conversation. Emily always gave the impression of being thoughtful and clever. She projected warmth and friendliness, and at the same time she had seemed *superior,* yet she appeared utterly insensible of her superiority. This remarkable confluence of appearance, demeanor, and ease had made her loved by virtually all who knew her. Some friend or other was forever inviting her to travel, and she spent nearly half the year, every year, away from home, off to London, York, Bath, Brighton, even Edinburgh and Cardiff. Everyone had wanted to be near Emily, and Mary Crawford had, if not precisely the same charm, something very like it.

"I assure you, I took no offense." Lucy made the deliberate decision not to introduce Mrs. Quince, in part because it felt quite pleasant to slight her, but also because she could not help but feel that she wanted this lady all to herself. "I come upon truly unusual business, Miss Crawford, and I hope you will forgive *me*."

"I am certain whatever you have to say will require no forgiveness. Please, sit down. Perhaps your woman will wait in the kitchen? Mrs. Emmett can fetch her a pot of small beer."

"I am content where I am." Mrs. Quince met Miss Crawford's eye, but she was not so bold as to sit herself.

"Of course," said Miss Crawford, who gave Mrs. Quince a sidelong glance that, to Lucy, suggested she understood everything.

Mrs. Quince had said she wished to do the speaking, but now Lucy believed it fell to her to explain her situation as best she could. "I hardly even know how to state this business, but there has been a strange incident at my uncle's house, and we have been advised to seek your aid." She went on to provide a summary of the evening's events, beginning with the arrival of the stranger and concluding with Mr. Snyder's recommendations.

"I have not the pleasure of knowing Mr. Snyder well," said Miss Crawford, "and I met him only briefly, so I fear he misunderstood the nature of my experience with the old knowledge. While I am something of a student of the hidden arts, I have no skill as a practitioner."

Lucy leaned forward, fascinated. "But you believe in magic? You think it real?"

Miss Crawford laughed, not unkindly. "If you had seen all I have seen, you would understand that it is not a matter of belief. From what you describe, you have seen remarkable things this night as well."

"What we saw was indeed remarkable," admitted Lucy, "but I am convinced there must be some manner of explanation."

"Certainly there is," agreed Miss Crawford. "Most likely, this man is cursed."

"What we have thus learned," said Mrs. Quince as she airily looked out the window, "is that you claim this man is bewitched, but you can do nothing about it. If that is so, I see no reason we should trouble your quiet any longer."

Lucy felt herself flush with shame, but Miss Crawford's smile remained fixed and kind and entirely directed at Lucy.

"I do not know that I shall be able to help this man, though I shall be able to tell you if he suffers a bewitchment or no with a high degree of certainty. Once we establish that,

45

well . . . then we shall see."

Miss Crawford had a carriage at her disposal, which she insisted they take the short distance to Uncle Lowell's house. They rode in uneasy silence, and Lucy could not help but suspect that Mrs. Quince, with her glowering mood, was the cause of it. Even in the dark, Lucy saw Miss Crawford cast her the occasional kind and conspiratorial smile, as though they were allies together against Mrs. Quince, and Lucy had the strangest feeling that she and this lady were friends, and that they had been for a great while. She knew it was but a flight of fancy, but she clung to the idea of having such a friend.

Upon their arrival, Lucy introduced Miss Crawford, believing her uncle must be charmed. He was, however, unimpressed. "Pretty for a witch, I'll warrant, but pretty don't signify," he said, apparently oblivious to Miss Crawford's presence or his unpardonable rudeness. "I'll not pay a farthing for gypsy tricks."

Lucy felt her face burn. "Miss Crawford wants no money" she said, using her most soothing voice. "Only to help if she can."

"It is what they say," replied Uncle Lowell. "If there is a bill to be delivered in the end, present it to the vomiting vagabond. I promise to pay nothing."

Lucy took a candle, and the four of them ascended to the guest room, which was cold

46

for want of a fire, and was lit by only two small oil lamps. There, in the gloom, they gazed upon the shadowy form of the stranger, who lay on the bed, curled up like a kitten on top of the counterpane, breathing in uneven rasps. Lucy took the opportunity to observe his uncovered misshapen foot — hooked and twisted like a beast's wounded claw. It was awkward to be so close to so handsome a man in a state of undress, and Lucy turned away.

Miss Crawford took the candle from Lucy's hand and crept forward to examine the stranger. She came within a few feet of him, held out the light, and then nearly dropped the taper. She stepped backwards, and her face twisted with surprise or perhaps fear.

Lucy ran forward to take her elbow. "Are you unwell?"

Straightening out and affecting a calm demeanor, Miss Crawford shook her head. "It is nothing, thank you. It is only that . . . I cannot say. There is something very wrong here."

"And it is now, I suppose, that you say you shall make everything right for a guinea!" cried Uncle Lowell. "You must think me the greatest fool who ever lived."

"I shall show her to the door," offered Mrs. Quince.

Lucy knew better than to apologize for her uncle. Instead she relied upon the tools she had always used to survive in his and the serving woman's company, which is to say, she ignored them as best she could. "What must we do, Miss Crawford?"

Even in the dark of the room, Lucy could see the concern upon the lady's face. "I cannot say what there is to be done. I can — I can try to do something. I must have some quiet. I beg you all to leave the room. All but Miss Derrick. You will stay with me, won't you?"

Lucy wanted to stay with Miss Crawford, certainly, though she did not know how she felt about staying with this undressed stranger.

"I shall remain too," announced Mrs. Quince, "to protect the interests of the household."

"I must request otherwise," said Miss Crawford to Lucy, ignoring Mrs. Quince entirely. "I do not think your woman's proximity will aid my concentration."

Mrs. Quince turned to Miss Crawford, and something hot and angry burned in her eyes, but she swept from the room, and Lucy indulged in a little thrill of triumph. It was childish, yes, but she did not care. *She* was the favored one now, and she watched with pleasure as Uncle Lowell and Mrs. Quince stepped away, so that only the two young ladies remained in the dimly lit room with the door closed.

Miss Crawford sighed as she set her candle down upon a little table near the fireplace. "Now I must do what I do not love. I must attempt to practice."

"Does it hurt you?" asked Lucy.

Miss Crawford laughed good-naturedly. "No, it is simply something for which I have no talent. I also hate to play at the pianoforte, for I am very bad at it, and the attempt makes me feel useless. I understand the principles of magic, just as I understand those of music, but I was not formed to excel at either. Even so, for the sake of your household, I will try."

Miss Crawford closed her eyes and stilled her breathing.

"You quiet yourself." Lucy had not intended to say anything, and she regretted the words the instant she spoke them. She hated when words escaped against her will. It was a feeling she knew too well. With Mrs. Quince, the consequence for a slip of this kind might be a pinch or a slap or a public scolding, and Lucy winced out of reflex.

Miss Crawford turned to her, the surprise visible upon her face even in the feeble light, but there was nothing dark or angry. "You know more of the cunning woman's craft than you admit."

"Only . . . only a little," she answered. "I attempted to learn to read the cards once, but I was not very good at it and — and it ended in a quarrel."

49

"With whom?" asked Miss Crawford.

Lucy surprised herself by telling the truth, though she had never before spoken of how Mrs. Quince treated her. She hated that the world would know how helpless she was, but now she found she wanted to tell Miss Crawford. "Mrs. Quince. She was kind to me once, long ago, but since that quarrel, she has not been my friend."

Miss Crawford clucked her tongue. "I don't believe I much care for your Mrs. Quince, so we may safely forget about her. I would like you to look for the source of this man's curse."

Lucy felt cold fear grip her. It was a near-blinding panic. Was it fear of Mrs. Quince or something else? She did not know why, but she did not want anything to do with helping this man. "I can't," she sputtered. "I know nothing of these things."

"You know how to quiet yourself," said Miss Crawford. "I cannot do it. At least I cannot do it well, for I have not the concentration. You must simply grow quiet and then, with your mind rather than your eyes, have a look about."

Lucy shook her head like a child. She had not attempted to enter this state of concentration, not since that afternoon, the last time she'd tried to read the cards with Mrs. Quince. She recalled it now in a jumble of images — Mrs. Quince's freckled complexion turning bright red, cards flying across the table, a crystal pitcher shattering. Mrs. Quince accusing Lucy of plotting against her. A slap across the face, shocking in its force and suddenness. Lucy had been unable to comprehend. She'd only known magic as something silly and trivial, something for street performers, or a kind of parlor trick practiced by wags like Jonas Morrison. She'd never understood why Mrs. Quince had taken the matter so seriously.

The thought of quieting herself filled her with a terrible anxiety, but she knew it was Mrs. Quince who made her feel this way, not the act itself, and certainly not Miss Crawford. As much as Lucy wanted nothing more than to step back and recede into the wallpaper, she was determined not to disappoint this lady. She bit her lip and squeezed her eyes shut for a moment. "I shall try."

Lucy took a deep breath and let it out slowly, and then repeated this action several times, slowing her breathing, trying to slow her heartbeat though it pounded loud and quick. She tried to silence the chatter in her mind. She felt the light of the candle. The proximity of Miss Crawford, and the strange man on the bed who radiated a dangerous warmth.

Then there was something else. Something red and black and angry. It burned, and yet, in her mind it seemed both cold and wet. On some deep level Lucy understood that if she paused to consider the contradictions of what she experienced, the sensation would vanish, like a vivid dream that dissolves into a jumble of images only seconds after waking. She held on to this experience by the thinnest strand of gossamer, and it nearly eluded her entirely. It was a glimpse of something that flickered like a candle and that she could only understand by putting together fragments. She had no knowledge of what it was, but she knew precisely where it was.

Breaking her concentration, Lucy strode forward. She opened the stranger's coat and, gripping the lining in both hands, she tore it, and there, tucked in the folds of the cloth, was a little package of white linen, no bigger than a crab apple, tied with what appeared for all the world to be human hair.

She began to reach out toward the bag when there was at once something between her and the bundle. It was dark and ill-defined and empty, and yet, for all its shapelessness, it seemed to Lucy to have a face — not composed of features precisely, but points within its blankness that stood in for features. It turned to Lucy and gazed upon her with its indistinct eyes and opened its absent mouth to reveal an even more black and undulating abyss within. There was something sick and wriggling about it, as swift and jittery as a beetle's legs as it lies upon its back. It was more terrifying than anything Lucy had ever imagined. It was terror itself, given a cold and shimmering nonform. Lucy's legs grew weak, and though she did not know it at the time, she would later realize she had nearly passed water where she stood.

If the encounter had lasted longer, Lucy would have been unable to resist the urge to flee, but from the moment she first saw the thing until the moment she acted, only a second or two passed. She had almost no time to feel the full brunt of the terror, and so she reached past the shapeless thing and grabbed the cloth sack and yanked it away.

She looked back and saw that the dark presence had gone, and the stranger was awake, staring at her with glassy eyes, but then he sank back to bed, unconscious once more.

Lucy took the little sack, and realizing she was no longer in the quiet state, she held it out to Miss Crawford.

The lady looked at the bag and then at Lucy. Her sea-green eyes were wide and moist. "Miss Derrick," she said, "that was most impressive."

Lucy held the package in her shaking hand. "What was that?" she managed, though her voice cracked as she spoke.

Miss Crawford put her own hand over Lucy's and smiled. "There are dark things in this world, and you have seen one of them, but it is gone now. Now we must get rid of the instrument that attached it to this man," she said. "A curse of this kind works upon the principle of sympathy. Whatever has linked the stranger to this bundle must still be in effect, so we must be careful how we destroy it. If we were to burn it, for example, it might cause that man to develop a fever or blisters, or possibly even burst into flame himself."

Miss Crawford took the package, set it down upon the little bed table, and began to untie it. The cloth unfolded as a square, and within in it, made of the same cloth, was a little effigy of a man, so bland and featureless as to be a model of any living person with four limbs and a head. Around its little cloth neck were tied strands of hair.

"Now we may safely destroy it," Miss Crawford said, clutching it in her hand. "It is inert. I shall toss it in the fire on my way out."

Lucy could not cease thinking of the shapeless creature she had thought she had seen or almost seen or sensed or whatever it had been. She opened her mouth to ask about it, but then decided it was better not to know. Already she began to doubt she had seen anything at all, to tell herself that her mind had combined shadow and smoke and fear and created a formless chimera. She liked believing this better than believing that the shape she had encountered was real.

To distract herself, she turned toward the man. "Ought he not to awaken?"

"I expect he will soon enough," said Miss Crawford. "Though free of the curse, he has been through an ordeal, and he will need time to recover."

They departed the room, and Miss Crawford put her hand on Lucy's arm in what felt like a gesture of friendship. Lucy looked up at Miss Crawford and saw her beautiful smile, and though she wished to hear more praise, she understood no words could ever capture the same force as that expression of respect and benevolence. Miss Crawford liked her. She approved of how Lucy had conducted herself. For the first time in as long as she could remember, Lucy felt as though there was a person in the world to whom she mattered.

4

Once Miss Crawford had departed, the fate of the stranger remained a matter of significant consternation for Uncle Lowell. He sent Mrs. Quince several times to investigate whether or not the stranger had yet awakened, and Uncle Lowell advised that she not be quiet when opening and closing doors. Still, as though a drunkard, the man showed no sign of rousing.

Lucy slept very ill that night, distracted as she was by her astonishing evening. Had she truly removed a curse from this man? Miss Crawford had seemed so sure of what she had said, and at the time Lucy had certainly felt that *something* had happened, but as each hour passed, she began to doubt that very much had happened at all. There had been no bright lights or shattered glass or other signs of wondrous things. The creature Lucy had seen, or believed she had seen, had been but shades of darkness, and it was possible, even likely, that the whole incident had been but an outburst of her imagination under Miss Crawford's guidance.

On the other hand, there was much that an overactive imagination did not explain, such as the stranger's peculiar outcries. He had said she must not marry Mr. Olson, but he had also said she must gather the leaves. She did not know what that meant, but the words echoed in her thoughts all night, like a haunting tune that, once heard, could not be forgotten.

Back and forth she debated with herself, pondering what was real and what was not, so the next morning at breakfast she was possessed of little appetite — in part from fatigue, and in part because, in the light of day, her situation with Mr. Olson seemed far more alarming than any supposed curse. Her life, which had been so unhappy, was on the verge of growing more terrible than she could imagine. There was no one to offer her advice, no one to tell her what to do, and this feeling of helplessness made her miss her father with such intense yearning that her stomach clenched and her lungs turned to stone in her breast.

Even as she felt his loss as an unbearable weight, she knew he'd been the man she cherished only in the last year of his life. Until her death, Emily had been his favored child; Lucy and Martha, the middle sister, had warranted little more than staccato bursts of conversation at meals. Mr. Derrick had room in his heart for only one of his motherless children, and Emily — clever, observant, and learned — was the obvious choice for a man who spent nearly every hour of every day sequestered in his library, tending to household business or losing himself in his books.

Lucy had never resented her father's overt preference. Her father's favoritism had always felt proper, so the emptiness she felt now had a familiar quality. Even when he had still been alive, for much of Lucy's life, she had yearned for him. She'd wanted him to talk to her, to tell her his private jokes, to invite her into his library and share his ideas and frustrations, but he had been always too busy with his solitude or with Emily.

Emily, for her part, had always appeared slightly embarrassed by her father's favoritism. Many times he would call for her and she would cry back that he must wait, for she was talking to Martha of a book, or listening to some gossipy story that Lucy was telling. It was Emily who taught Lucy the workings of the household, how to deal with merchants and tradesmen and laborers, who addressed her questions about the wider world and her own transition from childhood to adulthood. When she had been small, she went to Emily to cry over an injury or a slight from a friend. For a girl who had grown up without a mother and with a distant father, Emily had been the closest thing she had to a parent.

After Emily's sudden and unexpected death, Martha and Lucy feared their father would never recover. He shut himself away, barely ate, and spoke little but what the operation of the household required. Only once he had withdrawn entirely did Lucy understand how much of her father she had experienced through Emily — through the clever remarks no one but they understood, their conspiratorial whispers, the sounds of their laughter or spirited debates, muffled by the closed library door. Papa might have withheld himself from *Lucy,* but he had been there for Emily, and that had always been enough.

Then, one day, Lucy and Martha had been in the sitting room, sewing in mournful silence, when the library door cracked open, spilling forth sunlight. For weeks he had kept the curtains drawn, and now both sisters looked in wonder as their father walked to the door and stared for a long moment. "Lucy," he said, "I should like to speak with you."

She set down her sewing and entered the library, where he invited her, rather formally, to take a seat across from him by the window. They remained silent while Lucy breathed in the scent of tobacco and juniper. Mr. Derrick looked at his daughter, and Lucy stared out the window until she could stand the silence no longer. "We all miss her, Papa."

"Of course we do." His voice was clipped, almost impatient. "Tell me of the books you like to read."

The demand astonished her because it had no apparent connection to what had come before and because Papa had never before shown interest in what she read, or if she read at all.

"I like novels," she said.

"Novels are fluff," he said, hardly allowing her to finish speaking before he passed judgment. "Do you read anything else? History, philosophy, books upon the natural world?"

Lucy brightened, because she believed she could answer to his satisfaction. "I am now reading Mr. Lunardi's account of his balloon voyages in Scotland."

His eyes, long red from crying, grew wide, and faint creases grew at the side of his mouth. "Why do you read upon that? What is it that interests you?"

"There are machines that allow people to fly," Lucy said, filling her voice with wonder — perhaps intentionally, perhaps not. She was sixteen, and the distinction between performance and sincerity was not always clear, even to her. "How could I not be interested in marvels?"

He took Lucy's hand in his, and he wept unabashed tears, copious and silent. When he was done, he wiped his eyes with a handkerchief, smiled at Lucy, and let go of her hand. "I should very much like," he said, "to hear more upon the subject of ballooning."

From that afternoon until his death, Lucy had been his new favorite. She visited his library daily, talking to him of the books he gave her. He exposed her to the rudiments of ancient languages, Greek and Latin and especially Hebrew, upon which he instructed with an endless vigor. He directed her studies in astronomy, history, and particularly botany, keen that she be able to identify all manner of plants. He demanded that she learn the lives of medieval and Renaissance thinkers — dabblers in new science and old alchemy. She would struggle through these books all morning, and then her father would quiz her throughout the afternoons.

Then, after a few months of that, came the walks. Papa had always valued his privacy and quiet in his study, but now he took Lucy out into the woods surrounding their estate. He would bring his botanical books and test Lucy on her ability to identify barks and weeds and flowers and plants, making certain she could distinguish between common, Persian, and Algerian ivy or fringed, smooth, or hairy rupturewort. He talked of his love for those woods, of how he treasured the animal life, even the insects. Once he made her watch as an army of ants devoured a sliver of apple, for even when disturbingly savage, nature was always beautiful.

Never, not once, did he ask Martha to join them, and when Lucy suggested that she come along, he had dismissed the notion with a wave of the hand, as though the idea was too absurd to warrant a serious reply. Lucy found she wanted Martha's forgiveness for this sudden and unexpected elevation, but Martha refused soothing. "He's found comfort in you," she had said. "And so have I. And I'm glad it is you and not me."

"This is silly," Lucy answered. "It can be both of us."

"I am not like you and Emily," Martha said.

"I am not like Emily either," Lucy protested.

Martha had hugged her again. "You must not think I am jealous. I am only happy. Emily was bright, like the sun, and we could not see each other when she was here. But we see each other now."

It was true. In the weeks since Emily's death, Lucy and Martha had become inseparable. The idea that they had once been distant, while undeniably true, now felt absurd. It was why Lucy felt betrayed when Martha, shortly after their father's death, accepted a proposal of marriage from their relation, a clergyman named William Buckles. Harrington, the family estate, was entailed upon male heirs, and Mr. Buckles, a distant cousin, inherited the property. Martha believed she was looking after her sister as best she could, and when she'd broken the news to Lucy, they'd hugged and cried as though they had suffered yet another calamity. Lucy had looked at her sister, her quiet, bookish sister who never asked for anything, who never resented her siblings, who never dreamed that she ought to hope for happiness, and felt so gripped by love that it nearly broke her heart.

"You cannot marry him," Lucy had told her. "I know it is horrid to say, but he cannot make you happy."

"He can make you secure," Martha said. "How can I be happy otherwise?"

If Martha did not marry Mr. Buckles, she too would have nowhere to live, but Lucy believed this fact never occurred to her sister.

Papa, for his part, had detested the idea of the marriage when Buckles had first proposed it, for he detested Buckles as a simpering buffoon, but Papa died only a few months after the proposal, leaving the girls paupers. When Mr. Buckles renewed his offer, Martha accepted at once. In the end, the marriage did little to ease Lucy's situation, for Mr. Buckles would not have his wife's sister live in what was now his house. With no money, no prospects, and no parents, Lucy removed half a country away to Nottingham to live with an uncle, not even a blood relative, who did not much know her and had no wish to remedy that situation. Through no choice of her own, she rarely saw her sister, and now, her sister's infant girl. They were the only family Lucy had in the world, but Mr. Buckles did not much care for travel, or for guests, both of which were a bother.

Uncle Lowell's breakfasts were not the best. He served no bacon with his eggs and no butter with his bread. He preferred for himself a weak porridge and fresh fruit when in season, dried when it was not. He instructed Ungston to prepare small quantities of eggs as a concession to his niece, but he often observed that he did not love being put to the expense of serving what he did not eat.

Lucy, whose shape was not excessively slender, usually ate heartily, but today she only picked at her bread and pushed her eggs about with her fork while Uncle Lowell talked about the newspaper he read. Mrs. Quince sat near him. Having already eaten, her principal task was to refill Mr. Lowell's cup with chocolate and agree with his observations.

"More of your Luddites," he said to Lucy, as though her vague sympathy with their grievances the day before implicated her in their crimes. "A band of these brigands broke open a mill not twenty miles from here and destroyed every stocking frame within. They fired upon the owner and his man. What say you to that, Miss Lucy? Do you yet stand with these pirates and rally to the banner of their General Ludd?"

"I never said I stood with them," Lucy said as she speared a piece of egg with her fork and then removed it by scraping it against her plate. She did not like that he accused her of sympathizing with the Luddites, but at least he did not speak of the stranger or Mr. Olson. It was only temporary, Lucy understood, but if the man in the guest room would wake up and exonerate her, perhaps the whole situation might turn into no more than a marvelous anecdote, leaving her unscathed.

"If you no longer desire eggs," said Uncle Lowell, "you need but inform me. You may say, 'Uncle, I ask you not to beggar yourself with the expense of eggs, for I do not choose to eat them.' I do not think myself unreasonable in that regard. What, have you nothing to say, Miss Lucy? Have you no response to my sensible request?"

It is probable that Lucy would indeed have had no significant response under usual circumstances, but in this case she did not speak because she was staring at the stranger, who stood at the entrance to the dining room. He had shed his coat and wore only his trousers and his dingy white shirt, open to reveal his tanned skin and curls of dark hair along his broad and muscular chest. He wore no shoes, but his ruined foot was wrapped in a pillowcase.

"I do beg your pardon," said the man, his voice tinged, if not overwhelmed, with accents of the north, "but I wonder if you might inform me of where I am, what I am doing here, and why my clothing is tattered and my feet torn to shreds."

Lucy stared in amazement, Mrs. Quince clucked her tongue with distaste, but Mr. Lowell was instantly upon his feet. "If *I* might inform *you?*" he demanded. "It is you who must inform me, sir, who you are and what you are doing here. You must inform me why you have come to trouble my niece and why you have put me to the expense of doctors and witches and now, I suppose, food and drink."

"He disrupts a stranger's home," observed Mrs. Quince, "and then wants food and drink."

"Yes, of course." Lucy rose from her chair, almost catching her feet upon the table leg, for she found she was suddenly anxious. "Sir, please sit. You must be hungry."

"I confess I am famished and terribly thirsty," he said, "but you must indulge me elsewhere, for I am unused to being so dirty, and I fear I must offend you."

"You would put me to the expense of opening up another room for your convenience?

I've smelled the unwashed before, I assure you. If you will only sit at the far end of the table there — just there, yes, that seat farthest from my own — I am certain it will be well."

The man, who it now seemed was possessed of fine manners, bowed and took the seat. Lucy went to the sideboard, prepared for him a dish of eggs and bread, and rang the bell for Ungston that the stranger might be brought some small beer.

Though evidently famished, the gentleman restrained himself for a moment that he might give formality its due. "I beg the indulgence of introducing myself. My name is George Gordon Byron, Baron of Newstead in Nottinghamshire, and a member of the House of Lords. I tell you of my titles not in the hopes of impressing you, though we must admit that they *are* impressive, but because I am aware of my appearance, and I do not wish you to think me a vagabond."

"*Lord* Byron of Newstead!" said Lucy, now overcome with surprise. The handsome stranger — the one who had come to her, supposedly under a curse, to demand she not marry Mr. Olson — was a peer, their very own local peer. It was as though she'd found herself transported into a fairy story. She rose to give him a quick curtsy as she struggled to recall what other courtesies were required for this enigmatic gentleman, who, from his native neighborhood, was much absent and so the subject of enthusiastic speculation. "My lord, I am Lucy Derrick, and this gentleman is my uncle, Mr. Richard Lowell, and we are delighted to have you in our home."

"I am Mrs. Quince," said Mrs. Quince, who hastily rose to curtsy and add, "my lord."

Lord Byron who showed signs of surprise, took no notice of Mrs. Quince. He gazed at Lucy with new curiosity. "Your name is Derrick?"

"Yes," said Lucy, her voice catching in her throat. His gaze was intense, and she wished she could cease her blushing. She thought of him, before the front of the house, calling out her name, and she found herself wishing — wishing beyond all reason and hope — that he would show some of that passion once more.

"I should think you know her name, given how you cried it out like an oysterman last night," said Uncle Lowell.

Lord Byron looked about with evident confusion. "I do not recall that I did so."

"Very convenient," said Uncle Lowell. "I beg my niece to cease her bowing and scraping. A baron is a very shabby sort of peer, and Byron a shabby sort of baron from what I hear."

From his seat, Byron bowed at Uncle Lowell. "I am pleased, if somewhat surprised, that my reputation precedes me."

"It has not preceded you very far," said

Uncle Lowell. "Your seat is perhaps ten miles from here. Is that whence you've walked?"

"Ten miles . . . ," murmured Lord Byron. "But I came from London."

"You are in Nottingham now, my lord," said Lucy.

Lord Byron appeared very pale now. He raised his beer to his lips and sipped, though the vessel trembled vastly. "Perhaps I rode part of the way. I recall nothing. I have no notion of how I — but, only tell me, what day this is."

"It is the fourteenth of April," said Lucy, who then added, "eighteen hundred and twelve," because perhaps he didn't know the year either.

"I last remember the ninth," said Lord Byron, his voice distant and strained. "I was in London, upon an errand. I remember — I am not sure — but I think I arrived where I wished to go, and then I recall nothing. Except . . ." Upon turning to Lucy, he met her gaze with something like amazement. "Except you," he said. "I recollect your face, Miss Derrick. You did something to help me, did you not? I cannot recall what, but I have this notion that I am in your debt."

Feeling herself redden, Lucy turned away. "I do not know that I did anything."

"Stuff!" cried Uncle Lowell. "Can you pay for the expenses you've incurred or not? Baron of Newstead be damned, for it don't signify any silver in your purse."

With evident reluctance, Lord Byron turned from Lucy. "I shall pay my obligations, but I do not think myself well enough to return to London just yet. I will retire to Newstead and trouble you no more. Direct any expenses I have incurred to me there."

There was a moment of silence in which Uncle Lowell might have said that he must not rush, that he must remain a guest for as long as he might wish, but this offer never came. Instead it was Mrs. Quince who spoke. "But you must tell us, my lord," she said, in a rather disastrous attempt at a sweet voice, "what you wished with our Lucy, and what care you about Mr. Olson."

Lord Byron appeared truly puzzled. "I can see that any gentleman must wish for a connection with this charming young lady, but, to my knowledge, I have never seen her before I came to this house. As to this Mr. Olson, I do not know the name."

"You have no connection with Miss Derrick?" Mrs. Quince demanded.

"Regrettably, I have not that honor." Lord Byron studied his hosts carefully, and then allowed his eyes to settle once more upon Lucy's. "I am fatigued and not myself. I must remove to Newstead for fresh clothes and a bath, but before I go I should like to discover what it is precisely that I have done here."

■ ■ ■ ■

Mrs. Quince arranged for a coach to take Lord Byron to his estate, and while they awaited its arrival, she remained in the sitting room as Lucy provided the baron with a somewhat abbreviated account of his appearance at Uncle Lowell's house. She found herself looking out the window as she spoke, or at her fingers, or at Mrs. Quince because it was difficult to look at Lord Byron. He was not merely handsome, he was unnaturally handsome, and being near him made her forget how to act like herself. While she tried to remember where to put her eyes and her hands, and how to hold her body, Lucy recounted how he had arrived, begged Lucy by name not to marry, and spoke some other strange and inexplicable things. She thought it inappropriate to mention the vomiting of pins or removal of curses. Lord Byron appeared suitably mortified by even this redacted narrative, and his discomfort demonstrated that he was indeed mortified to hear of his conduct.

When she dared to look at him, Lucy saw Lord Byron cast disapproving glances in Mrs. Quince's direction, as though he wished the chaperone would leave. Perhaps she merely flattered herself. On the other hand, Lord Byron's reputation in the neighborhood was as something of a profligate, though details were vague, and virtually all handsome young noblemen enjoyed such reputations.

"My lord," Lucy said, once she had gathered her nerve, "you told me to gather leaves. What does it mean?"

He shook his head. "It appears I spoke a great deal of nonsense."

Lucy did not think it was nonsense The words kept returning to her, and she felt absolutely sure that she would, at some point, understand exactly what they meant. She could not say if she thought that good or bad.

At last, his hired coach appeared outside, and Lord Byron rose to excuse himself. "Miss Derrick," he said, "would you do me the honor of walking me to my conveyance? I would have a private word with you."

Lucy blushed, and she silently rebuked herself for doing so. This astonishingly beautiful peer was not going to say anything of consequence to her. She could not hope for it. And yet, he desired something, and she could not think what.

"There is nothing you may say to the young lady that you may not say before me," announced Mrs. Quince.

"You may keep watch upon us to make sure I remain a gentleman," said Lord Byron, "but I would say something that is for Miss Derrick's ears alone."

"And what might that be?" asked Mrs. Quince.

"Surely you see the paradox of the question," he said with a smile so condescending that Lucy had to bite her lip to keep from laughing.

As they descended the stairs, and Mrs. Quince glared at them through the window, Lord Byron leaned toward Lucy's ear. His breath was hot and distracting, and Lucy felt her heart quickening and her stomach muscles tighten. "Tell her I asked you for a kiss, and you refused," he said. "She will believe it and trouble you no more."

Lucy's face was burning from even the mention of the word *kiss*. A feeling of pleasurable warmth began in her middle and spread outward, threatening to overwhelm her. "What can you have to say," she managed, "that such a proposition is the disguise?"

"I have something for you, Miss Derrick. I found it upon my person when I awoke this morning. I cannot say how it came to me, but then much of my recent past is a mystery to me. As for this document, I know not your circumstances or what precisely this means, but I collect you are not happy with your uncle and his woman looking over you. Please, you need not respond. I merely wish you to understand why I thought it prudent to give you this in private. If I am mistaken, then by all means show this to your uncle at once. If I am correct, then I have done no harm and possibly some good."

"What can you mean?" The words caught in her throat.

"Come around the far side of the coach. I will have to hand this to you quickly, when the woman's view is blocked. You must then come back around where she can see you, so she does not become suspicious."

Lucy felt her heart racing. She was now involved in an intrigue, one that clearly had nothing to do with a peer choosing to make love to her. She followed Lord Byron to the far side of his coach, and he placed into her hand a thick collection of pages, folded three times. Instinctively, she stuffed them into the bodice of her gown, blushing all the while.

Lord Byron led her back to the other side of the coach. "Please, my lord. What have you given me?"

"Francis Derrick was your father?" he said in a quiet voice.

She felt herself grow faint and gripped his arm, though let go again at once as though shocked. She felt embarrassed at having grabbed him, and yet delighted, and wondered how she might find an excuse to grab his arm again. "Yes." It was hardly a whisper.

"You will forgive me, but when he died, what did he leave you?"

"Very little," managed Lucy. "He died with many debts, and what he had, he gave to my sister and her family."

Lord Byron nodded. "This morning, I found upon me the last will and testament of a Mr. Francis Derrick, and with that, some records of his finances. I did not read it overly closely, as it did not concern me, but the substance of these documents is that, beyond a few items left to this person or that, his sole beneficiaries for his personal effects and a sum of money he estimates as near ten thousand pounds, are his unmarried daughters, Lucy and Martha Derrick. I am sorry to tell you that it appears you have been the victim of a scheme to defraud you of your inheritance."

5

With Lord Byron gone, Lucy retired to her room to reflect in silence on all that had happened. What an astonishing and terrible two days it had been. She had met Miss Crawford, who, though a stranger, and one she would likely never see again, enchanted Lucy with the illusion of friendship. She had perhaps — or perhaps not — used actual *magic* to aid a handsome man in need, and that man had turned out to be a peer, one who gave every sign of flirting with her. This was an exciting development, particularly since it was entirely possible she had ended her engagement with Mr. Olson. And now this peer had handed her what appeared to be her father's will, which told a very different story from what the solicitors had presented.

Along with the will, dated only four months prior to her father's death, Lucy found a reckoning of her father's assets, which were far greater than the meager holdings and expansive debts of which the solicitor has spoken. According to the documents she held in her hands, Mr. Derrick had been possessed of investments that slightly exceeded ten thousand pounds. There was a matter of jewels that had belonged to Lucy's mother, as well as some plate and paintings and a few diamonds. There were other objects of value as well, including furnishings, rugs, and the contents of his considerable library. The will specified that, at the time of its composition, Mr. Derrick was free of significant debts, and he expected only trivial claims against the estate.

Lucy well remembered the misery of sitting in the parlor of her old home, Harrington, with Martha holding her hand while Mr. Clencher, the solicitor — a man so thin he appeared on the cusp of expiring — explained the nature and consequences of the will. The solicitor had told them in his dispassionate voice that Mr. Derrick had died with many encumbrances. Once these had been settled, a sum of approximately 240 pounds would be divided between Martha and Lucy, in addition to a few items of jewelry, which were of indifferent value. What objects that would not need to be sold to pay off debts were to stay at Harrington. The will specified that the house should remain largely intact.

Once she understood the contents of the will, Martha immediately wrote to her cousin, Mr. Buckles, to accept his standing proposal of marriage. She said nothing to Lucy until she received a favorable reply, and the contract was complete in all but deed. "It is the best way I know of to take care of you," Martha then explained to her sister. "You will live with us as long as you wish, and you will keep your things, and in every way you can, you will live as you have been used."

Lucy had wanted to beg her yet again to not marry Buckles, but there was nothing to be gained in expressing an opinion with which Martha was familiar. Martha knew Lucy's mind, and Lucy knew her sister's. Martha would marry to protect Lucy, and nothing Lucy could say would prevent her from doing so. If there had been someone Lucy could have married first, to stop her sister, she would have done it, but there was no one. She was powerless to stop her sister's sacrifice, and the best she could do was to honor it by pretending to be at peace with it.

Despite her good intentions, Martha had been unable to do much for Lucy. She and Mr. Buckles married at once, but no sooner had her new husband removed to Harrington than Lucy was made to depart. Mr. Buckles would not permit Lucy to join the household. His patroness, the Lady Harriett Dyer, whom he obeyed in all things, did not think it wise that so newly married a couple should be burdened with a troublesome and mischievous young girl, one whose reputation and loose morals presaged many difficulties to come. Martha rarely argued with anyone, and hated to quarrel with her new husband, but Lucy had heard the shouting as her sister pled her case, all to no effect. Mr. Buckles would not be moved. Lady Harriett had given her opinion, Mr. Buckles said. What did Martha mean by suggesting she not be heeded? Martha had no power over her husband, no wiles with which to force his hand. Lucy therefore went to the widower of her mother's sister, Uncle Lowell in Nottingham, and Buckles magnanimously granted her an annuity of thirty pounds per annum.

Now, more than three years later, she held this will in her hands, feeling her anger build. If these pages had been written by her father, then either he had established monstrous debts in the last few months of his life, or Lucy and Martha had been horribly cheated. Instead of living in misery and want, she ought to be a free gentlewoman of independent means. Her share of the fortune, five thousand pounds, was hardly a staggering sum, but it was enough to establish a comfortable and independent life. It ought to have been hers. It *was* hers, and someone had conspired to steal it away.

Lucy tried to imagine who that someone might be. Perhaps her Uncle Lowell, who valued money so highly, but that hardly made sense. He certainly did not want for money, and prized his quiet even more than his wealth. An extra ten thousand pounds would not significantly improve his lot, but a dependent niece had clearly altered it for the worse.

Also a suspect was Mr. Buckles, but, again, the fact that he was in a position to manipulate her did not mean he possessed motivation to do so. Papa's death meant that Mr. Buckles came into a comfortable and well-established estate that provided him with a healthy income from rents. If the new will were to be believed, Mr. Derrick had raised three daughters, set a handsome table, and stuffed a library full of books while managing to save ten thousand pounds. Surely the property itself was valuable enough to dissuade any man of some intelligence from such extremes. Beyond that, Mr. Buckles had the patronage of Lady Harriett, so if he had any serious wants, surely that lady would offer such assistance as he required. And above all else, forgery was a crime that carried the penalty of hanging with little chance of reprieve. No sane man would risk these consequences without a desperate motivation.

What of the solicitor Mr. Clencher? He would have been in an excellent position to deceive the courts, but Papa would never have done business with someone of so little integrity. If none of these men, then who? Perhaps some villain Lucy did not know. Of course, there remained yet another possibility — that the will she now held was the forgery — but who stood to gain from the creation of such a document? Lucy had nothing of her own to pay in the search for the truth, so this new will could hardly be part of a confidence game played upon her. More than that, the will *felt* right, just as the old one, she now understood, felt wrong.

All of which begged the question of what to do next. Lucy could not ask her uncle or brother-in-law for help because, though their guilt was certainly unlikely, they had nevertheless been the first two people she suspected. Similarly she could not ask Martha, since it would be wrong to set her upon a quest she must conceal from her odious husband and which, though it was but a remote possibility, might lead to her husband's execution. She supposed she might ask Lord Byron, and the idea was not without its attractions. Unfortunately, Lord Byron had a reputation for rakishness and distraction, and these were not the traits a vulnerable young woman sought in a legal adviser. Moreover, in light of her near elopement with Jonas Morrison four years earlier, arranging clandestine meetings with Lord Byron was altogether too dangerous.

There was but one person Lucy could think of — Mary Crawford. Though their acquaintance was new, Lucy believed she could trust

81

Miss Crawford. She had to trust someone, and a charming and independent lady of fashion, one whom Lucy had managed to impress, seemed to her the best possible choice. She hated to impose upon a stranger with something of this nature, but there was more in the balance here than mere money. Her father had wanted Lucy to have something, and an unknown person had interfered. Someone had thwarted her father's dying wishes, had cheated a man as his body lay cold and his heart sat still in his chest. A lady like Miss Crawford, who had shown unmistakable signs of goodness, would not want so grave a crime to go unpunished.

No sooner had she determined this course of action than Uncle Lowell came to visit her. He knocked upon the door, which was polite, but did not wait for a response before entering, which was not. He had previously observed that it was his house, and he did not see that he must demand permission before entering any part of it. He would never have barged into his niece's room at a time she might be dressing, but as Lucy was already dressed, he did not think she could be about anything he was not within his rights to witness.

He entered the room and paced back and forth for a moment, and then, at last, he spoke. "Now that the question of the man's name has been answered, you are to pen a note of apology to Mr. Olson and send it at once."

Lucy was in no mood to hear any demands from Uncle Lowell. "And what is it I must apologize for?" she asked, making no effort to soften her tone.

"Don't stand upon ceremony, girl, unless you wish him to withdraw his offer."

"I've done nothing wrong," answered Lucy, for whom the revelation of the will had fueled her sense of persecution, "and I care not what he does."

Uncle Lowell began to redden. His fists clenched and unclenched as he spoke. "That's a damned pretty thing to say. Do you think he's not heard of your whoring about with that scoundrel Morrison before you came here? Unless you wish him to believe the worst, you must convince Olson you are not engaged upon some adventure with that baron."

He now saw the document in Lucy's hand, and she observed that he saw it. She began to set it aside, though she realized too late that doing so was a mistake.

"What is that?"

Panic had her in its grips, and for a moment, Lucy could not think what to say. If she was made to hand over the will, everything could end at that moment. Maybe her uncle had stolen the money, and maybe he would simply not want the family name to become involved in a scandal over a few thousand pounds that were not even his. She could not allow him to make that decision, so Lucy forced herself to clear her mind and master her feelings. She held on to the will and met her uncle's eye. "It is a letter from my sister."

Uncle Lowell studied her carefully, perhaps sensing something amiss, but being a man too blunt for duplicity, he did not easily recognize it in others. After a moment he said, "I'll hear no more arguments. You will write to Mr. Olson."

Lucy felt strangely liberated. She very much liked the idea of playing a deep game, of keeping her options open, of possessing more information than anyone suspected.

"Certainly," she told her uncle. Relieved that she had preserved her secret, she was prepared to offer a concession. "I shall write him at once."

6

Her business would not wait. Lucy went out and walked to High Pavement in the hopes of finding Miss Crawford home. She told neither her uncle or Mrs. Quince that she was leaving, an omission that might come back to haunt her, but she could not trouble herself about that presently.

She found Miss Crawford at home, and her serving woman, the peculiar Mrs. Emmett, answered the door, beaming at her in her ebullient manner. Again, she wore her bonnet in a curiously low fashion, and Lucy wondered if she had some sort of scar or rash or disfiguration upon her forehead that she wished to conceal.

"My dear Miss Derrick!" cried Mrs. Emmett. "Miss Crawford will be so pleased you are here. And I am pleased too. Not that it can matter to you, but I am and I shan't hide it."

Lucy followed the cheerful woman into the sitting room and waited only a moment before Miss Crawford entered. She appeared, if anything, more beautiful in the full light of day than she had at night — pale and radiant, her hair almost unnatural in its whiteness. She again wore green, today a frock of verdant filigree upon an ivory background, and this too made her green eyes appear unnaturally intense.

"Miss Derrick, I am so glad to see you," she said. "I had thought to call upon you this morning and inquire after our stranger, but I did not perceive your uncle would welcome me."

"He does not welcome anyone," said Lucy. Her voice wavered as she spoke. She had not realized how truly apprehensive she was until this moment. She took a deep breath and steadied herself. She tried to slow her pounding heart. She did something that felt a great deal like . . . like quieting herself, she realized. She was here to find her own way, she told herself. This was her life, and if she had not the power to shape it as she wished, then she had at least the will to try.

Standing near her, Miss Crawford took Lucy's hand. "Are you unwell? Come and sit." She led Lucy to a chair near the fire, and she sat next to her and took her hand once more. "We have met but recently, but I hope we can be friends."

"I hope so too," Lucy said. "But I do not wish to abuse your kindness."

"Fear nothing of the sort. You must tell me all."

Lucy did. She took another deep breath and proceeded to tell her about Lord Byron's awakening, and his discovery of the will. "I very much hate to impose upon our acquaintance, no less because it is so new, but I have no one else I might turn to or trust."

Miss Crawford hardly took a moment to consider what she heard. "I shall be blunt and hope my bluntness does not offend you. I am a lady of independent means, but I have not always been so. I recall what it is to be dependent, so if it is within my power to aid you in anything, it will be my pleasure to do so. So you must tell me if you believe this will genuine."

Lucy nodded, nearly light-headed with gratitude.

"Would you entrust the document to me?"

Lucy did not want to let go of the will, but holding it in secret would accomplish nothing. If she did not entrust it to a stranger, what could she hope to do with it? "Of course," she answered after a long moment.

"Then I shall do what I can for you. I shall have my own solicitor make inquiries, and do so in a quiet manner. We do not want those who would cheat you to discover that you are aware of what they have done. You must know that forgery is a capital crime, and those who have deceived you must be willing to go to great lengths to protect themselves. You cannot risk anyone learning that you have discovered these irregularities."

Lucy nodded, feeling relief flood through her. She had someone to trust, someone who could help her. It had been so long since she had felt this. Not since her father was alive had she felt as protected as she did at that moment. "You are so fortunate to be your own mistress," she said, but she saw something dark in Miss Crawford's face, and she understood she had said the wrong thing. "I am sorry. Have I offended you?"

"No," said Miss Crawford, forcing a smile. "It is only that I should much prefer not to be my own mistress. I was married once. I have reverted back to my family name because I am not known here, and I do not wish to play the part of the rich widow."

"I am sorry," said Lucy. "I did not know."

Miss Crawford rose and adjusted a gilt-framed mirror above the fireplace. It was something to do, something to occupy her hands while she said something she thought she ought to say and did not wish to. "I shall tell you something, because I think it may help you someday. My husband and I were very happy together. I loved him beyond reason, though when he married me, he loved me only a little. He yet longed for another woman, and this longing was a barrier between us, but I married him because I told

88

myself I would make him forget her. Some would call me foolish, but I had faith in my love for him. In the end, he came to love me as much as I could have wished, and our days together were wonderful before death separated us. I tell you this not to be maudlin, but so you will know that love is a strange thing."

Lucy said nothing. There was nothing to say, and she could not imagine why Miss Crawford had told her these things. Did she somehow know about Lord Byron and wish for her to accept him on his own terms? Did she urge Lucy to marry Mr. Olson and learn to love him?

Miss Crawford walked back over to her chair and sat, making a great show of smiling and smoothing her skirts. "But enough of that. There is something else I would discuss with you. It is regarding what transpired last night with this baron."

Lucy did not want to discuss curses and magic and beings made of darkness as though they were real things. As long as she did not discuss these subjects with Miss Crawford, as long as they were but her memories alone, then she might convince herself that what she had experienced had been but mistake and illusion and the self-deception of the moment. "I do not wish to be rude, but I have not the time," said Lucy. "I must return, for I am not trusted to be gone long."

Miss Crawford scowled. "Why ever not?"

On an impulse, Lucy decided to tell her, and it felt strangely liberating to say the words aloud, to own the story, and, for once, to not feel ashamed. "When I was sixteen, I ran off with a young gentleman. He said he wished to marry me, but in truth he did not. It would have been the ruin of me, and the humiliation of my family, had the plan not been disrupted, but in my absence — I was gone but only a day, but in that time . . ."

Lucy did not know how to proceed, she did not know that she could. It occurred to her now that she had never spoken of the elopement to anyone. Everyone had always known about it. She had traveled north all day with Jonas Morrison, whose mood had become decidedly gloomy. He had always been wonderful with her — lively and witty and affectionate — but on their journey there had been no sign of that charming gentleman. There was no celebration of love, no kissing or hand-holding or eager chatter as they sat in the coach, and so as they drove, Lucy began to regret what she had done. Perhaps she would have regretted it anyhow, for it was one thing to dream of doing a naughty thing, to plan and make preparations for it, but it was quite another to act upon those desires.

Jonas Morrison hardly looked at her, instead staring out the window, or scribbling with a pencil into a tiny black bound volume he kept in his waistcoat pocket. Lucy felt his silence like an accusation, and a hundred times she turned to Mr. Morrison to tell him that she had made a mistake, that she wished to return, but something in his look made her fearful to speak. For months he had been the man she had always dreamed she would marry, but at that moment he had become someone entirely different.

It had rained that day, and the roads were not good. They made it only to Dartford before they had to stop for the night, but when they entered the inn, they found Mr. Derrick waiting for them. Lucy never discovered how he had overtaken them or known where they would stop, but he was there, standing by the fire, tears running freely, and she almost fainted as she thought that she had utterly broken her father's heart. She'd stepped forward to hug him, to beg his forgiveness and explain that she had done nothing wrong and they could go back to the way things had been, but something stopped her. She took two steps and froze because she understood that those tears were not for her. All at once, she realized he had come on business far more serious than her elopement.

"It is Emily," he said before she could utter a word. "Our Emily. She — this morning, she never awoke. She is gone. You were both gone."

Much of what came next was lost to her. Perhaps she swooned, but next she knew, she sat by the fire, her head down, a blanket over her shoulders and a cup of hot wine in her hand. She did not recall her father upbraiding Mr. Morrison for running off with his daughter. Instead, she had a vague memory of the two men talking closely together, whispering, as though Emily's death, and Lucy's reaction to it, required that men who ought to be enemies join together for her own good. Most inexplicably, she was almost certain she had seen her father shaking Mr. Morrison's hand. Lucy did not think it could have happened that way, but it was not a subject she had ever felt she could discuss with her father.

Mr. Morrison had once been a fixture in their neighborhood, friendly with Lucy's father, but after that day he simply vanished, ashamed to have been exposed, and wanting no more entanglements with a love-struck sixteen-year-old girl whom he had played with for his simple amusement.

Lucy told Mary Crawford a brief version of the story. When she was finished, Miss Crawford took Lucy's hand. "It was a youthful indiscretion that led to no harm. Whatever happened to your sister was none of your doing. You know that to be true, but it is time for you to *believe* it. You must cease condemning yourself for something you never did."

Lucy looked away, blinking back the tears.

"I cannot imagine how miserable they have made you," Miss Crawford said.

"They are not as kind as I should like," said Lucy, "and your words are most welcome, but that is not what affects me. It is that you have made me think of my father."

Lucy recalled the day, some weeks after he first invited her into his library, they reviewed together a book upon astronomy, and Mr. Derrick began to speak at great length upon the subject of Galileo and his excommunication.

"I am certain," her father said, "that this punishment affected him greatly. But Galileo reported what he believed to be true, and so I suspect that while the charge of heresy was unwelcome, he likely did not berate himself. Do you not agree?"

Lucy said that she did agree.

Mr. Derrick closed the book with a dramatic snap. "We must always remember not to condemn ourselves for what we have not done." Lucy had rarely felt more loved and understood. Now here was Miss Crawford, who was determined to be her friend. That would not be enough to help Lucy through whatever she must face in the days and weeks ahead, but it was something. It was something indeed.

7

When Lucy returned to her uncle's house, she was in a buoyant mood. Miss Crawford would help her to regain her inheritance. Perhaps, even at that moment, Lord Byron was thinking of her, considering the implications of courting a girl with no dowry, but Lucy would not be so penniless when her inheritance was returned. It was not the princely sum a peer might hope for, but he was only a baron after all and could not be so very choosy.

She knew it was foolish to count her father's inheritance before it was in hand, certainly before she had heard from Miss Crawford's solicitor. As for Lord Byron, he likely flirted with every young lady he saw, and she could not reasonably expect to be in his presence again. Even so, it felt wonderful to indulge in the fantasy, and she did not wish to stop herself.

Lucy had hardly ever troubled herself to imagine her life as Mrs. Olson. She thought of that future only as one in which she would be free of her uncle and Mrs. Quince, but Byron — that was something else altogether. She saw it at once, the two of them dressed in the height of fashion, traveling in his brilliant equipage, attending balls and routs and patronizing pleasure gardens. She could see herself hosting gatherings at their fine home, being greeted as Lady Byron. And she imagined the private times together, the walks, the quiet meals, the evenings before the fire.

Unfortunately, this new feeling of hopefulness had a price. Now that she could dream of other prospects, no matter how distant, the idea of marrying Mr. Olson had become odious. She did not love him. She did not like him. How could she promise before God to be bound to him forever? It seemed to her madness, madder even than agreeing to run off with Jonas Morrison. He, at least, had been handsome and charming. He had made her feel pretty and clever and delightful. Mr. Olson only made her feel . . . she hardly knew what. He made her feel, at best, nothing.

Prior to visiting Miss Crawford, she had, per her uncle's demand, sent Mr. Olson a note in which she explained Lord Byron's confusion and her innocence. She had done so as coolly as she could, but she had nevertheless expressed that she yet desired the marriage might proceed. It had been painful to write, for she wanted no such thing. She could hardly remember a time when she did wish to marry him, even though that time had been yesterday. Lucy understood, however, that it would be prudent to make no firm decision at present. If Mary Crawford could achieve nothing with her father's will, then it would be best to have Mr. Olson available. Did it make her a vile person that she considered her options with such a mercenary eye? She suspected it did, and yet what choice had she? She must survive. She must have food to eat and clothes and somewhere to sleep. And certainly no one judged a penniless peer who married for wealth. Why should she be held to a different standard?

All of her dreams burnt off like morning fog when, as she ascended the stairs, she heard Mrs. Quince calling for her in a birdsong voice. Lucy prepared a flimsy story of taking a walk to clear her head, but Mrs. Quince had no questions about where she had been. When Lucy followed her voice to the kitchen, she stood by a basket packed with food and a bottle of claret.

"I want you to take this to Mr. Olson at his mill," she said.

Lucy looked at the basket, not wanting to look into Mrs. Quince's pale eyes, which bore down on her with menacing intensity. "Perhaps that is not wise."

Mrs. Quince showed no inclination to listen to nonsense. In two quick strides she came to

Lucy and took her jaw hard in her pale hand, her long fingers gripping tight. "Your uncle wishes it."

Lucy attempted to step back and pull her head away, but Mrs. Quince pulled her closer, digging into her flesh with her fingernails. "You will go where I tell you, and you will marry whom I say."

Mrs. Quince let go. Lucy turned away, knowing she had no choice but to bide her time. There could be no ruptures, no major conflicts.

Choosing her battles, she nodded. "I will go."

Mrs. Quince harrumphed in triumph. "Better for you to have been good from the first."

Lucy took the basket and set out for the half an hour or so it would take to walk to the mill. It was a mild day, but still cool, and Lucy wore a long blue coat that she thought becoming, and it did a fine job of keeping her warm so that she could enjoy the stroll. She walked by Grey Friar Gate and over the footbridge and then along the rural ways that wound along the far side of the Leen, now swollen with spring abundance. She passed the hill the children called the "fairy mound," but there were no children playing there today.

She had visited the mill only once before, and that was with a large group from town and before it had been populated by machines and workers. Nevertheless, she had been down this road many times, and had often enjoyed the quiet, peaceful walk. Scattered along the way were rural cottages where the bulk of Nottingham's hosiery had once been made by artisans. When Lucy had first come to live in the county, these cottages had been vibrant places, full of comings and goings and the ceaseless noise of the interior looms. She had walked by to see children playing, women sitting together peeling turnips or sewing, men gathered to smoke pipes after a day's labors. Now all was altered. The cottages were dark and silent, or if she saw their inmates, they sat inert before their houses, watching her with hungry eyes, like wolves considering uncertain prey.

At last she approached Mr. Olson's mill, a large two-storied rectangular structure whose base was built of stone but the rest formed from unpainted lumber. A massive chimney belched dark smoke. When still fifty feet away she could hear the clattering of dozens of stocking frames — it sounded like an endless torrent of pebbles tumbling upon a wooden floor. There was a chorus of coughing and the muted sound of a single child crying.

Lucy had never before been inside a working mill, and did not know what constituted proper etiquette. Did she knock as though it were a private house or walk in as though it were a shop? Her indecision was answered when she observed one of the two main doors — for they were built like those of a barn — was open, and so Lucy merely stepped inside. What she saw left her breathless. The entire floor was an expanse of stocking frames — each one a rectangular machine as tall as a man and half as wide, fitted with twenty or more needles and wires into which quick moving hands fed the wool that produced the celebrated Nottinghamshire hosiery.

It was not the kind of work or the number of machines that horrified Lucy. It was, first of all, the gloom of the mill. There were few windows, and those were up high, letting in only thin shafts of daylight. These highlighted the amount of linen dust and debris in the air — the reason why nearly every worker paused several times each minute to cough. Even though she but stood at the threshold, Lucy's lungs grew leaden. Then there were the workers themselves: women, children, and the elderly. Three or four large men roamed the floor, looking for signs that a worker was not keeping a proper pace. Such a worker would receive a warning rap on the side of his or her frame from a cudgel. Lucy stood observing only a moment before the overseers beat an old man on his thigh and a child upon his back.

She did not mean to cry out, but upon seeing the brute hit the child, she could not help herself. One of the overseers, a tall man, and an extraordinarily fat one, of early middle years came over to her. He was nearly bald, with only a little fringe of orange hair about the back of his head, which was both over-sized and ruddy.

"What's here?" he asked. "Come to bring me what to eat, have you, missy?"

Lucy held herself erect and thrust out her chin. "I am looking for Mr. Olson."

He grinned at her, showing a mouth full of strong yellow teeth. "So's every girl in the county. A grim enough gent, I reckon, but now that he's got coin upon him, it's a differ-ent story, ain't it? But never you mind it. You want Olson, you come with me, miss."

Lucy followed him into the mill, and at once she felt her lungs constrict, as though someone had put a heavy woolen cloth over her mouth. The workers looked up at her as she passed by, and she noticed the cloth covering the basket's contents had come somewhat loose, and she felt dozens of eyes upon the bread that poked through. One little boy licked his lips.

"Something to eat, miss," he said.

The overseer struck his frame, and the boy returned to work.

At the far end of the building, the overseer knocked upon a single door set into the wall, and opened it without waiting for a response. Inside, Mr. Olson sat behind an expansive desk, writing out a letter. There were numerous other letters drying upon the desk, as well as ledgers and open books. Behind him, a door that he might come and go without crossing the mill, and a very large window allowed natural light to brighten the closet.

"Found this lassie looking for you," the overseer said.

"Yes, yes, send her in and close the door. I don't want that filth getting in here."

The overseer all but shoved her inside, and then shut the door tight behind him, leering at her as he did so. Lucy did not love being shut up alone with Mr. Olson like this, but the air was much cleaner and purer in here and the light was bright.

"Miss Derrick," said Mr. Olson. There was something peculiar in his expression. It was not precisely pleasure, for that would have been out of character. Nevertheless, Lucy detected a distinct lack of displeasure, and an attentiveness that she had not before seen in him. For an instant he appeared almost attractive.

"I know you are occupied," she said, feeling her face grow hot, "so I brought you your dinner." The words sounded forced and stiff.

He looked at the gift, which she set down on his desk. "It is an unexpected kindness."

Smiling somehow caused her throat to hurt, so she soon abandoned the effort.

"Please sit," he told her, and gestured to the chair across from his desk. "Though my mill is no place for a young lady."

"It seems an unhappy place," Lucy said, listening to the clacking, the staccato coughing, and the occasional thud she now understood to be the overseers' cudgels. She thought of her father's claim, that mills were a blight upon the land. She wished she could leave right then. It seemed to her urgent that she do so, but she could not think of how she could flee without humiliating herself, so she closed her eyes for a moment and tried to breathe. Perhaps Mr. Olson would not notice her distress.

He did not. "It is a place of business and not meant for amusement," he said slowly, as if explaining one of life's unavoidable distresses to a child.

Lucy swallowed hard, trying to fight back the feeling of nausea that was overtaking her. "But conditions appear so beastly for your workers."

"They must be so," said Mr. Olson, "if I am to make money. It is the nature of a mill. I cannot change how such matters are ordered, so I do not see why I may not profit from them."

It was certainly true that she knew little about the ways of business. The world was full of things better kept hidden — war, slavery, subjugation — and crying out against them would do nothing to stop them. And yet, for all that, she did not know how she

102

could be wed to someone who chose to perpetuate what any feeling person must agree is wrong. It is one thing to accept that one is powerless to stop the suffering in the world, but quite another to benefit from what brings misery to others.

She said nothing, for three years at her uncle's house had taught her the futility of arguing with a man a point that ran contrary to his interests. Instead, she said, "I hope you like cold chicken."

"I do," he said with the seriousness that suggested he liked cold chicken a great deal. "And whatever pleasure I derive from this meal, it will be nothing in comparison to that I take from your having brought it to me. I am not at all displeased that we are to be married."

Lucy struggled to think of a response. As she considered what combination of words might best extricate her from this situation, she noticed that something had changed. It took her a moment to find the source of the alteration, but then she realized what it was. The quiet. There was no clacking of looms. There was no coughing. She heard only the muffled cries of the overseers and now the near-perpetual thump of their cudgels.

"Has work ended for the day?" asked Lucy.

Mr. Olson removed and examined his watch and, seeing the time, appeared grave. He pushed himself from the chair, and ignoring Lucy completely, threw open the door to the office. The dust from the mill filtered in at once, as did the gloomy silence and the heat of so many bodies in close proximity.

"Get back to work, you mutinous bastards!" cried one of the overseers.

Lucy saw the balding red-haired man shouting and swinging his cudgel at the shoulder of a child not twelve years old who sat perfectly still, his hands in his lap. The cudgel struck with a dull smack, but the boy did not respond. None of the workers moved or spoke or so much as turned their heads. They sat entirely motionless, rows of them, silent and still as the dead, a mute audience with glassy eyes.

"You must make him stop it!" Lucy cried. She could not believe what she saw. The strangeness. The cruelty. This was not the world as she knew it, but some terrible, alien place, and she wanted no part of it.

Mr. Olson did not hear her. "What goes on here?" he demanded.

None of the workers spoke. The overseer stepped forward. "They on a sudden stopped. No reason, and all at once."

"I can have replacements for every last one of you before sunup," said Mr. Olson. "Do not think to test me."

No one answered. Somewhere within the building, a bird took wing. Mr. Olson balled his hands into childish fists. "This is Luddite business. These people have been put up to combining against me."

Lucy managed to take a step closer. One of the women in the row closest to her suddenly turned her head in a sharp and twitchy gesture, like a startled squirrel. She studied Lucy briefly and then opened her mouth. She paused for a moment and then spoke. "Gather the leaves."

The fear that had been building within Lucy now gathered its forces and engulfed her. The words spoken by the mill worker had been enough to stagger her, but there was far more here to terrify. Everywhere in the mill were dark corners, pockets of shadows. Every one of these seethed and pulsed with insubstantial creatures such as the one Lucy had seen when she'd removed Lord Byron's curse. Like that shadowy presence, these beings were composed of darkness, but they had distinctive shapes. She saw legs, spindly hands with wispy fingers, flickering tails, and vile teeth that rose from open mouths to dissipate like smoke. They were visible only from the corners of her eyes, and the instant she gazed directly at one of these forms, it vanished in the shifting light. Still, Lucy sensed them moving and throbbing and swarming like great clusters of slick and pulsating insect larvae. Instinctively, she understood that she alone could perceive these awful creatures. She had been touched by something, and now she could see what others could not. Perhaps what frightened her most was that she understood these things had always been there, lurking and watching and pulsing, and she too had once been oblivious.

Without thinking, she grabbed one of Mr. Olson's arms, but he shook her off as though she were an ill-behaved dog. The absent cruelty of that gesture helped her to clear her thoughts.

One of the other laborers, a little girl, also turned her head. "You must gather the leaves." She spoke the words, and the shadow creatures writhed and shifted and leapt from rafter to rafter, like clouds of darkness that passed over Lucy's head.

More mill workers now spoke. *Gather the leaves. You must gather the leaves.* Their sound was a cacophony, each speaking over the other, but all fifty of them said it again and again. An entire mill full of workers had ceased their labors to tell her something desperately important, and she had no idea what it meant. And while they spoke, the shadowy forms circled above them, all moving clockwise, as though forming a vortex that would suck them all upward, flying into oblivion.

"This is utter rubbish," Mr. Olson told her, "but it is Luddite rubbish, and therefore dangerous. You must go." He took her arm with an impatient grip and opened the outer door to his private room. Lucy cast one more glance at the mill workers, calling out as though mad, as though lost in religious ecstasy. She took in one more peripheral glance of the frenzied creatures, and then helplessly and gratefully let Mr. Olson lead her away. The cold air rushed into her lungs, the safety of the woods invited her. Lucy wondered if he had a private door for convenience or to allow for an escape should he ever face such an uprising.

"Have no fear," Mr. Olson said. "The mill will continue to produce."

He spared a brief look in her direction and then closed the door without further ceremony. Lucy stood in the cold, unable to determine what to do. The sudden silence, the stillness in the air, the absence of the host of insubstantial creatures now seemed odd and inexplicable. The quiet felt unnatural, like an accusation. How could it be that all those people spoke the exact words Lord Byron had said? How could those creatures be real? Was this truly — and she hardly wished to use the word, even to her herself — magic? It was like that moment, in the inn in Dartford when she'd seen her father standing by the fire, tears running down his face, and she'd understood, all at once, that the world was far different from what she had always supposed. Then, she had discovered the world's sadness, and today, she had discovered its darkness.

Lucy forgot to breathe, and then, against her will, she sucked in a thirsty gulp of air.

With nothing else to do, Lucy began to walk from the mill. She was afraid, but also curious, and so she swallowed her fear and circled around to the still-open front door. As she grew closer, once more she could hear the mumbled chanting, the rustling non-sound of the creatures' frenzied circling.

Frightened, but too curious to turn away, Lucy approached the front of the mill. The dirt and dead leaves and twigs crunched under her feet. She heard the distant hooting of an owl. The overlapping voices repeated their refrain until she was no more than twenty feet from the open door, and then, all at once, the chant stopped. For a moment there was only silence, and then came the clacking of a single loom, joined by another, and then a loud cough, and the busy thrum of a fully functioning mill. Lucy had the strange idea that if she were to step only a little closer the work would cease once more, the chanting would resume, and the shadows would again quicken. She believed it as much as she believed anything, yet she dared not put this notion to test lest she discover that she was right.

A hundred feet up the path, with the declining sun now in her eyes, Lucy saw a figure —

still and straight and tall with wide shoulders. She could not see his face, so glaring was the sun, but she had the distinct impression that he stared at her, that he *waited* for her.

Lucy thought of retreating to the mill, but she could not go back there, not with those workers, with their dead eyes and their monotonous chants. And this man had not threatened her. He might only be a farmer or a laborer on his way, wanting nothing more from her than to tip his hat and wish her a good afternoon.

The figure did not move. She could see almost nothing of him, and put a hand to her forehead in an effort to shield her eyes from the sun's glare, but it did little good.

"Good afternoon," she said cautiously.

He stepped closer. His movements were stiff and lumbering, and yet unnaturally quick. The whole effect of him presented a convoluted image, as though his limbs were attached in some wrong way and as though he, like the creatures from the mill, were made of shadows. He did not seem vile like those scattering, pulsating things, but he was somehow similar. And yet, unlike too, for despite all the shimmering obscurity, he was a lumbering figure of a man, dressed in rough clothes, and he held in one hand a massive hammer — the sort used for . . . for breaking things. He was, she now understood, a machine breaker. This man was a Luddite.

"Miss Derrick," he said in a voice deep and resonant and low, like the mournful note of a brass horn. She felt her bones vibrate. "Miss Derrick, you must gather the leaves."

Partly out of terror, and partly out of exasperation, she squatted down and clutched a handful of limp winter-worn leaves that remained upon the ground, holding them out toward the silhouette. "Will this do?"

The man laughed, and the sound was rich and throaty. "That is not what is meant."

"Then perhaps you will tell me what is meant," said Lucy. She dropped the leaves and slapped her hands together to knock away the dirt. She was beginning to find her confidence, and liked it. Whoever, *whatever* this man was, he was not like the black thing she'd seen last night; he was not a creature of void and darkness. "Who are you? And where are these leaves I must gather, and why and what must I do with them once they are in a nice little pile?"

His face was still hidden, but Lucy had the distinct impression that he smiled. "You will know when it is time. You have seen that there are those who do not wish you to succeed, and so you must wait until you are ready. You are not yet ready."

"Then why do you tell me to do what I am not yet ready to do?"

The hidden man cocked his head slightly, giving the impression that he smiled, though she could not know for certain. "So you will make yourself ready. Those who are to be your allies prepare themselves. You have seen the mill and the horror it brings. With what shall you counter something like that?"

Lucy said nothing. Fear and confusion and even a hint of excitement rendered her tongue inert. The man bowed deep and low before stepping out of view, not into the woods, but seemingly into the shadows, as though he pulled the shadows to himself, the way she might pull a cloak around her own shoulders. Lucy did not believe it while she watched, and she doubted her own recollection afterwards, but it seemed that the shadows around him were somehow physical — layered like the steps of a stairway or folds in a piece of fabric. Into these shadows the strange man vanished, leaving Lucy alone with the sounds of wind and birds and her own panting breath.

8

During her walk home, a resolution grew within her, and though that strange man was right to fear a bleak future of mills and oppressed workers living as little better than slaves, Lucy could think only of her own bleak future. The workers telling her to gather the leaves was odd — there could be no doubt of that — but perhaps it meant nothing. And the dark creatures she'd seen were likely bats or other animals that congregated in mills for the warmth and shelter. There had been nothing fantastical in her experience, and she would not let her imagination or her fear of marrying Mr. Olson convince her that the world was a place out of a story for children. But Lucy did understand something new. While she was hardly ready to join with the Luddites and their campaign of destruction, she could not build her own life upon the foundation of a mill such as she had seen. She could not be the wife of a man who beat children to make them work harder and longer and for less money. She could not establish her own domestic security upon a kind of slavery. However much she wished she could forget or discount what she had seen, she could not.

There was but one course for her. The moment Lucy returned to her room, she composed a letter to Mr. Olson, and upon finishing it, she stepped out and sent it at once, before she could reconsider or waver or delay. In this letter, she apologized for being indecisive, but she could no longer conceal her conviction that a marriage would not produce happiness for either of them. She thought well of him (certainly an exaggeration) and had no doubt that he would make someone very happy (there must be *someone*). However, she did not believe that she was that woman, and because she would not be happy, she did not imagine he could be.

She concluded with many more apologies and well-wishes, and begged that he not disquiet either of them by pursuing the matter further. In this she hoped to shelter herself for as long as possible from her uncle's wrath. As far as either he or Mrs. Quince knew, she had written the first letter of supplication, delivered a basket of food, and all was well. It was only a matter of time before they learned what she had done, and she could not imagine their fury, but Lucy hoped it would not matter. Any day, she told herself, Miss

Crawford would send for her with happy news. Lucy dared not consider what might happen if that news never arrived. All she knew for certain was that the moment the letter was gone from her hands, speeding its way to Mr. Olson, she felt light and free and relieved.

The day after her visit to that horrible mill, Lord Byron called upon Lucy. Given the great mistake she had nearly made with Jonas Morrison, Lucy would never have been granted permission to walk alone with any strange man, let alone Lord Byron, but she very much wished to speak to him. Anyway, why should she not? She had already burned her bridges by rejecting Mr. Olson, and so she hardly had more to lose. Therefore when he invited her out upon the street, she saw no reason to request permission. She simply accepted.

When filthy, his skin blistered from the cold, dressed in tattered clothes, and nearly ruined with exhaustion, Lord Byron had still been unusually striking. Now, there were hardly words to describe his beauty. His face was angelic, sensual, and amused all at once, his form broad and manly. He dressed in the London style of Beau Brummel, with buff pants, boots, a dark blue swallowtail coat, though he varied the form by wearing no neck cloth and keeping his collar rakishly open. One of his boots appeared made for the purpose of accommodating his clubfoot. Lord Byron walked with precision, and used his walking stick to help disguise his lameness.

They strolled through the streets, toward Nottingham Castle, and Lucy could not but enjoy that eyes were upon them. All looked and wondered who was this unspeakably handsome man — or perhaps they recognized him, for though not often in Nottingham, he was well known there. Lucy chose not to care what others saw or would say. She was upon an adventure. Here she was, having a marvelous afternoon. Perhaps one day all of her afternoons would be marvelous.

"Do you mean to stay at Newstead long?" she asked him. "The Nottingham assembly is next week, and I think you would make a pleasing addition to the company." Then, thinking of his foot she added hastily, "Though perhaps a man as busy as yourself has no time for our country dances."

He laughed, perhaps knowing too well what his presence would mean in such a place. "I should enjoy attending any dance where you are present, but sadly, I must return to London. I am new in the House of Lords this year, and if I wish to make a place for myself, I cannot neglect attendance."

"It was much talked of here when you spoke out in favor of the local hosiers over the mill owners," Lucy said. "There are those

115

who claim you are a Luddite yourself."

"I have no inclination for anything so awkward as machine breaking," Lord Byron said. "I gave that speech primarily to attract some notice. One must have outlandish opinions if one is not to fade into obscurity."

"Then you do not favor the workers over the mill owners?" asked Lucy.

"The cause of the workers is as good as any other. It is hard to care about such things overmuch, but I hear that this Mr. Olson you are supposed to marry is a mill owner. That is reason enough to side with the laborers."

What did he mean by telling her this? She hardly knew what to say. "I sense you are being flippant, but I imagine the Luddites appreciate your support, even if you do not mean it."

"I am fond of Nottinghamshire and would hate to see the county turned into some sort of wasteland of oppressed peasants. I like my laborers the way they are, thank you very much." When Lucy did not reply, he added, "Do not think that my departure will mean the end of our friendship. Not for my part."

That was *something*. He did flirt with her. Lucy felt a sharp jolt of fear or excitement or longing — she could not be certain which. Surely it was at least possible he felt some true interest in her. "You are very kind, Lord Byron," she said, pleased with how easy her voice sounded.

"I am, in truth, very selfish, and because I am selfish, I cannot deny myself the company of a young lady as captivating as you."

Lucy looked away to hide her flush of embarrassment. Her life had not taught her how to respond to praise with good graces. Byron was making his intentions clear, was he not?

"Have I told you that I am a poet?" His voice suggested only boredom with his own accomplishments.

"No," she said, not quite sure what to make of this new information.

"Yes, my *Poems on Various Occasions* is very pretty, I think, though nothing more. I created a bit of controversy three years ago with my satiric work *English Bards and Scotch Reviewers*. It was a clever piece, but there is no shortage of men who can write cleverly. I am now preparing for publication the first portion of a long poem I call *Childe Harold's Pilgrimage*. I wrote much of this while traveling in Greece. Remarkable country, and I think the sublimity of the experience is reflected in these excellent verses. The world, I do not doubt, will notice this effort."

"I am glad," said Lucy, still uncertain what Byron wished to convey to her.

"I do not tell you these things to boast. I don't believe in false modesty, and I know what I am. I am an exceptional man, and so I know of what I speak when I say that you are an exceptional woman. You see, I recall everything now."

The first thing Lucy thought of was the mill, and those voices calling out for her to gather the leaves, just as Byron had. Might he be able to tell her the meaning? "Do you know why you said those things to me?" she asked.

"No, not that. I remember what you did. I remember how it was you alone who could find the curse that was upon me. And then there was that *thing,* wasn't there? That dark thing. I remember lying frozen with terror, fearing — *knowing* — that . . . that . . . whatever it was . . . was going to reach out and clutch me with its . . . I don't know what. Not hands, but something. And then you stepped before it, defying it, and it feared your defiance. It was only an instant, and yet in that instant how many hours of terror did I experience. But you, Miss Derrick, had the courage of a lion. They may hold you cheap here, but I know better."

Lucy did not wish to deny what he said. She wished him to heap his praise upon her and bask in his attention, but she was also frightened, for what she had seen both with him and at the mill had all been real. She desperately wanted it all to be the product of her heated imagination, but if he had seen these things too, then how could she deny the truth?

They walked in silence for some minutes, but as they approached the center of town, Byron turned to Lucy. "I cannot say how I knew to warn you, but I must agree with my more distracted self. You cannot allow yourself to marry this Olson."

Her first impulse was to say, *Then I have delightful news, for I have rejected him!* Lucy knew better, however. She wanted to tell him everything she had done, and why, but she could not. She needed him to make his intentions clear. She yearned for it. She felt the need for it twist into a knot inside her, and the fact that he did not made her want to scream with frustration.

"You do not know him," Lucy said at last, pleased with her vague response.

"I know he is not worthy of you."

All at once, Lucy was angry — at herself and at Byron. She felt foolish. Who was he, a peer with an estate and a seat in the House of Lords, with his poetry and holidays in Greece, to tell her what she was free to do or not do? He knew she was not an independent gentlewoman. Unless he offered her some alternative, it was unconscionable of him to advise her against marrying Olson. Jonas Morrison had been much the same in his easy dismissal of the chains that bound her to propriety. She had been a child when she'd allowed herself to be persuaded by him, but she was a child no longer, and was furious with herself for dreaming a child's dreams of love and happiness.

"I have not the luxury of deciding who is worthy," Lucy answered, not troubling herself to hide her irritation.

"You have more options than you know," said Byron airily.

When they returned to Uncle Lowell's house, Lucy did not know what to do. She could not invite him in, for her uncle and Mrs. Quince to see. Nor could she simply send Byron away without risking rudeness. Her decision was made for her, however, as Mrs. Quince awaited her outside the house.

"Look at this," she said, setting her hands upon her hips. "Water rises to its own level, as they say. In this instance, it is the level of a gutter."

Lucy could think of nothing to say, but Byron bowed low to Mrs. Quince. "Mrs. Quince, if memory serves, and memory always serves well when it is beauty to be recalled."

She snorted. "I am not fooled by your nonsense, and I have no use for titled profligates. Come, girl. Your uncle wants you within, and asked that this gentleman accompany you."

Byron followed her inside, and there they found not only Uncle Lowell, but Mr. Olson as well. He did not appear surprised to see Byron, so Lucy surmised some neighbor had told him of Byron's visit.

Olson rushed to his feet with a rapidity that could only signal belligerence. "*Lord* Byron," he said, as though the title were but an affectation. "I demand you declare your intentions toward this lady. What do you mean by walking with Miss Derrick?"

Byron bowed once more. "What I mean is to talk to her, and as the weather is fine, we chose to talk out of doors. However, I must point out that it pains me to answer your questions, as we have not been introduced."

Mr. Olson did not much like this response. "I am Walter Olson, and I know you are aware of my intention to marry this lady."

"But I am not aware of any reason that your intentions are my concern," Byron replied.

"Then let us speak of *your* intentions toward Miss Derrick," Mr. Olson said.

Lucy observed that Byron but poorly hid his discomfort. He must now either propose marriage on the spot or declare he did not want her. Of course, men cannot be held accountable to all the women they do not marry, but neither should they be made to tell each one to her face that she has not been chosen.

"I have never before today spoken at length with Miss Derrick. It is absurd to ask such a question of me."

Of course he was right, but Lucy would have hoped for a less timid response. He was not a schoolboy, he was a peer, a member of the House of Lords, a *poet*. He was, by his own accounting, and by Lucy's, an impressive man, and yet he chose not to be impressive now. She understood his reasons, but she wished he might have said something else.

"And," added Byron, "my intentions are my own concern, and Miss Derrick's. Certainly not yours."

It took all of Lucy's will to suppress a smile. This was what she had hoped for. A hint — no more than a hint — of what was to come. It was enough for now, surely.

"It seems to me that you have no more to offer my niece than a lot of romantical fluffery," said Uncle Lowell, pronouncing his edict from his chair with all the gravity of an ancient lawgiver. "I beg you will excuse us. There are some private matters at hand, and we do not choose to speak of them in the company of strangers."

Lucy blushed with mortification. Byron said he would leave for London in a day or two, and she did not know if she would see him again. "Allow me to see him out," said Lucy.

"Ungston will tend to that," said Uncle Lowell. "You may sit, Lucy."

Though she shook with rage, Lucy was prepared to do as she was told. Byron, however, approached her and took both her hands.

"As we cannot say our good-byes in private, we must do so in public." As if interpreting her expression, he added, "I shall call upon you before I depart the county." He then bowed to the rest of the room, and took his leave.

Lucy took some small pleasure at his cool defiance of her uncle. Taking hold of Byron's calm as though it were her own, Lucy sat.

Uncle Lowell raised his head slightly, ready to present to the world another utterance of wisdom. "Mr. Olson," he pronounced, "wishes to say something."

Mr. Olson nodded. "Miss Derrick, I received your message, which I now understand you wrote without your uncle's knowledge or permission. It is not uncommon for young ladies to suffer a certain degree of confusion, and yours is without doubt an impulsive nature. The incident in which you nearly ran off with a rake was known to me even before I made my offer of marriage, though I thought you had matured beyond such things. It is time for you to set aside childhood, and so I have chosen to disregard your rejection of marriage. Your uncle and I have set upon a date six weeks hence for your wedding."

Mrs. Quince rose to her feet and held her arms out to embrace Lucy. "I am so happy for you, Miss Derrick."

Lucy turned away from Mrs. Quince. She felt dizzy, as though the floor shifted under her. This announcement was nonsense. She had severed ties with Mr. Olson by letter because she had wished to avoid a confrontation, but now a confrontation was upon her, and she had no choice but to accept their terms to argue. Perhaps accepting and remaining quiet for six weeks was the best course. By then she would have heard from Miss Crawford about the will. Once she had the means to establish her own household, she could say and do just as she liked.

But no, Lucy would not be so duplicitous. This was the moment to assert herself. She rose and looked at Mrs. Quince, who had by now lowered her arms, but still remained standing, staring at Lucy. She turned to Mr. Olson. "I beg your pardon, but I am resolved. I do not believe a marriage between us would lead to anything but mutual unhappiness."

There was a protracted moment of silence, and then it was Mrs. Quince who spoke. "The girl apparently believes she has some choice in this matter."

Uncle Lowell nodded and looked at Lucy. "You are mistaken to believe you may refuse to marry as we say."

Lucy was so astonished by this answer that she could hardly breathe. "I am of age," she said so quietly she wondered if they heard her.

They did hear. "And what shall that get you?" asked her uncle. "Have you money upon which to live? Have you the means to defend your position?"

Lucy said nothing. There was nothing to say. She had nowhere to go, no one to help her, not unless her father's estate came to her.

"The marriage shall proceed as planned," said her uncle. "You may go now."

Lucy affected anger and left in a sulky march, for if she did not pretend to defiance, she would certainly have succumbed to despair. As she crossed the threshold, she thought to turn back to glare at Mr. Olson, but then checked herself, and in that instant, she thought she saw something in the corner of the ceiling, concealed in the moldings, flickering in the firelight. It was but a hint of shadow, but it moved. It flexed. Then it was gone.

9

True to his word, Byron called upon Lucy the next morning. In the hopes of seeing him, she'd worn her best day frock, white with purple flowers, fitted perfectly to her form, with a plain low front. Seeing his coach arrive, Mrs. Quince stood near the door with her arms crossed so as to block Lucy's way. "You'll not go anywhere."

A week ago, Lucy would have retreated, but things were now different, and she would not obey. She could not even conceive how she might step into her previous timidity, and because retreating would do her no good, there was no direction but forward Lucy moved to push past Mrs. Quince.

Astonished, the serving woman lashed out and grabbed Lucy's wrist, digging in with her fingernails and drawing blood. Mrs. Quince yanked hard at Lucy's arm, attempting to knock her off balance, possibly to make her stumble. It was not a new maneuver, however, and Lucy was prepared for it. She stepped into the momentum, and then, stopping suddenly, she took hold of Mrs. Quince's arm, pulled hard, and then suddenly let go. Mrs. Quince fell upon her back, striking her head against the hard floor. And she lay there motionless, her face puckered with anger.

"I think," said Lucy, "that I shall go out."

By the time Lucy reached the door, Mrs. Quince was already upon her feet, but she did not approach. "What do you think you shall be when you are alone and without money or home?"

"I cannot know," said Lucy. "Could it be worse than what I am now?"

She stepped out into the street and met Byron at the door. Again, his appearance, his mere physical presence, astonished her. She had thought of him over and over during the night, she had dwelt upon how handsome he was, and yet, now that she gazed upon him, his beauty staggered her, as if she'd had no idea of it before. His dress was remarkably like that of the previous day, but the familiarity made him no less magnetic. He led her down the stairs, holding out his arm for her to take. "I fear I must leave in the morning, and I wished to call to see if you had survived the meeting of the Star Chamber."

"There is no longer any doubt," said Lucy, forcing herself to sound at her ease. She felt a trickle of blood on her wrist, but she did not inspect it, lest Byron see it. It would heal soon enough. Instead, she concentrated on the feel of his arm under her touch — warm and muscular and confident. "Mr. Olson has made his intentions clear. We are to marry in six weeks."

Byron sharply turned his face toward hers. "You must not do it."

"What choice have I?" asked Lucy, offering Byron the opportunity to provide her with an alternative. "I haven't the means to assert a preference. At least as Mrs. Olson I have some chance of a measure of independence."

"But no chance of happiness."

Lucy let go of his arm, for she found she was quite angry. "You go where you like," she said. "You visit with whom you like. You may marry whom you like or marry no one at all. I have none of those choices, so what right have you to tell me what I must or mustn't do?"

"It is the right of justice, Lucy," he said, unconcerned with her tone, and using her Christian name for the first time. "I have nothing but contempt for Olson now that I have seen him. I think anything must be preferable than a life shackled to that dullard."

"If you see an option that I do not, I pray you will tell me. Otherwise, I must ask you not to speak of what is not your concern." Lucy kept her voice even, her tone sharp, with no hint of the coquette, and yet, there

uld be no doubt that she now challenged
im.

At that moment they passed by an alley,
narrow and empty and so protected from the
sun that it was gloomy. Without signaling his
intentions, Byron turned in, taking Lucy's
hand and pulling her along with him. She
staggered slightly, and he righted her by taking hold of her shoulders, and then her waist.
A sensation of the most pleasant confusion
came over her, as if she did not know which
way was up, as if she were tumbling gently
through space. She felt the heat of his nearness, the masculine scent of his body, the
sweetness of his breath, and that warmth that
grew within her, within her very core, and
spread out like a fanned flame. And then, he
was kissing her. His lips were on hers, and
his hands moved down to her hips, and she
tasted coffee and licorice on his breath.

It took Lucy a moment to notice that she
was kissing him back. Her hands were around
his neck, and her tongue was in his mouth,
and she was trying to taste every bit of him.
She felt sure of herself, as though this were
not something entirely new and utterly
unexpected. She felt in control. She felt
vibrant and alive. She had not kissed anyone
since Jonas Morrison, who had claimed to
love her but had only sought her ruin. His
kisses has been tentative, gentle, even timid.
Byron's were greedy and urgent. He radiated

raw desire. It coursed through his body, and through hers.

This kiss was a kind of madness, but Lucy was not mad. It had to end before they were seen, before he pressed for more, right there in the alley, because she did not know that she could refuse him. It had to end, but not yet, not for another moment, because Lucy could not know that she would ever kiss him again, and she wanted to feel it, to burn the sensation into her mind that she might always cling to the memory.

It was Byron who broke off the kiss. He gently pushed her away and looked at her, his expression full of both tenderness and mischief. He touched her face with the back of his fingers. "You must come with me to London."

Lucy felt light-headed. It was all happening as she had imagined, and the collision of reality with fantasy overwhelmed her. It was what she had dared to hope for, but only in the foolish way girls hope for what cannot be, and now it had come to pass. She felt surprise and terror and delight, all in equal measure. "You must speak plainly. Do you ask for my hand?"

Byron met her eye and grinned with pleasure. "I am asking you to come be with me in London. We do not need to live by their rules, Lucy. We can live by our own and in glorious defiance. There is no limit to what we together can accomplish."

She could still feel the warmth of him on her lips, but now suddenly she was ashamed. She was a fool. She hardly knew this man, and she imagined he was the prince and she the princess in a child's fairy tale. Of course he would not marry her. She could bring him nothing. He was beautiful and he had a title. He would hold out for a young lady with a fortune to trade. And yet, for all that, she could not condemn herself entirely. He had misled her. He had made her believe he had a different kind of offer for her.

"You ask me to be your whore," Lucy said, her voice calm but dangerously brittle.

"Do not style it so," he answered. "That is the world's judgment, not our own. I can see you are no ordinary woman. Can you not see that I am no ordinary man? I cannot — we cannot — live the way the world demands. We must live according to our own law, or we shall be suffocated by their damned rules."

The selfish stupidity of his proposal infuriated her so that it was difficult for her to form words. She stepped out of the alley without troubling herself to see if he followed, hoping he wouldn't and hoping he would. When she heard him directly behind her, she stopped and spun around to face him. "You know nothing of me if you think I would stoop to such a thing. I am vulnerable enough living with my uncle. If I were to do what you propose, setting aside the propriety of the situation, for I know you hold that in contempt, I should be even more defenseless than I am now. What happens when you tire of me?"

"I will be your protector. While I live, you will want for nothing and fear nothing."

"While you live. And if you are taken ill or trampled by a horse? Your proposal insults me, sir, and I wish you had not made it. I wish — I wish I had not seen you more."

He reached out and took her gloved hand in his. "I want only that you rise above what these little fools demand of you. If I were as rich as your uncle, I would give you money to live independently. I would do this gladly because the world would be better for you living in it free and unfettered. I do not have such money, but I offer you what I can. I offer you a life with *me*."

"I must go," said Lucy, pulling her hand away.

She turned and walked hurriedly. Byron called out her name two times. He did not call out a third. She hardly had time to feel the pain of another avenue of escape closing itself to her, to make sense of her sadness and disappointment and disillusionment, when Lucy felt a hand fall hard on her shoulder. She turned to face Mrs. Quince who grimaced at her in mad delight.

"Now comes the reckoning," she said, and led Lucy back to her uncle's house.

10

Lucy remained in her room, not coming out for dinner, and not for breakfast the next morning, though by then she was famished. She did not want to face her uncle or Mrs. Quince. She felt ashamed for having kissed Byron, and yet she could not regret it. He was a wretched man, selfish and destructive, she understood that now, but she had kissed him before she knew that, and it had been wonderful. She could not, therefore, be sorry. Not entirely.

She remained hidden because she did not want to hear herself upbraided. She did not want to be called a slut. She did not want to listen to the story of her near elopement with Jonas Morrison recounted once more, revealed as the foreshadowing of all of Lucy's mistakes yet to come. Most of all, she did not want to be made to feel the full extent of her powerlessness.

An hour or two after she awoke, she heard Mrs. Quince's footsteps outside her door, and then the scrape of something being set down. Once she was sure no one awaited her in the hallway, Lucy peered out to discover a tray with some bread and old butter and dried prunes, along with a cup of cold chocolate. Lucy brought the tray into her room and stared at it for a long time, deciding if eating what Mrs. Quince had brought would amount to a capitulation. Eventually hunger won out, though resentment and helplessness dulled all pleasure the food might have otherwise provided.

Lucy set the tray out when she was done, and lay on her bed all day, staring at the cracks in the plaster and wishing Miss Crawford would arrive with news of her impending independence. Nothing of that sort happened. At dinnertime, Mrs. Quince left another tray, which Lucy retrieved, ate from, and then set out again. The same transpired in the morning, and Lucy began to realize that she was not so much avoiding an upbraiding as making herself a willing participant in her own imprisonment. Her uncle and Mrs. Quince now had from her precisely what they most wanted — to keep her locked away, passive and helpless, until the time of the wedding was upon her.

Knowing that she was complicit in her uncle's plans was not the same as knowing what to do about it, and Lucy attempted to devise some strategy that did not involve her

sitting in her room waiting to be dragged to
the altar or rescued deus ex machina by a
timely message from Miss Crawford — or
perhaps heroic intervention by a contrite
Byron, ready now with an offer of marriage.
These fantasies did not alleviate her suffering, but only rubbed salt in her wounds.

There was nothing to do but wait and hope
for the best. It had not been so very long ago
that she had been resigned to marry Mr. Olson. Would doing so now really be so terrible?
If she did not account for the will, the
inexplicable warnings, and the interest,
however inappropriate, of Byron, then perhaps hers was not the worst imaginable lot.
Maybe Lucy simply had to learn to look at
things as she had been used to doing before.
Certainly, if she remained in her room for
the next six weeks she would go mad. She
was therefore resolved to go downstairs and
face her uncle and Mrs. Quince. She would
endure the awkwardness of the first conversation, and then she could return to her old life
— at least until she devised an alternative.

Much of the morning and early afternoon
passed in efforts to screw up her courage,
and then she heard a carriage rolling to a stop
before her uncle's house, and then there were
the sounds of voices below — distant and
muffled.

Her uncle had so few visitors, and Lucy
understood that a rare opportunity presented

itself. If she were to face him and Mrs. Quince before callers, then surely their ire would be hidden, or at least dampened. And then, once these visitors left, the first encounter would already be over. Wanting to take advantage of this opportunity, Lucy dressed herself, tended to her hair, and made herself look as well as she could without aid, and went downstairs, a smile plastered to her face and feeling like an idiot.

When she walked into the parlor, a spike of dread pierced her. Sitting with her uncle and Mrs. Quince, both of whom appeared to be exceedingly uncomfortable, was Mr. William Buckles, her sister's husband, as well as that man's patroness, the widow Lady Harriett Dyer.

"Ah, yes, Miss Derrick," said Mr. Buckles, rising to his feet. He bowed deeply and awkwardly, for he was a towering, pear-shaped sort of man. He was dressed, as she had always seen him, in his clerical black and a white cravat, which always appeared out of sorts somehow with his perpetually red complexion. This, combined with his breathless way of speaking, gave the impression that Mr. Buckles had just come from running up several flights of stairs.

"Yes," he said, gasping for breath as he returned to his seat. "Yes, it is Miss Derrick. The young lady we've come to see." He took out a handkerchief and ran it along his high forehead — for his browning-apple-colored hair was receding like an army in full flight.

"Has Martha come?" Lucy asked, forgetting all manners, and not caring that she did so. "Have you brought the baby?"

"No," answered Lady Harriet, in her clipped voice. "*We* have business with you. Not your sister, and so she has been left at home to tend to the child." She did not rise when she spoke to Lucy.

Lucy did not trouble herself to hide her disappointment. She could not imagine why Mr. Buckles would come without Martha, and nothing could have cheered Lucy so much as a visit from her sister. But here, instead, was Lady Harriett, who owned an estate not ten miles from the home in which Lucy had grown up. Mr. Buckles had been Lady Harriett's curate before he had inherited Lucy's father's house, and in exchange for these attentions, he was slavishly devoted to her.

Lady Harriett looked well enough for a woman of her age, which Lucy supposed to be fifty or thereabouts. She was trim and fine-boned, with a sharp nose and tiny eyes that were penetrating for all their smallness. Her skin was white and vaguely waxy, and her lips extraordinarily red. Lucy always supposed she must have been pretty as a young woman, though she also supposed her unkind spirit must have dampened her attractiveness

138

considerably. Adding to her sour demeanor was a black gown and headdress, full widow's attire that might have been in the mode some time before the final quarter of the previous century. Lady Harriett had worn widow's black since her husband, Sir Reginald, had died a few years earlier. The precise details of his demise were unknown to Lucy, as it had happened when she was in mourning for her sister Emily.

Now here was Lady Harriett, glaring at Lucy with inexplicable contempt. Contrary to all logic, Lucy looked to her uncle for guidance, but he appeared nothing but uneasy, like a man who had released his dogs and now feared they would devour him. Mrs. Quince, for her part, sat with a look of smug satisfaction.

"Sit down," Mrs. Quince ordered.

Lucy sat. She longed to be defiant, but she wanted something substantial to defy, and sitting was probably the best course of action.

"It is rather a long ride from Kent," said Lady Harriett, "but I have come here to speak with you, and I will not brook any rudeness on your part. My late Sir Reginald knew how to manage a girl like you, and so do I. Do you understand me?"

"I understand your words," said Lucy, "but not the cause for speaking them."

"Already she is saucy," observed Mrs. Quince.

Lady Harriett paused a moment and said, "It is my understanding that you have defied your uncle's wishes regarding your impending marriage to Mr. Olson. Not only have you dared to refuse this marriage, but now you throw yourself at a profligate baron. Miss Derrick, the world well remembers precisely what sort of a girl you are. The sooner you are bound in matrimony, the sooner you will be safe — or at least safer — from your weaknesses."

Lucy seethed, furious and stunned by this intrusion. "I beg your pardon, Lady Harriett. You and I have been introduced, but we little know one another. I am not certain by what authority you direct me, or what has prompted you to make the long drive to do so."

"She is very rude," said Lady Harriett to Mr. Buckles.

"I did not expect this rudeness," agreed Mr. Buckles. "I am ashamed for her."

Lady Harriett folded her hands into an attitude of prayer and rolled her eyes to the ceiling. "Mr. Buckles is married to your sister, which makes his larger family my concern. I would not have you bring scandal upon Mr. Buckles through your improprieties. I believe that is how Sir Reginald would have ordered things were he alive, and it is how I shall do so."

A vein throbbed distractingly in Lady Harriett's temple. It hardly seemed likely that she came all this way out of concern for Mr. Buckles's reputation, which would be but little touched by Lucy's actions. But for some reason she did care. That much was evident. And Byron, under the influence of his curse, had also cared whom Lucy married. Lucy could not fathom of what possible concern this match might be to the world.

"Your interest in my future is most unexpected," said Lucy after a brief pause. "If I may speak bluntly, you are not my relation, and you have neither power nor authority over me. I beg you indulge me when I ask what shall happen if I choose not to marry Mr. Olson."

"You shall find I have power and authority over more than you suppose," said Lady Harriett. "If you refuse to marry Mr. Olson, then I will instruct Mr. Buckles to bar you from having any contact with his wife and daughter, whom you shall never see again."

Lucy stared in amazement, unable to believe what she heard. Martha and little Emily were her only family — for she hardly counted her uncle — left in the world, and she could not imagine Mr. Buckles could be so monstrous as to prevent his own wife from having contact with her sister. Martha would have no choice but to obey her husband's demands, but such an order would only fill their marriage with resentment and bitterness. "You cannot mean it," she said.

"Lady Harriett is, ah, very serious," said Mr. Buckles. "It would distress me to no small extent to give pain to my wife, but I will not . . . will not, shall we say, hesitate to do so for the good of my family. If you do not marry this Olson, you shall be cut off entire." He paused to wipe his brow in a dramatic and determined manner, as though the rest of the company must now pause to admire his brow-wiping prowess.

"I beg you recall the annuity which Mr. Buckles has been generous enough to provide," added Lady Harriett. She rose from her chair with the gravity of a queen vacating her throne and stepped across the room to stand directly before Lucy. "Your obstinacy is an insult to my late husband's memory, and I shan't tolerate it. If you continue on this course, you may remain in your uncle's house no longer. Consider your situation, young lady. Either you marry Mr. Olson, or you will be cast adrift, utterly alone and friendless."

Mrs. Quince nodded at Lucy, as though she herself had arranged everything that had happened and now gazed upon her own handiwork with pride and satisfaction.

11

Lucy comforted herself that Mr. Buckles and Lady Harriett chose not to stay. After their brief conversation, they set out at once to return to Kent. One good result of the visit, however, was that it effectively reintroduced Lucy to the routine of the house. Neither her uncle nor Mrs. Quince said anything of her walking with Byron or her brief confinement to her room.

Nevertheless, Lucy remained trapped. She *had* to marry Mr. Olson. She did not see how she could avoid it, not unless the new will proved valid and she came into her inheritance. Otherwise, she would be cast adrift with no money or refuge.

Oddly enough, in the face of these devastating consequences, Lucy found a new calm. Events were now out of her hands. She could hope the world might rescue her, and if it did not, she would float along on the tides of fate, much the way everyone else did. Who was she to think she deserved better? She would marry Mr. Olson, so dull and cold, but capable of providing her with a decent life. Women prayed daily for such a husband.

Lucy's efforts to resign herself to her fate were interrupted when Mrs. Quince pushed open her door to tell her that she had a visitor. "It is that Crawford woman. I did not know you continued to carry on with her. I believe I shall have to speak to your uncle."

Lucy would not have yet another connection taken away from her, but protesting would not serve her ends. Instead, she silently followed Mrs. Quince to the sitting room, where the ethereal Miss Mary Crawford stood looking out the window to the street beyond. She wore no green today, but a frock of white trimmed with light pink, and a broad-brimmed white hat with a matching pink band. With her fair hair and fairer skin, she glowed, almost like an angel.

"What is your business with Miss Derrick?" asked Mrs. Quince.

"She is my friend," said Miss Crawford. "Is she not permitted friends?"

"Of the proper sort," said Mrs. Quince with the sort of sniff she believed must make her appear more formidable.

Miss Crawford took a step forward. "Do you suggest something, Mrs. Quince? I beg you speak plainly."

Much to Lucy's surprise, Mrs. Quince retreated. Lucy had never seen her do so except in the presence of someone she wished to flatter. "I know of nothing objectionable," she said, and then walked toward the door, where she hovered for a moment, one last attempt to intimidate. Miss Crawford turned her back to her, however, and so Mrs. Quince departed.

When they were left alone, Lucy permitted herself to look at Miss Crawford, studied her face for signs of good news or bad. Miss Crawford met her eye, and her thin, vaguely sad smile suggested nothing good.

"The will is not real," Lucy said, holding on to the wall for balance. "It is false, and I have no cause for hope."

"It is real," said Miss Crawford, stepping forward to take her hand, "but the situation is complicated."

Lucy felt the most unexpected sensation, the warmth of pure affection that seemed to course from this woman's gloved hand. "You've already been so kind to me. I must thank you for making the effort, for attempting —"

"You need not thank me. Though we have met but recently, we are friends, and I will always do what I can for you. There is so much more to say, about this and about other things. Will you come with me, Miss Derrick?"

"Go with you where?"

Miss Crawford's countenance appeared

suddenly so serious that Lucy could never have predicted what she said next.

"To a picnic."

She had packed a basket in preparation, and they rode out of town, toward the southwest, in the direction of Gotham Village. It was a pleasant spring day, warm and dry — perfect for a picnic, but somehow Lucy did not think they were to sit out of doors because the weather was fair. In the carriage Miss Crawford tried to make idle chatter, saving the meat of her conversation for their destination. Lucy tried not to stare at her hostess, tried not to notice how her fair hair and pale skin seemed to glow in the dark of the carriage, tried not to notice her pure, almost painful beauty.

They came at last to their destination, near one of the old fairy barrows alongside the road. It was a hillock, much like the one on the road to Mr. Olson's mill. Already the brown grass was beginning to green, and some flowers were near blooming. A trio of rabbits scattered as Lucy and Miss Crawford approached and laid out a blanket and, upon that, a large basket. The lady had brought only a light meal of seedcakes, a loaf of bread, and a wedge of orange cheese. She had also packed a bottle of wine, the cork pulled and loosely replaced, and two pewter glasses. Lucy did not drink much wine, certainly not unwatered, and not in the middle of the day.

Miss Crawford removed some plates and prepared portions for them both. She then poured wine and handed Lucy a cup. Something felt almost ceremonial in her gestures, and Lucy somehow knew it would be wrong to refuse to drink. The wine smelled of earth and mushrooms and damp fallen leaves, but the taste was bright and fruity and delicious.

"My solicitor believes this will genuine," said Miss Crawford at last. "The one read after your father's death was false, and you were almost certainly cheated out of your inheritance."

Lucy let out her breath very slowly. This information was neither new nor surprising. She had suspected it from the moment she had first seen the new will, but to hear this fact asserted, without reservation, by another person — it made her feel faint. She set her cup down, struggling to balance it upon the ground.

"There are difficulties, however. Your father's solicitor, a Mr. Clencher, is dead, and so we know of no witnesses who can directly testify on the matter. The fact that the handwriting of this new will more closely resembles that of other documents by your father's hand is to your advantage, but it is a case that would certainly circulate in the courts for years, and cost thousands of pounds to bring to a conclusion. The resolution of the matter would likely cost more than the value of the inheritance. I know you must dream of a speedy reversal of this injustice, but the falsification of your father's estate is hidden behind legal barriers that make prohibitive the cost of revelation."

Lucy sat clutching her cup of wine so tight her fingers began to numb. She set it down with a trembling hand, and then wove her fingers together in an endlessly moving pattern. This life she lived was not hers, it was a fabrication, a falsehood, an unnecessary misery. She ought to be living in comfort, in independence, but that true existence was barred to her. This was the end of her hopes, and she would have to marry Mr. Olson. "There is nothing I can do?" she asked.

"You do have . . . options, though not perhaps the ones you imagine. I understand you hoped you could deliver yourself from your current situation, and that cannot happen with this will. But I believe I can offer you some help, if you will trust me."

Not daring to speak, Lucy only nodded.

"I think," Miss Crawford said, "we must begin by discussing the man who is most probably the architect of this fraud."

Lucy snapped out of her misery, her attention focused and sharp. At the same time, she observed, as if from a dispassionate position, how much more powerful was anger than misery. "Then you know who cheated me."

"There is a suspicious circumstance of a gentleman who shared the same solicitor as your father, and who hired this Mr. Clencher for a number of lucrative endeavors around the time of your father's death. These endeavors are poorly documented, and by all appearances, Clencher was paid for facilitating the false will and then keeping silent."

"Who was this other man?" Lucy rose without meaning to, hardly knowing she moved at all. She wanted to move, to act, to do. "Is it someone I would have heard of?"

"I'm afraid so," said Miss Crawford. "The man who has cheated you is very likely Mr. William Buckles, your sister's husband."

12

Lucy had considered Mr. Buckles a possible suspect, but it had been an abstract sort of speculation, and she had not really believed that her sister's husband, no matter how much she might dislike him, could have taken part in such a mad scheme. But now to hear it said aloud, to be told it was true — it was more than she could endure. She began to cry, first a stream of silent tears, and then convulsive waves. Her face was in her hands, and without knowing how it had happened, Miss Crawford was holding her, one arm around her shoulder, and Lucy sobbed into the sleeve of her gown.

"Shh," said Miss Crawford. "We shall make everything right."

"No, nothing will be right." To steady herself Lucy took another sip of wine. And then another. Her cup was empty, and Miss Crawford was refilling it. Lucy could begin to feel the effects of the drink. A soft cloud of indifference gathered around her thoughts.

What did any of it matter? "I must marry a man I do not like while I know I have been cheated out of what is mine. It is a nightmare, and I can do nothing."

"It is not so," said Miss Crawford. "I beg you to hear me. You have been much abused, but you are not powerless. I will show you that you *can* have everything. You can have your freedom, your inheritance, justice for those who have harmed you, and whatever else you desire."

Lucy stared at her as though she were mad. "I am not a child to believe that. I have so oft felt that my life is not my own, that I am where I do not belong, doing things I have no business doing, and now I find that it is so. The life I was supposed to have was stolen from me. And not only from me, but from my sister. Would Martha have married Mr. Buckles if she'd inherited her share of my father's fortune? Everything has been taken from us, and the courts provide no recourse. How can you lie to me so?"

"I tell you the truth. You can have what is yours and you can have justice, and you can set everything aright, but first we must speak of what transpired with that man — Lord Byron." Miss Crawford said his name as though testing out its feel in her mouth.

"What of him?" The last thing Lucy wished to think of was Byron. She hardly felt equal to discussing anything about him, and yet there was something in Miss Crawford's tone, in her manner, that she could not ignore.

"I believe you can help yourself with the same skills you used to help break that curse. I have no talents in that regard myself, only an interest, much as a person might be an indifferent singer or player, and yet also be a great enthusiast of music. Indeed, I came to Nottingham because it was predicted by another cunning woman, a very good one I met along the Scottish border, that I must come here. I was told that in your county I would find someone remarkable, and now I know I came here to find *you*."

Lucy hardly knew how to respond. Her cup of wine was empty again. She set it down behind her so Miss Crawford would not fill it again. She was beginning to feel things differently, sharper and more dull all at once. She liked it, but at the same time, she hated it. And she noticed things, as if for the first time. The wind blew a comfortably warm breeze across her face. The sun, which had been too bright a moment ago, vanished behind a cloud.

When Mrs. Quince had tried to teach her to read the cards, she had also said that cunning craft was like music or painting or acting. Everyone could do *something,* and, as in the various arts, only a few were possessed of sufficient talent to do a great deal. There were those for whom all the application in the world could produce only a mediocre result, and then there were those who hardly needed to apply themselves at all to achieve much. However, Mrs. Quince had come to the conclusion that Lucy was singularly ungifted. She called Lucy a clumsy oaf, too foolish and muddleheaded to grasp even the most basic of principles. Mrs. Quince's efforts to help Lucy learn to read cards had marked the end of those early days of friendship and the beginning of the long period of enmity.

"What is it you tell me?" Lucy asked. "That I might become a cunning woman? I know something happened with Lord Byron, and there were more strange events at Mr. Olson's mill. These things seemed real at the time, but then, that feeling fades, doesn't it?"

"Only because we wish it to," said Miss Crawford.

Lucy shook her head. "Do you suggest I might use *magic* to reclaim my inheritance?"

Miss Crawford nodded. "I believe that if you apply yourself, you will be able to master all aspects of your life. No one will ever command you again."

Lucy wondered what it would be like to no longer fear her uncle or poverty or her future, to have the means to right the injustices of her life. The thought of such power and freedom thrilled her, but it was a childish dream that she must abandon. To let Miss Crawford lead her down this path would only open her heart to despair.

Yet at that moment, Lucy forgot to be cautious. She forgot to protect herself and to be too cynical to believe. She even set aside her fear and rage. The possibilities all seemed so real when Miss Crawford spoke of them. Her eyes were wide and bright and inviting, and Lucy was ready to believe anything she said.

"We have a selective notion of truth. Look at this mound here." Miss Crawford took a sip of her wine. "Do you know what it is?"

"It is a fairy barrow."

"And do you know what a fairy barrow truly is?" asked Miss Crawford.

Lucy looked at the hill, green and bright. A butterfly hovered above it, not ten feet from where she sat. "A hill. No more."

"It is more, but also less. That is a story for another time, I think."

Lucy thought of what she had seen at the mill, what she thought she had seen in her uncle's house. "You don't mean to suggest there are actual creatures, do you?"

"In the mound? No."

"Because I saw something," Lucy continued. "I feel so foolish even mentioning this, but you seem to believe in these things, and I have told no one else. At Mr. Olson's mill, there were workers chanting the same strange words Lord Byron spoke. And there were creatures, dozens of them, made of shadow. And there was a man, a strange man, and he seemed made of shadow too. I sound mad. I know I do, and yet I saw all these things."

Miss Crawford rose to her feet. She walked away from Lucy and then back again. Her fingers moved, as though adding sums, and then she wiped her hands on her skirts. "You have already seen so much, and you have no training." She sat down again. "Can it be that you have truly never studied any sort of music?"

"I have read Mr. Francis Barrett's book, *The Magus*," Lucy said, referring to a popular book that had been published perhaps ten years earlier. After the unpleasant incident with Mrs. Quince, Lucy had sent off to London for a copy, spending money she could hardly afford. She had believed in a moment of weakness that if she could master magic, she would have a friend once more. It had been a silly notion.

Miss Crawford appeared amused. "Have you, now? All of it?"

"Some of it." Lucy felt her cheeks grow warm.

Miss Crawford did not respond to her embarrassment. She was, on a sudden, quite businesslike. "Have you attempted to make any of the talismans therein, or to cast any spells?"

She shook her head. "It all felt silly. Like I would be playing childish games."

Miss Crawford nodded. "And you would

have been. Barrett's is a popular book written for a general readership. His spells are fabricated or extracted from tawdry volumes meant for the ignorant. And such books are always obsessed with love magic, which you must never practice."

"I thought that was nearly the whole of what cunning women do," said Lucy. "Make this one fall in love with that one."

"Those spells are for dabblers with little skill. For someone with talent, it is a vile thing to make someone believe he feels what he does not, to induce him to make commitments that stand even after the effects of the magic fade. I cannot tell you how many unhappy matches, how many ruined hopes and lives, are the result of cunning folk playing with love magic."

Lucy nodded, though she might as well be promising not to fly too close to the sun with her waxen wings.

"If there is anything of value in Barrett," Miss Crawford continued, "it is cribbed from other writers, principally Agrippa. I daresay these are the sections you chose not to read."

"But I have read *of* Agrippa. My father had me read some histories of his life. I found them extraordinarily dull, but my father thought him important."

Miss Crawford's expression remained neutral. "Indeed he is. But you will have to know more than his biography. You will have to read and understand Agrippa's thinking, along with the ideas of a number of other writers even more impenetrable. Yes, I see the look upon your face. No one wants to spend her days and nights buried in dusty old tomes, especially those that are designed to confound, confuse, and defeat the reader, but there can be no true greatness without sacrifice. And, let me assure you, before I ask you to read anything too dull, you will have seen things, done things that will make you hungry to read the most tedious books in the world if they will advance your craft. Let me give you something."

Miss Crawford reached into her picnic basket and removed a little book, a duodecimo, and put it in Lucy's hand. It was hardly bigger than her palm, though it was heavy. It smelled of old leather and mold, and all at once it reminded her of her father. How at home she felt with Miss Crawford. A warmth spread over her, for here was another great protector, like her father had been, who loved her books. The thought of it made her feel safe, and for the first time in many years, it made her feel like she was somewhere she belonged.

"Are you well?" Miss Crawford asked her. "You have gone quite pale."

"I am well," said Lucy, who felt her eyes beginning to moisten. "It is just that I suddenly felt — I know this will sound odd —

but I felt as though, for a moment, I was living my own life."

"I understand you — more than you can know." She took Lucy's hand and squeezed it. They sat like that for a moment until Miss Crawford let go and invited Lucy to examine the book.

The first fifty or sixty pages contained densely written arguments about magical theory — Lucy could see that from the most casual of glances — but the rest of it was nothing more than various charts. Here were chessboards filled with letters, sometimes English, sometimes Greek, sometimes Hebrew. Some stood alone, some of the squares were embedded within circles, and these circles contained writing as well.

"You may recognize this sort of thing from Barrett," Miss Crawford said. "These are charms and talismans collected from major works on magic. Many of the charms included in those books are false, deliberately false, to deceive dabblers. There has never been a book of spells that was not at least three-quarters nonsense. In that book you hold, one of the better ones I could obtain, there are perhaps three hundred charms, and it may be that forty are genuine. Before you begin to read through material you will find challenging, why don't you attempt to discover which charms are real and make some of them work?"

Lucy examined the book. As she had when looking at the charms in *The Magus,* she felt vaguely silly, but at the same time she could not help but respond to Miss Crawford's gravity, and she held the book as though it were a piece of delicate and rare china. On the pages, the charms had labels indicating what they did, and most involved some sort of manipulation of another person. *To make another cleave to you in loyalty. To drive another from your presence. To inspire feelings of love in another.* Many required no other work than to copy out the charm and to hide it in the clothes or things or upon the person of the subject. Others required a small ritual or manipulation of objects.

"How will I know which are genuine?"

Miss Crawford merely said, "You must determine that for yourself."

"Must I choose now?" she asked, feeling slightly panicked and inadequate.

Miss Crawford laughed and her eyes appeared to turn darker, and then grow pale once more, like the moon appearing from, and disappearing behind, clouds. "No, I shall not make you perform for me, Miss Derrick. You take the book as a gift. Do not object. It is not rare."

Lucy hardly knew what to say, but she clutched the book to her chest. She wanted to bask in this new sensation of feeling special and important and of being someone of whom great things were expected. She had learned that very afternoon that she and her sister had been cheated out of their father's money, that their liberty had been stolen from them, and yet this awful knowledge was somehow mitigated by what Miss Crawford promised. This very notion of magic was foolish, but Lucy could hardly dismiss what she had seen. It *was* silly, she knew that, and yet she also knew it was real and suddenly all set out before her. With Miss Crawford, her friend, to guide her, soon everything would be different.

13

Things did not happen all at once. Lucy could find few enough quiet hours to take her book out of its secret hiding place and look it over, and perhaps she did not want to find the time. The mere thought of Miss Crawford's pale and pretty face was enough to fill Lucy with a kind of unrestrained happiness, but other times she would push the image away, not daring to hope that her life could be something more than what it was.

In the end, it was a feeling of responsibility toward Miss Crawford that drove Lucy forward. If that lady called upon her and asked how she had done, Lucy wanted to be able to report success, or, at the very least, report an honest and honorable failure. When she did examine the talismans, however, she found herself growing quickly frustrated. They all appeared equally plausible or implausible. They were mostly squares, subdivided into smaller squares, in which were written letters of Roman, Greek, or Hebrew, and occasionally some more mysterious runic symbols. Outside a square was often more writing, sometimes within a circle that surrounded the square. Many of the talismans were merely to be worn about the neck or placed upon the person one wished to affect. Others required more elaborate execution — combining the charm with particular plants or actions or items. She practiced copying them out, just to be sure that her hand could replicate the images, though she never produced a complete talisman, and always destroyed what she had made.

She sat in the one comfortable chair in her room, the light to her back, flipping through the pages for perhaps the fifth or sixth time, unable to see how she could determine a true talisman from a false. They were all different, all had their own characteristics, and nothing made some stand out and some fade away. Each was as opaque in its meaning as the next.

Perhaps because she was tired and not troubling herself with her feelings of hope or her unwillingness to feel hope, Lucy was able to clear her mind. She began to drift away from herself, something like the act of quieting herself she had learned, so many years ago, from Mrs. Quince. So it was in this half-quieted state that she turned the pages until she stopped hard. Her heart felt as though it would explode in her chest, for the charm upon which she gazed stood out as different — as powerful, as vibrant, as unmistakable. The charm upon which she looked was *magic.*

It was like an image in a book of trompe l'oeil etchings she had once leafed through with her sisters. These were pictures that, when looked at in a particular way, or with a particular disposition, would reveal a second picture hidden within. The means of uncovering these hidden images was beyond her ability to explain. When her sister Martha had begged Lucy to show her how to see it, Lucy could think of no way to instruct her. She could only say that Martha must look in different ways until she found it.

Now Lucy rapidly flipped through the volume, seeing the talismans for what they were, seeing which charms jumped off the page announcing their efficacy, and which lay flat and lifeless. She heard herself laugh aloud as she found one, and then she snapped the book shut and hugged it to her chest. What Miss Crawford said was true. And if there was magic, if it was real and Lucy could do it, what did it mean for her life?

In the end there were fewer true spells than Miss Crawford had said, only thirty-six. Many of these were to coerce love or loyalty or compliance — a few were so vile, Lucy could not imagine attempting to use them. There were a handful that would be worth trying, if only to see if the charms could be used effectively. Now Lucy wanted only an opportunity to try one, and so she determined to keep the book close at hand, waiting for the proper situation to present itself.

Some days later, the Nottingham assembly was upon her. Uncle Lowell did not wish to be put to the expense of preparing for an assembly when Lucy had already found a husband, but it was Mrs. Quince who argued for Lucy's attendance. Mr. Olson would be there, and he'd written to say he wished to dance with Lucy. Mrs. Quince observed that it would be unwise to allow so desired a bachelor to present himself before so many young ladies without Lucy present to maintain her claim. This argument won the day, and Uncle Lowell consented that Lucy might have a new ribbon for her hat, though the extravagance of this gift pained him immensely.

Lucy had no wish to go. She once loved the monthly assemblies, where she could see her friends and make idle chatter and pretend, for a few hours, to be happy. Now she had too much upon her mind, but as she had not the option to stay home, she would make the best of it.

The assembly hall on Low Pavement, but a short walk from Uncle Lowell's house, was a handsome building, inside and out, and very much grander than fashionable life in Notham, such as it was, required. Lucy did not mind, however, for it was bright and open and agreeable, and it always lightened her mood to be in a place so unlike her uncle's house. When she walked into the room — her entry was slightly delayed by a row concerning an attorney's clerk who attempted to gain entry to the hall, despite the rules forbidding such drudges from attending — Lucy was delighted to hear a competent trio of musicians were in the middle of a sprightly tune that had been enormously popular that year. Mrs. Quince inspected the people about her, making certain there were no conspicuous absences or presences worthy of gossip, and when she had exhausted such comments as she could muster, she retired with the other matrons to the card room. She would have remained with the younger people to keep an eye upon Lucy, but to do so would have been considered ill-mannered, and would have brought unwanted scrutiny on Lucy when it was to Mrs. Quince's advantage that Lucy look well.

Taking advantage of her freedom, Lucy soon found her little group of acquaintances — all of about her age, unmarried, and though she liked most of them well enough, none was a particular friend without whom she could not endure. Her position in Nottingham had always been one of a young lady of no prospects, and this had made particular friendships difficult. Lucy managed as she could with these ladies, for they approximated true friends well enough in situations such as these, when necessity required such an approximation.

This little group was led, with unanimous and unspoken consent, by a young lady called Norah Gilley, slightly taller than Lucy, thinner, with a narrow face, a sharp nose pointed down, and an unusually long mouth designed for sneering. Though not traditionally pretty, Norah had one of those plastic sort of faces that, had her disposition been sweet, her face must have seemed so too. She was, however, of a rather acidic nature. She was a lover of gossip, of finding fault, of being the first and the most eager to remark caustically upon another's defect. As a result, her countenance had a slightly unseemly cast, less ugly than alarmingly sensuous. She was a young lady whom gentlemen often wished to know, to dance with, to take to coffeehouses. Norah believed this must mean her destined to receive a very favorable offer of marriage, but Lucy understood the world well enough to know she misinterpreted attentions.

Norah stood now in the midst of the other girls, but also present was her father, a gentleman of about sixty years of age, with closely cut, thick white hair, the weathered remnants of a handsome face, and eyes so blue they almost astonished Lucy the first time she'd seen them. Mr. Gilley was an unusual sort of man for his age, because he enjoyed the company of people far younger than he, including his daughter and her friends.

Lucy's father had always made a great show of finding his daughters generally silly, and their friends even more so. In his study, however, when they talked of botany or astronomy or he reviewed her Latin, Papa became patient, understanding, sympathetic, and very interested in what Lucy had to say. Mr. Gilley, Lucy imagined, must be the opposite — pretending in public to find everyone of interest, whereas, she suspected, he scorned them all in private.

Now Mr. Gilley stood with his daughter and a dozen or so young ladies of her age, all of whom were laughing at a witty comment he'd made. Fans were out, covering mouths, and then, all at once, fluttering like a cloud of startled butterflies. Several of these young ladies, Lucy knew, had secret fancies for Mr. Gilley — a safe diversion, since Mrs. Gilley, while less social, was very much alive. For her part, Lucy had considered fancying the gentleman once or twice, if only as a means to relieve her boredom, but she could never quite summon the will. Mr. Gilley enjoyed the attentions of young ladies too much, and that ruined the effect.

Seeing her approach, he bowed deeply to her. "It is Miss Derrick," he said. "I had hoped to have the pleasure of greeting you here tonight. I should not have come out otherwise, for fear of catching cold. The weather is not yet sufficiently warm for me to feel entirely comfortable." According to local lore, Mr. Gilley had been deeply affected when, as a youth, he'd witnessed his older brother wake one morning with a slight cold and then die before noon. He now avoided cold weather, damp weather, and even cloudy days whenever he could. "An old man such as myself must take precautions."

Several of the young ladies protested that he was not so very old at all, and he raised his hand, waving away their objections, though it was impossible not to see how he relished them. That Lucy did not protest was not lost on him. He studied her very closely and attempted a different approach. "Certainly you are a sight worth making a man risk his health for, even a very old man such as myself."

Lucy wore a gown of ivory with gold French work in the front. It was not her best gown, for she had not wished to wear her best for this occasion, but she believed it did her no great disservice. Certainly the way Mr. Gilley looked at her suggested as much.

"We have the most wonderful news," said Norah, attempting to reestablish herself at the center of things. "One of the undersecretaries of the navy has died!"

"I congratulate you," said Lucy, who did not see how this could be good news, but she knew an opportunity for irony when one came along.

The other ladies giggled, and Norah affected appearing cross. "You goose. My father is to take his place. We are to remove to London within the month."

This truly was a reason for Norah to rejoice. Lucy had never been to London, had never been presented at court — which Norah had, of course — and a removal to London was what all country girls dreamed of. Now Mr. Gilley had received the patronage that he had long sought, and he was elevating his daughter along with him.

As was natural for any young lady, Lucy resented Norah's good fortune, but she knew it was small of her, and she knew what was proper. She hugged Norah and wished her joy and told her what her friend most wanted to hear — that she, Lucy, was green with envy.

"You will visit us, of course," said Mr. Gilley with the magnanimity befitting the station he would soon inhabit. "The city air is thick with coal in the winter months, and that is very dangerous to the lungs, but in life we must take risks if we wish to experience pleasures."

"Of course," said Sarah Nolin, one of the other girls. "We *all* must visit."

Mr. Gilley turned his full attention to Lucy, gazing at her with those incongruously youthful eyes. "I know Norah would welcome your company most particularly, Miss Derrick. Now, ladies, I know better than to impose myself upon you at any length. You will excuse me as I shall go sit nearer to the fire to warm my lungs."

When he was gone, Lucy hugged Norah once more. "You must be so happy. Of course we must miss you terribly, but you will not care for us any longer. You will have balls and routs and assemblies and all the company of very fine people."

"Must I not also congratulate you? I have heard that soon you are to be called by another name."

All the young ladies gathered around Lucy, eager for her answer. They pressed in, like pampered dogs surrounding a generous master with table scraps at the ready.

"I cannot understand your meaning," said Lucy. Her marriage to Mr. Olson was too painful a subject for her to feign joy, and so she chose to be coy rather than confirm or deny the report.

"Oh, come," said Norah. "We would never be so evasive with you, Lucy. Are you to marry Mr. Olson or no?"

Lucy did not want to say. The words would taste too bitter, so she only laughed and said,

"You know better than to believe idle gossip."

"So then, he is yet available, and any of us may dance with him if we choose? He is not *terribly* handsome, of course, but he is available, and they say soon to be rich. In Nottingham, that must be good enough." As Norah spoke she twisted her mouth into an attitude that was no doubt meant to seem ironic, but appeared to Lucy to be wanton. It was the sort of expression that led Uncle Lowell to call Norah *that girl who will, in time enough, turn whore.*

"You may do as you like," said Lucy, "though for a young lady about to remove to London, I should think Mr. Olson now too provincial for your tastes."

"London is weeks away," answered Norah, "and I should like to be diverted now. However, I would not trample upon what is yours."

"If you can win his favor, even if only for a month, I shall not resent it."

"I think she is being too clever," said another lady, Miss Bastenville. "She wants him for herself, but will not say, lest she be disappointed."

Lucy did not answer, for at that moment Mr. Olson himself walked into the room, and was immediately remarked by every unmarried woman there. Though his suit was unfashionable by London standards, it answered in Nottingham, and it was well cut and flattering to his squat form. He walked with a confidence that bordered upon grace, and he even bowed with a courtly air at the ladies he passed. As he did so, his eyes cast about here and there, searching the room, and Lucy knew he searched for her.

She felt cold, animal panic spread through her. She would not marry him. She would be a governess, or a serving woman. She would be like those characters in the novels who chose to do what is right and noble rather than what is expedient, and it was not because she was righteous, but because she now understood the easy thing is not easy at all. It is horrid.

She had been carrying Miss Crawford's tiny book of talismans with her everywhere she went — tonight she had left it in her pelisse — and now, Lucy thought, was the time for her to make the attempt. It occurred to her that she might make Mr. Olson fall in love with Norah, but she quickly dismissed the notion. Miss Crawford's words had affected her, and forcing two people to think themselves in love seemed to Lucy a cruel thing. Besides, that spell required hair and personal effects from both people, and obtaining these was not practicable. No, Lucy realized which charm she must use now. It would not solve her troubles forever, but if it worked, it would relieve her from the discomfort of dancing with Mr. Olson tonight. After this, she could throw herself on Miss Crawford's mercy, beg that lady for some means by which she could save herself from both frying pan and fire.

She saw Mr. Olson look her way, and Lucy felt her legs turn weak. Their eyes met, so she understood she was committing herself now to a path from which there could be no retreat. So be it. This was her life, and she would live it her way. If she had to choose between Mr. Olson and Miss Crawford, there could be but one decision. Lucy turned and fled.

First she went to the card room, from which she sent one of the attendants to fetch her pelisse. While she waited, she found a pen, a little bottle of ink, and a fresh piece of paper. This task was made more difficult because she needed to avoid Mrs. Quince, but that lady was much engaged in a card came, and by keeping to her back, Lucy managed to escape her notice.

Once she had retrieved the book, Lucy proceeded to the kitchen. The work in preparing the refreshments had long since been completed, so there was only a pair of serving girls standing about and speaking to each other in animated whispers. Lucy smiled at the girls and then walked to a far corner and set her items upon a cutting block.

Lucy consulted her book to make sure she recalled correctly what she needed, and saw that she required a lemon. She found one deemed too shriveled and moldy to be fit for the punch, but Lucy could not believe its poor state would affect her purposes. She took the lemon and a knife, and returned to the cutting block.

Setting out the book, Lucy began to copy the talisman precisely, as she had practiced in her room. This one was made of five rows of five Greek letters each, and long ago, under her father's tutelage, Lucy had learned to draw these letters, as well as Hebrew. Next came a circle containing a few words of Latin, and this surrounded the talisman.

On the surface, the writing out of a talisman was a simple thing — merely a set of symbols copied from one piece of paper to another. The reality was something else entirely. She intuitively understood it must all be copied precisely, the lines drawn in the correct order, this part before that, this word before that flourish. One way felt right, the others wrong. When she looked at the image in the book, she saw the natural process of the strokes of her pen. She used both hands, tilting the paper as she worked, keeping multiple things in her mind at once, solving and resolving puzzles, as though the talisman she copied were in perpetual motion, and she had to hurry to catch up to it before it escaped her.

Both Mrs. Quince and Miss Crawford had

compared magic to music, and though the idea had made sense, only now did Lucy truly understand. She lost herself in the process, and yet, at the same time, she was focused, intense, thinking of the present as well as her next move, ideas moving together, yet independently, like hands upon the pianoforte.

The process took perhaps ten minutes. The resulting drawing seemed tensed and coiled with energy, almost pulsing like a wounded fly that vibrated its wings at impossible speeds but went nowhere. The talisman extended out from the page, pierced the air around itself, sharp as a blade. She'd written very carefully and lightly, so she did not need to blot, only wait a few minutes for the ink to dry. Now, holding the knife in one hand, the lemon in the other, she began to quiet herself, blocking out the images around her, blocking out the two serving girls and the noise from the card room, and the more distant music and muted conversation from the dance hall. All disappeared but the knife and the lemon and Lucy's intent. Without commanding herself, but when the moment was right, Lucy cut the lemon in half, whispering, "Walter Olson," saying it only once, but with intent and force and perhaps even malice.

A sensation passed through her, like her stomach lurching in a dream where she was falling. She felt something cold, or maybe hot, but jarring and strange and familiar. She raised one half of the lemon and squeezed the fruit gently, allowing three drops of juice to spill upon the paper, and she understood the charm was made.

Lucy drifted off from her quiet place and glanced down at her work, pleased with herself. Then she looked up and was startled to see a man in the doorway looking at her. As soon as she raised her eyes, he was gone, but there was something familiar about him that struck her. She had seen only a flash of him, but though she could not say how, she was sure she knew him. And she was sure of something else as well, something unmistakable she'd seen in his eyes. It had been only an instant, but it was long enough to see that. Whoever he was, he knew she was working some kind of magic.

14

The man was gone in a trice, and Lucy decided she could not trouble herself with who he was or how she knew him. The notion that he understood what she was doing suddenly seemed absurd. She was like a child who, because she was naughty, believed everyone must know that she was.

Lucy folded up the piece of paper until it was no bigger than her thumbnail. Then, after finding her coat and placing the book with it, she strolled out to the dance floor.

Scanning the room, she saw that Mr. Olson was not dancing but sipping punch with Norah. His slightly stooped back was turned to her, and it seemed that it would be a simple thing to set the talisman upon him. She approached, hoping to avoid their notice, and slipped the piece of paper into Mr. Olson's pocket. Quickly reversing course, she went back the way she had come but, despite all her art, Mr. Olson turned to her and began to follow. She had taken only a few steps when he put a hand on her shoulder and spun her around. "You avoid me!"

"Avoid you?" Her pulse pounded in her neck. "What ever can you mean?"

"You fled from me not a quarter of an hour before, and now you flee from me again."

"When you first came in I was suffering a headache, and needed only a moment of quiet. After, you were in conversation with Miss Gilley, and I did not choose to disturb you."

"Are you jealous?" he asked with something like a sneer.

"You may speak with whom you like," she answered. "I've no inclination to intrude upon your conversations."

"Nor, it seems, to announce to the world our intentions. Miss Gilley informs me that we are not to be married. Have I not troubles enough without hearing such things? A mill in Heanor has just been burned to the ground by Luddites. For all I know, I could be next, and now you —"

He stopped. Mr. Olson opened his mouth as if to say more, but then froze. He looked up sharply, his expression like that of a man who has just, too late, realized he has bitten into a rotten egg. He took from his coat a handkerchief and wiped his forehead. "I — I do beg your pardon, but I am not well."

Lucy could think of nothing to say, so astonished was she to realize that her charm might be working. Then, all at once, a wave of guilt washed over her. The talisman was designed to make him wish to flee, but what precisely did that mean? Would he wish to flee from the room in which he stood, or would he wish to keep running forever so long as he wore that coat? What if he could not stop running? Had she unleashed a curse as malevolent as the one she'd removed from Byron? She wondered if she ought to remove the paper from his jacket, but it was far easier to drop a small thing onto a gentleman's person than it was to retrieve it.

All of these thoughts flashed through her mind in an instant, and then it was too late. Mr. Olson appeared to have something to say, but abruptly turned on his heel and walked with almost comical quickness from the hall.

Lucy stood staring after him, and then at the door through which he'd left, and whatever fear and guilt and regret she felt crumbled before the mighty power of her exultation. She had cast a *spell*. She had done *magic*. Such forces were true and vibrant and accessible, and she had commanded them. It was not her imagination or some silly fancy. It was all Lucy could do to keep herself from laughing out loud, from clapping, from jumping up and down like a little girl. She was not powerless and weak. Not anymore.

She was thinking to herself all the things

she might now do, when a man passed before her. "Lucy Derrick, you do look pleased with yourself. I can't think of a better way to express your happiness than with a dance."

Lucy looked up and knew at once that here was the man who had watched her make the talisman. It took all her will not to cry out or gasp or stagger back or faint. A thousand incoherent thoughts burst in her mind, wild and discordant and impossible to sort. Standing before her was Jonas Morrison, the man who had convinced Lucy to run away with him four years earlier.

Lucy had not seen Jonas Morrison since he had left their neighborhood, but she had heard that he had married very well. Apparently a beautiful and wealthy woman had succumbed to his charms. She wondered how miserable this lady must be today.

Now he held out a hand and Lucy took it, hardly aware of what she did, too confused even to think of resisting. Before she could clear her thoughts, she was upon the dance floor with him.

"Bit of a surprise I imagine," he said as they danced. "For me as well. Surprises all around, yes?" He reached up to her ear and seemed to produce a brightly colored egg, which he then showed her with a grin.

"You are much mistaken if you think your little tricks are of interest to me," said Lucy.

"I thought it was rather a good trick. Egg from an ear? People usually like that sort of thing. People who aren't humorless, I mean." He spoke quickly, as he often did when he was excited, she recalled. Or perhaps he only affected excitement. If Lucy knew anything about Jonas Morrison it was that she had never really known him at all.

"However," he continued, "I am far more interested in a different kind of magic. Tell me why you cast a spell upon that man."

Lucy's first impulse was to pretend to ignorance, but what need had she to justify herself to him? Four years earlier, Mr. Morrison had nearly seduced and ruined a sixteen-year-old girl. He had come into her life and destroyed it, altering her prospects forever. She hated him, hated him more than she hated anyone, and she owed him nothing.

"I would avoid creating a scene by condemning you in public," said Lucy through clenched teeth, "so the moment this dance is over, you will walk away from me, and I will never see you again. I despise you, sir."

He was silent for several steps. Once or twice he opened his mouth to speak, but it felt like a long time indeed before he found his words. Lucy dared to look at him, and what she saw surprised her. Like Byron, he wore London fashions, and his hair was only a few shades lighter, but they were very different in appearance. Mr. Morrison's good looks were less monumental, less devastatingly magnetic than Byron's, and he had a wry, ironic cast to him, as though he thought everything a great joke. He lacked Byron's gravity, but he struck her as more grave than he had been in the past. He still had the same easy grin she recalled, but it was replaced, from time to time, by a somber expression.

He, apparently, had also been evaluating her. "I see you are not the girl you once were."

"I have not been allowed to be."

"Do you know what? I think you are right to be angry with me. I behaved horribly. Truly terrible stuff. And I am content for you to hate me all you like when we have finished speaking, but I am here upon a serious concern now that may be just a bit more important than who did what to whom many years ago. I wish to know why you cast your spell upon that man. And don't pretend to misunderstand me. I don't mean batting your eyelashes or simpering and acting coy. I mean a *spell*. Abracadabra! You meant to repel him, and now he's gone."

Lucy felt shame and confusion and fear, but did not wish to demonstrate any of these emotions. She wanted to know how Mr. Morrison had discovered what she had done — how it was that he knew about magic at all — but she refused to appear weak before him. Instead, she said, "It is no concern of yours, I promise you."

"It is no concern of mine why you wish him gone. No surprise either. I had a good look at him. Bit pruney in the face, so ship him off, by all means. It is my concern, however, if you live or die, and you are placing yourself before dangerous and powerful forces."

Despite herself, Lucy gripped him tighter Then she let go. "I hardly think Mr. Olson is dangerous," she said with a forced laugh.

"No, he's harmless, but he has crossed paths with some very bad . . . well, *things* I suppose is the right word. Things. Yes. You do not want your fortunes entangled with his."

"Our fortunes are already entangled, for he and I are to marry," Lucy answered, if only to demonstrate that he had no sway over her.

For a brief instant it seemed as though Lucy had genuinely surprised Mr. Morrison. He gave the impression of a man whose words had been quite knocked out of him. But he recovered quickly enough. "Your spell bodes somewhat ill for domestic happiness, I should think."

Lucy could offer no response to this sound observation.

The dance was over, and Mr. Morrison bowed. "I haven't the time or inclination to justify our past, but you must listen to me, Lucy. If you must continue to cast your country-witch spells, cast no more in Mr. Olson's direction. You are putting yourself at great risk."

With that he bowed again, and walked away, leaving the hall altogether. He had hardly stepped away, and Lucy had not had time even to consider anything beyond the fact that *Jonas Morrison* was here, in Nottingham, dancing with her, before Norah rushed over to her. "Dear Lucy, who was that? He is the handsomest man I have seen this age, and he had eyes for no one but you. I suspect dear Mr. Olson would be angry were he still here."

Lucy had other concerns besides Mr. Olson, and even besides Jonas Morrison. Coming toward her from across the hall was Mrs. Quince, her face red with anger. Lucy made her way toward the door, lest Mrs. Quince grab her and drag her out as though she were a wicked child.

15

Mr. Olson was not known to be a drinking man as a matter of habit. He was too concerned with his business to waste time and money upon such foolishness, but after Lucy had humiliated him at the assembly, he was in a state. He hadn't wanted to go home, but rather the urge had come upon him to walk and walk and walk until he at last wished to settle, and settle he did at the Little John Tavern. There he drank silently and heavily until the publican told him he had to leave that they might both go to sleep. Mr. Olson managed to stumble home, and he fell into a thick slumber upon his bed with his clothes yet upon him. It was not until the next morning when he woke up, feeling a pain in his head at once dull and sharp, that he discovered the terrible truth: During the night, every stocking frame in his mill had been broken.

It was the work of machine breakers. He had no doubt once he saw the damage. If he did have doubts, they would have been put to rest by the message chalked upon his door in a surprisingly neat hand:

Sing not songs of old Robin Hood
His feats I but little admire
I will tell of our own General Ludd
Now Hero of Nottinghamshire.

Underneath this bit of doggerel was drawn a circle composed of a string of nonsensical runes, and within the circle was a grid of squares containing Greek letters. But Mr. Olson hardly knew what to make of it, and spoke of it to no one, not out of fear or confusion, merely out of indifference.

It took little time for word of the destruction to spread.

"This is your fault," Uncle Lowell told Lucy. "Had he not been drinking away sorrows heaped upon him by you, he would have been home to protect what was his."

"She snubbed him," added Mrs. Quince. "In public too." She looked directly at Lucy and smirked. Mrs. Quince knew she had been rude to Mr. Olson, and she also knew Lucy had danced with another man, though she did not know that the other man was Jonas Morrison. While Mrs. Quince might know his name, no one in Nottingham knew Jonas Morrison by sight, or so Lucy hoped.

She felt horrible guilt over what had happened to Mr. Olson's mill, and yet Lucy could not help but feel elated and excited too. Her spell had worked, and Jonas Morrison, for whatever reason, had confirmed that she was working magic. She did not know what he was doing in Nottingham, and she did not love all his cryptic warnings, and she hated that fate had placed him in her way once again, but none of that mattered. What mattered was that Lucy could cast a spell that worked, and she wanted nothing so much as to finish her breakfast and return to her room to study.

When she left the table, however, Mrs. Quince followed her into the hall. She put a hand on Lucy's upper arm, but did not squeeze hard. "Who was that man at the assembly?"

Lucy, feeling emboldened by her use of the talisman, decided to play ignorant. "He was handsome, was he not?"

"What was his name?" Mrs. Quince's already-high voice cracked.

"It does not much matter. I shan't see him again soon."

"You danced with a man to whom you had not been introduced?" As the serving woman became angrier, her voice grew lower.

"Oh, we were introduced, but I don't recollect his name. He was only passing through, so I did not think it worth recollecting."

Mrs. Quince let go. "You are particularly stupid today." As though it were an afterthought, she slapped Lucy in the face. It was sharp and stinging, and then cold, and finally hot. Lucy did not move. She did not cry out. She waited for the tears to come, but they did not. There was nothing but a deep and burning anger, and the resolution never again to experience anything like it.

A week after the Nottingham assembly, Lucy was approached by Ungston, who told her that a carriage belonging to a Miss Crawford awaited her. Lucy hardly paused to examine herself in the mirror. She rushed outside, only to find the coach empty. The driver informed her that she would be taken to Miss Crawford's house anon.

Miss Crawford met her at the front door, and embraced her warmly as though they were old friends. Her cheerful pale face was surrounded by a nimbus of white-blond curls. "My dear Miss Derrick, how I have missed you. I do wish I could have seen you again sooner, but I have been so terribly busy."

Miss Crawford led her inside and called for the tea things from Mrs. Emmett, who shrieked with delight when she heard that Lucy had arrived. Her eyes widened under her low bonnet, as she hurried into the room, wiping her floury hands on her apron, as eager as a puppy. Lucy had the distinct impression that had her hands not been covered with flour, Mrs. Emmett would have embraced her as her own daughter. Soon she sufficiently recovered herself, collected the tea tray, and set it down, surveying her work like a proud squire upon his dominion.

"You two will have so much to discuss," said Mrs. Emmett. "I shall leave you to it. Only" — and here she pivoted toward Lucy and smiled as though she might burst with pride — "only let me look upon you a moment, Miss Derrick."

Lucy felt herself frozen with confusion and embarrassment at this notice. "You are too attentive to me. I do not deserve it."

"You make me laugh," said Mrs. Emmett, who then removed herself so, as she said, the two young ladies could speak of their young-lady business.

"Now," said Miss Crawford as she handed a cup of tea to Lucy, "you must tell me all you have been doing. Have you had any success with that little book I presented to you?"

Lucy told her how she had learned to identify the talismans, and how she had used one upon Mr. Olson to powerful effect. "I did not think I could do it. When Mrs. Quince tried to teach me to read cards, she assured me I was utterly without talent."

"Mrs. Quince must be a mere dabbler who has no idea of what she sees. Many women with a strong feel for magic have difficulty

189

with divination. If anything, your inability to master the cards is a sign of your native talents. Either she did not recognize what she saw or . . . or she was testing you."

"Testing me for what?"

Miss Crawford looked away for a moment and then met Lucy's eye. "It is an old trick cunning women use to test those they believe may have talent. Nearly anyone can read the cards, so if a person is useless with them, it can mean she has enormous potential."

"Why would she wish to test me?"

"I don't know, Lucy, but you cannot trust her."

"You may be certain that I do not."

"Good. You must be careful with your trust. You are talented, and so you must attract attention if you are not careful. I fear you will have to learn much, and quickly too. I must call you Lucy. We are such good friends now, and you must call me Mary."

"I shall love to do so," said Lucy, whose heart hammered at the proffered intimacy.

Mary smiled in the way of unhappy people. "I told you I am no cunning woman, but I *can* read the cards a little. I know that changes are coming, and we must be ready to face them. Dark and terrible things, things such as what you saw with Lord Byron and at the mill, but those things are but minor disturbances, harbingers of beings much more dangerous."

"But what has any of it to do with me?" Lucy asked.

"You have seen these beings," said Mary. "They are drawn to you and you to them. They speak to you, and I believe it is because you are already connected with them. I don't know how, but I suspect they sense that you will be there to stand against the very worst of them."

Mary could not speak with any certainty or authority about the peril that brewed around them, but she believed in her soul it was real. "For now, you must continue with your studies. You must learn as much as you can, and be ready for what dangers may come."

Lucy did not much like the sound of that. She did not like vague threats and uncertain menaces, but Mary seemed disinclined to say more. "I don't know how I shall continue to study if I have nowhere to live. My uncle has threatened to cast me out if I do not marry Mr. Olson, and after what passed at the assembly, I believe he may now finally withdraw his offer."

"Hush, my dear," she said. "We will manage it. Your uncle may be affected by your influence. You know that now. You have taken the first steps down a path that will burden you with many responsibilities, but there are privileges now too. You need be at no man's mercy. You can be mistress of your own life, and want neither for money nor shelter nor protection. These things will all be yours in time, and with application."

Lucy did not quite know if she should believe that these prospects could be realized, but Mary telling her that they could made her feel better, made her feel protected.

"Again, for now," Mary said, "you must continue with your studies. I have chosen some books for you to read, and you will take them with you. They may be rather dry reading, but it is important that you understand the basic principles of how magic works and what it is."

Mary rose and returned with a pile of half a dozen books, each far larger and thicker than the little volume she had presented to Lucy last time. "You must start with Agrippa's *Three Books.* After Agrippa, I urge you to master Paracelsus's *Philosophia Adepta.* It is the best of his writing. Then you may wish to attempt this English translation of the *Sefer Raziel HaMalakh,* though you must keep in mind that cabala is made to be confounding, and your utter bewilderment will be no reflection upon you, but upon the nature of the material. Knowledge comes sometimes only through the struggle to comprehend the incomprehensible. Oh, and this is interesting — a curious take on Mesmer's animal magnetism that should work nicely with your natural charms. And do look at this translation of *Abra-Melin*. I sense you have a particular talent for talismans, and his squares may amuse you."

Staring at the books, Lucy felt overwhelmed and frightened. "When may I see you again? I am sure I must have questions."

"I shall do my best to send for you more frequently than I have, but you must not come here if I do not call for you. I do not wish to sound arbitrary, but there are matters I will explain later that I cannot discuss now. I must have your word on this, that you will not call upon me."

"Of course," said Lucy, who could not but feel hurt at this.

"Have no fear. I shall make sure you have all you need. And now, let us see about keeping you safe in your uncle's house."

It was easier than she could have supposed. A talisman found in the first book Mary had given Lucy resolved the issue: *To make others comply with your wishes.* Lucy copied it out with great care, feeling the supple lines come alive as she drew them, feeling the strokes of the pen meld and link themselves to one another. She then allowed some sugar, melted in a spoon, to fall upon the talisman. When it hardened, she rolled up the paper and sealed it with a thread from one of Uncle Lowell's coats. She then approached him, and slipped it into his pocket.

"Uncle," she said, "regardless of Mr. Olson's plans, you will not cast me out."

"Of course not," he said. "Quite right. It would be unseemly for you to make your way in the world when you have an uncle who can look after you."

The next day she heard her uncle and Mrs. Quince arguing loudly, and Lucy heard her own name mentioned several times. Whatever else her uncle discussed, it was clear that he did not know why he had said what he had to Lucy earlier, and he did not know how he might take it all back.

16

A few days later, Lucy awoke to the sound of Uncle Lowell shouting quite angrily. She had been up late at night, attempting to read and understand Agrippa, which was challenging indeed, but the knowledge that it was *real,* that she had real power of the secrets of the universe, provided a compelling motivation. Sometimes her concentration would slip not because of this difficulty of the material, but because she would think about her father. She recalled sitting and reading with him in his library, and after hours upon hours of struggling, she would lose herself in understanding, only to emerge from her trance and see her father, across the room, looking at her over his little spectacles. How his face had glowed with pleasure, and how her heart had been heavy with happiness to be the daughter who made him so pleased. What, she had wondered, would her father think of her studies now?

Attempting to hold on to all the theorems

and speculations and arguments, she dressed hurriedly and descended the stairs to find Uncle Lowell still in full pique shouting at Mrs. Quince.

"It is more than I can endure," he pronounced with a gravity designed to end the conversation. It did not.

"*She* approves of the visit," said Mrs. Quince. "Sir, if you think your quiet is threatened by a little disruption of your home, think what would happen should you earn her enmity."

"What is happening?" asked Lucy, who stood at the entrance to the dining room.

"You — all of you! — have conspired against me to rob me of the one thing I love best, my quiet," answered Uncle Lowell. "I will not have it."

Mrs. Quince turned to Lucy, and flared her nostrils like a horse scenting the wind. "Your sister, Martha, is coming, and she is bringing her infant."

"And her husband and no doubt a nurse and a maid and jugglers too," said Uncle Lowell.

Lucy could not have been happier. Martha had emerged from her confinement a few months earlier, and Lucy had gone to visit her shortly after, but she had not seen her sister or the baby — called Emily — since.

A dark thought occurred to Lucy. "Lady Harriett is not coming, is she?"

"I hardly think so," said Mrs. Quince, "after the insults you've offered her."

In her exuberance, Lucy turned to her uncle. "Oh, I'm so happy. Little Emily will be near six months now. It is a charming age for a baby."

"These infants scream and cry and they make a great deal of mess," said Uncle Lowell. "I hope the wet nurse will tend to everything." He had evidently reconciled himself to the visit.

"Martha nurses Emily herself," said Lucy. "It is the new fashion."

"How dare you speak to me of such things?" demanded Uncle Lowell.

Martha, Mr. Buckles, and little Emily were to arrive in less than a week, though the day was not set, for Lady Harriett had not yet announced when it would be convenient for her to release Mr. Buckles from his many duties as her curate. Lucy's life was now filled with all manner of expectations — some things wonderful, and others dreadful. She would soon see her niece. She would also be forced to face Mr. Buckles for the first time since learning of Mary's suspicions. And as for the matter with Mr. Olson, they had heard nothing, but it was known throughout the county that his prospects were ruined, and so Uncle Lowell presumed the marriage was off. Though he still openly blamed Lucy, his wrath simmered rather than raged. Lucy had been used to living upon thin ice, and she understood that she could not depend upon the calm lasting, but for the time being, she chose to enjoy it.

Meanwhile it seemed as though the world was changing all around them. Throughout Nottinghamshire, the machine breakers continued to strike, destroying stocking frames, burning houses down, and in one case firing upon a mill owner while he sat at the supper table with his wife and children. In each case, they left notes proclaiming themselves to be followers of Ned Ludd, their general and king. It was violence and chaos and upheaval, but many feared it was more than that. The revolution in France had begun, after all, with violent outbursts among the lower classes, and some sensed a similar uprising could be brewing in England. Only recently had England's mad king been pronounced too deluded to remain on the throne, and now the profligate Prince Regent ruled the land.

The war with France had taxed the nation for too long and showed no signs of abating. Because many markets in Europe, the colonies, and the former colonies in America were now closed off, the home trade suffered horribly. The country endured its second disastrous harvest in as many years. Everywhere there was suffering and deprivation as even the oldest could not recall having seen in their lifetimes. In contrast to this misery was the extravagance of George, Prince of Wales, the so-called prince of pleasure, known for his gambling, his immoderate drinking, his excessive eating, and his association with scandalous women and outrageous men. He ruled with an oblivious indifference to the suffering of ordinary men. Though she did not wish to think of such things, Lucy understood that conditions were ripe for upheaval and revolt.

Jonas Morrison had said he had business in Nottingham, and that business had something to do with Mr. Olson, so Lucy feared she must encounter him again, but after so many days, she began to feel more at ease. He'd made an impression upon others at the dance, and so she'd heard rumors among her friends about which inn he'd chosen for his lodgings, and Lucy was careful to avoid passing too close to any suspect establishment. Not seeing him, she soon discovered, made it much easier to pretend she had never seen him at all.

Lucy spent as many hours as she could manage with the books Mary had lent her. Sometimes she studied until her eyes stung, but she read, and she reread, and she took notes, and she paced and reread again until passages once as dense as oat porridge began

to make sense to her. Never had she worked
so hard to understand what at first appeared
impenetrable, but never before had she possessed such motivation. Power and independence, and all she needed to achieve these
things, resided in the knowledge the books
contained. She could endure, she discovered,
because she had reason to endure.

One night during this period there was a
gathering at Norah Gilley's home on Castle
Gate. It was a large affair with several dozen
people in attendance, all meant to display
before the neighborhood Mr. Gilley's glori-
fied status before he decamped for London.
There would be food and punch, some dancing, and, no doubt, much preening of the Gilley clan. Lucy had no desire to attend, but
Mrs. Quince insisted she go. "You cannot
hide in the house forever," she said. "It will
make you look pitiable. And we do not know
for certain if Mr. Olson has thrown you over.
Best to be out and show no shame, no matter
how shamefully you've behaved."

The Gilleys lived but a ten-minute walk
from Uncle Lowell's house, so no coach
would be called, despite the inevitable late
return. She had Mrs. Quince to look after
her, and that would have to be enough.

The gathering was the usual assortment of
Nottingham men and young ladies of mar-
riageable age, and a few married couples for

variety. A card room was set up for the older ladies, and after inspecting the room to make certain that there was no one of concern about, and warning Lucy not to turn slut once again, Mrs. Quince withdrew to play at cards with her friends.

Norah, in an elegant blue and yellow silk tunic, greeted Lucy with a brittle hug and expressed how much she must miss the pleasure of her company once she was removed to London, how all the balls and fashionable friends and marvelous diversions could not make up for what she must leave behind. It was horrible, unthinkable really, that she should go off to such delights while Lucy was left in dreary Nottingham, but what was to be done? Norah then let Lucy go so she could embrace another newly arrived girl, and deliver much the same speech. Lucy chose to put her freedom to good use and fixed herself a plate of food from the table, ladled herself some punch, and quickly sat with her friends that she might better engage in the ritual of looking at the men, pretending not to look at the men, and giggling.

Lucy's heart was not in it, distracted as she was by her recent conversation with Mary, but she kept up her end for form's sake, and when a game of lotteries was announced, she rose to join in so she would have an excuse not to dance should someone ask her. As she walked to the table, however, she observed a young man amusing a crowd of young ladies with a series of tricks involving brightly colored balls, which he was in the process of making vanish and reappear in a variety of unlikely places — in inverted teacups, under hats, bundled into scarves. It was Jonas Morrison.

Mr. Morrison appeared to notice Lucy out of the corner of his eyes, and he hurriedly announced the end of his performance, to the complaints of the young ladies, whom he tried to comfort with promises to show them more anon.

It all struck her anew. The anger she felt toward him, the blame she set upon him, and the helpless embarrassment she had felt upon their last meeting. She had loved this man once, or believed she had, and he had destroyed her life for his own amusement. She could condemn Byron for so much, but not duplicity. He said what he believed and lived by his own law, selfish and wicked though it might be. Jonas Morrison, however, was a thousand times worse for pretending to feelings that were not his so that he might prey upon an innocent young girl.

"Miss Derrick. Keeping clear of danger, I hope?"

"I am doing so this minute," she responded, attempting to walk around him.

Shockingly, he reached out and took her by the wrist. It was not a rough grip, but it was firm and undeniable. "No need for that. There are few enough places where we may talk without arousing suspicion. Look, I have brought you a peace offering."

He unfolded her hand, and she discovered a single red rosebud pressed against her palm. Another one of his silly tricks.

"I have not interest in your games," she said in a harsh whisper, pulling away from him. She continued to clutch the flower, for though she did not want it, she did not know what else to do with it. "You've brought me nothing but misery, and the world knows of it. If these people knew your name, my reputation would never recover. How is it you are even here? No one knows you."

"As for that, people can be made to forget whom they know and whom they don't. You should know of such things by now, I think. And you must believe that I regret that what happened caused you so much pain," he said, "but those days are past, and I must speak to you about what is happening now."

"And that is why you come here?"

"That and the food, yes."

Lucy did not want to hear any of his flippant remarks. "You told me I must not involve myself in what did not concern me, and now you tell me it does concern me."

"I have learned things since then. Please, Miss Derrick. Dance with me. People are beginning to stare at us."

It was true. Their conversation was evidently heated, and eyes were upon them. With the rosebud now pressed between her fingers, for she had nowhere else to put it, they stepped out onto the area reserved for dancing. Soon they settled into the rhythm of the dance.

"You know of these Luddites, and the one they call General Ludd?" he asked.

"Of course," said Lucy. "Everyone does."

"Yes, well they have heard of you. Apparently they speak of you a great deal."

"What does that mean?" Lucy demanded, suddenly quite terrified. What did the Luddites know of her? Why did she matter to them?

"Oh, well, that's rather difficult to say. Could mean anything, I suppose, but I'd like to know myself. I am here in pursuit of their leader, so what interests him interests me."

"You mean to hunt Ned Ludd?" asked Lucy, intending to mock him.

Mr. Morrison, however, showed no signs of understanding the humor. "Yes, that is precisely correct. I am here to hunt Ludd."

Lucy was sure he must be teasing her, and yet there was nothing but seriousness upon his face. "There is no Ludd. He is but a story. Everyone says so."

"I've discovered that it may not always be sound to accept what everyone says as the truth. You may depend upon it — Ludd is all too real, and my order has sent me to stop him."

Lucy could not restrain her curiosity. Had Mr. Morrison become a monk? "Your order?"

"You must understand that I am not the man you once knew. I was never that man, really, but I'm even less he than I once was."

"Yes," said Lucy, turning to hide her disgust. "I heard you married, and married well."

"That is true." He looked away. "I convinced a young lady, beautiful and rich, that she ought to marry me."

"And yet you are dancing now with me and not your wife."

"My wife is dead," Mr. Morrison said.

Lucy swallowed hard. "I did not mean to be cruel. I am sorry."

"She was murdered."

Lucy gasped and stepped away from him. He pulled her back toward him, and when he spoke his voice was low and intense, but somehow gentle. "You cannot know. You cannot understand what this did to me. She was my wife, and I loved her, and someone took her from me. I do not dare think what I would have done or become — I might have become the greatest of villains, I might have destroyed myself — were it not for my order."

"Have you become some sort of devotee of religion?"

"Not religion, no. I am an acolyte of knowledge, a brother of the Rose-Cross."

"I've not heard of it," Lucy said.

"We are also called Rosicrucians," Mr. Morrison explained. "We are a society of men who persue ancient knowledge and wisdom. The head of my order has sent me to destroy Ludd. After that, I may persue my own goals."

"And what are they?"

"To take my revenge upon my wife's murderer. If nothing else, I am a man who believes in revenge."

Lucy hardly knew how to respond. She did not feel comfortable speaking to him of his wife, particularly when his grief was still so evident, so she chose to speak of other matters. "What danger do the Luddites pose? Perhaps the Luddites attempt to save England from the destruction of nature and of the souls of its workingmen."

"Is that how the cunning women see it? Well, I suppose there is some sense to that, even if it is a bit muddled. Your kind have always tended to the individual, and so the worker who must labor for more hours than he chooses or earn a few shillings less than he would like — that must cause you grief. My kind looks upon nations, not men. If these Luddites are unanswered, they will bring about a revolution in England such as there has been in France, and I promise you the streets of London will run just as red with blood as did those of Paris. Is that not harm enough? If not, let me paint you the picture of another future, one in which every nation on earth advances its technology. Every nation but ours. There are new ways of manufacturing, new goods we have not yet conceived, but the Luddites will keep England from participating, and so we will fall behind. Then we will have no trading partners, and the nation will fall into poverty. That means suffering, starvation, want, and misery. This is the future the Luddites offer."

The music now ended, and Mr. Morrison led Lucy to the punch table for refreshment. Lucy was about to ask more questions, particularly why he believed she had some involvement with these Luddites, but their conversation ended abruptly. A hand grabbed Lucy by the shoulder and spun her around roughly. It was Mr. Olson, and hurrying close behind him, Mrs. Quince, who appeared to be doing her best to keep him away.

"I feel certain this is but a misunderstanding, Mr. Olson," said Mrs. Quince. "A young lady may dance when asked."

Olson turned to her, his expression dark and hard and unforgiving. Lucy had not seen him since the destruction of his mill, and whatever he had endured since that night was inscribed upon his countenance. He looked older, and there were heavy bags under his red-rimmed eyes. His hair was unkempt, his neck cloth stained and frayed. His fingernails were caked with dirt, and his face was unshaven.

"I thought I might find you here," he said, his voice loud, almost shrill. "But I did not think to find you had taken up already with another man."

"It is but dancing," said Lucy. Then, because she did not like the frightened waver in her voice, added, "It is no concern of yours."

"It *is* my concern," said Mr. Olson, making no effort to keep his voice low. "You are to be my wife."

"You see," said Mrs. Quince. "All is as it should be. Lucy, you must thank Mr. Olson for his goodness."

"Mr. Olson is mistaken," Lucy answered in a quiet voice. "I do not wish to marry."

Mr. Olson took an unsteady step toward her and gripped her arm tight. "I do not care what you wish. Your uncle promised you to me and I will have you. And what is that? A rose? This man gives you flowers?"

Lucy attempted to pull free, but could not. Mrs. Quince hissed something at her, but she was not listening, because now Mr. Morrison was advancing, attempting to wedge himself between Lucy and Mr. Olson.

"Sir, you ought to reconsider your approach," he said. "Certainly you ought to remove your hand from the lady. That would be an excellent first step. And a fine second step, if I may be so bold, would be to cease

208

behaving like an ass. If there is any more conversation to be had upon the subject, I think it best we conduct it in private. That way, if events should turn badly, no one need see you beaten like a dog. So what say you? A little private chat?"

Mr. Olson gave a hard tug on Lucy's arm, forcing her out of the way, but Mr. Morrison moved to block Olson's path. The two men were of about the same height, but Mr. Morrison was the leaner of the two, and Mr. Olson showed every sign of interpreting his slighter build as weakness. "I'll not be intimidated by a dandy who would take what is mine. Who are you, sir?"

Mr. Morrison gave the briefest of bows and opened his mouth to speak.

To Lucy, it felt as though time had slowed down to an agonizing crawl. She looked about the room, at the food and drink and guests, who were now gathered around, watching the row with scandalized delight. What could she do to prevent him from speaking? If Mrs. Quince were to learn that this man before her was Jonas Morrison, *the* Jonas Morrison, then she might be cast from her uncle's house at once. No mere charm could protect her from that. Had she a glass of punch in her hand, she would have thrown it in his face. Had she a plate, she would have struck him in the head. She had nothing, she could do nothing but watch with horror as

Mr. Morrison spoke his name.

She fully anticipated that Mrs. Quince's jaw would drop, that she might squeal in delight, or grin malevolently. What she did not anticipate is that Mrs. Quince would take a step back, as if in fear, crashing into the punch table, and upsetting the bowl so its contents ran down the back of her gown. She righted herself, and Lucy saw her face had gone pale, her eyes wide. She stood for a moment, punch running off her gown as though she had passed water on the floor, and then fled in what Lucy could only imagine was confusion.

While the spectacle of Mrs. Quince occupied the guests, Mr. Morrison did not allow his attentions to be divided. He stared down Mr. Olson. "Miss Derrick is not your property. Take your business elsewhere while you better recollect how to speak to a lady."

The argument between these two men, Mrs. Quince's scene, and the revelation that she had been dancing with Jonas Morrison — it was all too much for Lucy. She could remain there no longer, and made her way to the front door, ignoring the open stares that followed her. She thought she heard Mr. Morrison call after her. Lucy went out into the dark street and did not run, but walked quickly, thinking only of how much she wished to return to her uncle's house. She would think of nothing else, for then she would have to consider how this dispute must be discussed even now, what would be said of her as a result of Mr. Olson's rudeness and Mr. Morrison's clumsy efforts at chivalry.

Snow was falling lightly, and the cold was bitter, the streets slippery with ice, making it difficult to walk as quickly as she wanted. Lucy had gone only to the corner of Grey Friar Gate when she observed a group of men heading toward her. There were some seven or eight of them, rugged-looking men of the laboring order, the sort she did not wish to encounter by herself under any circumstances, and least of all at night. They spoke and laughed loudly, radiating drunken pride and bravado. They were precisely the sort of men, in precisely the sort of state, to do what they must later regret. Lucy was suddenly afraid, but she believed if she turned to run, they would notice and follow — even if she could run upon such slippery streets.

Lucy turned away from them, toward the church and Pepper Street. She felt like a wounded bird attempting not to attract the notice of a cat, and thus far they'd shown no sign of concerning themselves with her. These were men in rough homespun clothes, and they all carried bulky objects upon their shoulders — tools and equipment and materials of some sort. Perhaps they were just workingmen, happy to have employment, done with their day's labors, and wanting nothing so much as to see their wives and children and hearths. Perhaps her fear was without meaning or substance. Lucy turned her head for a better look and saw, in the dim streetlights, that what they carried with them were poles, pikes, hammers, and mallets, and all at once she understood. They were Luddites.

Lucy turned to run, but it seemed as though time changed and distorted around her. They were half a block away, and then they were encircling her, obstructing her — tall and menacing, smelling of earth and old sweat.

"Here she is then," said one of them. "Miss Lucy Derrick."

"What do you want from me?" Her voice was high and cracking. Lucy could feel her heart in her throat, hammering loud and hard, as though it might break free of her body. It seemed to her that something had shifted in the world. The rules she had always known, with the quickness of snuffing a candle, no longer applied.

"Oh, we don't want to hurt you, girl," one said. "You ain't an enemy of the workingman, now are you?"

"I — I have no reason to be," Lucy stammered. "You have not given me a reason."

"But which side are you on?" asked the same man. "Do you favor the man who wants only to work for his bread, or do you favor the men who would build machines that crush us — men like that man you was to marry?"

"She ain't marrying him," said another. "She's made her choice, so don't frighten her."

"I don't want to scare her," said the first man, "but I won't have her quieting up on me, will I? Now, lass, do you mean to walk away from this Olson for good? Tell me now."

"You're the ones who broke his stocking frames," she said.

He laughed. "Course we are. Who but us? Did it pierce your heart to see him suffer?"

"Enough!" The voice came from the back of the group. It wasn't loud, but it was commanding, and every man in the group stopped. None looked, but they all ceased their motions and waited. Lucy felt herself freeze too. His voice made her uneasy. It had an unnatural sound that seemed almost to disrupt the workings of her body. It was foreign and somehow impossible.

It was the man she had seen outside Mr. Olson's mill, and yet now he appeared somehow greater than what he had been then. There was something in him that terrified her, like a thing that she was not meant to look upon. He was the tallest man she had ever seen, and the broadest, and yet he did not look like a giant in a roadside show. His proportions were right and true. He appeared

213

veiled in darkness, as though the shadow sought his face or was part of his face. For an instant she saw him in bits and pieces — his eyes, his mouth, his brow — and then he moved and the shadows rested upon him again, drawn like metal filings to a magnet.

"We are not here to frighten you," he said in a voice deep and rumbling. "We know of you, and now you know of us. You understand what we stand for, do you not?"

"To whom do I speak?" cried out Lucy in a voice she hoped made her sound bold.

"You speak to our king and our general," answered the first machine breaker. "He who shall tear down the rotten planks of this country and build it up afresh. You speak to Ned Ludd."

Whatever this being was, Lucy understood he was not a man. He was something different, something terrifying. "Sir, I know of your cause, and I sympathize with your suffering, but I cannot join a revolution against my king."

The strange shadowy man stepped forward, but then stopped and seemed to shake his head like a dog who has received a blow. His eyes were wide and bright, not glowing, but something near it. In a flash too quick for Lucy's eyes to follow, he lashed out and grabbed her wrist, and with his other hand, pried open her fingers. It was the second time this had happened that evening, and the second time Mr. Morrison's flower revealed itself.

Lucy had forgotten about it, but it was clearly no trivial thing. Ludd took it from her, pinching one petal with his thumb and index finger as though it were too dangerous to grip as she had gripped it. He whispered something at the flower, and then dropped it into his other palm. He closed his fist and opened it again an instant later, revealing a handful of dust. It reminded Lucy of one of Mr. Morrison's little tricks, but this was no trick. It was magic, ancient and unfathomable.

"This is Rosicrucian work," said Ludd.

"Then she sides with the enemy," said one of his men.

"She cannot choose a side," said Ludd, "when she does not yet know. We don't ask for you to join us, Miss Derrick. We only want that you will not stand against us, and that you do your part. Can we ask that of you?"

"I do not know," she said, "but I will do what I think is right."

"See that you do," said one of the others.

"Remember that pledge when you gather the leaves," said another Luddite.

There it was again. "What does that mean?" asked Lucy. "Why do you tell me that, and tell me nothing of what it means?"

"You will know," answered Ludd. "When you are ready, you will go to Newstead. But

215

do not enter the abbey until you are prepared to fight for what you love."

He and his followers now walked on, stepping into the darkness without further word, leaving her alone upon the street to wonder and doubt and marvel in her confusion.

17

Word of the incident at the Gilley house spread with astonishing rapidity, but Lucy was preoccupied with the knowledge that she had actually met the supposedly mythical General Ludd, and that he had a particular interest in her life. To her, this revelation was far more important than an embarrassment with a man she did not wish to marry. Nevertheless, she was soon enough made to confront issues that preoccupied others. At the breakfast table, her uncle could not bother to swallow his dried prune before confronting her directly.

"What do I hear of a row between you and Olson and some rogue?" he demanded.

It appeared that Mrs. Quince had revealed what her uncle was likely to hear on his own, but no more than that. If she'd told Uncle Lowell about Jonas Morrison, he would certainly be ranting about it already. Lucy could not understand why she would keep her knowledge of Mr. Morrison a secret.

Before Lucy could answer her uncle, Mrs. Quince entered the room and leaned against the doorjamb, crossing her arms. "Once again, Miss Derrick humiliated Mr. Olson by dancing with another man. The same man as at the assembly, if I am not mistaken."

Again, she did not speak the name. Mrs. Quince now showed all the glee and triumph she did not display last night, as if to fool Lucy into forgetting her unguarded response. But Lucy could not forget the sight of Mrs. Quince, staggering backwards, staring, as though she gazed upon a ghost, oblivious to the punch trickling down her frock.

"I did not humiliate Mr. Olson," said Lucy, playing along for now, if only for her uncle's benefit. "I did not know he would be there. He arrived after that man asked me to dance, and I had no good reason to deny him."

"All very good for you, but how do you explain the row?" asked her uncle.

"It was none of my doing," said Lucy. "Mr. Olson was very rude to the stranger."

"At least there is no harm done. Despite your rudeness to him, Mr. Olson has in no way indicated that he wishes to end his engagement to you," said Uncle Lowell as he slurped at his chocolate. "He wrote to me this morning and made his intentions plain. You are to continue to regard him as your intended husband."

That Mr. Olson was now ruined obviously

mattered little to her uncle. Lucy did not raise this point because it was not an argument she could win. More than anything she wished to speak to Mary about her encounter with Ludd. The rules were clear, however, and she was not to visit Mary without an invitation. She spent the morning with her books, though she could but little concentrate on Paracelsus, and much to her surprise, her wishes were soon enough satisfied. Ungston knocked upon her door to tell her that Miss Crawford had sent her equipage and requested the pleasure of Lucy's company.

When she arrived at the little town house, Mrs. Emmett ushered Lucy inside as though she were late for an appointment. She found Mary waiting for her, dressed in a frock of green and white, and looking particularly pale. Even her hair appeared whiter than Lucy recollected. Despite her pallor, she seemed quite pleased to see Lucy.

Mary took her hand in her own. "I am sorry I have not been able to see you more and hear of your progress. You must tell me everything at once. What have you been learning? What has captured your imagination?"

Lucy had wanted to tell Mary of her encounter with Ludd, of the revelations about Jonas Morrison and the Rosicrucians, but Mary wanted to hear of nothing but studies, and Lucy was content that there would be plenty of time to speak of those other matters later. So Lucy began to speak of what she had been reading, and before she knew it, her studies were all she could think of. She went on for the better part of half an hour about what she had read, what had intrigued her, and what she could not understand.

"I knew you would do nothing but amaze me," Mary said when Lucy had finished her breathless recitation. "You learn and understand like no one I have ever heard of."

"That cannot be so," said Lucy. "Everything is so hard to understand."

Mary shook her head. "Come, tell me how the effigy we found upon Lord Byron could affect him. What principle was at work? Was it magic truly?"

"I hope I express this right, but the things I have done, I have seen — they are real. I don't doubt that. But they are not *magic,* in the sense that people mean when they use the word, are they? *Magic* implies some sort of exception from the rules that govern the world, something outside nature, but if these things were magic in that sense, these spells could not be written down. There could be no knowing if a spell would work from one time to the next. But these things you teach me to do — they are governed by laws. A spell cast in the same way, under the same conditions, with the same level of concentration — it will work the same every time. If that is so, is not magic simply another kind of natural philosophy, though a more obscure one?"

"Yes," said Mary. Simple and direct. "You have grasped the most powerful secret of all, and one that eludes so many who seek to master these skills. Now tell me, what rules governed the curse upon Byron?"

"I believe it is the natural sympathetic link between all things. If I understand Agrippa, then everything in the universe is a miniature representation of the whole, and that by affecting certain things mimetically, you can cause those effects to reflect back upon what you desire. There is a phrase I have seen frequently in many of the books: *As above, so below.*"

"You speak of Agrippa's law of resonance," said Mary. "It states that all things which are similar are also connected, and so they are drawn to each other's power. You affect the universe by affecting the miniatures of the universe to be found within everything."

Lucy smiled. "Agrippa writes that you can intensify the natural attraction between things by augmenting charms with items that come from, or belong to, the target and by using items in nature that best conduct what sort of energy you wish to apply. Different objects in the world contain different kinds of energy, and so the charm I used upon Mr. Olson called for a lemon, for its natural bitterness.

The charm I used upon my uncle to persuade him not to cast me out of his house required sugar, for its ability to conduct sweetness — in taste and disposition. It is why so many spells call for parts of frogs or toads or newts. These are creatures that change form over the course of their lives, and so they possess a natural transformative quality."

"You explain it all with perfect clarity."

"I wish it could be explained to me in perfect clarity."

Mary laughed. "Those who write of such things wrap their knowledge in obscurity to keep the uninitiated from understanding and attempting."

"It is so much to understand, and to accept. And there is so much we have not even discussed. Many of the writers have lengthy sections upon the summoning of spirits and demons. Am I to learn to do such things?"

"No," said Mary. "While you are my student, you will not try anything of the sort, and if you are wise you never will. Commanding such creatures is not safe, and you have challenges enough before you."

Mary rose and retreated to her library, from which she returned with a slender folio. It was bound in faded calf's leather, slightly scuffed, and held closed with a tattered red ribbon. Mary's dexterous fingers untied the ribbon as she spoke. "I meant to wait many weeks, perhaps many months, before showing this to you, but danger is coming quickly, and we must act to stop it. You know of the machine breakers? You have heard of their General Ludd?"

"Of course." Lucy's pulse raced. They were moving toward something of moment. "I believe . . . I believe I saw Ludd last night. He spoke to me. And it was not the first time. I saw him outside Mr. Olson's mill, though I did not know it was he at the time. And I have seen other things, creatures of shadow, even in my uncle's house. I am so confused and frightened, Mary."

Mary paced the room, playing her fingers along the slender volume's ribbon. "I am not surprised he has come to you. I told you there is something coming. A great change for good or ill, but a change that cannot be prevented, only shaped. The machine breakers are a part of this."

"Of the ill?"

"Of the good," said Mary. "Do you understand what these machines represent? Already we hear tales from all over the country of how coal smoke blackens the skies and soils the waters. There are those like your Mr. Olson who would take men and women who once labored of their own hands to produce their own goods in their own homes and remove them to mills where they labor for endless hours for little money in the most monotonous and tedious and unimaginative

223

of work. They blacken nature and turn men into machines."

"But there are only a few such places."

"There will be more, more than we can imagine. Anything that can be made will be made by machine. Already some of these machines are powered by steam and coal, and someday they will all be. When that happens, there will be no more artisans and craftsmen, only mill workers ground down by their machine labor until they are sick or dead, and replaced by others equally nameless and faceless — one man or woman or child no better or worse than another. It is an end to our English way of life, an end to nature as we know it, and if nature is blighted, then so is magic as we know it."

"Things in the world can shape the world," Lucy said, thinking aloud. "Agrippa's law of resonance. You mean that changing the landscape changes the nature of the world itself?"

"That is exactly what I mean. You have seen what transpires in Mr. Olson's mill. Imagine that multiplied by a thousand, or a thousand thousand. Imagine forests destroyed for fuel to feed the mills, rivers blackened with their wastes. Generation after generation of children who know nothing of childhood, but only long hours of labor. Imagine men who are virtual slaves to mill owners, who dictate conditions and wages. I have seen these things, Lucy. The world is not merely going to change, it is going to be remade."

"But why must I stand against it?" asked Lucy.

"I don't know," Mary said. "I cannot say why Ludd seeks you out, or why you can see the creatures of shadow that are invisible to nearly everyone else."

"Can you see them?" asked Lucy.

"If I look for them," Mary answered sadly. "They are part of the world, just as we are."

"And Ludd? Is he part of the world too?"

"He is something else, I think. But he is drawn to you, just as the shadow creatures are. You have become some sort of magnet, Lucy, drawing things in. I do not know why, but I do know that you cannot ignore your centrality."

Lucy said nothing for a long time. The idea that she had some power, some responsibility, to stand against mysterious forces and great changes seemed absurd, and yet her friend believed this.

"What must I do?" she asked.

"You will start by opening this book." Mary held it out. The untied red ribbons dangled free.

Lucy took the book and knew at once she did something momentous and important. With a trembling hand, she leafed through the pages, few that they were, and saw the book contained a series of engraved prints, images of men, angels, animals, and all sorts of odd beings. Expressions were curious, often pained or amused or oddly lascivious, and often without cause. Men flew through the air on wings. Animals rode horses or baked bread in ovens. Activity of some sort abounded, though it was hard to tell precisely what these figures were attempting to achieve. They poured liquids in bowls, weighed substances, mixed and measured, and while all of the illustrations had clearly been done with the same hand, some seemed to Lucy silly and trivial, and some struck her as serious, even important. They demanded her attention.

"This is the *Mutus Liber*," Mary said, sitting at last across from her. "The wordless book. It was published in La Rochelle in the seventeenth century, and it is said to be the most precise book ever printed on the creation of the philosopher's stone. Do you know what that is?"

"Is it not the key to alchemy?" Lucy asked. "I understand it to be a stone in name only, but I've seen it represented as the key both to transmuting base metals to gold and to achieving eternal life."

"Yes," said Mary. "The stone is not a stone at all, of course. It is sometimes said to be a powder, sometimes said to be a process with no physical shape — a spell or a set of actions, a state of being, or even the body or mind of the alchemist who understands the workings of these secrets. The *Mutus Liber* dared to set down processes never before committed to print, because it set them down metaphorically. Only someone who is attuned to the hidden arts could understand the instructions embedded within the pictures. And what is more, the pictures make themselves known to those who have the right of understanding. The book is said to favor the wise and the learned, particularly if someone wise and learned is the book's rightful owner. It is always most powerful in the hands of the person to whom it belongs."

"Do you mean to say that once I understand these images, I would have the secret?" asked Lucy as she turned the pages, noticing the particulars of each print. Some appeared pregnant with meaning, but others struck her as merely odd. "That I could, with enough study, make the philosopher's stone, whatever that may be?"

"No," she said. "Because this book, the one printed at La Rochelle, is not the true *Mutus Liber*. It is always thus, isn't it? Secrets within secrets. There are dozens, perhaps hundreds of copies of this book in circulation, but they are all false. The true book contains only twelve prints, not sixteen like this one. It is said that three of those found here are real, but no one is certain which three. That this edition is not the true *Mutus Liber* is a secret possessed by very few, and even those in possession of that secret cannot say which of these prints are genuine."

"Prints five, ten, and thirteen are true," Lucy said, not a little pleased with herself.

Mary stared at Lucy, her face unreadable. "How can you know that?"

"How did I know which spells were real in that book you gave me?" she asked. "It is the same. I cannot prove that I am right, but I know it."

She did. Those prints *felt* different to her. It was as though they gave off heat, but it was not heat at all. It was as though they sang to her, but there was no sound. It was a kind of energy, almost like the feeling that someone's eyes are upon you, even though you have not yet turned to see that it is so.

Mary smiled. "I doubt it is the same. What you have done here is far more impressive. These pages are designed to elude detection. And yet, I knew you could solve this riddle, even if I did not believe you could do so with such ease."

Ease was not precisely the word Lucy would have chosen, for it had not been easy so much as it had been natural, like struggling to remember something long forgotten. But now that she saw these pages for what they were, she found she wanted to see more. Perhaps she would have done a great deal to see more. "Where is the true book?" she asked. "The complete one."

Mary shook her head. "I can only tell you what is rumored. There was said to be a whole copy in this kingdom, perhaps the only one in the world, guarded by the Brotherhood of the Rosy Cross — the Rosicrucians. You know who they are?"

"I have heard of them," Lucy answered, afraid to say more.

"I have heard that the leader of a powerful Rosicrucian lodge had the book, but he believed dark forces would use the book against England, and so, to protect it, he had one of his agents take the book apart and hide its pages. If there is a true *Mutus Liber* left in the world, the pages are separated by great distances."

Lucy was only half-listening, because as interesting as were Mary's words, the pages were so absorbing. There was something in the curious etchings, something she could almost see. The first thing she observed was that these pages somehow went together. It was no coincidence that these three were left in the book. They were a set, and someone who perhaps believed he might choose pages at random could choose these three, not seeing how they belonged with one another. But there was something else, too. The patterns, the images, took hold of her thoughts, pulled them, led them like a boat upon a river's strong current. There was meaning here, clear meaning, though it took her a moment to see it.

At last she looked up at Mary. "There is a principle of magic we have not discussed," Lucy said. "The principle of sacrifice."

Lucy understood at once that she had said something significant, for Mary dropped her teacup. It struck the floor and shattered, while the lady herself gripped the sides of her chair as though preparing for a great wind that might rip her from where she sat. Mary said nothing, merely stared at Lucy in wonder. Lucy was afraid to ask what it meant. They sat there, frozen in the moment, until roused by a pounding upon the door. Lucy listened as Mrs. Emmett answered, and then, after a moment, Mrs. Quince rushed in, with Mrs. Emmett behind her. Lucy had only enough time to close the *Mutus Liber* before Mrs. Quince could glance in its direction.

"Miss Derrick must come home at once," announced Mrs. Quince.

"What is it? Is something wrong?" asked Lucy.

"You will worry about anything," said Mrs. Quince. "No cause for alarm, except as it affects our peace. Your sister and her family have arrived, and Mr. Lowell does not wish to have them about without you present."

"Oh," said Lucy, who was still so intrigued by Mary's reaction that she momentarily forgot to be thrilled at the news that her sister was there at last. Thus she allowed Mrs. Quince to lead her away without saying a proper good-bye or even understanding precisely what had happened.

18

All the strangeness of her most recent encounter with Mary was forgotten the moment she walked into her uncle's house and saw her sister in the front room, holding her baby, little Emily. Lucy rushed over and carefully hugged her sister, so as not to crush the baby, and then peeled back the blanket to afford herself a better look at the child, who was awake but gurgling peacefully, swaddled as she was in a blue blanket embroidered with silver lace.

Lucy looked at her sister and her niece, and hugged them both again. She felt the tears running down her cheeks, but she did not care. She was so happy to see them. This was her only remaining family, and how she loved her sister, and how she loved her niece. "Oh, Martha, she looks just like our Emily. The resemblance is remarkable."

Emily had clearly brought Martha a full measure of happiness. Prior to having her baby, Martha had looked too thin and drawn and unhappy, but now she appeared plump and rosy and cheerful. She favored their father more than Lucy did, but she shared Lucy's dark hair and rosy complexion. Her face was longer, however, more pinched, giving her the studious look she had taken so much to heart before her marriage.

She patted her baby's back. "I do think she is the very image, though Mr. Buckles believes she favors his side of the family."

"It matters not for a girl," said Mr. Buckles, by way of greeting. He had walked in when Lucy was occupied with the infant, and was busy wiping a cloth along his forehead. "Were it a boy, it would be preferable that he favor his father."

Lucy looked at Martha, for an instant forgetting that Martha did not know about her husband's treachery. She expected that they would share a look of disdain or disgust, but Martha only looked away, appearing grave. She clutched her child closer to her breast. Lucy understood at once that Martha had come to hate her husband. It was there upon her face, and it made Lucy unspeakably sad. Even though such hatred was only just — even if Martha did not know that Mr. Buckles had altered their father's will — Lucy did not want Martha to suffer.

She looked over at Mr. Buckles, who simpered foolishly at Uncle Lowell, and Lucy felt her face redden with rage. He had stolen what was hers, what was Martha's, what was her father's, and paraded about as though it were nothing. He made his insipid observations and commanded Lucy's sister as though he were not a villain. She swore to herself that he would pay for his crimes. And then, because his hand was outstretched, she took it and welcomed him back to Nottingham.

Lucy spent the next morning in seclusion with her sister and niece. Often her thoughts turned to the aborted conversation with Mary the previous day. She had obviously said or done something to alarm her friend, and she wished more than anything else to know what it was before seeing her again.

So Lucy was relieved when she received a message from Mary asking her to meet her in the marketplace that afternoon. Martha appeared insulted when Lucy excused herself, observing that it must be a very particular friend who would call her away from her sister and niece, whom she sees so seldom. Lucy assured her she was, and that Lucy only needed a little time to assist her friend in purchasing a new hat for dinner that night. Martha clearly wished to be invited along, and Lucy dreaded that she would speak her desire aloud, but she did not, and Lucy comforted herself that she would have plenty of time to spend with her sister.

Lucy met her friend in the crowded marketplace at noon, and Mary took both of her hands somewhat awkwardly, for she held a little leather bag by a string in one hand.

"I know you have not much time," said Mary, "but we were interrupted at such an awkward moment yesterday, and I wished to speak with you before more time passed."

"I have longed for the opportunity," said Lucy. "If I said something to offend you, Mary, I am so very sorry."

Mary laughed and then hugged Lucy. "Offend me indeed. Hardly. You astonished me, that is all. I have never met anyone, heard of anyone, so perceptive as you."

"But I hardly knew what I was seeing or what it meant."

"I know," said Mary, walking Lucy over to a little bench where they could sit. "You must understand that the pages of the *Mutus Liber* contain certain truths about the magic of the philosopher's stone, about the principles that make it function. The pages, though in various locations, always seem to be grouped according to one of these important principles. It is almost as though the pages will not allow themselves to be separated. Perhaps it is not so surprising. We talk about the most powerful magic in the universe, for it is the ability to transform one thing into another thing. Most of the magic that even the most skilled cunning women or hermeticists practice is no more than the natural push and pull of the universe. But this is something different."

"Is it dangerous?" asked Lucy.

"Oh, yes."

Mary opened her leather bag and removed a piece of paper, an ink pot, a quill, a flat piece of wood, which Lucy divined was for her to write upon, a book, and a plump red rose. She then took the small volume and leafed through it briefly, looking for a page, which she soon found.

"This is a charm to kill plants," said Mary. "It is dangerous magic, traditionally used for evil, and it involves changing the nature of something. Plants are made up largely of water, and this spell works by moving the water from one location to another. If you would make the attempt, please."

Lucy examined the image in the book. It was a very simple square of seven boxes across, each containing a single Roman letter, the top line spelling out "KONOVON." In form, it would be an easy charm, but she sensed there were tricks and hidden pitfalls. There were flares in the letters, and she understood almost immediately, purely as intuition, that the letters could not be written in order. Feeling almost certain she was copying it correctly, Lucy took several minutes to duplicate the charm. She then looked up at Mary, for there were no instructions upon the page.

"Toss it upon the rose," said Mary.

Lucy looked around the marketplace. People hurried about their business, and no one paused to consider a pair of young ladies huddled in conversation. So, in that public setting, Lucy did as she was told. Nothing happened. She sat there for a moment, waiting for instructions.

"You copied the charm perfectly," said Mary. "Have no fear upon that score. You have a wonderful hand and excellent instincts. The charm did not work because it is not powerful enough to work upon its own. It needs some added force, like a mule that requires a push to begin its labors. And that added force can be provided by a sacrifice."

Lucy felt uneasy. She had images of mad Picts slitting the throats of lowing cows. "I do not know that I wish to perform a sacrifice of any kind."

"I will not ask you to sacrifice living creatures," said Mary, her voice soft. "I have no interest in causing any living thing distress, but there are other kinds of sacrifice. Your choices can constitute a sacrifice. Denying yourself something, or taking on tasks you would choose not to. For now, I will show you a more direct, simpler kind."

She picked up Lucy's charm and handed it back to her. "I want you to try again, but this time, pick that flower, and focus on converting its energy to the charm."

Mary pointed to a dandelion that grew between the stones at their feet. It was a bright yellow and the weight of the flower burdened the stem so that it bent over slightly. Lucy knew from her reading that a tea made from the dandelion could be used as a diuretic, and the juice of the crushed plant was good for removing warts.

Lucy had never before hesitated to pick a flower, but thinking of it as a sacrifice made her uneasy. Picking it seemed suddenly brutal, barbaric.

"You wish me to sacrifice one flower to destroy another."

Mary smiled. "It does seem a little tasteless."

Tasteless indeed, but Lucy had a strong wish to see if there was anything to what Mary said, so holding the charm in her right hand, she picked the dandelion with her left, concentrating, as Mary had said, on its energy. The moment she picked the flower, she tossed the charm upon the rose.

There was no sign that anything had happened, but when she lifted the charm, she saw the rose had been reduced nearly to powder, and that it lay in a little pool of dampness. The water in the plant had been leeched out entirely.

Lucy stared, hardly able to speak. Every bit of magic she had done until now had been vague and general, hard to prove, and leaving no physical result, but here was something else entirely. She had, using magic, physically altered something in the world. Even after all she had seen and done, this struck her as difficult to believe.

"I think you understand now," said Mary. "The information contained in the *Mutus Liber* is dangerous, and if it should fall into the wrong hands, it would be very bad indeed. And that is why we must hope it falls into your hands. You see, that was but a minor charm, and your sacrifice was but a small one, but it was enough to push the energy far enough to work. With a powerful sacrifice, almost anything is possible."

"Well, I shan't go around destroying life for power," said Lucy. "I won't."

"No, you will not," agreed Mary. "I would not trust you with this information if I thought you should, but as I have shown you, there are many kinds of sacrifices, including the sacrifices others make for you. Those can be the most powerful kind, and you would be well to remember that. If a friend sacrifices something of value out of love, it can render powerful the most impotent spell, it can break the strongest ward, change powerful enemies. To understand the principles of sacrifice is to understand when the time is right to act, when others have made you something better than yourself."

■ ■ ■ ■

After putting her items back in the leather pouch, Mary began to walk Lucy back to her uncle's house. "I don't wish to keep you from your sister long," she said. "But you need to understand what is happening. There is no book on earth so dangerous as the *Mutus Liber.* Its secrets are devastating."

"But you said it contains the secret of eternal life. Surely eternal life is not a terrible thing."

Mary adjusted her wide-brimmed hat to keep the sun off her pale face. "Alchemy is transformation, Lucy, not addition. Man is born to die, and mortality defines man's nature. To possess eternal life is to be human no longer. Those who have pursued this secret must undergo a terrible alteration. They lose their souls and so become vile creatures, evil, mere shadows of themselves. They feel no regret. Murder, theft, violence, destruction — none of these things give them pause. Whatever terrible, monstrous person you can imagine — that is nothing compared to one who has become immortal. These transformed creatures may do the most horrendous things and think about them no more than you would think of the grass upon which you trod as you go on your way. They live for nothing but to continue, to indulge their pleasures, and to remain hidden."

Lucy felt a chill, and drew her cloak around her. "Do you believe that there are such people? That what you speak of has truly been done?"

"I have seen it," said Mary. "I have seen more than you could credit unless you'd seen it yourself. That is why I brought you to the fairy barrow, for it was such a fit place for our first discussion of these things. Do you know what those mounds truly are?"

Lucy shook her head. First immortal people, and now fairies. She did not know what to think.

"They are ancient graves, tombs of people from so long in the past that their bones are likely nothing but dust. They tell us that the ancients knew what we have forgotten. Stories of fairies are as old as this island, but their nature in our stories has changed over time. However, I assure you, such creatures are real, but they are not what you imagine. I do not speak of silly, sprightly, mischief-makers. What the ancients called fairies are the dead, returned to life. They are revenants, given existence with the most ancient of alchemy."

Lucy looked upon her friend with un-abashed incredulity. She had seen things, done things, that most people would have thought impossible, but what Mary spoke of now was beyond her ability to accept. "In asking me to believe this, you ask too much."

"I know these beings are real as much as I know you are. These fairies — these revenants, if you prefer — have long wielded their influence over this kingdom, but their influence has been waning. They fear to increase their numbers, because they fear the power and vigor of those who are young, and yet the old ones, powerful as they are, grow torpid, weary of life and fearful of death. But in their limited influence they have funded and supported the rise of mills. Clothing mills and iron mills and pottery mills. Mills that make everything once made with the careful eye and hand of the artisan. These revenants have lost their humanity, and now they seek to rob the rest of us of ours."

Lucy felt her breath catch. Had not her father used nearly the same words to speak of the mills themselves? "But if they are creatures of magic, why should they wish to see magic banished, as you say it must if these mills rise?"

They now stood outside Uncle Lowell's house.

"I know you must go, and there will be plenty of time to discuss these matters further, though perhaps not tonight." At this she smiled. "For now, what you must know is that they are indeed creatures of magic, Lucy, but magic alone can unmake them. They fear nothing else, for they cannot be destroyed by any weapon, by any disease or any accident."

242

"Then nothing can stop them?"

Mary shook her head. "I heard a story once of one of these creatures that contained itself in an elemental circle — something far more powerful than a magic circle. The nature of the elements is a guarded secret, but once inside, it took its own life as a means of destroying the life of another of its kind. And there are other rumors of powerful elemental magic that can be used against some of them, but these secrets are closed to us."

"Then what would you have me do?" asked Lucy.

"Continue to read and learn and hope you are ready. Ludd has sought you out, and I believe these revenants will seek you out as well. It is only a matter of time, and I don't know that you can ever be prepared, but you must try your best. I fear to think what will happen otherwise."

19

The next day was warm and beautiful, and Lucy did not wish to remain in the house with Mr. Buckles and her uncle. An excursion was just the thing, and she believed she knew the perfect place.

Like many country estates, both the grand and the ancient, Newstead Abbey was open to visitors certain days, particularly when its master was not on the premises. At Newstead, only the grounds were open, as the main building itself was largely in a state of disrepair, unfit for visitors or even, some said, inhabitants. Locals knew that Lord Byron could afford to restore only a minimal number of rooms, and so he kept the building closed to outsiders out of embarrassment and concern for their safety.

Ludd had told her to gather the leaves in Newstead, whatever that meant, but Lucy had no plans to do any leaf gathering. She had no plans to enter the house, only to look around, get a sense of things, to see if she could gain any insight into what Ludd wanted, and perhaps to gain some insight into Byron himself. She had to admit that visiting his estate offered a special thrill. He would not be there, of course, but it was his home, and she liked the idea of seeing it.

Martha was certainly curious about Byron, having heard a heavily redacted, and so somewhat nonsensical, version of his visit to Uncle Lowell's house. In the end, she understood only that a dashing, perhaps slightly dangerous, baron toyed with the idea of pursuing Lucy, and *that* was the reason Lucy did not wish to marry Mr. Olson. It was certainly only part of the truth, but it was a story that clearly pleased Martha, so Lucy allowed her sister to believe it.

While she did not anticipate anything unusual might happen, Lucy still preferred to limit the excursion to the two of them, and so she was quite relieved when Mr. Buckles demonstrated no interest in attending. "I have seen Lady Harriett's estate," he told Lucy. "I have been a guest there many times, and so have no need to see the estate of some minor baron."

They packed a basket and hired a coach to take them the ten miles or so to Newstead. The two sisters were so delighted to be alone, truly alone, in each other's company. Little Emily was with the nurse, and while Martha missed her child, as new mothers are inclined to do, she also relished the luxury of a few hours to herself.

That she also enjoyed being away from her husband was painfully obvious to Lucy, but she would not press this matter. Martha had sacrificed herself because she believed it was the only way to keep her sister from poverty. It had not worked, and now she was shackled to him until one of them was dead. It was too horrible to think of. It was no wonder that Martha loved her little baby to distraction, for Emily must be the only thing in the world to give her pleasure.

Had they not received directions, they would never have found the abbey, for its only indication from the High North Road was a white gate and a small post house. Once through the gate, they traveled for perhaps half a mile through thick woods, some of the last remnants of the long-since destroyed Sherwood Forest. Once the turrets and parapets of the ancient gothic structure began to appear above the trees, Lucy could not help but think how appropriate so imposing a ruin should be housed in a wood that was, itself, a remnant of the past.

Newstead Abbey was massive and imposing and beautiful and in a state of unspeakable disrepair. Walls crumbled, roofs were collapsed. It looked unfit for habitation, and yet, for all that, it was breathtaking. A decayed wall enclosed a wild garden to the north and east. To the west lay a massive lake that sparkled in the sunlight. Lucy had never seen anything so simultaneously magnificent and gloomy.

Martha too appeared momentarily transfixed. After gazing upon the main building with wonder, she took Lucy's hand. "I think that to be mistress of Newstead might be something."

Lucy smiled at her sister. "Certainly something I shall never know."

The grounds were reasonably orderly — and massive — and the two sisters wandered from fountain to pond to topiary to well to crumbling statuary, giggling and pulling each other by the hand as though they were girls again. Some heavy clouds passed before the sun, and the air turned moderately colder. Their cheeks became apple red, and their breath puffed into the air with their laughter. Lucy could not recall a time when she had been happier. She forgot about magic and dark beings and leaf gathering. For this one day, she was determined, she would be but a young lady, thinking young-lady thoughts, visiting with her sister and diverting herself.

They wandered the grounds for two hours, ate their lunch, and walked until they were quite fatigued. They saw no other people and no animals of consequence — the rumors of Byron's menagerie thus far being unproved, for they saw no bears or wolves or giant tortoises, and certainly not the ghostly dog said by locals to haunt the grounds. Lucy had wanted to gain some sense of what Ludd had meant by sending her to Newstead, but when Martha suggested they return home, Lucy began to feel that the excursion had been a wonderful failure. She had learned nothing. There were no clues or hints or cryptic messages.

As she considered these matters, Lucy noticed a stranger approaching. He was an older man, in his sixties at least, and dressed like a tradesman in plain woolens. He walked with a stick, and wore an expression upon his rounded face of such kindness that it never occurred to Lucy to be cautious. He grew closer, and his grin widened, and when he was close enough he paused and removed his hat.

He bowed to Martha, but then turned his attention to Lucy. "Are you the young lady for whom I am looking?"

"I cannot know," said Lucy, who suspected that she must be precisely the young lady for whom he was looking, though she hated even to wonder why.

Martha tugged on her arm, perhaps alarmed by something in the man's appearance, or, more likely, his mode of address. Lucy, however, ignored her sister. She could not know who the man was or what he wanted, but she felt certain she had nothing to fear from him.

"Quite a lot of ghosts upon this estate, do you not think so?" he asked.

"I saw none," Lucy said.

"Not even the dog?" the old man asked. "He is quite friendly for a dead dog. Ghost dogs are often so quarrelsome, you know. I saw him frolicking by the water. He must enjoy it for now, for his time of enjoyment will come to an end soon, perhaps. So much of it will."

"What do you mean?" asked Lucy. The man's voice was light and easy, but his words chilled her.

"The world is changing, young lady. You must know that. The things that play in the forest about here — they will play no longer. And sport no more seen on the darkening green." He paused for a moment. "Oh, dear. I do hate when I quote my own writing, but I just now understand what I was saying, and it is such a surprise when things become clear."

"Lucy!" Martha hissed just above a whisper. "Do you know this *gentleman?*"

The older man removed his hat and bowed. "I do beg your pardon. I seem to have forgotten my manners. My name is William Blake, engraver, and I am at your service."

There was no doubt the man was peculiar, but Lucy's instincts told her that she had nothing to fear, so she curtsied and smiled at the man. "I am Lucy Derrick, and this is my sister, Mrs. Martha Buckles."

"Very charmed, ladies. And I believe it is you, Miss Derrick, that I have come all the way from London to see. And having completed my task, I must return to London and my work. I do hate to be away from my home and my dear wife. I only wished to come here to make your acquaintance."

"I am very sorry," said Martha. "You traveled more than a hundred miles to meet someone you did not know, and having said hello to her, you return from whence you've come?"

"You have it precisely," Mr. Blake answered with great cheer. "Now I have ordered it so that when Miss Derrick and I meet again, we will no longer be strangers."

"That is nonsensical," said Martha.

"If you subscribe to the narrow reason of Bacon and Newton and Hume and men of that stripe, then I suppose it is," answered Mr. Blake. "I choose not to let the devil's logic interfere with God's truth, not when it is before my eyes."

Martha turned to Lucy. "You appear remarkably unperturbed. Do you know something of all this?"

Lucy shook her head. "This sort of thing happens to me a great deal these days. But sir, can you tell me nothing more of your business with me?"

"I cannot because I know nothing of it," he answered. "I have no doubt we shall know in time. But the green is darkening, is it not? The mills come, belching smoke and ash, grinding men to dust, and nature prepares to decay. You know it too, I think."

"Lucy," Martha said again, the urgency evident in her voice.

Lucy was about to respond, but she suddenly heard weeping, and she observed that Mr. Blake heard it too. It was a soft sound — a delicate, feminine sobbing — nothing menacing, and yet Lucy understood that the afternoon had turned. The air grew cool, and the hair on the back of her neck bristled. Everything around her refined and sharpened into vivid colors. She heard every twig and leaf crunch under their feet.

They traveled some fifty feet down the path and found, sitting under a tree, a young woman in a dingy white dress, rustic by the look of it. They could not determine her age, for she had her back to them, but she wore her coppery hair loose and unruly under her bonnet, and by her size — tall and very thin — Lucy imagined her to be in her late teens. There was something about her look, about her misery and the way she held her head in her hands, that reminded her of herself weeping after the death of her sister. She remembered one afternoon, some weeks after the day her father had admitted her to his study, when she had been walking behind the house, and Emily's death had struck her fresh, like a blow. She had understood, as if for the first time, that her sister was gone, that she would never see her again, and the emptiness of this realization overwhelmed her. She had fallen to the ground and wept, unable to stop herself, unable to find the will to try.

She knew not how long she lay there — hours perhaps — lost in her own misery, until she'd felt hands upon her shoulders. She'd shrugged them off, but they were insistent, and when at last she looked up, Lucy saw that it was her father, out of his study, pulling her to her feet. He was not used to being an affectionate man, and he did not love to touch even his children, but he took her into his embrace and let her weep against his shoulder for long minutes, until she felt smothered by the scent of wet wool. She did not know if there was ever a moment when she'd loved her father so well, or needed him more, or was so glad to have his guidance.

Now she looked upon this strange girl as she sat hunched over, a mournful, almost bovine sound escaping her lips, and Lucy wanted to comfort her, wanted to offer her some small portion of what only another person can provide in such moments of grief. As they approached, the girl did not regard them at all, and they saw she was bent over a book. The text must be passing melancholy,

Lucy thought, to elicit such a response.

Martha hung back, but Lucy circled around, and Mr. Blake walked by her side, a look of pure concern upon his wrinkled face. When they could see the girl's face, they noted that she was pretty, with a fair countenance, somewhat marred by freckles and a nose broad and flat at the bridge, but with large, very beautiful hazel eyes — red and moist with tears though they might have been.

As Lucy and Mr. Blake approached her from the side, the girl suddenly started and scrambled to her feet in a terrified scurry, more animal-like than human. Once she rose, however, she appeared somewhat calmed by the sight of the two young ladies and the kindly older man, who anyone could see posed no threat. There was, however, a marked look of incomprehension on the girl's face. Her mouth hung slightly open, her eyes squinted as though willing the world to form into some intelligible shape.

Curiously, the girl wore a slate around her neck, held on by a piece of thick cord, and in her hand she held a piece of chalk. The book she'd been reading lay on the ground, and Lucy read the spine. It was Byron's *Poems on Various Occasions*.

"Hello," Lucy said cautiously. "We are sorry to have startled you."

Martha had now come around to face the

girl, who had begun to mark up her slate with furious speed. *I am Sophie Hyatt. I am deaf.*

Lucy gestured that she would like the slate so she might respond, but the girl shook her head and gestured toward her lips. Lucy had read of deaf people who could understand words by watching a speaker's lips, though she had never seen the thing done herself. Overwhelmed by the wonder of it, Lucy said, speaking slowly and moving her mouth in exaggerated gestures, *"I am Lucy, and this is Martha and Mr. Blake."*

The deaf girl laughed, and in her laughter, she appeared remarkably beautiful. *Speak as you are used,* she wrote on the slate, and held up the sign with her eyes twinkling. *Not so slow.*

"I am sorry," Lucy said. "I did not mean to offend you. Or to startle you. We heard you weeping, and wished only to make sure you were not in distress."

"Not in distress," said Mr. Blake. "In love."

She wiped at her eyes with her fingers and wrote, *Yes.*

Unable to help herself, Lucy said, "Not with Byron, I hope."

Sophie took a step backwards. *Do you know him?* she wrote after a moment's reflection.

"Only a little," said Lucy, not wishing to set herself up as a rival to this deaf girl, though she *was* pretty, and a certain kind of man liked a vulnerable woman. Was Byron such a man? Would he prefer this poor creature to Lucy? She hated herself that such thoughts occurred to her, and she summoned the will to set them aside. In this she was very near successful. "I do not know him well enough to be invited to Newstead. I come merely to look at the grounds with my sister, and we met Mr. Blake along the way."

Do you love him?

Lucy and Martha exchanged looks. Lucy liked him, certainly, but she was almost entirely confident that she did not love him. Martha took the uncertain look upon Lucy's face as amusement, and began to laugh, and Lucy laughed too. She did not wish to mock the deaf girl, and tried to stop herself, but to her surprise the girl laughed with them.

I am very jealous, she wrote. *It is silly, for he does not love me.* She paused for a moment, studying Lucy, her head cocked like a bird's. *I think you are like me.*

"What does she mean, Lucy?" asked Martha.

Sophie smiled. *Three years ago they came. They showed me the wordless book. Very powerful, but I pretended not to know the good pages from the bad.*

Lucy felt a sudden pang of paralyzing fear. These phenomena were unavoidable. These people were ubiquitous. It seemed as though she had been living in a fantastical world her whole life, one that willfully ignored the magic all around. She had been too blind to see it, but now that her eyes were open, it was everywhere.

"Who came to you?" asked Lucy.

A lady, very proud, all in black, as if mourning. A simpering man. A curate.

Lucy put a hand to her mouth. It had been Lady Harriet and Mr. Buckles. It could be no one else, and they too were interested in the *Mutus Liber,* the book with the false pages. They wanted it for themselves. It could only be that Lady Harriet wanted the power of eternal life. She wanted to become one of those revenants of which Mary had spoken — a broken, inhuman thing. It seemed to Lucy that Lady Harriet was already upon her way.

Martha took her hand. "You look so pale, Lucy. And I cannot understand a word the two of you exchange. This is more curious even than Mr. Blake, if you will forgive me for saying so. What is all this?"

Lucy forced a smile. "Just local lore, too tedious to explain." She looked at Sophie and gave another easy smile. "Have you been in the house?"

No, said Sophie. *When I go, it will be with you.*

Martha stepped closer, looking concerned. "Do you want anything? Food? A ride somewhere? We have a coach just at the roadway."

The girl shook her head. *I live close. I am done here.* She gathered up her things and wandered into the woods without looking back.

Mr. Blake watched her go and then rubbed his hands together. "What a remarkable day! But now I have a long journey back to London. May I see you ladies off?"

He escorted them back to their coach, and waved kindly as they rode off, as though he were an uncle or an old friend. Several times Martha turned to Lucy to ask questions, but each time she stopped herself. It soon became evident that, whatever she might wish to ask, she was not certain she would want to hear the answer.

20

It was a strange day, full of new people and new information, and when she returned to her uncle's house, Lucy excused herself, claiming fatigue, and retired to her room, determined to be alone until dinner. There was so much to think about. Lady Harriett Dyer and Mr. Buckles had, three years earlier, shown the *Mutus Liber* to the deaf girl Sophie Hyatt. It was evident they had been searching for someone who could identify the true prints from the false. Did they know that Lucy could do that? Was there a link between Lucy's natural talent and Mr. Buckles's theft of her property? Did these new facts somehow explain why Lady Harriett had been so adamant that Lucy marry Mr. Olson?

Much to her own surprise, Lucy found herself feeling jealous that this deaf girl had been shown the pages. *Her* pages. She wished Mary had lent her the book, because she longed to look at them. She closed her eyes and tried to recall the complex images she'd seen, but they were too elaborate, too elusive to be summoned.

Since his arrival, Lucy had done her best to avoid Mr. Buckles, either by staying out of any room that he might occupy or by directing all of her attention to the baby when he was around. He had, she was now certain, stolen her birthright and her independence, and she hated that she must pretend he had not. But now, it seemed to her even worse. It was not simply that he had stolen from her out of malice and greed. If Lucy's suspicions were right, Mr. Buckles was involved in a complicated and long-standing conspiracy against her — a conspiracy whose scope and goal was beyond her understanding.

After she and Martha returned from Newstead, Lucy had excused herself by saying she was tired so that she might go to her room and pursue answers in her books. She had found none. She did not even know what she looked for, but she could not bear to do nothing. After several hours, she abandoned the effort and joined the family in a late dinner.

That night, after her sister had retired to bed, Ungston once again informed Lucy that Miss Crawford awaited her in her carriage. Lucy rushed outside, and even in the dark, the lady's grim expression was evident.

"Mary, is something wrong?"

"Not wrong, no," said her friend. "Please step inside for a moment. I must speak with you."

Lucy entered the coach and sat next to Mary, hardly knowing what to expect.

The lady turned to her, eyes seeming to glow in the gloom of the coach. "Matters are serious, Lucy. I am afraid I cannot long stay. I have business that I must attend to, and it may be many days before I return. Since I saw you last, grave circumstances have come to my attention, and I must speak to you before I go."

"I have learned things too," Lucy blurted out. She wanted to be more patient, to wait to hear Mary's news, but she could not contain herself. "Mr. Buckles and Lady Harriett have been looking for the *Mutus Liber* too. Everything is connected, though I don't know how."

Mary appeared little surprised by this news. "I know you are frightened, Lucy, but the book has always been important. It is more so now. That is why you must find the scattered pages before our enemies do."

These words struck Lucy as dire and true. She was supposed to find the missing pages. Now that she heard it, it made perfect sense. She formed the words, though they felt thick and bitter in her mouth. "I must gather the leaves."

"Yes, that is what you must do."

A strange calm came over her. It was not as though she understood why these things happened, but at least there was purpose. She must find missing pages of a book. It was a task, and tasks could be accomplished. "And when I have them?"

"Then we will determine what to do together." She leaned in to hug Lucy. Her skin was icy cold. "I know this is much to ask of you, and I hate that you must do it alone. I will be by your side again as soon as I can, but I am needed elsewhere. You must remember, Lucy, that the *Mutus Liber* is strongest in the hands of the person to whom it belongs, but . . . things have become so complicated. And never before has it been more important to trust me."

She handed Lucy a writing tablet, upon which was set a piece of paper with dense writing on it, too small to read in the dark. Mary then set forth a quill and an ink pot.

"What I must ask you now will sound outlandish, but I beg you to trust me. You must sign this, Lucy."

"What is it?"

"A will."

Lucy could not believe what she heard. After everything that had happened with her father's will, did Mary believe Lucy would sign a will in haste, without reading it?

"In this will you leave everything to your

sister, which is I know what you would wish. Everything except any pages of the *Mutus Liber* that you might find. Those you entrust to me."

Lucy opened her mouth, but she could not even think of the words she would say if she could.

"You must wonder why," said Mary. "And I shall tell you. If you do not sign this, the revenants will kill you. If the pages are left to me, they will not. It is that simple. I am your friend, and I would do anything to help you. You must believe me. I want you to leave me the pages for that reason and for no other — because your enemies would risk anything than that I should become the true owner. To protect you, we must make the consequence of your death terrible to those who seek to harm you. If you have ever trusted me, trust me now. I know not what I can do for you if you will not."

There was such pleading in her voice, such desperation, that Lucy could not but believe her. This was Mary Crawford, the one person in the world who knew her secret, the one person, besides her own sister, she trusted. Though unable to understand the request, Lucy decided she had to believe in her friend's good intentions. She signed where Mary directed her. They blotted the signature, and then Mary rolled up the paper and handed it to Lucy.

"I do not need it. I would not have you think I am about some deception with it. Only, keep it safe. The will must exist to protect you." She hugged Lucy again. "Remember, I am your friend. Do not doubt me." She then handed Lucy the copy of the *Mutus Liber* she had shown her previously. "Hold on to this. Add pages to it as you can."

Dazed, Lucy stepped out of the coach, and watched it drive away, holding in her hand a paper that granted, upon her death, the most powerful book in the world to her only friend.

Lucy rushed inside, only wanting to retire to her room, but Mrs. Quince confronted her on the staircase. She had been avoiding Lucy since the encounter with Mr. Morrison at the Gilley house, but now she stood, blocking her way, a disdainful expression upon her face. She knew something. Lucy was sure of it.

"Some secret nighttime assignation, Miss Derrick? What do you have planned? I wonder. What do you think to do? No money, no husband, no friends? Do you believe your little tricks will work forever?"

Rather than retreat, Lucy took a step forward. The knowledge that Lady Harriett had been scheming against her for years made her angry, and her anger emboldened her. She leaned into Mrs. Quince's face and said, in a bold whisper, "Jonas Morrison."

Mrs. Quince flinched and stepped away.

"You are brazen," she said, attempting to act unperturbed, "to flaunt your whoredom before me."

"I had no wish to see him, and hope I never set eyes upon him again," Lucy said, stepping close again, "but you fear him. Why?"

"You are mistaken," said Mrs. Quince as she smoothed her apron.

"Then go tell my uncle," said Lucy, wishing to test Mrs. Quince, perhaps wishing to hurt her. "Tell Mr. Buckles. Tell them all with whom I danced. Go on. Tell them."

Mrs. Quince did not move.

Lucy pushed past her, entered her room, and closed the door.

Her triumph over Mrs. Quince, glorious though it may have been, left Lucy more confused than happy. What was Mr. Morrison to her that she should be so frightened? And what did it mean that Lady Harriett had been seeking someone to identify the *Mutus Liber* in the past few years? Was there some link between that and Mrs. Quince's failed efforts to teach Lucy to read the cards? And now came this will that Mary has asked her to sign. She did not suspect Mary of trying to cheat her, but she did believe her friend knew more than she was saying, and that made Lucy uneasy.

Lucy slept badly and was awakened by the baby, whom she could hear fussing through the walls. Martha was not at the table when Lucy went downstairs for breakfast. There was only Mr. Buckles and Uncle Lowell, who appeared very angry indeed. Lucy glanced at Mr. Buckles, but he offered only a foolish smile before turning away. Was it hard for him to look at her, she wondered, to see the young lady whose life he had stolen? Lucy doubted his thoughts were ever troubled by such things. She did not believe him even conscious that he had done wrong. He had done it, and now it was over, so he thought no more of it.

After a brief period of silence, and then the baby began its shrill wail again. Mr. Lowell slammed down his fork. "I cannot see what your baby is doing, crying so violently."

"It is usually very placid," said Mr. Buckles. "Even Lady Harriett has condescended to observe how very . . . how, ah, very placid it is."

"It weren't placid last night," said Uncle Lowell.

Lucy set aside her breakfast and went up to see Martha, who was still in bed, but quite awake. The bags under her eyes testified to the difficulties of her night, but she brightened considerably when she saw Lucy.

"I shall go quite mad," said Martha. "Poor little Emily is really not herself. She's never been like this, and I fear she may be ill."

Lucy brushed some unruly hair from Martha's face. "Does she nurse?"

"Like nothing I've seen." She lowered her voice to a whisper. "I am quite bruised. Emily is ravenous, and has taken to biting me with the little teeth she has. Why, it seems she has grown more teeth overnight, which may explain her sadness. In truth, if she does not cease hurting me, I will have to hire a wet nurse after all."

Just then the door opened, and the nurse came in with little Emily wrapped in a blanket.

"How is she?" asked Martha.

"She won't settle, mum," said the woman. "I reckon she wants her milk."

"It cannot be," said Martha. "She has done nothing but eat."

"She's been trying to nurse off me, mum."

Martha reached out and the woman handed her her baby, and as she did so, some of the blanket fell away. It was all Lucy could do not to scream, for instead of little Emily, there was a monster, a foul thing of skin so white that its bulging, pulsating blue veins showed through. It had pink eyes, little tufts of black hair curling from its head, sharp and narrow eyes, pointed ears, and a predator's sharp teeth. It looked at Lucy and grinned.

Lucy looked to the nurse and then to Martha, but neither of them noticed anything unusual about the child. Neither observed that it was not Emily at all.

Lucy saw what was invisible to the others — that baby Emily had been replaced by some foul thing, by a changeling. But how had it happened, and where was the real Emily?

"My sweet, you must not hurt your mama so," said Martha to the thing as it suckled greedily upon her breast.

Lucy swallowed hard, and tried to speak. She failed and made the effort again. "Martha," she said a ragged voice, "when did the baby begin to fuss?"

"Now that I think on it, it was right after we went to visit your friend, Miss Crawford."

Lucy took another step backwards. "You saw Mary? When did you see her?"

"After we returned from Newstead and you retired to your room — to nap, I presume. Your friend sent her coach around, inquiring after me. She said she had no wish to disturb you, but she longed to meet her friend's sister and niece. I cannot believe I neglected to tell you, but it is almost as though I forgot about it until this moment. How odd."

A secret meeting between her sister and Mary — a meeting her sister happened to *forget!* And Mary had said nothing to her when she had seen her after this meeting had taken place. Now Emily was gone, replaced by a changeling. And all of this after Mary had insisted Lucy leave the still-undiscovered pages of the *Mutus Liber* to her in a hastily composed will. Could Mary have been deceiving her all along? Lucy found herself trembling with the realization that the one person in the world she trusted, other than Martha, had betrayed her.

She excused herself, not caring how she surprised Martha with her abruptness, and ran downstairs and out of the house. She ran down the street, pushing past and over and around whoever or whatever came across her path. She cared not how women stared or tradesmen shouted. It was nothing to her. She ran as fast as she could across the square to High Pavement.

When she arrived at Mary's house, she knocked heavily upon the door, but received no reply. She knocked again and again, and finally she peered into the window.

What she found made her heart thunder in her chest. The house was all but cleared out. There was nothing upon the walls, no furniture upon the floors. The rugs were gone, and the curtains too. All was closed up and removed. Lucy saw but one thing, a single crate with a piece of paper attached to it, and upon the paper was written "Miss Lucy Derrick."

Trying the door, Lucy found it unlocked. She rushed inside and unfolded the paper, but it contained no information. It merely denoted that the crate and its contents were hers. Lucy looked inside and saw it was a large collection of books upon the practice of magic.

Lucy remained frozen. Martha's baby, dear little Emily, was gone, replaced with some goblin monster, and Martha did not know it. Mary was gone, and it seemed that she had played some terrible role in all this.

Lucy staggered backwards and felt tears coming on, but she fought them back. No, she thought. No more crying. Mr. Buckles and Mary Crawford and Uncle Lowell and Mr. Olson and even General Ludd — Lucy would discover who was set against her, and she would give them cause to regret it. She would take back what was hers, what had been robbed of her father — and she would find Martha's baby. For so long she had been powerless, but not now. She would save her niece. She did not know how she would do it, but she would find a way. By force or by stealth, she would challenge those who had made themselves her enemies, and she would have victory over them, because Lucy understood that at the center of all these events was the *Mutus Liber,* a book whose authenticity she, and perhaps only she, could determine. They wanted it, and Lucy would have it, and once she did, she would be in a position to dictate terms, terms they would not like at all.

21

It is one thing to be determined to act, and quite another to know precisely what needs doing, and so Lucy spent a long and sleepless night as she weighed her options and considered her alternatives. In several trips, so as to avoid the notice of anyone in her household, Lucy removed the books from Mary's house to her own room. If Mary were her enemy, why would she give Lucy these books? And yet all evidence suggested that Mary had played some part in Emily's being replaced by a monster. There was nothing to do now but study, learn what there was to be learned, what paths there were to explore. It all had to be done soon — very soon — for Lucy could not endure that Martha must live another day with that vile, grinning monster suckling at her.

She could find in Mary's books nothing of use about changelings — only myth and folklore, stories that rang of falseness and ignorance. What Lucy needed was to learn how to banish a changeling and how to retrieve the stolen child. If there was little to be discovered about changelings, however, there was much written on other sorts of beings. In Lucy's new library she read of the dark things that stalked the world, the spirits of Agrippa's *Fourth Book* or the demons of the *Lemegeton.* Lucy had learned nothing of spirit summoning, and Mary had warned to stay away from such magic, but books teaching the methods of such summoning were among the books Mary had left her, and now those warnings fell flat. Mary had abandoned her, possibly betrayed her. Martha and Emily were in trouble, in terrible danger, and only Lucy knew that this was so. It fell upon her shoulders to do something.

With no one to guide her, with no hints to help her follow the right course, Lucy had no choice but to find her own way. She spent the day closeted away with her books, looking for what she ought not to look, and found what appeared to her promising. It was in a volume that Mary had given her, marking off certain sections as the only ones worthy of her attention, but there were other sections as well, including one dedicated to the Enochian magic closely associated with John Dee and Edward Kelley. This author had gone back to the source text, the *Heptameron,* and proposed a simplified method of calling down spirits, demons, and angels.

It felt dangerous to Lucy, but it also felt *real,* like something she could do, and yet the creatures in the book terrified her — foul, twisted, distorted things, drawn in broad, renaissance strokes, like the monsters who inhabit the lost islands of unknown seas. Attempting habitually to master beings of this sort would be foolish, but surely she could do so once. She needed only to call a creature of knowledge, command it to tell her how to banish a changeling and restore her niece, and then she would send it off. She would do it quickly and cleanly, and the danger would pass so swiftly it could hardly be accounted danger at all.

The book explained that the creature would attempt to deceive her, to punish her for the insult of summoning it to her realm. It would attempt to trick Lucy into setting it free, and it would then destroy her in one of a thousand painful ways that would appear to the outside world a natural death. Lucy was certain she was too clever for that, too focused. Men summoned these beings out of ambition and power, and these desires were their undoing. A woman who summoned a spirit for benevolent purposes would be more cautious.

Lucy would have thought she must roll up her rug and fashion a magic circle in chalk upon the floorboards, but that turned out not to be the case. The book said that it was best to limit the size of the manifestation of an otherworldly being, and that circles were best drawn on pieces of paper in ink — the smaller the better, but never so small as to compromise accuracy. Errors in the circle would allow the summoned creature to break free, and that was always fatal.

When she began the work, Lucy felt much as she did when copying out a talisman, not that she was drawing something, but more that she was reassembling an object that had been taken apart. The lines and circles and runes seemed to fit together like boards perfectly cut by a carpenter's skilled hand. Or they did not feel that way, and so she twice destroyed her work because the circle simply *felt* badly constructed even if she could not find the error. When she was at last finished, she knew what she had done was perfect. She examined it over and over again in the rushlight, for it was now late at night, but her eyes only told her what she already knew — that her work could not be improved upon.

Lucy had put a great deal of effort into choosing a creature that might be most easily summoned and best controlled, and settled upon an angel whose name she could not pronounce (it was written out in Enochian runes, which looked like a strange combination of Hebrew and Latin letters), and whose particular virtues were said to be power, knowledge, and vengeance. Lucy wanted only one of those, and hoped the other two would not get in her way.

The summoning was simple. She would need to quiet herself, banish the world from her thoughts, and recite the simple sentence written in the Enochian tongue (helpfully transliterated by the author), while drawing forth a drop of her own blood. Very direct, very easy. With the circle written on so small a piece of paper, it made the whole affair curiously portable. She could bring her angel of destruction with her wherever she went, Lucy thought with the kind of crazed humor of the exhausted. It would make a pretty diversion at a ball.

Suppressing her giggles, bringing herself into the right frame of mind, Lucy — having memorized the incantation — stood before the circle, a knife ready to draw across her finger. And that was when everything went mad.

The door to her room burst open, and a dark form was on her at once, knocking her down and ripping the knife out of her hand. Lucy fell backwards, snapping her head forward in time to avoid knocking it upon the floor. Instead, she slammed her forehead into that of her assailant. Lucy grunted in pain and surprise, but the person on top of her made no sound.

She was held down by a large figure, round

and soft, and who smelled strangely pleasant, like a warm wool blanket on a cold winter day.

"Are you hurt, Miss Lucy? Tell me you are not hurt."

Lucy scrambled out from under the bulky form. "Mrs. Emmett?"

Hurrying to close the door, Lucy turned to see the plump woman getting to her feet, straightening out her bonnet, which she wore in her customary low fashion so it pressed her hair flat against her forehead.

"Lord, how I had to run to make my way here in time! Did not Miss Mary teach you any better than to fool with such things as summoning? One mistake in that circle of yours, and it would seek out the most arrogant living thing in the room, for these creatures hate arrogance above all weaknesses, and they can smell it the way a dog smells a rabbit. You may be certain that if you are alone, the most arrogant person in the room is you."

"What are you doing here?" Lucy demanded, attempting to keep her voice low. "How did you get in here? How did you know I was summoning a spirit? And where is Miss Crawford?"

"So many questions," said Mrs. Emmett with a good-natured laugh.

Checking the clock upon one of the side tables, Lucy saw it was near three in the morning. The house, however, remained silent. Mrs. Emmett's arrival apparently had awoken no one.

"Then let us take one question at a time," said Lucy. "Where is Miss Crawford?"

"Oh, I am certain I don't know that. It's got nothing to do with me."

"Nothing to do with you?" asked Lucy. "Is she not your mistress?"

"You are my mistress now."

"What can you mean? I cannot pay you."

Mrs. Emmett smiled. "I need no money."

"But what will Uncle Lowell say?"

"He'll say nothing," said Mrs. Emmett. "I'll not stay here. You don't need me, Miss Lucy. Not yet. When you do, I'll come to you. It is no hard thing."

Lucy shook her head at the nonsense. She was too tired to understand. "When did you last see Miss Crawford?"

"To that, I cannot say. My memory isn't good for such things."

Lucy circled around Mrs. Emmett. If this examination disturbed the good woman, she did not show it. She only turned her neck like an eager puppy to follow Lucy's movements. "How did you know I meant to summon a creature?" Lucy asked.

"How could I not know it?" Mrs. Emmett asked.

Lucy let out a long sigh. "Take no insult, Mrs. Emmett, but what are you?"

"I am Mrs. Emmett," she said with much cheer.

"And you now serve me?"

"Yes, Miss Lucy."

"You serve *me* and not Miss Crawford?"

"Yes, Miss Lucy."

It did not yet make sense, but Lucy suspected she was moving closer to some kind of clarity. "When we first met, you knew you were to serve me? Is that why you embraced me?"

"Oh, yes, Miss Lucy. I know everything that will happen to me. I even know when I shall be no more."

"You know when you are going to die?" Lucy asked.

"I know everything that is going to happen to me."

"Then can you not alter things to make your life easier?"

"It is not my life, it is yours."

This exchange was making Lucy uncomfortable. "What shall I do with you?"

"You need not worry for that. I have saved you from being destroyed this night, as you must have been — for there is an error in your circle. Your talent is great, but it is not flawless. You have come far by trusting your instincts, and you have come to see that your instincts do not lie, but it does not follow that you know all."

"Miss Crawford warned me not to summon, but I cannot know that she is my friend — that she ever was. My niece is gone — replaced with something vile — and as much as I wish I did not think so, I fear Miss Crawford had a hand in this."

Mrs. Emmett took her hand. "You must not doubt that she is your friend. You have none better. You cannot know what she has done and what she is yet prepared to do. She does not wish you to know, but you may depend upon her friendship."

"And what of my niece? What of Emily?" Lucy demanded. "She has been replaced by a changeling. What do you know of it?"

Mrs. Emmett shook her head. "I know nothing of how it was done or who did it."

"Do you know anything of changelings, of how I may banish it and retrieve my niece?"

"Only what is commonly known," said Mrs. Emmett.

"Nothing is commonly known," snapped Lucy. "Tell me what you can."

"I know that when a child is exchanged, it is hidden away, placed out of time as we understand it, so that months may pass for us, but only seconds for the child. If one were to banish the changeling, the original child would take its place, and to someone who knew not how to pay mind to such things, it would appear only that the child's disposition had changed."

"And how is this to be effected?" Lucy

demanded. "Can you tell me how?"

"Not I," said Mrs. Emmett. "I know nothing of alchemy."

Lucy stepped forward. "It is alchemy?"

"Of the most powerful kind, yes. If a spirit creature chooses to replace a human child itself, that is another matter, but to effect such a change requires the most powerful of alchemical knowledge. One must create a kind of spiritual doorway, and make it strong enough to last. Anyone who could build such a thing could create the philosopher's stone itself."

Lucy took hold of Mrs. Emmett's shoulders. "Then if I were to possess the *Mutus Liber,* I could retrieve my niece?"

"I daresay yes," agreed Mrs. Emmett.

Lucy let go of Mrs. Emmett and collapsed into her chair. The *Mutus Liber* was the key to everything. Her enemies wanted it, but she must want it more, and she must have it first. The course she was already on was the course she must continue to follow, only now with greater urgency and determination.

She looked down at the piece of paper on which she had drawn the complex Enochian circle, which she still clutched in her hand. "And what of this? Do I simply burn this? Is that a safe way to destroy it?"

"Do not destroy it," said Mrs. Emmett. "Keep it. Keep it with you always."

"Why? It is corrupt and dangerous. You said

so yourself."

"Because sometimes you can use danger and corruption for good ends," she said. Mrs. Emmett then leaned down to give Lucy a hug and departed the house, as unseen and unheard as she arrived.

She at last fell asleep in the predawn hours, and awoke late in the morning. By the time she emerged, the house was in disarray. In her room, Martha's nurse was busily packing her trunk, while downstairs Mr. Buckles was giving Ungston loud and utterly unnecessary orders — "Do not muddy my linens!" Martha sat in a felt armchair of faded green near the window, and the sun glowed against the white curtain at her back, making the wispy strands of Martha's black hair shine as though she were an angel. And yet, how unlike an angel was the creature that crawled up her shoulder. Its back was to Lucy, but she could see its scaly white skin and the strands of greasy, brittle hair that escaped the tiny bonnet, which did not quite conceal its pointed ears.

"What do you do?" cried Lucy. "You are not leaving."

"We are." Martha's voice cracked, and the bags under her eyes were dark and heavy. She appeared to have aged years in but a single night. "Uncle has said he cannot endure Emily's wailing, and though his doctor can find no ill with her, I should much like if our own man could look her over. She has no fever, and she thrives, yet she must eat all the time and will not settle."

The creature turned to Lucy and leered at her with its narrow eyes. Its mouth opened to show sharp teeth, which it licked with its flat and leathery tongue.

Martha rose to her feet. "Oh, here. Hold her for a moment."

She thrust out the baby, and Lucy had no choice but to take it. It clung to her shoulder, and its claws thrust into her flesh. Lucy felt a sharp jolt of pain and the faint moisture of blood trickling down her back. The creature nuzzled close to her ear and emitted a burst of staccato breaths — something like laughter. Its body, cold as ice and strangely loose, like a bladder of wine only half full, pressed against her. The urge, powerful and demanding, to pull the thing from her body and fling it to the floor shot through her with the force of a sudden and irresistible blow. Holding a rat or a venomous serpent to her breast would have been no more unnatural than this. Yet Lucy mastered herself. She could not attempt to tell Martha the truth, for she understood her sister would not be able to accept it.

"I thought you would want her," said Martha, sensing her discomfort.

"I am tired today." Lucy pried the creature

loose and handed it to Martha. Its tiny claws were wet with Lucy's blood. "I slept poorly last night, and now I am distracted. Oh, Martha. You *must* stay here." Lucy's plan to summon a creature to help her cast out the changeling was obviously finished, but she could not allow Martha to leave. As long as she could keep an eye upon the creature she could hope to do something about it, but Lucy could not bear the thought of Martha going off with it, having no idea what it was, that it was not her Emily.

Martha shook her head. "For Emily's sake, I cannot stay. I wish you could visit with us. Oh, how pleasant that would be if only . . ." She did not finish her sentence. She did not need to. Mr. Buckles had forbidden any further visits from her family until the baby was older. He believed Martha's relations would distract her from her duty.

In two hours, Lucy stood outside her uncle's house while Martha and the creature entered the loaded carriage. Before stepping through the door, Mr. Buckles paused and approached Lucy, gently leading her aside by taking hold of her arm in one of his long-fingered hands. His skin was so wet with perspiration, it was as though he'd just withdrawn it from a bucket of water.

"You've been, ah, shall we say, a terrible — let us say it direct — a terrible disappointment to your sister, and, if I may add, to Lady

Harriett," he said. "All very shameful. I trust there will be no more difficulty — difficulty or trouble, to be sure — with your marriage to Mr. Olson."

Lucy could not stand to have him speak to her in that tone, to treat her as though she were a fool and a child. Most of all, she could not endure that he would attempt to manipulate her powerlessness when it was he who had rendered her so.

"Mr. Buckles," she said, keeping her voice calm, "I have seen the original of my father's will. I am not a fool, and I know the difficulties in righting this injustice, but I will not be dissuaded. Ere I am done, I shall see you dangle from the hangman's noose."

Mr. Buckles blanched. He raised a wet hand to his cheek as though she had actually slapped him. "You would not dare," he said, his voice hoarse.

"I would not dare what?" asked Lucy, emboldened. "Seek justice? I would not dare to reclaim what is mine?"

"Such unnatural feeling!" he exclaimed. "I am your sister's husband."

"And I am your wife's sister," Lucy answered in return.

"I shall speak of this to Lady Harriett," said Mr. Buckles. "Would you oppose *her?*"

"I believe she and I are already opposed," said Lucy.

At this, he laughed. "I can tell that it is not

so. Shall I tell you how? Because you are yet alive." Mr. Buckles bowed, and then entered his carriage, leaving Lucy feeling as though she had made a terrible mistake.

Martha was gone, and so was the changeling. Each tick of the clock, each chime of the hour, was like a blow to Lucy, and so it would be until she had rescued her niece. She tried not to feel it, to dull the anxiety that boiled in her stomach, for she knew there could be no easy or quick resolution. She would live this way for days, perhaps weeks and months; she would have to endure it, for there was no one to do the work but she.

Lucy sat in her room at her secretary with her books, making notes and marking pages, working until the last of the sunlight was gone, and then, working late into the night by rushlight. So she strained her eyes as she copied out runes and magic squares, as she made lists of herbs, as she memorized Latin for spells. At last, when the clock struck one in the morning, she could do no more, but she did not believe more was required, and she believed it would serve. Lucy dressed for bed, extinguished the rush, crawled under the warmth of her heavy counterpane, and let exhaustion take her.

The next morning she awoke early and took from the pantry a small quantity of dill and rosemary, as well as an apple, of which she needed only a bit of the juice. She found also some dried flowers that Ungston used to make a sweet-smelling potpourri, which he put into bowls and set about the house. There she found rose and violet, as she required for the two spells she intended to cast. The first would be easier, for it involved the placement of a talisman, and she had grown quite adept at the creation and deployment of the cunning little engines. The second would be far more dangerous, and ethically problematic, but she could not scruple over safety and ethics now.

With her work done, Lucy traveled to visit Norah Gilley. The house was all in disarray as they prepared to travel to London. Lucy had believed they were not due to depart for several weeks, but it seemed that the schedule had been accelerated, for servants were busy running up and down the stairs with folded clothing and packages of household goods. Much of the house was being closed up, and in every room but the parlor, the furnishings were draped with sheets.

Norah greeted Lucy with a kind of cold imperiousness, as though her impending relocation to London were something of a coronation. An extended hand would not do for what Lucy had in mind, so she pulled her friend into a hug. This provided the opportunity to slip a tiny piece of paper into the folds of her gown.

Soon they sat. Norah asked at once if Lucy would like tea and cakes. Lucy almost answered, but then caught herself. It would be the first request she made, and so if she asked for refreshments, the charm would guarantee that Norah did not rest until they were delivered, but it would do no more than that. Instead, she turned to Norah and smiled.

"You leave for London in a few weeks' time, is that not so?" said Lucy.

"The precise day has not been determined, but I believe it will be sooner than I had supposed," said Norah. "We await only the final word from the ministry."

"Would not London be so much grander if you brought a friend with you, and would not you be best served if I were that friend? You must ask your father if I may come with you."

Norah appeared struck by this. The impending move to the capital was what elevated her above her friends, and to share that elevation would be unthinkable, and yet she now considered the matter seriously. "I cannot doubt that I shall make friends without delay, in particular with Papa's important office and his connections, but even so, how much more lovely it would be to share my joy with you. I shall ask him at once." She leapt to her feet.

Lucy remained alone in the parlor, her body almost shivering with nerves. Only now did it occur to her that she ought to have used a charm upon Mr. Gilley as well, for what if he did not want his daughter to bring a friend? But not five minutes passed before Norah rushed into the room, bright with glee. "He says he thinks it a marvelous idea," she said, and hugged Lucy. "He only tells you that you will have to be careful of your lungs." Both young ladies giggled at Mr. Gilley's fear of catching cold. It was as though they were little girls. Then they called for cakes, and then ate far too much as they talked of the thousand things they would do together. Lucy cared for none of it; she had no interest in balls and milliner's shops and grand houses and pleasure gardens. Perhaps a few months ago these would have seemed the finest things in the world to her, but now they seemed to her only to facilitate a small step toward a larger goal. She only spoke of them to keep Norah excited and happy. It was the least she could do after so deceiving her friend.

The next phase of her scheme required that Lucy do something she would once have considered unthinkable. She directed a note to the inn at which Mr. Morrison was lodged, and invited him to meet her at a chocolate house off the market square. Lucy had to steal a glass of wine from the kitchen in order to sufficiently steady her nerve, so much did her hand shake upon her first attempt to write the note. The kind words, the implication of forgiveness, even of admiration, made her sick in her soul, but Mr. Morrison had important information, and if Lucy were to succeed, she would need as much information as she could find.

As she prepared to leave the house for this rendezvous, Mrs. Quince hurried from the sitting room to bar her way from the door.

"Where do you think you go?"

"I have business," Lucy answered. "It is none of your concern."

"Is it with that vile Mary Crawford?"

"I shan't answer your questions, so stand aside. I am soon to leave for London with Miss Gilley, and you have no further power over me."

"Leave for London," repeated Mrs. Quince. "Does your uncle know?"

"What does it matter? Both of you have wanted me from this house, and I shall be gone."

Mrs. Quince took hold of Lucy's wrist in a tight grip. "What of Mr. Olson? You are to marry him."

"It's time you ceased to trouble yourself about my affairs," Lucy said, feeling the anger take hold. She was Lucy Derrick, a cunning woman, collector of the lost leaves of the *Mutus Liber,* and she would not be treated like a street urchin. "If you do not take your hand off me, I swear I shall make you bleed. Do not doubt me."

Mrs. Quince let go but did not step away. "You will regret having crossed me."

"Thus far," said Lucy, as she shoved the woman aside, "I'm rather enjoying it." She opened the front door and stepped out into the street without troubling to look back, though she very much wished to.

Lucy was not certain Mr. Morrison would obey the summons, and could not have said how she would respond if he did not, but he arrived on time, his face betraying his curiosity. It was crowded at that time of day, the room's bigger tables filled with large parties ranging from smiling elders to screaming infants. There were a variety of smaller tables, meant for couples, and Lucy had taken one of these in the back. She knew her presence there with a young man was a risk. People might talk. They probably would, but Lucy had more important things to consider, and she would be gone from Nottingham soon enough.

Finding Lucy at her table with two steaming bowls of chocolate before her, Mr. Morrison bowed and told her formally that he stood ready to obey her commands. If he were surprised by her invitation, he did not show it.

"Please sit," said Lucy. "I have taken the

liberty of ordering for you."

"And you are thoughtful to have done so," he said, rubbing his hands together before he took his seat. "I've always loved chocolate. Very good of you to recollect that."

"I did indeed," said Lucy, "and since I did not know how willing you would be to accept my invitation, I thought it best to provide an incentive."

"I confess I am surprised at all this," he said. "Pleasantly surprised, to be sure, but after our last encounter, you did not appear to wish to say more to me. But I am glad you summoned me, for I am to leave soon, and I did not wish us to part on such poor terms."

"Where do you go?" His pronouncement had now caught her by surprise, and she did not know how or if it would affect her intentions.

"I await my orders. All I can tell you, really. These things are best kept secret."

Lucy did not reply, and Mr. Morrison took a sip of his chocolate.

Lucy watched him, making certain he swallowed. She thought about what she was doing. This spell would make him love her, and that love would last until she broke the spell or until something happened to stagger him free of the spell's influence. She would be manipulating another human being, which was a terrible thing to do. But this was Mr. Morrison, and so she told herself that if she could make him an unwitting agent in her service, it was the least he owed her. Accordingly she said quietly, "Thus you are bound to me, Jonas Morrison."

Mr. Morrison set down his own cup and put his hand to his temple. "My God, Lucy. Did you just now — ?" He looked away, out the window, then back to her. "I beg your pardon. I don't recall what I was saying."

"You spoke of your orders," said Lucy, as she watched his face for some sign that the spell had taken effect.

"Yes, I must go soon," he said, "and I do not want to. You must know that I do not want to leave you. Do I shock you? I am sorry, I cannot help it. You cannot doubt that I am in love with you. I know that I used you falsely in the past, and you are right not to trust me. Only you must trust me this time. You must."

Lucy swallowed hard, suddenly aware of all the ambient noises that surrounded her — the other conversations, the rolling of carriages upon the street, the ticking of the clock, the birds, the cries of vendors, and the thundering of her own heart. She hated Jonas Morrison, but to toy with him this way was monstrous. She humiliated him and herself, and the consequences of her actions would likely prove disastrous. She understood that, but even as the waves of regret washed over her, she also knew she had no choice. She needed to know what he knew, and everything else would wait until her niece was safe. That is what mattered. Emily was missing, and her sister cared for a horrible creature, and no one anywhere knew or was prepared to do anything about it. No one but Lucy, and she would do what she must. She would crush and humiliate and deceive a thousand Jonas Morrisons if she had to.

Lucy rose to her feet. "Do not say such things," she managed. When she had imagined casting this spell upon him, she had not considered how she would respond to such a declaration.

"I know you resent what happened between us, but I am ready to make amends, to show you my true self. I ask only that you allow me the opportunity to prove myself."

Lucy turned to him, steeling herself for the bitterness of the words she must speak. "If you love me, you will trust me, and if you trust me, you will tell me what you know. I must understand what is happening, Mr. Morrison. I must understand everything. If you love me, you will not leave me in the darkness of ignorance."

Mr. Morrison considered what she said, and seemed to measure her words for their reason. Then he reached forward and gently took her hand, wrapping her fingers in his as though she were made of something brittle, and he feared to break her. They both sat down again.

"I can deny you nothing that is in my power to grant," he said. "There are dark matters of great importance of which I cannot speak, which I have sworn to withhold from all but other initiates, but what is within my power to tell you, I will."

His touch disgusted her. No matter how she might regret manipulating him, she could not help but despise him for what he had done to her. Nevertheless, she did not pull away. "What are you doing here, Mr. Morrison? Why have you come to Nottingham?"

He leaned forward, as if to lessen the distance between them. "I was to keep my eye upon the man you were to marry, Mr. Olson."

"But why?"

He took a deep breath. "There are forces in motion. Dangerous forces. Chief among these are what people are apt to call fairies or elves. Do not laugh, for this is serious."

Lucy thought about Mary's words, as well as the changeling creature she had held in her own arms. "I assure you, I am past laughing."

Mr. Morrison appeared surprised by her reaction. "You know of them already?"

"They are the spirits of the dead, returned and given flesh. They are revenants."

"You are unusually well informed," said Mr. Morrison. "Quite impressive. Almost no one outside our circle knows it. There are some historians of our folklore who have commented upon the fact that what we call fairy barrows are often burial mounds of the ancients, but that is the closest I have ever seen to things becoming common knowledge."

"I have uncommon sources," she said. Unable to any longer endure it, she removed her hand from his light touch. She was gentle, however. Lucy knew that a jarring experience or emotional confusion could destroy the effect of her spell. She would have to tread lightly.

Mr. Morrison looked at his hand, as if unable to comprehend what had happened, and then straightened himself. "Yes, I have no doubt. They have been among us as long as anyone can recall, bound to these isles. They are part of who we are, part of what it means to be British. For many years they have walked among us, scattered through many powerful families in the land. There have always been those who sought to join their number, who dream of power and immortality, and little imagine the cost. And too there are those who seek to constrain their power and influence, such as my order does now."

"What do these creatures want?" asked Lucy.

He shrugged. "Sometimes nothing more than to exist as they please. They play their games among themselves and, at times, they toy with us. Sometimes their schemes are trivial, and other times they seek to manipulate our lives in ways we cannot tolerate. They are strange and vile, Lucy, and to encounter one is to be altered by its strangeness."

"Our mortality makes us what we are," said Lucy, echoing Mary's words.

He nodded. "How could I help but love a woman as wise as you? Yes, that is the thing. Even the ones newly returned are so altered as to be different creatures than the beings they were in life. They are inscrutable and arbitrary and terrifying."

"Mr. Morrison, why is any of this important? You say that these beings have long walked among us. Why is your order acting against them now?"

"The world is changing, Lucy. Everywhere we see the rise of new machines, new methods of making and building and transporting. The world is about to enter an era in which man and machine will hold dominion over nature. In this, the revenants have allied with us. They have been providing us with intelligence against the Luddites."

"Do you mean to say that you stand with these monsters?" Lucy was horrified. She knew that Mr. Morrison and his Rosicrucians believed that Britain must not fall behind the rest of the world as mills replaced men in the production of goods, but to align with creatures that Mary described as pure evil — that seemed too much.

"Not quite so much standing with them as finding ourselves upon common ground."

Mr. Morrison's hand had been creeping back toward hers as he gathered the courage to hold it, but Lucy snatched hers away. Now that she knew what he stood for, she could feel far less guilty about having placed this spell upon him.

"Have you seen these mills?" she asked him. "Do you know what they are, what it is to work in one? Do you understand what it is you defend?"

"I have seen them," he said, and indeed he looked shaken. "They are terrible. I know that, Lucy, and your outrage does you credit, but Britain cannot stand alone, defenseless in the past while other nations march forward. We will be backwards and defenseless."

"That is a poor excuse," said Lucy.

"We have no choice. If these Luddites are unchecked, their uprising will lead to rebellion. Do you want to have happen here what has happened in France? We must move forward in peace or fall backwards in violence. What course would you advise?"

"A third way," said Lucy, who spoke without thinking, but as the words escaped her mouth, she knew it was what she believed. There had to be a third way, some kind of compromise position that steered the nation between the Luddites and the revenants. *That* was what Lucy endorsed. And, much to her own surprise, she found that she cared about it. It meant something to her. Finding her niece was the most pressing issue upon her mind, but this — this compromise was important too. She could not have said why, she could not have said how her opinion on the fate of the nation could be of consequence, but she felt sure that it was.

"What is that third way? I pray you tell me, for if you can think of it, I shall urge my superior to pursue it."

Lucy smiled. "I don't know. Yet. Give me a little time." She placed her hand back on the table. The idea that he would again touch her, would even think of touching her, was sickening, but Lucy had set these events in motion, and she would have to let them unfold. "What has Mr. Olson to do with all this?"

"We are not entirely certain. The truth is, the revenants give us half-truths and partial intelligence. They attempt to aid us against the Luddites, but also to manipulate us for their own ends, perhaps even ends that have nothing to do with this cause. We believed that Olson was to play some role in the rise of these mills, but since his frames were destroyed, it may no longer be so. In any event, I am upon a new mission now."

"What is that?"

"There is a book," he said. "An alchemical book that supposedly contains the secret of both making and unmaking revenants, of enslaving and banishing magical creatures. It contains much more besides: the secret to warding against magic, and to breaking the wards of others. It tells of things not imagined, and yet so simple, it is hard to believe they could be unknown. But most of all, it contains the secret of bringing the dead back to life — or, perhaps more accurately, to giving them a new kind of life. It is, in short, the most terrible book in the world. The only known copy of the book has been torn apart, and its pages scattered. My superior has charged me with finding these pages. I don't know precisely why, but the book is likely something we can use to bargain with these revenants."

Lucy tried to look only vaguely interested, but her hands began to shake. She could use the *Mutus Liber* to cast off the monster that had taken the place of her niece. She had to find the missing pages, and she had to do so before Mr. Morrison did — a man who enjoyed the resources of a secret international organization.

She took a deep breath to clear her mind. "Do you know where to find this book?"

"It has been broken up into many pieces," he said, "but I believe I have recently discovered where to look for at least part of it, and

I must leave soon."

There was no help for it now, and so she spoke words she would never have believed she could utter. "Will you take me with you?"

Finally he found the courage to take her hand. Mr. Morrison smiled at her, and his eyes moistened. "I should like nothing better than to have you with me, but it is far too dangerous."

Lucy swallowed, preparing her to say the words she had to say. "If you love me, you will take me with you."

He looked down at the table for a long time. Finally, he met her eyes. "My search for the book will take me far away, to many different places, and I cannot harm your reputation by asking you to go with me unmarried. And I cannot now marry you. I should like nothing better, Lucy, but until this matter is resolved, my superior would not give me permission."

No one is asking you to marry me, thought Lucy bitterly, and yet, she could not help but consider this offer as though it were serious, as though it were brought on by something other than her magic and her will. Mr. Morrison was a gentleman, he had money and certainly influence of some kind. He was charming and clever and handsome. Ought she not to set aside her past antipathy and encourage this line of conversation?

"However," he said, snapping her out of

her thoughts, "before I travel, I must look for some of the missing pages close to hand. It will be dangerous, but you are a woman of some skill, so if you do precisely what I say, I will venture to bring you with me."

It was better than nothing. It was a start. "Where do we go?"

He made a face of disgust. "To a vile place, Lucy. One as full of demons and ghosts as anywhere on earth. We go to an estate whose every stone is permeated with evil and dissipation. It is the ruined home of a corrupted baron who is more devil than man. The place I speak of is called Newstead Abbey."

22

They would go at night, Mr. Morrison said, as the servants of Newstead would not remain the night in the absence of their master. Slipping in at night increased their chances of finding the book and remaining undiscovered. Lucy knew she would need to bring whatever talismans and protections she could muster against fairies and other dark things. Newstead, as she already knew, was supposed to be haunted by several ghosts. The entire neighborhood spoke of Byron's deceased dog, whom Mr. Morrison said was called Boatswain, and according to local gossip there were earthly creatures to fear as well. Byron was known to keep a menagerie of wild animals upon the grounds, including a bear, a wolf, and, perhaps less menacing, a tortoise. Lucy was determined to prepare for all of these, and for dangers yet unimagined.

Yet, if danger could be avoided, why should they risk breaking open the abbey? "Can we not ask the master of Newstead to give you or sell you what you seek?" Lucy asked.

"The master of Newstead, as you style him, will not behave like a gentleman. If he knows we desire the pages, he will withhold them for as much money as he can demand."

"And why not pay him then? Surely your order has resources."

"We do," said Mr. Morrison, "and I believe if we could depend upon him to conduct himself according to the dictates of reason, we would buy the pages, but this man is half mad, a capricious and dangerous fiend who will ally himself against his nation for the simple pleasure of rebellion. We dare not risk letting him know that we are aware of the pages and desire them."

Byron had shown her every sign of being a kind, generous, and open gentleman, but he had shown her another side as well, and Lucy too would hesitate to depend upon his goodness. Still, she found herself irritated that Mr. Morrison would speak so ill of him. Who was *he* to judge anyone else's actions after his crimes and after he and his kind had sided with revenants and mill operators? Lucy thought it entirely possible she could persuade Byron to give her the pages. He lived by his own law, and it was a dangerous law for her, but perhaps with the aid of the right talisman, Lucy could get him to surrender whatever she wished.

That was all speculation, however, for

Byron was in London. If the pages were here in Nottinghamshire, it was better to take them with Mr. Morrison's aid. She hated that it was he with whom she would share this adventure. It would be far more delightful to sneak into Mr. Morrison's estate with Byron as her coconspirator. Byron had insulted her, that was true, but in his mind he had not meant his proposal as an insult, and his regard for her appeared genuine, not brought about by magic and charms. This was, however, all building castles in the air. There were to be no adventures with Byron, and Lucy would have to order things as best she could to protect her niece. Later she would worry about who was right in this conflict between Mary Crawford's ideas and Mr. Morrison's.

Byron would surely have had no difficulty in asking Lucy to slip from her home in the dark of night, but the idea did not sit well with the far more prim Mr. Morrison. He wrestled with the impropriety of it, torturing himself over his near elopement with her four years before. In the end, he was forced to make do with many assurances of his good intentions. "You may depend upon my behaving honorably," he told her. "Do not think I will confuse love with license."

Lucy absently thanked him and at once began to consider which among her gowns would be best suited for a midnight adventure to a gothic castle.

■ ■ ■ ■

Lucy contrived to slip into everyone's supper a combination of herbs to induce a heavy sleep. She also placed little bundles under the pillows in each bed, bits of lavender entwined with each person's hair, and a drop of wine. They would wake under natural circumstances, but they would be disinclined to hear her slip down the stairs and opening the front door. Upon the clock striking one in the morning, Lucy, as Mr. Morrison had directed her, removed herself from the house and he met her upon the street. There was to be no carriage, only a single horse, onto which Mr. Morrison helped her. Then, without ceremony, they began the slow and steady ride into the night.

They spoke little, but Lucy felt the awkward weight of his body against hers as they rode. He did not press up against her on purpose — nothing so vulgar as that. If anything, he shifted away from her, avoiding contact, but only because he so much desired it. Lucy hated him still — of course she did — but she also felt a strange kind of pity for Mr. Morrison. He was a melancholy creature, and showed every sign of being genuinely affected by the death of his wife. Lucy, with her spell, would only make him more melancholy still.

At last they turned off the main road and

continued the next mile or so until the looming shape of Newstead Abbey began to appear in the shadow of the near-full moon. Mr. Morrison's pace did not slow, but she sensed a tension in him as he approached.

"Have you before been to the abbey?" she asked him.

"Once." His voice was cold and clipped. Lucy understood that there was something between the two men, something Mr. Morrison chose not to speak of.

They followed the road past the great lake and around the southern wing of the castle to approach by the western front. Lucy thought of what Mr. Blake had said about ghosts, and though she had taken precautions, she could not help but feel the thrill of fear. Yet, for all her anxiety, it was a pleasant night with a bright moon and a soothing quiet. The horse trotted along the road until they reached its broadening, right before the door. There, they dismounted and Mr. Morrison tied his horse. He took from his saddlebag a lantern and a tinderbox and struck a light.

When Mr. Morrison raised the light, Lucy almost screamed with surprise. Upon the steps to the main entrance was a crumpled figure in white. For an instant, Lucy had no doubt that she beheld a ghost. Then, while her heart pounded in her chest, she recognized the wild auburn hair and frail limbs.

She let out a gasp of relief and rushed over, even as Mr. Morrison called out for her to stop. Lucy felt no fear, however. She knelt by Sophie Hyatt's prostrate form, and saw that the deaf girl was not hurt, only sleeping.

Lucy took her exposed hand, which felt as cold as ice. Sophie awoke with a start and sat up, looking both confused and disappointed to see Lucy staring at her.

"Hold up the light," she said to Mr. Morrison, who was now behind her. "She must see my lips to understand me."

Without inquiring what she meant, he obeyed.

"Miss Hyatt," said Lucy. "What do you do here?"

She did not shiver. The elements appeared to have no effect upon her. With a steady hand, she took her slate, which rested by her side, and found her chalk upon the ground.

I love him, she wrote.

Lucy took her hand. "I know you do, but you will catch your death. Are you not cold?"

The fire within warms me, she wrote.

"Improbable, I should think," said Mr. Morrison, who removed his greatcoat and draped it over the girl's shoulders. It looked absurd upon her — she was like a kitten lost in tangled bedsheets — and she reacted to the added warmth not at all. "You are acquainted with the shivering deaf girl, Miss Derrick?"

"We have met before," said Lucy. "She has bound herself to Lord Byron."

"Tell her to come with us, but to make no mischief," he said. "When we are through, we will see her someplace safe. I won't leave her here to be pounced on by bears or nibbled at by tortoises or whatever else can happen at this wretched place."

Mr. Morrison's concern surprised Lucy. It would have been more consistent with her idea of him if he had been content to leave a damaged girl such as Sophie to her fate, particularly if it were a fate she had chosen for herself. Perhaps it was the spell Lucy had put on him that made him more caring than was his nature.

They attempted the front door, which was locked.

Mr. Morrison retrieved from his pocket a long, ornate gold key. "Association with my order has certain advantages. We know so many marvelous people, including lock-smiths."

He rotated the key in the lock, and the heavy door swung inward.

Lucy expected something vile and cold and heavy to wash over her, but it was only a large hall, dark and empty and badly kept. They had taken only a few steps inside before her lungs began to feel heavy with dust, and if there was nothing inherently frightening she saw or felt, she nevertheless started when she felt Sophie's frail hand tug upon her gown. When she turned, the girl held out a pebble no larger than a raisin.

Sophie twisted the slate that hung around her neck and scratched out a few lines. *Eme-thist. For spirits.*

Lucy nodded. She had her own amethyst upon her to protect against ghosts, but she did not want to reject the girl's generosity. She took the stone and squeezed Sophie's arm by way of thanks, and then stood back while Mr. Morrison held up his lantern.

"Amethyst?" he asked.

"Yes," Lucy said.

"Smart girl."

"Smarter than you," said Lucy, who held up the small amethyst pendant that she wore around her wrist.

"Think you so?" asked Mr. Morrison, who removed an amethyst on a chain from his pocket. "It appears that the deaf girl is the only one of us generous enough to share."

"I presumed my gem would be sufficient for all of us," Lucy answered sulkily. She did not like to be accused of being unkind.

"It will. I should not have let you come if I were not prepared for what we might find," said Mr. Morrison. "I don't much care for ghosts — bit of a bad history there — and the ones here are more unpleasant than most."

Lucy laughed nervously. She was eager to move on. "You know the way to the library?"

"He has no great library," Mr. Morrison said. "But I know where he will have such books as he possesses — in the old drawing room."

Again, there was that tone in his voice, but Lucy did not ask questions. Instead, she took Sophie's hand and followed Mr. Morrison into the great expanse of the entryway. Here was a vast, cold stone room with vaulted arches. There was little in the way of decorations or wall hangings, and Lucy perceived it was but an entrance to the abbey proper. Somewhere in the distance she heard a slow drip of water.

Mr. Morrison turned back to her. "This is the crypt."

"Splendid," she answered.

They turned right and proceeded up a great and broad stone staircase, the steps wide enough to be negotiated without much difficulty by a horse. Horse droppings scattered about the floor gave evidence that Byron had actually ridden indoors. Lucy also observed overturned plates of food upon which rats nibbled, occasionally turning to stare at them brazenly. There were, however, no ghosts in evidence.

At the top of the staircase they entered the great dining room, which showed more evidence of horses, discarded food, and overturned and shattered bottles of wines. Cobwebs tickled their faces, and they heard the scurry of little animal feet — more rats most likely, but this being Newstead, there could be no assurance that they would not be poisonous lizards or African monkeys or anything else Byron's imagination might desire and his credit might procure.

Through a carved doorway they entered a corridor which took them to a short set of steps, and then a door, which Mr. Morrison pushed open. They followed him inside.

It was a massive room, sixty feet long, and almost half as wide, and it was the most orderly and well-kept space Lucy had yet seen in Newstead. There were paintings upon the walls, and comfortable furnishings near the ornate fireplace. Along the far wall, even in the dark, Lucy could perceive bookshelves. Relief washed over her. Their journey was near an end.

"This is the great drawing room," said Mr. Morrison. "Byron keeps his collection here. Nothing like what a gentleman would call a library, but a few hundred volumes, so this may take some time. Let us see if we cannot find some candles or lamps to light to make the work go faster." He raised up his lantern and then began to let out a long string of uncharacteristic curses.

Lucy saw at once his reason. The shelves along the wall, where Byron's books ought to have been, were completely empty.

"Damn him," said Mr. Morrison. "I should have known he would do something of this sort."

Lucy tugged on his sleeve.

"You will have to endure my language," he said. "And the deaf girl cannot hear me."

"Not that," said Lucy. "By the door."

Mr. Morrison turned his lantern toward the door. At first, he saw nothing in the gloom — Lucy watched him shift his light about in search of what had alarmed her — and then he saw it, the massive gray wolf, its yellow eyes reflecting the lantern's glow. Even in that dim light, they could see that its mouth was open, its head low to the ground. The animal let out a low, rumbling snarl.

They stood on the far side of the furnishings, so the sofa and chairs and tables were between their position and the wolf's, but that would do them little good. Very slowly, Lucy reached into the inner lining of her cloak and removed a small felt pouch. Loosening the drawstring, she began to sprinkle its contents on the floor around them while she muttered an incantation. She hoped it did not need to be spoken clearly, for she was still slightly embarrassed to do such things in front of other people.

"Monkshood," she told Mr. Morrison when she was done. "The wolf won't like it."

"Very clever, bringing that with you," he said, "though we're in some trouble should we decide to leave the circle."

"What happens then?"

"Then," said Mr. Morrison, "then we shall resort to other means."

The wolf moved closer to them, and Sophie gripped Lucy's arm. Mr. Morrison, for his part, remained motionless and apparently unperturbed.

"You are most calm, sir," said Lucy.

"I have taken you at your word that it is monkshood," he said. "You are certain it is?"

"My father taught me to recognize and distinguish plants," she answered.

"Then it is monkshood," said Mr. Morrison.

The wolf walked slowly, casually, around the furnishings, and approached the circle with a cautious snort. It stopped and sniffed again at the thin line of monkshood and let out a whimper, taking a few steps back. When it was perhaps twenty feet distant, it stopped and turned toward the door, but it did not move. Instead it watched something else with great interest, and it took Lucy a moment to see that there was a light approaching, moving raggedly as whoever came ascended the stairs. Then a figure appeared in the doorway holding a candle in one hand. It let out a whistle, and the wolf ran to it.

"Ah, well done, boy," Byron said to the

312

wolf, patting it upon the head with his free hand. "You have caught the intruders."

Byron's delighted grin reflected the two lights. He wore a dressing gown, open to the waist, revealing his muscular chest. Lucy noted the gown was unusually long, trailing to the ground so as to conceal his clubfoot.

Sophie began to breathe heavily, and she pulled away from Lucy. The wolf, seeing this, turned and growled at her. Lucy grabbed the girl to keep her from leaving the circle, though she pulled wildly and began to let out low animal noises.

"What have you done with your books?" Mr. Morrison demanded.

"I do make Newstead available from time to time that the commoners might view it, but I assure you that this is not a convenient hour. And Miss Derrick, I am surprised to see you here in such company. Last time we spoke, you made it clear you did not wish to see your name compromised. I cannot think late-night excursions with such a man to be wise."

"Byron, don't poison this lady with the sounds of your voice," responded Mr. Morrison coldly. "Tell me, where are the books?"

Even in the poor light, Lucy saw Byron's face darken and his expression contort into pure rage. He jabbed a finger toward Mr. Morrison as though he thrust a sword. "You don't demand anything of me!" he shouted, sounding very much like a madman. "This is my home. Mine! You are an intruder. Thank me for not shooting you dead, Morrison."

In her surprise and fear, her grip slackened, and Sophie broke away, running toward Byron. The wolf turned and leapt at her. Lucy wanted to look away, but she forced herself to look and saw Sophie unclench her hand and toss a handful of something at the wolf. It must have been monkshood, because it was as though the wolf struck something in mid leap. It yelped and fell to the ground, where it began licking its haunches. The girl, meanwhile, had hurled herself at Byron and clung to him. He put his arm around her and patted her affectionately, like a man with his child. There was something else there too, Lucy thought. His movements were slow and sensual and knowing, and Lucy understood that Byron had already taken full advantage of this girl's devotion to him.

"Lord Byron," said Lucy, somehow emboldened by his outrageous behavior with Sophie. His defiance of all morality made her trespassing seem insignificant. "We should never have come here without your leave if we thought you were home, but we believed you in London, and the matter too important to wait. Please, you must tell us. Where are the books?"

"Oh, Lucy. If you had come to me, I could deny you nothing. You know what is in my heart. But I cannot abide your aiding this man."

"Your heart?" Mr. Morrison demanded. Now he retrieved from his pocket a pistol, which he pointed at Byron. "What feelings do you pretend to have for this lady?"

This, clearly, was the "other means" to which he had alluded. "Please," Lucy said to Byron. "I know not what is between you and Mr. Morrison, but you must understand this is a matter of the utmost importance to *me.* It is for my sake that we have come here. I beg you send away the wolf and tell us what we want to know."

Byron appeared to soften at this. He said something to the wolf that Lucy did not understand, but apparently it did. It rose upon its legs and trotted out of the room.

With his arm still around Sophie's shoulders, Byron faced Lucy and Mr. Morrison. "My means are not what I would wish. Consequently, I sold my library."

"To whom?" demanded Mr. Morrison.

Byron grinned at him. "I shan't tell you. Now, what shall you do about it?"

Mr. Morrison snorted. "You think we won't be able to find out?"

"I suppose we shall see."

Sophie refused to go with them. When Lucy approached the girl, she simply clung tighter to Byron and turned away.

"This is unworthy of you," she told him.

He smiled at her. "This is who I *am*, Lucy. I live by my own law, not the world's, but I like to believe my code is not without honor. I do not harm or deceive her. She wishes to be with me upon such times I find agreeable, and I cannot tell her that she ought not to wish it."

"She loves you," said Lucy. "What will her life be when you walk away with hardly a recollection of her?"

"She knows I will not remain," he said, "and she chooses to stay."

They turned to go and Sophie ran over to Lucy, giving her a warm hug. When they broke off, she scribbled something on her slate. *Thank you. I will be well.*

"I hope so," Lucy said.

Sophie took her chalk once more, her hand moving quickly over the slate. She held it out, this time at such an angle that, even at a distance, Mr. Morrison would be unable to see. It read, *Books sold to Hariet Dier, Kent.*

Lucy struggled to keep her face from showing her surprise. She knew at that instant that she would not tell Mr. Morrison. He wanted those pages for his order. He wanted to stop the Luddites. Lucy was still uncertain about the Luddites themselves, and how wholeheartedly she endorsed their cause, but she knew that even if Mr. Morrison wanted to help her, once his order took hold of the *Mu-*

tus Liber she would never have another chance to take the pages herself.

She hugged Sophie again, wished her well, and departed with Mr. Morrison, adopting his mood of disgust and defeat.

Outside Newstead, Lucy walked with Mr. Morrison, neither of them speaking for some time. At last he said, "I don't recall you mentioned that you knew Byron."

"Nor did you," she answered. "You and he appear to loathe each other."

"And you and he appear to have feelings of another sort."

Lucy felt herself stiffen with anger. "How dare you presume to judge me, sir! After what you did to me. And — and I was only sixteen, and you —" She turned away, shaking, feeling tears burning upon her face, and not wanting him to see.

She did not hear him walk toward her, but when he spoke, she sensed he stood directly behind her. "I am sorry, Lucy."

"You are sorry," she said, not troubling to turn to him. "You have the luxury of apologizing and forgetting, but I have not. I am reminded of it nearly every day of my life."

It occurred to Lucy she was being unfair. Mr. Morrison might well have been more sensitive had she not cast a love spell upon him. It might not be his fault entirely that he was so callous about what he had done to

317

her in the past. More important, the spell might well be broken if she distressed him too much, so she attempted to calm herself. She wiped her eyes with her hands and turned to him.

"I aided him once," she said, trying, not entirely successfully, to keep her voice from trembling. "Using the cunning craft. It made an impression upon him, and he chose to express his feelings by making me a very improper offer. I hope I need not add that I rejected it as the insult it was. That is the extent of my history with him. What is between you?"

Mr. Morrison appeared to mull over what he had just heard. Then he sniffed. "You have met him. You have seen how he behaves, how he treats women — even those too unfortunate to know their own interest. I cannot abide such a man, and circumstances have thrown us together enough times for our opposing natures to clash."

"What is your next step?" asked Lucy, making every effort to lighten her voice. She wished him to believe her anger had passed.

"I cannot yet say. I will report to my order and we will formulate a plan."

Lucy let out a sigh as they approached his horse. "At least we did not need the amethyst, for we encountered no ghosts."

Mr. Morrison let out a laugh. "Miss Derrick, the amethyst is the only reason we did not."

23

The following morning word arrived from Norah Gilley that they were going to London two days thence, and Lucy began to make preparations to leave her uncle's house. While she packed her things, a boy arrived at the house with a note from Mr. Morrison, who begged she meet him once again at the chocolate house. When she arrived, he was loitering outside and looking agitated and demonstrating no particular interest in chocolate.

"I must leave Nottingham at once," he told her, moved nearly to tears by what he said. He took both her hands and looked directly into her eyes. "I ought to have gone already, but I could not leave without seeing you."

"I go to London in two days, with Miss Gilley. Where do you go?"

"I have sworn an oath of secrecy. I can tell you only that I leave England."

Lucy took a moment to consider this news. If there were parts of the book outside

England, she could never retrieve them herself. Maybe it was best not to ask too many questions. Better he should go, find the pages, and then hopefully she could persuade him to give them to her. She hated to let him leave with the love magic still upon him, but for the sake of her niece, Lucy had no choice.

"Perhaps," she said, "when you have completed your quest, you will find me in London."

He let go of her hands and began to pace in short strides. "If there is a way to do so without compromising the safety of this nation, then I will find you, Lucy. As soon as I can."

After saying this, he proceeded to make many declarations. He spoke of how they would be together once this dark hour had passed. If he noted that she did not encourage, or even respond to, these speeches, he made no sign of it. At last, greatly moved by his own sorrow, he departed, and Lucy wondered if she would ever see him again. If she wanted the missing pages of the book, she supposed she would have to.

Shortly before she left for London, Mr. Olson came to call. She longed to say that she was unwell and to send him away, but he had suffered much, and even if he had also caused suffering, Lucy did not wish to be cruel. More than that, he had loved her after his own fashion, and she must not hate him for that. On the other hand, he had never declared he no longer wished to marry her, and she did not want to hear him press his case. However, Lucy knew she would likely have to face many things, many people, she would rather avoid. Best to get into the habit.

She went downstairs and found him in the parlor, sitting with his legs pressed close together, hands in his lap, looking uncomfortable, and yet, for all that, he appeared, if not precisely happy then at least contented. His eyes were wide and bright and attentive, his suit new and neat and clean. He had cut his hair into the fashion of late, and it was neatly combed. As she entered the room, he rose to his feet and bowed at her, and he had the air of a man who believed in his own significance.

"Miss Derrick," he said when they were seated, "I understand you are to leave for London for the remainder of the season."

"Perhaps not so long. Perhaps longer," she said. "I do not yet know."

He nodded. "I thought it would be wrong not to take my leave of you. I know that matters did not end between us as I had wished, and I spoke some words which I now regret. Nevertheless, I hope when you think of me, you will think well."

Apparently Mr. Olson had set aside any intention of pursuing the wedding, and he'd simply neglected to mention that fact to the bride. In any case, this was good news, making her inclined toward generosity. "With all my heart. I have never said how sorry I was to hear of your mill, and the reversals you suffered. I do not love such enterprises for their consequences to the men of Nottingham, but I never wished that you should face these difficulties."

"On that score you need have no fear," said Olson. "My machines were destroyed and I had no money to replace them, but opportunities have arisen, and I now construct a new mill in a new location. From this adversity, great things have arisen."

He forced a smile at her. Perhaps he wished to show her what she had neglected to seize, but Lucy did not think so. She believed he was just as relieved to have escaped her as she was to have escaped him.

"I wish you much prosperity."

"I cannot see how we can fail," said Mr. Olson. "Lady Harriett, my patroness, has a good head for such matters as these — a remarkable trait in a woman."

Lucy stood up and wrung her hands, and seeing that he stared at her she sat back down again. She opened her mouth, to say that he must not take her money, must not do business with her, but knew how it would sound, and she had no means of convincing him. Nothing she could say would be creditable, and so she put her hands in her lap and looked away. "I can only wish your business brings you the success you desire."

"Thank you, Miss Derrick," he said, seeming to find nothing odd in her behavior. "I am sanguine it will all be well. You see now, you would not have suffered for being married to me."

"And yet," she offered. "I sense that your feelings have altered."

He nodded. "It is the strangest thing. You must understand that I know you are a pretty girl, but I have never valued such things in a wife. I have never wanted to marry for anything but property. It merely happened one day that I thought I was in love with you, and then one day I thought I was not. I suppose love is strange in that way."

He rose to his feet, blushing and announcing that he had taken enough of her time. She saw him to the door and shook his hand, so they parted with declarations of friendship. Yet Lucy was deeply troubled, for now it seemed to her obvious that someone had placed a spell upon Mr. Olson to make him love her, and she could not imagine who that person might have been. It did seem curious, however, that Lady Harriett still had designs on Mr. Olson. Lucy wondered if she had been manipulating him all along. It hardly mattered, though. Soon Lucy would be gone, and this would no longer be her concern.

■ ■ ■ ■

Two days later, Norah arrived at Uncle Lowell's house in a handsome coach, drawn by four yellowish horses. Her parents had traveled on ahead, and it was to be just the two young ladies and Norah's woman. With great difficulty, Ungston and the coachman loaded Lucy's trunk, which contained no small number of books, including her mostly false copy of the *Mutus Liber.* In addition, there were magical implements, herbs, and, of course, as many of her clothes as she could manage.

Her uncle sat in his study, reviewing some letters, and took his leave of her coolly. "You've quite disappointed me in your conduct with Mr. Olson," he said. "I hope you shall do better in London. You'll be returning here in the end, I suppose."

Lucy curtsied. "I have not troubled myself to think of the future."

"No, I suppose not," he answered, and then turned away.

Outside his study, Mrs. Quince waited for her. "Enjoy your travels," she said with a pinched smile. "Do try to bring no more shame upon yourself."

Lucy studied her, feeling unnerved by her restraint. "I have no notion of why you have treated me as you have, but in the end I will find out. You may be certain of that."

Mrs. Quince stared in wonder, unblinking and unmoving, and remained that way until Lucy was inside the coach.

When Lucy and Norah approached the equipage, Lucy observed Insworth, Norah's servant, hunched over her botched knitting, muttering gloomily under her breath as she teased out false stitches. She had been in the Gilley family for a long time, and no amount of ill humor or ineptitude could prove sufficient cause for dismissal. She was a remarkably sour woman, with an offensive smell, and so best not confined to a coach for a long period of time, but it was not she who gave Lucy her surprise. It was the woman sitting across from her: Mrs. Emmett.

Lucy paused, unable to think of what to say, so it was Norah who spoke for her.

"Your woman is here already," she said, her mouth compressed into a pinched smile. "I did not know you possessed such a person."

They climbed in, each lady next to her own servant, and soon the coach began to roll. Mrs. Emmett only looked out the window, and occasionally turned to Norah to smile beatifically. Lucy felt a boiling medley of emotions — anger, confusion, and most of all, curiosity, but she could ask nothing in front of Norah, and she postponed all her questions until a convenient time arrived.

Satisfaction, such as it was, had to wait until their first stopover at an inn in Leicester. Lucy found cause to take Mrs. Emmett aside. "What are you doing here?" she demanded.

"You can't go to London without your serving woman," she said cheerily.

"Did Miss Crawford direct you to come to me?"

"Oh, yes. Long ago, but I am your woman now. I told you that, Miss Derrick."

"How is it that Norah seems to know you?"

"She knows me because I am your serving woman," said Mrs. Emmett.

Further inquiry produced only answers of an equally unsatisfying and circular nature. Lucy learned nothing of Mary's whereabouts. The best she could get out of the serving woman was that she, Mrs. Emmett, had *always* worked for Lucy. Lucy simply had not known it.

The remainder of the journey was without much amusement or event. On the first night they stayed at an inn in Bedford, where a trio of officers made much of the ladies, even if they made slightly more of Norah, perhaps because Norah made much more of them. Lucy had matters on her mind other than officers, but she did not judge Norah, for she recalled what it was to have nothing of import to occupy one's thoughts. If anything, she felt a pang of jealousy for her friend's freedom to indulge in these simple pleasures.

They were on the road again before first light, though Mrs. Emmett was asleep again soon enough, snoring so loudly that at first it was comical, later maddening. Before nightfall, Lucy could make out the approaching city looming on the horizon. The farmland around them became less expansive, the people less rude, and the air less clear. Indeed, shortly after lunch the windows of the coach began to cloud over with gray soot, and the air they breathed grew heavier with London's belching chimneys and coal smoke.

As they entered the city, Lucy gripped Norah's arm, for the scene around them was not one of refinement, but horror. London had always had its poor, but the new mills built upon the river, spewing forth thick clouds of black smoke, seemed like something out of Dante's Hell. It was like the poverty of Nottingham, multiplied a thousandfold. A boy walked shirtless against the cold evening air, his body so gaunt Lucy could all but identify his organs. A woman, almost equally uncovered, held her naked baby upside down by its feet while she shouted at a leering, finely dressed man. Two gentlemen laughed while they slapped an insensible woman's face. A young man, with no hands, held up his begging bowl between the raw stumps of his wrists.

This was the worst of it, but not the whole.

Gangs of thieves roamed the streets, their occupation so obvious it might have been emblazoned upon their coats. Likewise the whores made no effort to disguise their trade. The most brazen of them exposed their breasts to the coach before realizing it was inhabited by ladies, at which observation they would spit or hurl turds. Lucy had never seen such filth — the animal refuse that gathered in the street, the human refuse that did likewise, and besides came flying out of windows as they passed. The stiffly moving rivers of kennel that made their slow, muddy way down the street. Dead dogs, dead cats and rats and horses — the latter being dissected by a gang of feral boys after meat — lay everywhere. And everywhere was soot — so deep and thick and inescapable it caked Lucy's throat and nostrils and made her long for a bath.

Norah laughed to see Lucy's response. "Oh, this isn't really London. We shall go to places in town where these sights do not exist. I don't trouble myself to look."

Lucy nodded, not because she agreed or saw the wisdom in pretending that people did not live so, but because she dared not speak, dared not say what was on her mind. Here, in this terrible place, Lucy understood that the Luddites were right, that Ludd, whatever he might be, was right. The machine breakers, the revolutionaries, those who raged against what they could not stop — all of them were right. And Mary Crawford — whatever role she may have had in replacing her sister's child — she was right too. What terrible thing would Lucy herself not do, would not any sane person do, to turn back the tide upon these horrors, to stopper up the vomiting chimneys, to wipe away the soot and ash and dirt that fell from the sky like snow.

Then, as Norah predicted, their surroundings improved. The streets became wider and cleaner and less populated in general, less populated with mendicants and felons and whores in particular. Suddenly there were broad, glorious houses, gentlemen with ornate walking sticks, ladies in fine gowns, servants with neat little children in tow, or happy little lapdogs in baskets. There were elegant horses and majestic equipages. There were parks and lawns, fields where careless children played, watched over by mastiff-faced nurses. The air was still heavy and thick and dirty, and the occasional wretch still crossed their path, and the occasional whore still leered as she searched for willing coin, but even so it was a different world, and Lucy found herself pretending that the other place did not exist — not because she wanted to, but because she did not know that she could do otherwise and survive.

Not an hour in London, and Lucy was

becoming a Londoner.

Mr. Gilley had rented a large, luxurious town house in Crown Street, perhaps not quite so close to Hyde Park as Norah would have liked, but close enough to be somewhat fashionable. The interior of the house seemed even more massive than its exterior suggested. The rooms were well lit and beautifully appointed, with the most fashionable furnishings and window treatments and paintings. There were too many servants for Lucy to learn their names at once, and she had the choice of three unoccupied rooms to call her own. Both of Norah's parents were home, and while Mrs. Gilley greeted Lucy with cool indifference, Mr. Gilley appeared delighted that Lucy was there, and gave her a lengthy lecture on how to protect herself from catching cold while walking about London. He fussed over her in a thousand ways, begged her to make any adjustments to her room, inquired into her preferences for dinner, and promised her that she would enjoy the delights of London or he would alter London to her liking. A room below stairs was found for Mrs. Emmett, and so there was an end to all the necessary adjustments. Mr. Gilley cared not how long she remained because he liked her, and Mrs. Gilley cared not because she had no regard for her at all. Lucy could hardly have asked for more, and the charms she had brought to effect these ends might, perhaps, never have to be unpacked.

Lucy's next order of business was clear. It was far easier to make her way to Kent from London than it was from Nottingham, but now that she was in London, she began to realize just how little she had planned. Besides determining how to get to Kent, she would need to determine the best possible course for getting inside Lady Harriett's house undetected, discovering the pages of the *Mutus Liber* from Byron's library, and then getting out again.

That she would be no closer to saving her niece saddened her immensely. Mr. Morrison, after all, was no doubt deflowering virgins in some foreign land as he searched for other pages, and if he found them, would it do Lucy any good? He would return to her if he could — her spell would see to that — but would he have the pages with him when he did? There was no point worrying about what she could not control, however. She would find the pages, one at a time if she had to. She would study and learn and experiment and practice until the pages were hers.

Lucy had hoped that Mrs. Emmett might prove to be of some use in these matters, but she appeared utterly confounded when Lucy asked her for advice. "I cannot say anything as to that, Miss Derrick," she answered. "I only know when it is time for you to go to Kent, you will go."

"Then you know I will get there?"

"I cannot tell you that, Miss Derrick," she said. "I can only say that if you are meant to go, you will go, and at the time you are meant."

"Meant by whom?" Lucy asked testily.

Mrs. Emmett appeared to detect none of Lucy's irritation. She only smiled and looked off to the distance, as though the person or force she referenced was just beyond her vision. "By them who mean such things."

Only after her arrival did Lucy realize that she had somehow expected Mrs. Emmett to ease her way in London, but that would not be the case, and she was hardly better prepared for the confusion of the metropolis than if she were on her own. How precisely did one get to Kent? How much did it cost? Lucy had her quarterly allotment of ten pounds, and she had to spend with caution. Money could be made by other means. She knew that, but she was reluctant to practice cunning craft when she did not have to. Every spell cast required herbs and paper and pen and ink — things that cast money or might be missed. More than that, she'd never felt comfortable with the idea of using magic to earn money. What came into her purse must exit from another's, and how could she say whose need would be greater?

So she told herself that she did what she could. She learned what she could learn, and she planned as best she could plan. She was who she was — a young woman of limited means and almost no freedom, and she could not help being that. If she truly were at the center of things, as so many had told her, then would not the right opportunity present itself? Fate had sought her out in quiet Nottinghamshire. She could hardly be said to be hiding in London.

Meanwhile, the routine of fashionable London life soon settled on her, and a week had passed before she knew it — a week in which her sister, Martha, lived with a monster and her poor niece was held captive somewhere by something Lucy dared not even contemplate. Instead of searching for lost alchemical books or battling creatures from the invisible world, she browsed in dress shops, attended music recitals, and visited fashionable homes to view art and collections of curios. There was more in her future too: the opera and the playhouse and the tea gardens. On all of these excursions, Mrs. Emmett accompanied her, as though she were Lucy's chaperone, and dutifully allowed herself to be sequestered in kitchens and servants' rooms when they were not in transit. Servants began to complain of her, however. They spoke to Norah, and Norah, in turn, spoke to Lucy.

"She makes them uneasy," she said one afternoon as they sat in the parlor. She kept her voice down, as though afraid Mrs. Emmett would overhear her, even though she had been sent halfway across town upon an errand. "They say she never eats and never talks except when directly addressed, and then she says only the most absent and polite things."

"You make her sound like the perfect serving woman," Lucy said.

"She is certainly not the sort of serving woman to be found in fashionable homes, and I'm afraid she'll have to go."

Lucy did not pay Mrs. Emmett, and did not know how to dismiss her or even if she could. She had visions of the woman mooning about the town-house door like a stray dog, or worse — sneaking inside. There would be constables and bailiffs and magistrates. She could not allow any of that.

"I don't know that I can do without her," said Lucy.

"Of course you can," said Norah. "There are a hundred women in London who will do for you a thousand times better than that country oaf."

"I cannot part with her," said Lucy, and because she did not know how to argue the point, she left the parlor and fled to her own room.

The next morning, Mr. Gilley found her descending the stairs, and took her by the elbow to the empty parlor to discuss the matter. Lucy did not like that he touched her so freely. Something about his expression suggested an intense and disproportionate pleasure in the act. It occurred to her, as he led her into the room, that she had never before been alone with her friend's father, and did not much care for this development.

"I understand there is some difficulty with your serving woman," he said to her.

"Norah says the others don't like her. I know she is odd, but I cannot let her go." Lucy kept her eyes lowered because she wished to appear pitiable and because she did not care to see how Mr. Gilley looked upon her. She could all but feel the heat of his gaze upon her skin.

"If it is a matter of money," said Mr. Gilley, "I can offer some assistance and send her off. She can offer no objection."

"It is not that," said Lucy. "I cannot do without her. If she cannot remain, then I must return home."

Mr. Gilley said nothing, and Lucy felt the quiet of the room, and the warmth that came from the fireplace and the nearness of Mr. Gilley's lurking form.

Mr. Gilley looked at her and pressed his lips together in a tight approximation of a smile. "That shall not be necessary. My servants will be more tolerant. You must never fear that I will fail to look after you, Miss Derrick."

"Thank you, sir," said Lucy, curtsying. It was the most formal, distancing thing she could think to do, but it was too late to correct her error. She had put herself in the power of a man who was determined to extract from her what he could, and Lucy did not know that she could ever again let down her guard while under his roof.

While the crisis with Mrs. Emmett had been building and resolving, the rest of the household had been attentive to but one thing: the assembly at Almack's, to which Mr. Gilley, with some pains, had secured tickets. The Wednesday assembly was the most fashionable event in all of London, and only the grandest people went. If it were known that Lucy had never formally been presented at court, she would have been barred entry, but Lucy chose not to raise the point, and Norah conveniently forgot to tell her parents — likely less out of concern for Lucy than for the difficulty such a revelation might present.

Lucy's joy at the prospect of attending was incomplete. Shortly after arriving at the Gilley house, she'd received a letter from Martha in which she made every effort to put a happy face upon her suffering, but Lucy had no doubt that Martha was worried to distrac-

337

tion about what she believed to be her baby. Even Martha's handwriting appeared unsteady and distraught.

Lucy had to find a way to get to Kent and to the next pages of the *Mutus Liber,* even if it meant exposing herself to horrible rumor and speculation. The day after the assembly, she told herself, she would go. She would find some way, no matter the cost. She would be under too much scrutiny before then, but after, when everyone was exhausted and self-satisfied, she would find the opportunity to escape.

Norah insisted upon new gowns for the both of them, and when Lucy announced she did not have the money, Mr. Gilley offered to pay for hers, explaining that he should love to see her in a new gown above everything. She hated to put herself in his debt, but it was too awkward to refuse, and so she accepted with many thanks. Lucy walked away from the experience with a trainless, stomacher-front gown of a beautiful coral color, flattering to her shape, perfectly matched to her complexion. Accompanied by a shawl of a charming ivory shade, and with her hair dressed up and curled, precisely to the fashion, and then covered with a prim little hat with a saucily small brim, Lucy felt very pleased with herself indeed. When Norah, who looked fine in her somewhat less-flattering tunic of too bright a red — a color she had loved in the milliner's shop, but now required constant reassurance that it had not been a mistake — told Lucy she looked "well enough," that was sufficient to feel like a triumph.

Lucy had to feign enthusiasm for the assembly, but her apathy vanished when they walked into Almack's ballroom — beautifully lit, as bright as day, full of the most fashionable ladies and the most handsomely appointed men that either she or Norah had ever witnessed. The room was perhaps four times the size of that any dance the Nottingham, and it was peopled with likely ten times the number of occupants. Unlike the Nottingham assembly, where one conversed with farmers and small landholders and petty merchants, here were lords and ladies, men and women whose every act was written up in the newspapers, the stupendously wealthy by birth, nabobs freshly returned from India, actors and actresses who graced the London stage, poets and novel writers and painters and celebrated musicians.

"It is safe to say," Norah told her, "that if a person is fashionable, and if he is in London tonight, then he is here in this room."

The ladies had no choice but to remain in tow behind Mr. Gilley, but if Norah yearned to be asked to dance by some fashionable gentleman, Lucy was content to witness and observe and be unobserved, for she feared any conversation must expose her country ignorance. After introductions to a near endless procession of peers and foreigners of significance and a sprinkling of navy men, Mr. Gilley fell into close conversation with a handsome man in his sixties. He was dressed quite beautifully, Lucy thought, in a plain dark suit that both bowed to and defied the current London fashions. The man's hair receded, his face was wrinkled, and he was short, thin, and quite pale, and yet there was something appealing in his face that was hard to deny. Lucy had little doubt that, in his youth, he had been striking. In his old age, he remained charming.

After exchanging jovial words with Mr. and Mrs. Gilley, he demanded to be introduced to the ladies.

Mr. Gilley cleared his throat and turned to Norah. "My dear daughter, Miss Norah Gilley, allow me to present to you Mr. Spencer Perceval."

Norah conducted herself with excellent grace, and curtsied low. Lucy, for her part, was taken by surprise, and gasped quite openly. She did not follow politics closely, but there was no avoiding the knowledge that she was about to be introduced to the prime minister.

When Mr. Gilley turned to Lucy, the prime minister, perhaps ready to be finished with these introductions, about which he cared so little, was already shaking Lucy's hand.

"And this," said Mr. Gilley, "is my daughter's particular friend, Miss Lucy Derrick."

Mr. Perceval squeezed Lucy's hand hard enough that she let out a little gasp. Then he let go at once. "Forgive me," he said. "Only, miss, I know your uncle. May I have a private word?"

Lucy felt oddly out of place in her own life. "Of course," she said.

Mr. Perceval took her arm and led her away from the Gilleys. "I don't truly know your uncle," he said amiably enough. "I do, however, know of you from the reports of my agent, Mr. Morrison."

"Do you mean to say that Mr. Morrison is a Tory?" Lucy said with surprise.

The prime minister let out a boisterous laugh. "My party is not so fortunate. Mr. Morrison is a brother of the Rosy Cross, and I am the leader of more than this government."

And now Lucy understood. Spencer Perceval, Prime Minister of England, was also the head of Mr. Morrison's band of Rosicrucians. It was from him that the orders came.

"Mr. Morrison is bound to report everything to me, you know, and so he has been made to tell me about you. I hope you do not find this too shocking. You are lucky to have had the experience of serving with him."

Lucy did not consider herself lucky. "And

341

why is that?"

"Because," said the prime minister, "Mr. Morrison is a great hero to this country. He has, quite literally, done more for England than any man alive."

Lucy snorted, thinking of his silly tricks, his easy charm, and how he had deceived her four years earlier. "I find that difficult to credit."

"Most young ladies are rather taken with him. In any event, he wrote of how you have found yourself in the thick of things, and even how you aided him in his efforts to retrieve the pages to a book we seek. Perhaps he had no choice but to impress your services, but you must know that your part is over."

"I did not know that I had a part circumscribed to me."

"You do," he said, his voice gentle but firm. "We all do, my dear. And please do not think I mean that we are an august group of savants and you are some meddling child, for that is not it at all. What I mean is that you have served your country and done far more than any of us would have dared to ask, and now we wish you to step aside. The earth itself is moving, Miss Derrick, and it would grieve me to see you crushed beneath it."

Lucy did not much like being told what to do by a stranger, even if that stranger was the prime minister. "I shall certainly keep your advice in mind."

"You would be wise to do so," he said. "Have you any idea who are the players in this game? Have you any notion of what this Ned Ludd is?"

"No, Mr. Morrison did not tell me."

"Of course he did not. It is not for you to know. Allow me to assure you that your ignorance is a gift. Relish it, and seek to learn no more. I say that out of concern."

Lucy remained motionless, daring to neither move nor speak. Could it be true? Was she truly risking her life if she pursued the matter? And yet, what choice had she? She could hardly cower in fear while Emily was locked away in some unimaginable dungeon. Nor could she turn away from events of global magnitude when she had some role to play. Mr. Morrison and the prime minister, in their arrogance, decided that the future of Britain depended upon the enslavement of its laborers, but Lucy did not believe that. It was true that she did not know precisely what Ned Ludd wanted, but did it matter? Whatever his nature, was not he in the right and the Rosicrucians in the wrong, and so was she not obligated to stand with Ludd?

"By gad, Spence, do you mean to bore that poor girl all night?"

Lucy looked up, and walking toward her was — and there could be no mistaking him, even though she had never seen his face before except in prints and woodcuts — the

Prince Regent, directly in front of her, gesturing toward her with a wineglass. Lucy was about to meet the Prince of Wales himself. Yet it was not he that made her uneasy. On one side of the prince stood a remarkably handsome, well-appointed man she did not know, and on the other side of that man stood George Gordon, Lord Byron.

24

A brief round of introductions followed, though Lucy would later have a difficult time remembering the specific details of what was said and who said it. For here, shaking her hand, was the Prince Regent, the man who would someday be king of England, who now was all but king. To his left was a man of almost equal fame, the notorious George "Beau" Brummell, the prince's close friend, and the person who, through example, had single-handedly changed men's fashions in London. Owing to Brummel's precedent, men now wore trousers rather than breeches, close-fitting coats, and exquisitely knotted cravats. It was said that dozens of men came to his home each day simply to watch him dress, a process that was rumored to last hours. Lucy had read in one of the magazines that Brummell employed three separate tailors for the construction of his gloves alone.

And then there was Byron, dressed like the other three gentlemen in buff pants, white shirt, and dark jacket. He, however, wore no cravat, and kept his shirt open, his chest wildly exposed. He was, without doubt, the most beautiful man in the room, and it seemed that every woman there looked at nothing but him. It therefore surprised Lucy that he looked only at her, and there was such an intensity in his gaze that it embarrassed her. Everyone in the room must see how he gazed at her, and she felt herself grow hot and dizzy all at once.

For a moment, she thought that Byron would take her in his arms there, that he would kiss her before everyone, and if he made the attempt, would she be able to stop him? Would she wish to try?

She did not have the opportunity to find out, for, after waving off the prime minister, the Prince Regent stepped in front of Byron and up to Lucy.

"I thought I knew all the young ladies of note in London," the prince said to her. "How can it be that we have not met?"

Lucy curtsied and stammered out an introduction. Only a few days ago, she had been trapped in Nottingham, victim of her uncle's stinginess and Mrs. Quince's cruelty, and now, here she was, meeting the Prince Regent himself.

"Your Majesty is too kind," said Lucy.

"Too drunk, I should think," said Mr. Brummell, coming closer and examining

Lucy as though she were a painting at an exhibition. "She is pretty enough, I suppose, but no more. I cannot see why she commands your attention."

Lucy felt as though she had been slapped. She had seen the cruelty of fashionable life in London — the barbs and asides and whispers behind fans. Lucy never doubted that fashionable ladies insulted her from a safe distance, but she never dreamed that anyone would speak to her in such a manner to her face.

The moment hung in the air. Perhaps it was only a second or two, but for Lucy time ground to a halt as she struggled to understand how she must respond to this abuse. Should she do nothing and show herself a meek and toothless thing? She wanted to. More than anything she wanted to walk away, but it seemed to her that there would be more than her share of struggles ahead, and she must learn to show courage when the situation called for it, not merely when she had prepared for it.

"If the prince wishes to speak to me in any manner he chooses, it is my duty as his subject to submit," said Lucy. "You, sir, are rude."

Brummell took a step back and put a hand to his mouth in mock horror. "It is like the cobra of India. Pleasing to behold, but deadly in its strike."

347

"Shut up, George," said Byron.

"Mon dieu!" cried Brummell. "Your Majesty, this upstart just addressed you by your Christian name and told you to shut up. I think it is time to have him dragged away in chains."

The prince laughed and winked at Lucy. "When there is conversation among three men named George, there is never an end to the confusion."

"The confusion ends," observed Byron, "when two have titles, and one is a commoner."

Brummell touched his fingers to his chest. "The entire world is commoner than I."

The prince laughed again and turned to Lucy. "He is a buffoon, but he amuses me. I am sorry if he injured you with his inappropriate tongue. How shall I punish him?"

Lucy looked at Mr. Brummell long and hard, and thought she saw something there very sad, like a piece of crystal — beautiful and exquisite, but so delicate that it must, in time, shatter. "I believe," she said, "he shall punish himself in due course."

There was an awkward moment of silence among the three. Then Byron turned to Brummell. "If this lady says such a thing to you, then you are a fool to ignore it." To Lucy he said, "It is time to dance."

Before she could object, or perhaps before she could have time to decide if she wished to object, Lucy was upon the dance floor with

Byron, lost in a massive swirl of expensive clothes and even more expensive perfumes. One could hardly hear the music, fine though it was, over the low hum of conversation, for every couple spoke in low and meaningful tones, and Lucy wondered who around her was planning an illicit assignation. Everyone? Was she? She could hardly think so, and yet here was Byron, and for all the terrible things he had said and done, she enjoyed his company, enjoyed being near him. And she understood all too well that his beauty was, in itself, a kind of magic.

"You have no idea how I've missed you, Lucy," he said to her in a low whisper, almost a growl. "I've thought of you every minute."

Lucy said nothing. Part of her found him revolting, disgusting, vile. Another part, however, saw him as something far greater.

"You are not still angry with me, I hope? You cannot be jealous of that girl at Newstead, as you had already rejected me."

Lucy could only shake her head. That he would say such a thing, imagine that somehow she had come to see his way of life as normal as he did, struck her as amazing. However what would have seemed like madness only weeks before — spells and talismans and magical components — was now perfectly normal. Byron's own dissolute life must seem the same to him. And if it did seem normal to him, no more than the way he lived, then did it make him evil? If he saw no harm in what he did, and no one resented him for his actions, was he a bad man or merely a different kind of man?

"That poor girl loves you, you know," Lucy said. "It is not a simple diversion to her. It is everything."

"More women love me than you would suppose, Lucy," he said utterly without pride. If anything, he sounded weary.

"You need not take advantage of them."

"How advantage? Are they not human beings, free to make choices as well as I? Poor deaf Sophie, as you would style her, is not a child. Her deafness has not injured her mind. She is a clever young lady who knows what the world is, how it condemns those who spurn its petty rules, and she made her choice with her eyes open. I made mine, and I say you are in no position to judge. Indeed, you insult Sophie by presuming to know her life better than she does."

Lucy shook her head, half in disbelief and half in amusement. "Lord Byron, you are truly an unusual man. You could argue that up is down, and I fear I would believe you ere long."

He laughed. "If Lucy Derrick believes I am unusual, then it must be so. Tell me, what are you doing in London with those awful people? It is one thing to associate with your uncle, which you cannot help, but Gilley is the worst sort of climber, and his daughter looks like a wily slut."

"I shall, for the moment, refrain from responding to your insults upon my friends. I am here because it is the only way I could get to London, and so have freedom. Or so I thought. I must get to Kent."

"To find whatever book you and Morrison wished to pilfer from my library?"

"What is between you two, if I may ask? Why do you hate him?"

"I hate no man," said Byron, "but I think him an insufferable prig, and he never hesitates to find fault with how I live."

"But that is enough for you to dislike him so?"

"To dislike a man such as he is its own pleasure. But now it is my turn for a question. Why were you with him? Why did you break open my house in search of a book in my library? It obviously matters to you as well as to him."

Lucy wanted to trust him. He was so astonishingly beautiful and, in his own strange way, completely forthright. What offended her most about him was his very truthfulness, and, when looked at from a certain perspective, that could not be offensive at all. "Lord Byron, I can only tell you that it is important to me, but to say more would strain your credulity and cause me to suffer in the relating. I will also say that Mr. Morrison is no friend of mine. I may have deceived him as to my feelings, but it is no more than he deserves."

Byron smiled at this revelation. "I had not thought I could like you better, but I now do. Deceiving Morrison for your own ends indeed. How can I serve you?"

Lucy took a deep breath. "I must get to Lady Harriett's estate, and I do not know how to go about it. I have no one to ask. Except — except you. Can I impose on you to inquire how I would find a coach to take the shortest, fastest route to Kent?"

The dance was now over, and Byron led her away from the dance floor toward the periphery, perhaps choosing the spot in the room farthest from Mr. Gilley and his daughter, who were, even now, straining their necks in search of Lucy. Lucy and Byron stood near the wall thick with paintings, and he smiled down upon her.

"I shall do better," he said. "I shall take you to Kent myself."

Lucy felt, all at once, terror and excitement. To go off alone with Byron! Why, it was scandalous, but perhaps no less scandalous than taking a coach by herself to Kent.

"You are truly kind," said Lucy. "I know not if I should accept your generous offer."

"Oh, your virginity is safe with me, Lucy. I will not again declare my feelings, and you need not worry that I will attempt to persuade you into circumstances that are not to your liking. You have seen for yourself that I need not resort to cruel measures to find solace in this world."

Lucy blushed so deeply she feared she might swoon. No man had ever spoken thus to her, and yet there was something reassuring in it. With Byron there was no dance of pretense and posture and performance. He said what he meant and expressed how he felt. Perhaps that made him the safest companion she could find.

"You can tell no one what you do. I may be fool enough to trust you, but no one would believe such a voyage to be an innocent thing. I cannot sacrifice my reputation."

"Of course, I will tell no one. You will have to manage to explain your absence to your hosts. That is your concern. I can only take you where you wish to go, and do it with all the discretion you desire."

"Then I shall gratefully accept your generous offer," said Lucy, already thinking about how she would conceal this visit from Norah and her family, and thinking that the time would come, very soon, when she would be alone with Byron, with no one to supervise or interfere or object. This notion thrilled her as much as it terrified her.

It was at that moment that Norah arrived, with her parents in tow. They looked slightly winded, and Mrs. Gilley straightened her gown, as though the effort of finding Lucy had tired her. Nevertheless, now that they had found her, they chose to act as though all was well.

"Ah, Miss Derrick," said Mr. Gilley. "Here you are at last. I did not know you would walk off so readily with a stranger." The moment he stopped speaking, his face drew into a tight line, and he gazed upon Byron through narrowed eyes.

Byron bowed at Mr. Gilley. "Hardly strangers, sir," said Byron. "Miss Derrick is my near neighbor in Nottingham, much as you are, and as you and I are acquainted, it is odd that you should think I do not know this lady's family."

"I see," said Mr. Gilley. "I was unaware there was a connection. In any event, Miss Derrick, you alarmed us by disappearing as you did without a word."

Lucy curtsied. "It is merely that the room was so crowded, and we were separated by the crush of people." Feeling herself blush once more, Lucy turned away. She had vanished for a few minutes in a crowded gathering, and already they implied she had behaved inappropriately. What would they suggest when she vanished, for days perhaps, with Byron? The trick, of course, would be arranging things so that no one would find out.

25

Byron could not depart for two days. It was longer than Lucy wished to wait, but less time than she would have had to wait without his help, and so she did not complain. It seemed to her that her time might be put to good use. Indeed, the more she thought about it, the more she realized she needed these two days to prepare, and so she asked Byron if there was a shop in London that specialized in books upon subjects occult. She had books aplenty, but she hoped to purchase ingredients she could use for her trip to Lady Harriett's estate. She'd spent long hours sewing secret pouches into her frocks, poring through her books, memorizing spells and talismans, imagining every situation and how she might respond.

There was no guarantee she would find useful materials. Any such shop might be run by charlatans or cynics who sold books and trinkets in which they had no belief, seeing their customers as simpletons. If that were

355

the case, Lucy would have lost nothing.

This left Lucy with the question of how to slip away unnoticed, but a few hours of study revealed this to be an easily mastered problem. When Norah and her mother wished to attend tea at the home of a lady of fashion — yet another wealthy woman with Tory leanings who would pretend not to be condescending while passing a stilted hour with strangers for whom she had nothing but contempt — Lucy affected a headache and said she would stay at home. She did not know how long her expedition would take, and she did not know if she could be home before Norah returned, so Lucy concealed her absence with a talisman. She directed Mrs. Emmett to remain behind in the event something went wrong, that she might best concoct a story to explain where Lucy had gone. Next, she directed one of the footmen to find her a hackney coach, which she took to the Strand, and found the shop Byron had mentioned, off the main thoroughfare on Bridge Street. It was a respectable old building, well maintained and orderly, and when she went in she was surprised to see that it looked like any other London bookstore, of which she had visited quite a few since arriving.

A kindly old gentleman in a spotless white apron smiled at her when she walked through the door. "Can I help you?"

"I hope so," said Lucy. "What have you for breaking open houses?"

When she had finished her business, the shopkeeper cheerfully wrapped her purchases, and wished her a good day. When Lucy opened the door onto the street, she came face-to-face, much to her surprise, with Spencer Perceval, who had his hand out and was preparing to knock. His handsome face formed an *O* in surprise, and his slight form took a step backwards.

"Miss Derrick," he said.

"Mr. Perceval," she responded. Then, on a whim, she curtsied, because she did not know how one ought to behave in the presence of the prime minister.

He could not help but smile. "I see my warnings have had little effect."

"I was but looking at some books," said Lucy, who focused all of her will into not looking like a child caught stealing sweets. "Is that now a crime?"

"Your crimes are none of my concern," he told her. "However, I wish to make certain you do not interfere with our affairs. Your visit here has nothing to do with the events we spoke of the other night, does it?"

"Of course not," said Lucy. It never occurred to her not to lie, and it was this facility that made her so good at deception, especially if the man she deceived thought her pretty.

He studied her carefully, ostensibly for signs of dissembling, but Lucy had the feeling he used this examination to look at her because he liked to look at her. Lucy did not think of herself as vain about her appearance, but she knew when a man admired her, and she saw no reason not to use this advantage to keep Mr. Perceval off balance.

"The order cannot tolerate your interference," he told her. "The next time I see you, I hope it is someplace less suspect than this."

"I hope so too," said Lucy. As she walked away, she had the distinct impression she had gotten away with something.

When Lucy returned to Mr. Gilley's town house, Lucy handed her coat and hat to a servant, went to her room to set down her things, and then proceeded to the parlor, where Mrs. Gilley and Norah were playing cards. Lucy sat near them, with her back to the fire, and opened a novel that happened to be sitting there. Both ladies said hello, and neither asked where she had been or how she had passed her day. The spell had worked flawlessly.

It did not work forever, however. It would last no more than two sunsets, and so that meant when she climbed into Byron's carriage the next day, she would have to reach Lady Harriet's estate in Kent — a distance of some fifty miles — discover what she could there without being detected, and return to London before two days had passed. It seemed to her that this should be possible — provided nothing went terribly wrong, but there were any number of things that could go wrong, particularly when one traveled such a long stretch of road in such a hurry, and when one was involved in such risky undertakings as breaking open the house of a wealthy and influential lady, and doing so with a notorious rake.

Lucy collected all she might need for charms she might be forced to make or spells she might have to cast. Most of these she put in a small travel bag, but some she secured in a secret pouch she had sewn in the gown she would wear. She meant to keep emergency provisions in that, and perhaps use it to secure from the world what she did not want the world to see.

Mrs. Emmett declared that she would stay behind to cover Lucy's absence. The good woman wept at the prospect of being apart from Lucy for two days, but she also insisted that she could not go, though she would not say why. Lucy wanted her there as a buffer against Byron, but Mrs. Emmett would not be persuaded.

Byron collected her in the predawn hours, somehow looking perfectly rested and impeccably dressed, despite the early hour. Lucy had been full of apprehension, afraid that he would attempt something inappropriate the moment she entered the coach, but though he smiled at her and snuck glances at her in the dim light, his behavior was entirely unobjectionable. After the first hour, Lucy began to relax and feel as at ease as she would if they were in the presence of a chaperone.

After they rode in silence for some time, Lucy explained her time limitations, and Byron merely smiled and told her that he would certainly have her back by the hour she desired. And perhaps he meant it, but it also occurred to Lucy that he would not be particularly troubled if he did not. Perhaps he would determine it to be in his best interest that she did not return in time. Once revealed as the sort of woman who would run off with a rogue for two days, she would have nothing to lose by accepting his scandalous proposals. Lucy would be on her guard.

Their conversation at first centered around trivial things, as though they were but two unremarkable people upon an exceedingly unremarkable journey. They talked of the gathering at Almack's, of some of the people Lucy had met since arriving in town, the sights she had seen, and the plays she hoped yet to see. Byron talked of his forthcoming volume, *Childe Harold's Pilgrimage*, which would be published soon, and how many voices had agreed that it was apt to bring him significant attention. He was buoyant and witty, and pleased with Lucy's company. He was, in short, very much the man whom Lucy found so charming when she first met him in Nottinghamshire and the man she wished he had remained.

"I cannot thank you enough for helping me in this regard," said Lucy.

"I am happy to offer my help," he said. "If only because I willingly sold a book to Lady Harriett that I would have been so much happier to give to you as a gift. And yet you seem reluctant to tell me what book it is and why it is so important."

Lucy sighed. "The affair is complicated, and so unbelievable. Even having seen what you have seen, you would think me mad if I told you the truth. I would think myself mad. I have spoken it aloud only to Mr. Morrison, and it nearly broke my heart to do so."

"You would tell him what you would not tell me?" He sounded more arch than angry.

"Only out of necessity."

"Then I shan't force you," he said. "But you need not fear for my belief. I have also seen many things. The ghost of my dog, Boatswain, haunts my estate at Newstead, and people think me mad when I speak of it, but that makes it no less true. I would add that I am bound to accept anything that comes from your lips as the absolute truth."

It was this ease that prompted her. "I had an older sister whom I loved very much, and she died very young. My other sister, Martha, named her first child for her. I cannot tell you what that child means to me, and now she is gone, replaced with a vile thing, a changeling. I know how it sounds, but I have seen it, even if no one else has. The book I seek will give me the knowledge I need to banish the changeling and return Emily to her mother."

Byron said nothing for several long minutes. "I am sorry that such a book was in my power and that I let it go. I only wish I had known."

"I did not know until recently. Have you ties to Lady Harriett?"

"Her family is old and established," said Byron, "and because of my title, I am often in the company of such people."

"Do you think she would give you what we seek as a favor?"

Byron shook his head. "Lady Harriett does not do favors, and I recall she was curiously eager to buy my collection, which is a poor one. I think she must have known what I had. If she truly wants this book for herself, she will never give it over. Do you have a plan that does not require asking politely?"

"Yes," said Lucy. "It involves breaking open the house and stealing the book."

"Oh," said Byron. "I hope it works better than it did at my home."

362

Lucy smiled at him. "That effort was planned by Mr. Morrison. I shall plan this one, and I assure you, it will go far better."

They dined that evening at an inn, and who was to know that they were not husband and wife? It was, for Lucy, a wonderful feeling: powerful and anonymous. The eyes of all the ladies in the room were upon Byron in admiration and upon her in envy, and it seemed to her that she knew, if only in the smallest way, what it would feel like to be Lady Byron.

They remained at the inn until past midnight, and Byron drank more wine than Lucy would have thought wise, but she did not believe it her place to advise him on such matters. As he drank, he talked more about his forthcoming volume, which he both praised as brilliant and dismissed as having been effortlessly tossed off in odd moments. He felt sure that the book would secure him eternal fame, just as he felt sure it would make the world despise him.

When the time was right, they drove on, and Lucy watched the dark countryside pass before her. They were not far — less than sixteen miles — from Harrington, where she had grown up, and she knew the road well enough for it to make her melancholy. She was determined not to feel sorry for herself, however. Mr. Buckles had deceived her, and rather than pitying herself for the life she had lost, Lucy was determined to steel herself for revenge. She was not accepting her fate, but striking back, taking control of those who would order the world around her. Lucy liked how this sense of command felt.

They arrived in the vicinity of Mossings, Lady Harriett's estate, but it was not yet late enough to attempt a forced entry, and so they sat in the coach until another hour had passed. Byron assured Lucy that the lady had a reputation for being a woman who went to bed early, and by one in the morning they could be certain that she, her staff, and any guests she might have would be long in their beds. It was only a matter of reaching the library and identifying the book or missing pages, and escaping before they attracted attention. Unfortunately, Byron did not believe he would be of much use in identifying books from his own collection. It seemed to Lucy a rather odd thing for a poet to so little know his own books, but Byron appeared to take a certain pride in his indifference to works that were not his own.

"I've brought a few tools that should help me to find it," said Lucy, "and if I don't know where it is, I will certainly know it when I see it."

"It may be risky to take the time to search the library. The longer we are there, the greater the chance someone will notice that there are lights or will hear the noise we make."

"No one will notice us," said Lucy as she grabbed her bag. "Let us go."

The estate was large, and Lucy felt exposed and conspicuous as they crossed the expansive lawns, thankfully not populated by dogs. They passed fountains and gardens and shrubbery, until at last they reached the main house, massive and stately, built in the unadorned style that preceded the reign of Oliver Cromwell. All was quiet upon the grounds, and in the dark, the house looked like a lonely mountain, or perhaps a sleeping giant, passive and still, but coiled tightly with danger.

They walked around to the servants' entrance, moving slowly, cautious of dogs or any other unwelcome surprises. None came, and they at last reached the door, which was bolted shut. Lucy reached into her bag and removed something dark. Next she withdrew a tinderbox and made a light, which she applied to several candles attached to the object.

"Are you certain you wish to make such a light?" asked Byron.

"Oh, yes," said Lucy, who affected far more confidence than she felt. Here she was, breaking open the house of a dangerous and powerful woman, attempting to commit a crime that could lead to her going to jail, to standing trial, to humiliation beyond anything she could imagine. She swallowed her fear because she had no choice.

Only by quieting herself, as though she prepared to cast a spell, could Lucy keep herself from shaking uncontrollably. She did this for Emily, she told herself. She did it for Martha and her father and she did it for herself.

The light revealed that the object she had retrieved was a sort of mummified hand that had several candles molded onto each of its fingers, and a wax base attached to the stump of the wrist, that it might be set down.

"Good Lord, what is that?" demanded Byron, probably in a voice louder than was wise.

"A hand of glory," said Lucy, who wished to sound as though she thought this a very ordinary business for a sophisticated woman such as herself. "It is the pickled and roasted hand of a hanged murderer, upon which the proper incantations have been spoken. The intruder who holds the hand of glory may trespass without hindrance or detection."

Even in the dark, Lucy could see Byron's disbelief. "Does it work?"

"Let's find out." Lucy pushed against the servants' door and found it conveniently open. They stepped inside.

The house was pitch-black, and their hand of glory provided a jumbled chaos of flickering light and overlapping shadows. She thought of all the remarkable things she had seen and done since the day Byron had pounded upon her uncle's door. This was not the first adventure she'd had. It was not even the first house she'd broken open. Ought she not to be used to such things by now? Her heart pounded, and her hand trembled, and she wished only that she might finish and flee.

"Where do you think the library would be?" asked Lucy.

"These houses are all upon the same plan," said Byron. "I believe I can find it." He reached out to take the hand of glory himself, but then recoiled, not wanting to touch it. Instead, he pushed on through the dark and led Lucy up a set of stairs and then down a long hallway. At the end of it they found a series of open doors, one of which led to the library — an enormous room that very possibly could have contained all of her uncle's house.

Byron closed the door and, without actually touching the hand of glory himself, led Lucy over to various candles to begin to light the room. He took one of these and lit sconces and chandeliers until the space was quite bright.

"We will be visible from the outside, and from that wing of the estate," he said, gesturing toward the window at the parallel wing. "But if everyone is asleep, and that horrid thing does what it is supposed to do, then it should not much matter."

Lucy now removed from her bag a little divining rod she had made at home, to which she had applied the juice of a freshly cut apple, a drop of her own water, and a cat's whisker. She then spoke a few words over the divining rod and held it upright in both hands.

The feeling was subtle, almost too subtle to be certain it was not merely her fancy, but she followed the impulse toward a section of books across the room and to a particular shelf of books. Lucy took every one of the books down and set them on a well-lit table and began to leaf through them. Byron picked up a volume as well, but it soon became clear that he had no idea what he was looking for, and so set it down again.

After the first two books, Lucy picked up a third and set it down unopened. Then another with which she did the same. After two more books, she reached out for another, and a sharp sensation ran through her fingertips, a shock of something living and powerful. It was almost as though the book called to her. No, not that. Something *in* the book called to her. She felt it wanting to be found, and had no doubt that this was what she had sought. She opened the book to almost precisely the middle and there, sewn irregularly into the volume, were three prints in the dreamy, discordant style she recognized as that of the *Mutus Liber.* Here were floating men and naked women and dancing animals. Here was a bear with the head of a mouse, combining mercury and salt. Here was an ancient and bearded man, like an artistic rendering of God, pointing his divine finger at a flower — a bluebell, Lucy believed — as it sprang from the ground. The images felt alive and needy, and what they needed was Lucy, and Lucy was happy to take them. It was though she was reunited with a long lost piece of herself.

Just as the pages Mary had shown her had in them instructions upon the subject of sacrifice, so too these wanted to tell her something. It was something just out of her grasp, like a word she had forgotten that would come to her at any moment, but she had not time to puzzle over it now. She would not stay in Lady Harriett's house a moment longer than necessary.

Without waiting any longer, Lucy took her penknife and cut the pages from the book. She folded them and placed them within the hidden pouch in her gown, and then set the damaged book back in its pile. Now she had to decide if she should trust Byron or pretend to continue looking and convince him she must walk away disappointed.

She moved some more books about and then turned to Byron to see how he occupied himself, but as she did she saw two people standing behind him. One was an odd-looking man of middle years, wearing an out-of-fashion and rumpled tan suit. He had unruly hair that stuck up at strange angles, and unnaturally large eyes that appeared wild and gave the impression of being propped open against his will. His hands shook, and he bit his dry and peeling lips. He frightened Lucy, but not nearly so much as Lady Harriett Dyer, who stood near him, wearing her usual widow's black. Her gray hair flowed about her shoulders. She stood with her arms folded across her bosom, and she gazed upon the scene with evident disgust.

"Can you really suppose that I would not have wards in my house to protect against something so trivial as a hand of glory?" said Lady Harriett. "Did you not know it is possible to keep another's charms from working within your own walls? Miss Derrick, you clearly have no idea with whom you are dealing. And you, Byron" — she moved across the room, her stride swift and purposeful, and stood before the baron — "have you no wish to live that you would defy me like this? I was under the impression we understood each other."

"Lady Harriett, this is a silly misunderstanding." Lord Byron showed her his best smile.

He managed to proceed no further, however. Lady Harriett struck him across the face with the back of her hand. The blow was impossibly swift, and equally strong, for Byron was lifted off his feet and traveled his body length through the air, landing upon the hard floor with an alarmingly solid noise.

Lucy rushed over to Byron, but her eyes were on Lady Harriett, who was evidently far more than what she appeared.

26

Byron had been motionless for a moment, but then groaned and with Lucy's help managed to bring himself to the sofa, where he sat looking gloomy while his fingers repeatedly tested the tender skin of his face.

"Your beauty is bruised, not broken," said Lady Harriett. "Reckon yourself lucky I did not snap your neck."

Byron said nothing, only leaned against Lucy as if for support, though she could not imagine what sort of support a sitting man required. What was Lady Harriett that she had such strength? And what could Lucy do about it? She began to think of all the spells she knew, all the talismans she had memorized, all the tools she had hidden upon herself. There was one to induce weakness and vulnerability, but she had not brought it. She would certainly have one ready if she were ever to face Lady Harriett again. There was the failed summoning circle, which would kill the most arrogant person in the room, but Lucy could not be sure that person was Lady Harriett and not Byron himself. And then there was the matter of Lady Harriett's wards. Lucy had read of wards, but knew little of them, and had never had the time or inclination to make inquiries into that branch of knowledge. Would anything she knew work here?

Lady Harriett paced the room, and the odd man remained still, standing near the fireplace, watching them, twitching and scraping dry skin off his lips with his teeth. Lucy told herself that she could find a way out of this disaster. Lady Harriett clearly possessed powers terrible and dangerous, but Lucy had three pages of the *Mutus Liber* hidden away, and she would escape with them. Emily depended upon it.

"I have yet to decide what to do with you," said Lady Harriett. She turned to the man. "They come into my home, the home of my late husband, and violate it with their presence. Do you see, Mr. Bellingham? Do you not see what sort of enemies there are here? They have come to do you harm. They have come to keep you from receiving your *money*."

"I want what's mine!" This Mr. Bellingham shouted at them. It was like an eruption. He was quiet and twitching, then his mouth opened, his eyes expanded, and he shouted with incredible vehemence. Then back he shrank to his previous meekness.

"Of course you do," said Lady Harriett. "And you shall have it if you do as I say. Now, get some sleep, Mr. Bellingham. I shall manage your enemies."

"You are very good, Lady Harriett. Yes, quite good." He shambled out of the room, bouncing upon the doorframe as he departed.

Lucy watched him depart, not knowing what to make of him, but understanding intuitively that Lady Harriett played upon his madness in order to get something from him. Lucy had always thought her vile and self-serving, but she had not imagined her capable of this sort of manipulation. She dared not wonder why Lady Harriett toyed with this Mr. Bellingham. There were bigger matters that concerned her — primarily, escaping with the pages in her possession.

No sooner was he gone than others began to drift into the room. They were undeniably corporeal beings, but they moved with the distracted, otherworldly indifference of ghosts. There were three men and two women, all of different ages, all well dressed, though every one of them had some sign of indifference in attire — a ribbon not tied properly, a loose cravat, buttons hanging by threads. They entered the room and stood looking at books or out the window. One picked up a marble bookend and held it up to the wall sconce to better examine the veins.

Lucy looked at Byron, who shrugged and put an exploratory finger to test the severity of the bruise upon his cheek.

"Lady Harriett," Lucy began, but managed nothing further. The moment she spoke all five of Lady Harriett's guests turned to her with a suddenness that verged on terrifying. The marble bookend fell to the rug below as the man who had been holding it took three sudden steps toward Lucy, stopping only a foot away. He bent forward, putting his face near hers, staring with great intensity.

Lucy could not help but notice that he had a rather nice face — beautiful even, if pale and slightly gaunt — but his eyes were wide, unusually colorless, and unfocused. His hair was thick and the gray of an overcast sky.

"She ought not to be here," he said in a dreamy voice. He stood up straight again, and began to examine his thumbnail.

"I know that, Mr. Whitestone," snapped Lady Harriett. "I shall deal with her."

An old woman of perhaps forty, who had previously been staring out the window, leaned forward. "We are counting on you to do precisely that."

"Yes," answered Lady Harriett. "And now you must let me proceed as I see fit."

"She intends to gather the leaves," said the first man.

"I *know* that," snapped Lady Harriett. "This girl will accomplish nothing."

The other woman, a bit older than the first, remained at the window. "If we kill her, we need not think of her anymore. Is that not so?"

Lucy's pulse thrummed in her neck. If Lady Harriett wished to kill her, Lucy did not believe she knew of anything that would prevent her.

"If that were true, then I would have killed her before now," said Lady Harriett, her voice so cold that Lucy had no doubt that this assertion was true. "She has protected herself, so if we kill her, we shall be worse off than we are with her alive."

"Perhaps we can keep her locked away," said Mr. Whitestone. He put a finger to his cheek. "What?" he asked no one in particular.

"I know what needs doing," said Lady Harriett, "and I shall do it. Now, off with all of you. I shall meet with you presently."

The group appeared slightly surprised, but not offended. They exchanged looks. One of the men shrugged, and without further conversation, they drifted out of the room as curiously as they had drifted in.

Lady Harriett, Lucy, and Byron remained silent for some moments afterwards. Lucy wished Byron would speak, but when he did not, she took the burden upon herself, affecting the sort of bravado she wished she possessed. "I am sorry to have intruded upon your menagerie of madmen, but it is time we left."

"I don't know that you shall ever leave," said Lady Harriett. "My late Sir Reginald would not have hesitated to execute justice by his own hand. Perhaps there can be no better way to honor his memory."

"Come, Lady Harriett," said Byron who had begun to recover himself. "Let us not make more of this than we ought."

"You must think me a fool, Byron," said Lady Harriett. "After all I have done for you, that you abuse me in this manner is unthinkable. I cannot say what I shall do with you or your little slut. For now, you shall have the run of the house, for you can do no harm, but do not think that you can walk out of the building." She smiled at Lucy. "Perhaps you would care to try."

Lucy attempted to rise from the sofa, but she could not. There was something clammy on her wrists, on her knees. It felt as though there were hands upon her, countless tiny hands touching her, feeling her flesh in places no one had ever touched her. She could almost see them from the corners of her eyes, the shadowy creatures from the mill, things of darkness and ambiguity. She could not look at them directly, but as she turned away, she saw dozens of wispy fingers tugging upon her skirts. These things, she realized, were Lady Harriett's creatures, or at the least, hers to command. Fear and nausea shot through Lucy, and she understood at once that she was out of her depth.

"You are nothing, girl," said Lady Harriett. And now she cried out, but not to Lucy. "Oh, stop it! Hands off the girl until I tell you otherwise or she attempts to escape."

The shadowy creatures were suddenly gone. Relief washed over Lucy as she realized she could move once more. "Who are you," said Lucy, "that you can command such things?"

Lady Harriett laughed. "I thought you worth my attention, but it seems you know nothing."

"I know only of my sister and my niece," said Lucy, "and what I must do for them."

"There are millions of sisters and millions of nieces, and their fate is in the balance," said Lady Harriett. "I care nothing for your family."

"Though my sister be Mr. Buckles's wife?" said Lucy.

"Buckles is useful because he is so eager to please. Now, I shall have one of my girls show you to your rooms — or you may share a room if you like. I care not if you play the whore with this man. In the meantime, I shall have to consider what to do with you."

"If I am not back by tomorrow evening, I shall be missed," said Lucy.

"Not my concern," said Lady Harriett. "But you have no need to fear ruin, for I shall

summon Mr. Olson. I'll have Buckles officiate at your wedding, Miss Derrick. You and
Mr. Olson shall, at last, be joined."

Nothing that had happened that night filled
Lucy with as much terror as this announcement. With a clergyman to officiate, and one
loyal to Lady Harriett and who could be
depended upon to swear whatever she demanded, the wedding would be valid.

"Mr. Olson no longer wishes to marry me,"
protested Lucy.

"You know as well as I that his opinions
may be managed," said Lady Harriett. "Rejoice, for soon you will be a married woman.
May you be as happy as my Sir Reginald
made me."

The servant showed Lucy to a massive room,
painted gold, with a gold carpet and gold
velvet curtains. The dangers of the evening,
combined with the intensity of the color,
began to make her head ache. Byron's room
was next to hers, as though Lady Harriett
were daring them to behave shockingly, but
Lucy had no capacity for mischief of that
sort. She had hardly sat on her bed, preparing herself to think of her situation, shielding
her eyes from the room's unrelenting color,
when there was a knock upon the door. Lucy
rose, feeling like a somnambulist, and opened
the door to find Byron standing there, appearing grave, one half of his face bright red.

"May I come in?" he asked.

"Yes," she said, her voice heavy with fatigue, "but you must leave the door open."

He stepped in but closed the door behind him. "I do not know that I wish for anyone to hear what we have to say."

"I see not what difference it makes." And yet, Lucy did not rise to open the door again.

"I am sorry things have gone so badly," he said.

Lucy shook her head, unable to find the words to express her despair.

Byron took a half step forward, but remained some five feet from her. "I swear I shan't let that marriage take place. You are a resourceful young woman of remarkable ability, and I shall not have you abandon hope. We shall get you out of here, and if it is too late to return undiscovered, what of it? What they say of you means nothing. You decide what it means to be Lucy Derrick."

"I cannot have this conversation once more," said Lucy. "It means nothing to you because you have the luxury of it meaning nothing. I must live in the world as a woman, and if I am not returned before that spell expires the situation will be grave indeed."

Byron's hands on her shoulders felt hot. Lucy felt herself flush. The blood was now full in her face, and she felt a strange, delicious energy building inside her. She did not know what would happen next, and for the moment she did not care. Perhaps her life was all but ruined with nothing before her but shame and exile. Should she not find pleasure and comfort where she could?

"Should the worst happen," he said, "and you fail to return on time, then you must burn in the scorn of the world and emerge from it anew, a phoenix reborn, to live by your own law." He retreated a few steps. When Lucy raised her eyes to look at him, he met her gaze with a smile. "And yet, I do not believe it will come to that."

She hated that he was so beautiful, that she could not look at him and talk to him without thinking, even for a second, that there was no man to match him. "What is she?" Lucy managed, attempting to master herself. "How can she do what she does? Who were all those strange people who listened to her as though she was their master?"

He shook his head. "It is you who must tell me."

"I think you know her better than you allow," she said in an intentionally stern tone. "She takes liberties with you that she would not with a stranger."

He shrugged. "Lady Harriett acts as she wishes." He encircled her fingers in his hand, his grip loose and warm.

Lucy pulled her hand away. "What if I cannot stand against her?"

Byron had no answer for this, so instead he

kissed her. Their lips met, and she offered no resistance. His fingers gently clenched her shoulder. He pulled her closer until his broad chest pressed against her breasts and she felt the power of his thundering heart. His breath was hot and sweet, and she had never known anything so intoxicating. She wanted him, to possess him, to have him upon her and over her and for him to smother her entirely.

"Yes," he said. "We shall comfort each other."

Though it took all her will, Lucy pushed him away. With only a few inches between them, she looked into his beautiful, wild face and staggered back a few steps. "The world may yet choose to despise me, but I will not despise myself."

"Lucy," Byron began.

"I am tired," she said. "I must be gone from here by noon tomorrow or I shall be married or ruined. I have few resources. You may have made a career out of sacrificing everything to your pleasures, Lord Byron, but I cannot."

He reached out, stroking her face with the backs of his fingers. "Lucy, you are confused."

"No!" she shouted, not caring who heard, not caring if Lady Harriett and all her servants were awakened. She walked away from him, toward the fire, as though its heat might burn away her shame and desire. "I am tired and I am frightened and I am desperate, but I am not confused." She took a deep breath and ran a hand over her face. "Do not attempt to seduce me again, or I shall hate you. I must sleep and clear my mind, and in the morning, I shall escape this house. My niece, my flesh and blood, is held prisoner somewhere, and the monster that has taken her place sucks the very life out of my sister. I will not sacrifice them on the altar of gratification. I cannot fail my family again. Are you my ally or not?"

He bowed in response. "You must never doubt that I am. I shall obey your wishes and meet any challenge you may present to me."

"Will you obey me?" asked Lucy, thrilled by her anger and her sense of power and authority. She had neither lied nor deceived nor used vile magic, and he was still hers. Women *were* magic. "Will you do as I ask without question or hesitation?"

He bowed again.

She thought of the things she had yet upon her, the knowledge she yet possessed. She had three pages of the *Mutus Liber,* stolen from Lady Harriett's library, and neither that witch nor Byron nor anyone else in the world knew she had them. Even now, those pages called to her, sought her attention, like an itch inside her mind. There was a puzzle, a riddle to solve, and she would solve it. She was more dangerous than anyone knew. Lady Harriett's words meant nothing. She was mighty, she told herself, and she would not be stopped.

"These walls shan't hold us," Lucy pronounced, feeling her courage form into something material and adamantine. "Lady Harriett and her allies and her imps can do nothing against us."

He turned to open the door. "Then I shall see you well rested in the morning, Lucy."

"I wish you good night, Lord Byron."

He began to walk out and then turned to her. "As a point of clarification, do you say that I must never try to seduce you ever, or not while we remain here?"

The thinnest smile, constrained but quivering, danced upon his lips, and Lucy could not help but laugh. "Here to be sure," she said. "We shall see what comes later."

The smile blossomed fully. He bowed one last time and closed the door behind him.

Sitting on her bed, Lucy listened to the ticking of the tall case clock outside her door, and she heard nothing else. Perhaps ten minutes passed. Perhaps twenty. When it seemed like enough time, she removed from the folds of her skirt the pages she had cut from Lady Harriett's book. By the strong light of several tapers, she began to unravel their meaning, which came into sharp relief. *Persuasion.* She could not escape the word, just as with the first set of pages she could not escape the notion of sacrifice. But Mary was not there to tell her what it meant or how to apply it to her needs, so Lucy had no choice but to discover that for herself.

Before allowing herself to sleep, Lucy had opened her curtains so she would awaken at first light. Nevertheless, she remained in deep slumber perhaps later than she wished, not rising until an hour or so after dawn. She refreshed herself as best she could with water from the basin, dressed, and began to go through her materials that she had collected the night before, organizing her notes and charms. She had fallen asleep before finishing, too exhausted to go on, so she finished her work now, writing for as long as she dared. When the clock struck eight o'clock, she knew she could wait no longer. She had perhaps four hours to escape Lady Harriett's estate.

Though she had slept only a few hours, her mind was much clearer, sharper, focused by anger and desperation. Lucy opened up the bag she kept hidden in her gown and examined once more the herbs, the tools, and the ingredients. What she hoped to do was possible. From memory, she made a talisman of vulnerability. She would not be surprised again by Lady Harriett's strength.

Placing her bag within the secret compartment in her gown, she left her room and knocked upon Byron's door, and found him dressed and ready to attend to her.

"Let us then see if Lady Harriett will offer us breakfast," she said.

Here they had a bit of good fortune, perhaps the only good fortune upon which they ought to depend, so Lucy embraced it most gratefully. Breakfast was, indeed, set out — a series of chafing dishes with eggs, toast, bacon, porridge, and meats. There was salt, which Lucy required, and she saw a parsley garnish, which she quickly pocketed. Upon the table was a vase containing a variety of wildflowers, including, Lucy noted, bluebells. Lady Harriett was careless to leave such things lying about.

They were not to dine alone, for sitting at the table, enjoying a plate piled high with sausage and bacon, was none other than Mr. Buckles. His tall frame was stooped over his plate while he worked his knife and fork with determined fury, slicing and smothering. His face was slick with perspiration, as though the act of cutting and eating taxed him to his limits.

He looked upon Lucy, took a bite of sausage, and then spoke while he chewed. "I hear I am to wish you, as they say, joy, Miss Derrick. To become Mrs. Olson after all. It is very grand, and more than you deserve, if I may be so bold. But it is Lady Harriett's will."

"Where is Lady Harriett?" asked Byron, touching his cheek. It had begun to bruise, disrupting his beauty like paint spilled upon a portrait.

"Lady Harriett and her associates have departed," said Mr. Buckles. "Something happened with that John Bellingham fellow — some disaster that she blamed upon you, Miss Derrick. I am hardly surprised you would have something to do with that madman. A twitching sort of person, and always off upon what he is *owed*."

"When shall Lady Harriett return?" asked Byron.

"Her ladyship did not, ah, shall we say, trouble herself to tell me what is surely none of my concern. She has instructed me to marry you to Mr. Olson upon his arrival, whether she is here or no."

Byron looked at the food and then at Lucy, and she nodded. She did not much feel like eating, but she required strength and did not wish to find herself in a dire situation too depleted to do what she must.

Lucy served herself a healthy portion of eggs and toast — the meat did not appeal to her today — and sat at the table as far from Mr. Buckles as she could while still able to conduct a conversation. Byron, for his part, put but little food on his plate — some sausage and porridge. Lucy sensed that, for a man of great appetites, he was an abstemious eater.

"How does my sister?" Lucy asked Mr. Buckles.

Mr. Buckles put a large piece of bacon into his mouth. "She is well."

"And your daughter?"

He paused for but a second. "She is also well."

"You know that for certain?" asked Lucy.

He smiled in his simpering way. "How should I not, ah, know?"

"How indeed?" asked Lucy. She drank a glass of water. She wanted neither hunger nor thirst to inhibit her in the time ahead.

"I must tell you," Mr. Buckles said, "how, let us say — I believe the word is *mortified* — yes, how mortified I am that you would treat Lady Harriett Dyer in this fashion. In light of the attention she had condescended to show you, both in offering advice in your affairs and in permitting her servant to marry into your family. Now, you break open her house. I hardly know how I shall look at my wife again given what her own flesh and blood has done."

He went on in this manner for some time, permitting neither his chewing nor the repetitive nature of his subject to interfere with his discourses. As this conversation required not a word from anyone else, Lucy allowed him to proceed as he pleased until she was done eating. She then set down her utensils, pushed back her chair, and walked over to Mr. Buckles. Taking a deep breath, she raised up her hand and struck him across the cheek as hard as she could. She had not the power of Lady Harriett, and Mr. Buckles did not fly from his chair as he might have done in her imagination, but even so, the sound rang out with a reverberating crack, and Lucy could not be dissatisfied. Her own hand stung from the force of it, but she cared nothing for that.

Mr. Buckles remained motionless, tears in his eyes. He looked utterly bewildered, like a little boy who has discovered his father kissing the kitchen maid, and suddenly sees that the world is not what he has always believed it.

Lucy turned to Byron. "Be so good as to restrain this man."

He rose and did as she asked. He stood behind Mr. Buckles, holding his arms so that they were pinned behind the chair. "If Lady Harriett's creatures should choose to interfere," Byron said, "I may not be able to do as you ask."

"Lady Harriett said we have freedom of the house," said Lucy. "Let us use it."

Mr. Buckles was beginning to find his voice. "How dare you!" he thundered. "How dare you lay hands upon me and restrain me. Do not think that Lady Harriett Dyer will not punish you most severely."

Lucy struck him again. It hurt her far more this time, for her hand was now quite tender. What ought she to feel in striking her sister's husband, the man who had cheated her out of her inheritance, out of the life that should have been hers? Shame? Rage? Revenge? She felt none of these things, only a hard resolve.

"Mr. Buckles," she said, "be so good as to remain quiet until I ask you to speak. You are in the service of a monster, but you are far worse, for you would sacrifice your own child for your mistress. You disgust me, sir, and I have not the time to visit upon you the punishment you deserve for defrauding me of my inheritance. For now, I wish to know where I can find my niece."

"I am instructed to tell you nothing, and I will tell you nothing," he answered.

Lucy reached forward and began to unknot Mr. Buckles's cravat. He look at her in shock, and Byron cocked an eyebrow in curiosity, but she would not pause to explain. Once the cravat was gone, she unbuttoned his vest, took the top of his shirt in each hand and ripped it open, exposing his pale, flabby chest, hairless and slick with perspiration.

"Stop this!" cried Mr. Buckles.

Lucy felt as though she stood outside herself. Never before had she done anything so audacious. Never before had she violated the bounds of decency with such determination and disregard. In this place, at this time, propriety did not matter. Lucy would do what she must, would do what she liked, to save her niece, and she would take the consequences as they came.

She reached over to the center of the table and pulled from the vase a single bluebell, just as she had seen in the pages of the *Mutus Liber.* Those pages were meant for her. The flower was meant for her. All came together with ease and precision, like pieces of a broken dish. "Lean the chair back, if you would, Lord Byron."

Byron leaned back the chair and Lucy showed Mr. Buckles the object in her hand.

"What do you do with that flower?" he asked with a horror perhaps inconsistent with Lucy's instrument.

"It is a bluebell," she said. "They grow near graves, you know. My father taught me that. And there is no greater truth than death. The bluebell, when used properly, will render you incapable of lying or with-holding what I ask of you. The only difficulty is that it must be held over your heart, and I am not altogether certain you have one."

"How did you learn such things?" Mr. Buckles demanded.

"I learned them from the *Mutus Liber,*" she said.

Mr. Buckles let out a shriek, like a frightened child. Then he swallowed hard and attempted to blink the moisture from his eyes. "I'll tell you nothing," he croaked.

"Let us find out." She slapped the flower upon his chest and, losing herself in the process, moved the bluebell in a circle until the petals began to crumple and ball. She absented herself, muttering she hardly knew what, but words the pages of the *Mutus Liber* seemed to hint at. She pressed the flower into his breast until his skin ringed red from pressure.

At last, she came back to herself. "Now will you tell me what I wish to know?"

He opened his mouth and moved it back and forth. His jaw vibrated, his lips quivered. Then he spoke, his voice low and forced. "Yes."

She smiled. "Much better, Mr. Buckles. Let us discover all your secrets."

27

Byron continued to balance the chair backwards while holding Buckles still with one arm. "I realize you are enjoying yourself," he said, "but we cannot know how much time we have before Lady Harriett returns. Besides which, holding the chair this way is rather uncomfortable. I suggest you ask what you must so we might depart."

There was not much time, Byron was certainly correct in that, and there were so many questions that needed asking, but only one that mattered. "You may lower the chair, Lord Byron." When he had done so, she looked at Mr. Buckles. "Where is your daughter?"

He did not hesitate before responding. "I do not know."

"Then Lady Harriett did not take her, has nothing to do with her disappearance?"

"No."

"But you knew she was gone, that she had been replaced?"

He paused for a moment. "Yes, of course I knew."

"Does Martha know?"

"No."

Lucy sucked in her breath.

"Do you know who took Emily?"

"One of Lady Harriett's rivals. That is all I know."

"And why? What did this rival want?"

"To keep Lady Harriett from doing what she wished with the child."

"And what did she wish to do?"

Mr. Buckles worked his jaw for a moment. "She wished to kill her."

Lucy could no longer control her anger. She could no longer pretend this was a logic puzzle. "Your own daughter. Why did you not stop her?"

"It is not my place," said Mr. Buckles. "She is a great lady, who condescends to let me serve her. How could I refuse her such a thing? It was not a boy."

"Do you know how I can find your daughter?" Lucy asked.

"If I knew, Lady Harriett would have her by now."

"But why does she want your daughter dead?"

"Because talent runs crossways through families, particularly from aunt to niece. There was too great a likelihood that she would have the same sort of inclinations you do, and Lady Harriett could not endure having another such as you to contend with."

"Another such as me," Lucy repeated. "I would be nothing to her if she had not condescended to interfere with my life and abuse my niece."

Buckles snorted. "Even Lady Harriett can meet her destiny while running from it."

"We should go," said Byron, his voice strained.

"Yes, one moment," said Lucy. "What is Lady Harriett? Who is she that she can do such things as she does? I must know."

Mr. Buckles barked out a cynical laugh. "There has never been a more ignorant girl. You would never have dared to meddle with her if you understood who she is."

"Then enlighten me," said Lucy.

"There is no time for this," blurted Byron. "We must run while we can. Ask him how we circumvent the guards upon the doors."

"I need none of his help for that. Who is Lady Harriett?"

"If you don't need his help," said Byron, "then let us go."

"Not yet," snapped Lucy. "Tell me, Buckles. What is Lady Harriett?"

"She is my mistress," he said with a grin.

"What *is* she," repeated Lucy. "What is the nature of her power?"

"You poor, silly girl," said Mr. Buckles. "You really don't know. Lady Harriett is of that order of beings you are foolish enough to call fairies. These are not the tiny imps in children's tales, I assure you. They are the dead, Miss Derrick. They are the glorious dead, the triumphant dead, returned to earth with timeless flesh. Lady Harriett has walked this island, governed this island, for centuries. There are not many of her kind, but they are powerful, and they will not stand to see all they have built brought down by a rogue who thinks himself wiser than they."

"Ludd?" asked Lucy.

"Yes, Ludd. Lady Harriett and her kind have always maintained their power with a gentle hand, bending rather than breaking. Ludd and his followers do not understand this, and so they must endure abject defeat. Just as you shall be destroyed for what you have done here."

"I am sure there are circumstances in which your threats are more effective," Lucy replied. Then to Byron, she said, "Tie him up, and we shall go." Looking around the room, Lucy found a window sash, yanked it from the curtain, and tossed it to Byron. He quickly tied Mr. Buckles to the chair, and then used a table linen to gag him.

"It won't hold him long, but it will do for now," he said. "You must understand that you have made an enemy of someone very deadly."

"It is she who has made an enemy of me,"

Lucy said, not believing her own bravado, but enjoying the sound of it all the same.

They approached the front door with a certain trepidation. Lucy reached into her bag and retrieved a small pouch, which she held at the ready. She held back and turned to Byron. "Try the door."

He bowed and put his hand on the door-knob. Nothing. He waited a moment, startled as the clock struck ten. Then, catching his breath, he turned.

At once he shouted in surprise and pulled his hand back in pain. Four rivulets of blood were trickling across the back of his hand, looking like slashes inflicted by invisible claws.

Byron turned to Lucy in horror and confusion. "What do I do?"

"Try again," she said as she tossed at the door a handful of herbs that she'd assembled, using the ingredients she'd had upon her, as well as what she'd been able to find in the house. As the mixture struck, Lucy felt a shrinking, a movement in the air as though what had been there was there no longer. "Try again," she repeated more forcefully. With evident reluctance, Byron took the handle and turned. This time the door opened and the light of a gloomy, cold, and overcast day struck them as the most beautiful thing they had ever seen.

Lucy tossed another handful of herbs in

their path and they exited the house. They went perhaps ten feet forward along the walkway and turned around.

"Will those creatures follow us?" Byron asked.

"I think they have been ordered to keep us in, not retrieve us if we get out. Besides, they will not want to cross the line of herbs upon the threshold. Beings of that nature don't like thresholds to begin with, and I've made it that much more unpleasant."

"What precisely did you toss?" he asked.

"Dried fennel, dill, salt, sage, and garlic."

"After you are done defeating the evil spirits," Byron said, "perhaps we might pickle some cucumbers."

Lucy could not help but laugh. "Let us find your coach and get back to London."

They turned to walk down the path, but Lucy then froze and grabbed Byron's arm. It took all her will not to scream. Something ran toward them, hard and fast. It was black and foul and terrifying, a great mastiff, obscenely and almost absurdly oversized. It was the largest dog she had ever seen, near as large as a pony and all over a glossy, total black. Its mouth was open, baring its sharp, glistening fangs, slick with saliva, and in the gloom of the day they could see its eyes bright, almost luminescent.

"Back to the house!" Byron cried. He grabbed her hand and they ran toward the open door. Lucy hesitated, but only for a second. She did not want to return to that prison, but she did not want to be devoured by a monstrous dog either, and if they had escaped once, they could escape again. When Byron pulled her hand a second time, Lucy allowed him to lead her back to the house.

They'd covered half the distance when the door slammed shut, and Lucy felt a ripple in the air that she was certain was silent, malicious laughter. The house stretched out in either direction for hundreds of yards, but there was nowhere to hide. If they ran, it would extend their lives by a few extra seconds of terror.

Lucy struggled to think of a way out. The dog appeared physical enough, but that did not mean it was not a thing of spirit. She had heard of legends of the black dog, the barguest, that was said to be like a ghost or a demon. She had no choice but to treat it as though it were precisely that and hope for the best.

Lucy drew out another handful of her herbs. "We had better hope this works. It is all we have." She poured what remained into Byron's hand, and they both readied their fists, planted their legs, and sucked in their breath. Lucy had seen many wondrous and fantastic things, but she never quite believed her spells or talismans or herbs would work until she saw it happen, and never quite believed it had worked even seconds after. Before they'd seen the dog she was already beginning to doubt that she had freed them from the guard of evil spirits. As she stood there, shoulder cocked back, uncovered hair blowing in the growing wind, Lucy did not expect the herbs to defend them. She believed she was about to die, cruelly and painfully. There would be no one left to rescue Emily, and the sadness, the disappointment, and the anger at that out-weighed the fear, as mighty as that was.

The dog leapt into the air to attack, and Byron shouted, "Now!" as he hurled his herbs. Lucy needed no prodding, and she tossed but an instant later, wanting the dog to be but a little closer. The herbs spread out into the air, lingering like a cloud, and the dog, mouth open wide, impossibly wide — its tongue wagging like a grotesque wave — seemed to flinch its massive head just slightly as it passed through.

Lucy braced herself for agony and oblivion, but instead there was a loud cracking sound as beast and cloud met, and the dog let out a yelp and bucked in the air, turning sideways, and now suddenly coming toward them like a massive projectile. Lucy grabbed Byron's hand and pulled him out of the way while the dog, which must have weighed thirty stone, slammed into the door, cracking the wood. It fell to the ground with a sickening wet noise, still and lifeless and bloody.

"My God," said Byron. "I hoped for something, but surely even you did not expect so definitive a result."

Lucy stared at the dog, confused and uncertain, for it did not appear to be a thing of spirit at all, but flesh and blood — and a great deal of the latter. The animal's abdomen was torn open, and blood pooled around its lifeless body. Then Lucy noticed an acrid scent, like that of a gun just fired. She turned and looked down the path where a woman stood holding a long-barreled hunting weapon. She was just now lowering it. She was perhaps two hundred feet away, but there was no mistaking her tall form, elegant shape, pale complexion, and the ethereal white hair that hung free, billowing in the wind. It was Mary Crawford.

28

Lucy hardly knew what to say or what to do. There was Mary Crawford, who had vanished, who had left her, who had perhaps taken Emily and replaced her with a monster. She had also just saved Lucy's life. There could be no doubt about that.

Her legs felt unnatural, not her own, unsteady and heavy at once, but she forced herself to walk to Mary, who stood with a grim smile upon her face.

"We must hurry," Mary said. "I know not when Lady Harriett will return."

"Who are you?" said Lucy, her voice now sharp. "What are you? Was it you who took Emily?"

Mary took Lucy's hand. "There will be time for answers, Lucy. I swear it to you, but if we do not go — *now* — it may be too late."

"Mary is right," said Byron. "We must go."

Lucy spun in astonishment. "You are already acquainted?"

"I know not what you mean," Mary said. "I

perceive that you are alone here. I saw no pathetic excuse for a man cowering while you attempted to rescue him."

"Mary," Byron said in his most soothing voice, "this is no time for recriminations."

"If you think," Mary snapped back, "that I will not put a bullet through your knee rather than let you follow, it proves how little you understand me. I care nothing if you suffer. I care only for my friend, whom I love — an emotion you do not understand but as it pertains to yourself."

Lucy pivoted her head between the two of them. More than ever, she felt like some child being dragged about by adults she neither knew nor understood. It seemed now that Mary too was familiar with Byron, and not happy in the acquaintance, though she had betrayed none of that when they had first met before his unconscious form at her uncle's house. It took no great leap of the imagination to suppose what Byron had done to Mary to incur this anger, nor why she would keep such a familiarity a secret. He was the man he was, and he made little pretense of being otherwise, but he was also beautiful and charming, and more than once Lucy had known the temptation he could inspire.

"I won't leave him," said Lucy. "I asked him to take me here, and he aided me when I needed it. I will not turn my back upon him."

"Damn it!" Mary spat. "I will take him off the grounds — to the inn. No more than that. Let him say but one wrong thing, and I shall give him a second bruise to match his first."

They rode in Mary's coach for the twenty or so minutes it took to return to the inn. No one spoke, and Lucy spent much of the time stealing glances at both Mary and Byron. The lady did nothing more than look out the window, her face hard and stony. Byron, for his part, appeared chastened, and looked to Lucy like nothing so much as a child who had been caught doing something naughty.

Lucy wanted to speak, to try to mend things between these two friends, these two people who, above all, had made her feel important and special and powerful — these people she liked, possibly loved, and whom she could not trust.

When they reached the inn, Mary opened the door herself. "Get out," she said.

Byron did not look at her. Instead, he turned to Lucy. "You need not stay with her. I will see you back."

"Too many times," cut in Mary, "have I had you in my power and spared your life. You must think me softhearted, but I promise you are mistaken. Leave now if you value your flesh."

Byron spared a glance for Lucy, and a sort of sheepish half smile, and then departed, gently closing the door behind him.

"You do not know him if you would put your trust in him," said Mary.

"I know what he would have of me," Lucy said, "but I do not offer it."

"You know nothing," Mary said. "He will take what he desires, do so without remorse or regret, and think himself mighty for indulging his appetites."

Lucy gasped. "Is that what he did to you? Did he force himself upon you?"

"It does not matter. If he can be of use to you, then use him, but never put yourself in his power. He is weak and vile, but he is dangerous because he is beautiful and believes himself exempt from the law of men. In truth, he is a capricious madman. I shall say no more of him, so do not ask."

Lucy did not recognize in Byron the man Mary described, but she understood there was no point in arguing. "If you will not speak of Lord Byron, then speak of my niece. Do you know where she is? Did you take her, Mary, and replace her with that creature?"

"Yes," she said. "I did that, and I did so out of love for you."

"Because Lady Harriett would have killed her?"

"Yes." Mary made an effort at a sad smile. "I cannot guess how you learned as much, but I have no doubt it involved an impressive application of cunning craft."

"Lord Byron held Mr. Buckles still while I used the knowledge of persuasion from the *Mutus Liber* to force him to speak the truth."

Mary took Lucy's hand. "You make me proud, my sweet girl. You must know that. I could not have put my faith in anyone better."

Lucy yanked her hand away. "You did not put any faith in me. You stole my niece and told me nothing."

"I had no choice, Lucy, just as I had no choice but to go into hiding. Lady Harriett would destroy me if she had the chance, and you must not doubt that she has the power. You have seen only the smallest fraction of what she has at her command. I risked everything — far more than myself — in coming to your aid today. It was only a coincidence that you happened to be there when I came to liberate a man she held prisoner in her home."

"That madman, Mr. Bellingham?"

Mary nodded. "He is a madman, but he is of use to our cause. Lady Harriett knew that, which is why she tried to keep him hidden, and that is why I freed him. He has a purpose yet. Now her plans are thwarted, and she will be very angry with both of us. Perhaps you think she is a foolish and vain old woman, and at heart she is those things, but she is much more than that."

"A revenant," said Lucy. "A fairy."

"Yes, but these are just words. Most people have no real knowledge of what they are, of what they do."

"I shall relish the history lesson," said Lucy, "when I have my niece safe."

"Your niece is safe nowhere that you could get her," said Mary. "Nor are you safe, but you can defend yourself. Emily is helpless, and you must endure being separated from her while these troubles rage, because that is the only way to keep her alive."

"Can I see her?"

"You cannot go there."

"Go where?"

"I shall not tell you."

"This is all nonsense. What is that creature that torments my sister? Will it harm her?"

"No," Mary said. "It cannot help being what it is. It is monstrous, I suppose, but not deadly, and it is loyal to me. It will do as I have bid it, and it will keep my secrets, and though it will feed off your sister — for its kind is voracious — it will not hurt her."

Lucy shook her head. "That is not good enough. I don't want Martha to suckle a monster. I want to know why she must. I don't believe Mr. Buckles's story that Lady Harriett fears Emily. She fears me, though I don't know why."

"Perhaps she does not believe she can kill you," said Mary, "but what Buckles told you is nonsense. No doubt he believes it, that it is

407

what she told him, but the truth is far more elemental than that. His wife, his child, have power over Buckles and Lady Harriett resents it. She would kill Emily as a sacrifice, because of the power contained in her most loyal servant willingly surrendering his own child. It is no more than that. While the child lives, she will seek her. You cannot imagine what sort of monster she is."

"Then tell me," said Lucy. "But tell me as we drive to London, and quickly too. I must be back by sundown."

Mary did not ask why, did not request the details. She understood it mattered to Lucy, and that was enough. She spoke to the driver, and they were on their way.

"To understand what you face, what your enemy is, and why I act against her, you must understand her nature," began Mary. "I have told you a little, and you must forget all you know of fairies. Disregard fairy tales and Shakespeare and Spenser and all the poets and romances. They are but lies and superstitions and silly stories meant to make sense of something strange and unknowable. What the ancients first called fairies are creatures that stand between two worlds, spirits of the dead, brought back, given new flesh, and made immortal."

"With the *Mutus Liber?*"

"With alchemy, and by use of the philosopher's stone, yes. The *Mutus Liber* contains the description of that method, a method so elusive — elusive, I say, and not complex, for it is both natural and easy — that it cannot be contained in one's mind. It is a myth that the philosopher's stone can bring eternal life to a living man. It can return a dead man to flesh, and he shall remain in that form for eternity. But there is a price."

"What price is that?"

"Eternity itself," said Mary. "No one, not even the revenants themselves who have been dead, know what lies beyond death. There is something — we know that — for otherwise there would be no soul to call back. But we also know that once the soul is attached to this immortal flesh, the world beyond is forever barred to it. If the revenant dies here in this world, its soul is blasted out of existence. If there is a hell or a heaven or communion with a great and loving deity, those things are lost. The eternal life of the *Mutus Liber* is a terrible curse. It robs these beings of their humanity and makes them truly vulnerable, for they can be unmade, and in their unmaking is true destruction. You may fear the unknown beyond life, but that fear is colored with hope. For the revenant, there is no hope, only terror."

"And Ludd? Is he one of them?"

Mary shook her head. "No, he is something different. Long ago there was a king named

Lud — with one *d*. He lived during the Roman period. Very little is known about him, but Geoffrey of Monmouth writes that he built a series of fortifications upon the Thames, one of which, his favorite, was Caer Lud, or 'Lud's Fort.' You know, of course, what that fort became over time."

Lucy swallowed. "London."

"Yes. In fact, Ludgate is named for him. But that king was more than a man, he was something else, the manifestation of a Celtic deity worshipped as Lug or Lud."

"You mean to say that the man I met, whom I spoke to, is a god?"

"He is a creature worshipped as one, which is a different thing. But he is the embodiment of the spirit of this land, and he has been summoned many times during periods of danger and crisis to lead his people to victory."

Lucy studied her friend's face. "It was you, wasn't it? You summoned Ludd."

"I did," said Mary. "I used dark and dangerous magic, the kind I have asked you to avoid. The summoning of spirits is a fool's game, and it could destroy you, but I had a purpose beyond myself to serve. The revenants have long walked among men. They have used their power sometimes for good and sometimes for ill, and sometimes the judgment of such things depended upon your politics or which claimant to the throne you favored.

Their influence has always been over what must be viewed in the great scheme of things, as petty politics — a powerful faction in a system that must be called an oligarchy."

"How many of these beings are there?"

"Not many," Mary said. "Perhaps a dozen in positions of power. There are a few more who have separated themselves from this group, who exist as they choose."

"And Lady Harriett leads these beings?"

"Lady Harriett may seem like an old woman, but she is the youngest of them, and so the most vigorous. It is why she is their leader. The others have lived so long, they are disconnected from their own lives, from the world around them. They depend upon Lady Harriett to guide and protect them. Do not underestimate her. We have risked much by setting ourselves against her."

Lucy did not doubt it. "And our own nation sides with them," she said, thinking of her conversation with the prime minister.

"It does, because the men who make these decisions do not understand the bargain they make," said Mary. "They believe an era of machines will bring prosperity and security, but they don't understand what so cold a world would look like. They don't understand that the revenants want to usher in this era of machines because it will, necessarily, put all but an end to the age of magic. In standing against Ludd, these men do not do evil knowingly, but they do evil just the same. Once the ways of magic are stifled, the revenants will have nothing to fear. There can be no threat of alchemy to unmake them, and they will be safe in their eternal flesh. They care only for their security. Their dark minds will not be disquieted while machine replaces man, while craftsmen are turned into beasts of burden, while children starve and beg. They see not how the world they usher in will be a kind of hell. Their lungs will be choked by the soot and ash of production; their minds themselves will be lost to indolence and laziness. I was willing to risk myself, my life, to try to stop this nightmare they would bring upon mankind, and so yes, I summoned Ludd."

"But why does all of this involve me?"

Mary shook her head. "I don't know, and I am sorry for it. I know only that all roads on this journey begin and end with Lucy Derrick. You are everything in this. You do not want to be, and I cannot blame you, but you are. And if you wish for your niece to return in safety, you must defeat Lady Harriett."

"By finding the *Mutus Liber.*"

"Yes. You have already done a great deal by stealing pages out from under her nose."

Lucy thought about the pages. "She said her house was warded, and magic would not work there, and yet it did work. Was that because of the *Mutus Liber?*"

"In part, yes. The pages called to you, did they not?"

Lucy nodded.

"You've already discovered that they come in groups, and each of those groups conveys an important component of the whole of the book's teachings. But each page is separately enchanted, drawn to the others, and drawn to the person who possesses them. Twelve pages and twelve enchantments. Simply to hold them in your hand and to know what they are will make you both powerful and dangerous. Possessing only some of them is less desirable than possessing the whole, but you will still benefit from these enchantments. You will have more power and more luck."

"Would not Lady Harriett know that?" asked Lucy. "Would she not make every effort to protect herself accordingly?"

"As old as she is," said Mary, "she still does not understand magic. Not really. Lucy, when you were a child, did you know someone who was a very fast runner?"

"Of course," she said. "We had a friend, Eliza, who would always win when we raced."

"Always? Did she never lose?"

"Well, sometimes, of course. What has this to do with the wards?"

"Eliza may have been fastest," said Mary, "and she may have been reliably so, but that did not mean she would always win. You

413

might depend on her to win against one of your friends, or even a stranger, and most of the time she would. But sometimes someone could be faster, or perhaps her legs would be tired or she would be hungry."

"Wards get tired?"

"They grow strained and frayed, like old rope, or stronger and weaker, like winds. Her wards will work most of the time, but they did not work this time, because you are powerful and she is old. She is strong, Lucy. Very strong. She is stronger than you can imagine, but *not* as strong as she thinks, and that is our only advantage."

"The journey continues," said Lucy as she looked out the window. Suddenly, she felt a sharp terror. "Where are we? I do not recognize this road. Is this the way to London?"

"No," said Mary. "We are returning to Nottinghamshire."

Lucy gripped the side of her seat in panic. "No! Did you not hear me? I must return to London. If I am not back by sunset, I will be discovered missing. They will know how long I have been gone. Why have you tricked me?"

"Because I knew you would not listen," said Mary. "I knew you would still go because you care too much for what the world thinks of you."

"You speak more like Byron than you would credit."

"You will not say that to me," she snapped.

Her anger was sudden and terrible. She was like a jungle cat, crouched as it readied itself to pounce. Her face flushed dark and her eyes widened and her pupils narrowed. Teeth showed through parted lips. "I am nothing like him, and you will never say such a thing to me, nor even speak his name to me if you can avoid it. I will —" She then began to weep, and she pulled Lucy to her breast. "Forgive me. Your comment was innocent, and my anger unjust."

Lucy pulled away. "You may not wish to be likened to him, but you are as careless with my name and reputation as he is. Who are you to decide if they are worth preserving? My reputation is mine, Mary. I do not wish to let it go so lightly. I have no means, I have no name, I have no station. I cannot live as a whore in the eyes of the world. I am not so foolish that I don't understand that the world's thinking it so shall make it truth in the end. I may try to resist it, but I must have bread, and in the end, I will become what they say."

"There is no fate that can be thrust upon you but what you permit," said Mary, beaming like a proud parent.

"I thank you for your confidence, but I must go to London. Turn us around while there is still time."

"You cannot go to London," said Mary. "Things are going to happen, and they will be beyond even your control. London will soon become a city of chaos."

"My friends are in London," Lucy said.

"Many people are in London, but there is no helping that," Mary answered. "It is time for the change to begin. It has to happen in some way, and revolution can never be quiet or peaceful or easy. I wish that it could be, but it cannot. Revolutions must be bloody. You may condemn me for a monster, but the men who have allied with the revenants are willing to endure suffering for their cause, and so there is no other way. I have set things in motion, and we are now powerless to stop what we have begun. We have no choice but to flee from its destruction."

How much of this was metaphor or speculation or sheer nonsense? Lucy did not know. Mary did not lie to her — she believed that — but she withheld much when it was convenient, and Lucy was tired of being manipulated and moved about like a game piece. It was time to make her own decisions.

With hardly a thought of what it would mean, Lucy leapt up, hurled open the door of the coach, and threw herself out onto the grass. She landed more violently than she would have expected, and she felt the sharp scrape of something cut against her cheek. Her arm struck something hard, and she heard herself cry out in pain as she rolled, and then she rolled again. The world passed by in a nauseous blur of grass and tree and rock, and Lucy understood that she had jumped out upon the top of a hill. From some unfathomable distance she heard Mary shouting and then horses crying out their complaints, but Lucy was tumbling — tumbling fast and hard and with terrifying speed; the gray of the sky rolled past her eyes as she gained momentum and a strange calm came through her. She thought she was at the center of things and that all roads began and ended with her, and yet here she was, about to have her head broken open by a rock and a tree.

And that was when she landed into the nearly frozen stream of water. She opened her mouth to cry out, but water filled her lungs. She thrashed, hardly knowing which was up or down, but managed, owing to the shallowness of the stream and nothing else, to lift out her head and find cold, welcome air. She cried out in relief and confusion, only to realize her head lay only inches from a horse's hoof.

Lucy raised her head to see a great black and brown stallion, and atop it, smiling without humor, sat Mr. Olson. Then Lucy's world went dark.

Lucy awoke feeling surprisingly warm. Her dreams were filled with cold water and mud, but now she was dry. She felt aches in her arm, her back, both her legs. Her face stung, and she remembered leaping from Mary's coach. And she remembered Mr. Olson.

She opened her eyes.

It could well be that Lucy possessed some sort of expectation of what she would find when she opened her eyes, but whatever it was, surely this was not it. She sat in a rough-hewn wooden chair near a fire in a rude cottage with a dirt floor and nothing upon the walls. She could see through the windows that it remained gloomy outside, and in the cottage all was dim and shadowy. Her gown was dry and brittle, much stained and caked with hard mud. So was her skin. Her hands were clotted with dirt, making them hard to move. They were also bound behind her back.

Across the cottage, at a long table, sat Mr. Olson, wearing a mud-splattered riding coat. He sat working at a piece of wood with a knife, but sensed that she gazed upon him. He set down the wood, but not the knife, and looked at her. Even in the dimness of the cabin she could see his face was set in something like anger. He was red-eyed and haggard, and had three or four days' worth of beard upon his face.

"You woke up," he said in a heavy voice, deep and scratchy.

Fear thudded in her chest. She needed to get free. She needed herbs and plants and a pen. She needed to make a charm and escape.

It almost made her smile to think how magic was now the first thing she thought of in a crisis.

"Please, Mr. Olson," she said. "I am hurt, and I must go. I must be in London as soon as I may." Time was running out, and she was stuck here, with Mr. Olson who appeared not himself. Lucy gritted her teeth with anger. She would not cry. She would find a way out of this. She was at the center of things, and she would find a solution.

Mr. Olson pushed himself from the bench by the table and stood menacingly over her. "I am shocked by your behavior. Lady Harriett summoned me to her home, and when I arrived, I saw the damage you had done. Breaking her door, killing her dog. All was chaos. You had only just departed, and Lady Harriett just returned, but she made everything clear. I understood that I had to go after you. I was so tired, but I had to have you, Lucy, and now I do. At last, you are mine."

"I am not yours," said Lucy, trying hard to sound both determined and reasonable. He did not seem the cold, unfeeling, methodical man she had known. There was something unrestrained about him, darkly passionate. He seemed like a madman. "I do not wish to be here. Whose cottage is this?"

"As to that, I have no knowledge. I found it, and so it is mine, as you are."

"Listen to me," said Lucy. "You must let

me go at once, or there will be consequences."

"What consequences can there be?" He looked about the small house, straining his neck theatrically in a grotesque mimicry of humor. "Soon we shall be married, and that shall be the end of it."

"You said you did not want me," said Lucy, hating the desperation in her voice. "You said your feelings were altered."

He shook his head and grinned like a panting dog. "I never said that. I only dreamed I did." He placed his hands upon her shoulders and then reached around and began to unlace the ribbons of her frock. "We must wait to be married in law, but not in deed."

Lucy pushed herself back into the chair, but there was nowhere to go. She pulled against her restraints, but they would not be moved. She had thought herself powerful and mighty, but there was no magic, there were no charms, that could help her now. And this was truly happening. Mr. Olson, vile and mad and under Lady Harriett's monstrous spell, was undressing her, and she could not stop it.

There were three ties, and the first two went easily. His clumsy fingers struggled with the third. He grunted rudely and pressed his body against hers as he pulled at the ribbons, trying not to make the knot tighter. Finally, it came loose, and he grunted in appreciation.

He pulled at the shoulders of her gown so

that it hung loose upon her, but it yet hung. "Has any man before seen you? Has Byron?"

"Please," Lucy said. She strained against the bonds holding together her hands. She felt them rub her skin hot and raw. She felt blood trickle down her hands, and yet she fought though she knew it would do no good. It would only cause her more pain, but she fought because she could not be a woman who did not fight. "You must let me go. It is not too late. Nothing is done that cannot be undone. You must see reason."

"Are you a maid or aren't you?" he asked, now sounding angry. "Did you give yourself to that man you ran away with, or did you whore yourself off to Byron? I should not be surprised. It will go better for you if you are a maid. I shall not forgive you if you are not, but you shall be mine all the same."

Lucy could find no words. She felt paralyzed and cold and distant from herself. Everything was about to end. The life she knew would be blasted out of existence, and she would be something else, something lesser, something violated. Even when she escaped from this fiend, and she had no doubt she would do so soon enough, she would be filthy and used. She would be contemptible, and none of it was her fault. She wanted none of this, and she would pay the price for his crimes.

She thought of the pages newly acquired

from the *Mutus Liber,* hidden away now. The images had swirled together, unfolded like a flower. She had deciphered them like a puzzle, like a riddle, and she understood some of what they said, what they told her about the magic of persuasion. It was like mesmerism, or mesmerism was like this. It hardly mattered. If she could but get free, if she could but use a few herbs, or make a quick charm, she could make Olson leave her be, but it did her no good to think of what she would do if she could.

"You won't answer? Well, I'll have answers soon enough. Now, let's have a look at you." He reached to the front of her gown, and sucked in a deep breath as he prepared to pull away the gown.

And then Lucy heard the voice behind her.

"Olson, you have never been so close to death as you are at this moment. Step away from the lady." Byron stood at the door with a pocket pistol drawn. Lucy strained her neck to see him, but she wanted to see his beautiful face, set in determination, blazing with anger and perhaps exertion. He looked wild and demonic and angelic all at once.

"I must thank you for giving me an excuse to shoot you," Byron said. "I've wanted one, so I shan't ask again."

Mr. Olson turned to Byron and made a low, gurgling sound in the back of his throat. "She will never be yours. She is mine."

Byron's expression changed not at all. "I did warn you." He fired the pistol.

A loud bang filled the room, and a rosette of blood blossomed on Mr. Olson's thigh, darkening his already filthy breeches. He let out a howl as he clamped a hand to the wound. "Damn you!" he cried. "You've shot me."

"I am only getting started," said Byron, striking him in the head with his still-smoking pistol.

Byron rushed to Lucy and began to cut her restraints with the rough knife from the table. In a moment, the rope snapped, and Lucy was free.

"I know not how long I was unconscious," she said, the words coming out in a mad jumble. "How long have I been here? Hours? Is it too late? Tell me it is not too late."

"It is not too late," Byron said, gently pulling her to her feet. "I followed you in Mary's coach, and I saw you jump. Now I have come for you, and I shall return you in time." He placed his hands upon her shoulders, and turned her around. Gently, he tied the ribbons of her frock. She felt his fingers, warm and dexterous, brushing against her, and she closed her eyes in pleasure and relief.

It was she who kissed him. Her lips found his, and she raised a hand to touch his warm face, rough with stubble, and she lost herself for a moment in his sweet taste and the feel of his arms around her. He had come for her. He had saved her. Whatever he was, whatever cruel and selfish things he did, whatever he wanted from her, it was he who had rescued her from destruction. How could she not kiss him? How could she not want to give him whatever he asked?

Then she pushed herself away.

They stood in a filthy shack with Olson upon the ground, bleeding and wheezing but a few feet away from them. Byron made her right and whole and safe, and if circumstances were different — if they were someplace safe and clean and quiet, she did not know if she could have refused him anything, but they were not in such a place.

"I can never thank you enough," she said in a strained voice.

She then walked over to Mr. Olson and squatted down better to examine his leg. It bled steadily, but not alarmingly, and though the sight sickened her, Lucy knew what had to be done. She could not leave him to die, no matter what he had done. While Byron busied himself with reloading his pistol, she found a cloth, stiff from drying, near the fire, then crouched next to him. Gritting her teeth as though the act would cause her pain, she ripped open his breeches and used the cloth to bind the wound tightly. Let someone else clean the wound. It was more than anyone would ask of her. It would have to be enough.

Without warning, Olson opened his eyes and looked at her. Lucy leapt backwards, nearly falling over as though startled by a great rat.

"You are to be my wife, Lucy. I command you not to leave me."

She had no answer for him. She rose and nodded at Byron. It was time to go.

They turned to the door, but found it blocked. Standing before them, smiling in an absent way, like an amused child playing with toys, was the strange gray-haired man from Lady Harriett's estate, the one called Mr. Whitestone.

"I can't remember what I am doing here," he said to Lucy. He sounded amused, not at all upset. "Do you think that odd?"

"You are supposed to be protecting me, blockhead," said Mr. Olson, still unable to get up from the floor, but now dragging himself toward Lucy, like a desperate soldier upon the battlefield.

"From which one?" asked Mr. Whitestone.

"From the man, you dolt."

"Oh, yes. That is what Lady Harriett said."

Quickly, impossibly quickly, he closed the distance between the door and Byron, and lifted Byron in the air, holding him under his arms the way a parent might lift a beloved child. Then Mr. Whitestone tossed Byron hard against the wall. His body struck upon the shoulder, and Byron cried out as he bounced off. Something fell from his pocket, landing upon the dirt floor with a thud. An instant later, Byron landed himself, hard upon his shoulder. He cried out again. His teeth were now covered with blood, and his eyes looked wild, desperate, and enraged.

"Like that?" asked Mr. Whitestone.

"It is a start," snarled Mr. Olson, panting heavily, taking a break from crawling toward Lucy. "Now, rip his head from his neck."

"Oh," said Mr. Whitestone. "Are you certain? I don't love to kill."

"It is what Lady Harriett said," answered Mr. Olson. He winced and snapped his teeth together, fighting off a wave of pain. "In her name, in the name of her late husband, Sir Reginald, I command you to pull Byron's head from his shoulders."

"No," said Lucy, stepping forward, placing herself between Mr. Whitestone and Byron. "You will not hurt him."

"He did mention Sir Reginald," said Mr. Whitestone. "We take that very seriously."

"But you do not love to kill," said Lucy.

"Do I kill the lady as well?" Mr. Whitestone asked Mr. Olson.

"No, not kill. You may strike her, though not in the face. Nor the breasts. I do not want her breasts bruised."

"Oh," said Mr. Whitestone.

Lucy had no time to think. No time to

consider. She saw that the object that had fallen from Byron's coat was his pistol. Darting forward she grabbed it, and not taking a moment to think — for she dared not hesitate, dared not consider — she pointed it at Mr. Whitestone's chest, cocked the hammer, and pulled the trigger.

The pan flashed and the gun blasted forth its ball, bucking in Lucy's hand and jerking her wrist back so hard that at first she feared she had broken it. The pain lasted but a second, however, and she reached back and pulled Byron to his feet. He staggered, but he seemed more disordered than wounded.

"Dear Christ!" he cried out.

Lucy followed his gaze and looked at Mr. Whitestone, and she came close to swooning. She had missed his chest by quite a bit, and the ball had struck his face. Almost everything above his mouth — nose, eyes, most of the forehead — had been blasted away or crushed. Nothing remained but a mass of bone and blood, oozing freely, and yet Mr. White-stone remained standing.

"Oh," said the bloodied but unharmed mouth. And then Lucy saw something else. The skin around the wound began to repair itself, to grow. She saw the skin moving, stretching, increasing, so that it appeared as though his face crawled with a thousand ants.

She yanked on Byron's arm. "Can you run?"

He nodded.

They ran.

They had but a single horse, and she sat behind Byron, clutching him tight. Riding on horseback was both faster and less comfortable, and given all her bruises and injuries, Lucy felt each step of the journey, but she willed the horse to run faster. She tried to think of nothing but the journey. There would be time later to think of the horrible spell cast over Mr. Olson and monstrous Mr. Whitestone, clearly an immortal revenant, whom she had shot in the face. She shook the image from her mind. Instead, she managed to pry her watch from her bag, and what she saw there filled her with hope. It was only just before noon. They could make it in four hours. She looked wretched, inexplicably filthy, but she would worry about that later. She only needed to get to Mr. Gilley's house in time.

The sky remained steel gray and dark, so she could not chart the passage of time, but she felt they must be covering a great deal of ground, and though she hurt and the cold cut through her, she told herself all would be well. Her wounds would heal, a fire would warm her. Little else mattered. Not now. The things she had seen, the things she had done, they would all wait. That is what she told herself as they rode and time collapsed into itself and minutes became hours or perhaps the other way around. They could only ride. Thinking and worrying and wondering accomplished nothing.

As they turned at a crossroads, Byron slowed sufficiently that she was able to remove her watch and observe the time again. A quarter after two. "How much longer?" she called.

"Not an hour and a half," he answered.

She would be at Mr. Gilley's house by five o'clock. The sun would set likely about an hour after that, so she would have half an hour or so to spare — closer than she would have liked, but that did not matter. She would be there.

They crossed into London and Lucy found that a reckless man on a horse could move about the city far more readily than could a carriage. Soon they arrived at Mr. Gilley's street. Byron dismounted and helped Lucy to the ground.

"I cannot thank you enough," she said to him.

He was bruised and beaten and disordered from the road. His teeth were still stained with his own blood. Nevertheless, when he bowed he looked as regal as any king could wish. "The tables turned soon enough, and you did save me as well," he allowed. "Yet, I think we can agree that mine was the more impressive rescue."

"There is much I would know," she said. "Mary would not explain her disposition toward you, and I feel you conceal things about Lady Harriett and her kind as well. We saw things today — impossible things — and yet I do not think you were as surprised as you should have been. I know you have secrets, Lord Byron, and yet I owe you more than I have ever owed any man save my father."

He bowed again. "The secrets I keep are not my own. That is all I may say as a gentleman. As for the other matter, I have tried to impress upon you that there is nothing I would not do for you, Lucy. Perhaps now you believe me."

"I do indeed." Lucy laughed. She was perhaps vaguely giddy from the thrill of having survived what she had, of having escaped Lady Harriett and Mr. Whitestone and ridden all this way. Only a few weeks before, she had felt herself helpless in her life, and now look what she had accomplished! She had seen and done and learned so much, and she now possessed three more pages of the missing book. Along with the original two from the false *Mutus Liber,* that meant she had five of the twelve. Perhaps she truly was mighty.

Byron, however, turned quite serious. "I will not speak ill of Mary Crawford, Lucy. I can only say that lady's heart can lead her to make judgments neither wise nor warranted.

She may be a good friend to you, but in this matter, I would ask you not to heed her overmuch. And then there is the business of her abducting you."

"She claims that something terrible is going to happen in London, that I am not safe."

"I have not observed you to be safe anywhere but with me."

Lucy felt herself blush. "Good afternoon, Lord Byron, and I thank you once more."

He bowed. "I hope you will someday value me as you value my services."

Lucy's face felt hot, but she yet spoke what she felt. "Our disagreement is not regarding your worth."

Byron stepped forward and reached out to touch her, but then withdrew. They were upon a public street. "Then come to me," he said in an urgent whisper. "Come to me soon, or I shall die from this torment. I know what is in your heart, and you know what is in mine. What else matters? I beg you to come to me." With this, he turned, mounted his horse, and rode off.

Lucy remained still for a moment, thinking of Byron, his beauty and valor and all he had done for her. Could she love a man such as he? She did not know, but she knew she wanted to be with him, and she did not know that she could risk being alone with him.

This was hardly the time to dwell on such things, however. Lucy turned and entered the house. She knew she looked terrible, and wished she had yet upon her tools that she might craft one last charm, something to help her get to her room unnoticed that she might wash and change and appear before all as clean and poised as they must expect. If they saw her now, she must tell some story of being knocked down in the street, and it would engender a great deal of fuss, and perhaps even make it more difficult to move freely, but she would meet that challenge when she came to it.

When she walked through the door, however, she understood something was wrong. Mr. Gilley, Mrs. Gilley, and Norah all stared at her as she entered the house. Only Mrs. Emmett appeared happy. Beneath her low bonnet and curling hair, her obscured eyes were wide with pleasure. "Welcome back, my dear," she said. "Oh, there has been a fuss."

"Miss Derrick," boomed Mr. Gilley. "Where have you been?"

"I was knocked down in the street," she said. "It is not so bad as it appears."

"Where have you been these two days?" demanded Mr. Gilley.

Lucy could think of nothing to say. She looked at the tall case clock in the corner, and it confirmed her suspicions. It was not yet four. So how could it be that they had discovered her absence? Lucy thought over the charm she had constructed, racking her brain to recall some misstep or error. Understanding her mistake would not help her now, but she was numb with surprise and fear, and it was all she could think to do.

Then she heard a familiar, high-pitched voice speak her name. Lucy turned to see Mrs. Quince walk into the parlor. She held in her hand a piece of paper, torn in two, and from across the room, Lucy had no trouble recognizing it. It was her talisman.

"Miss Derrick, our mutual friend Lady Harriett asked me to look in upon you and make certain all was well. She will be quite disappointed to discover you have shamed yourself and your family." She walked over to Lucy and handed her the ripped talisman. "Some trash of yours, I believe. I found it upon the floor."

"I am sorry your visit could not have been more pleasant," said Mr. Gilley.

"No fault of yours, I am sure," answered Mrs. Quince. She folded her arms across her breasts and smiled.

Lucy locked eyes with Mrs. Quince, making an effort to keep her own expression cold and dangerous. "There will come a reckoning," she said.

"No doubt," answered Mrs. Quince. She curtsied and moved toward the door. "As I said, I cannot stay, Mr. Gilley, but I thank you for listening to me."

"I am grateful for your intelligence," he

answered, and then turned to Lucy. "An excellent woman."

Lucy said nothing, though Mr. Gilley's expression suggested he anticipated she would have much to say, perhaps on the topic of Mrs. Quince's excellence. When she did not speak, he coughed theatrically and straightened his posture.

"This is very serious, Miss Derrick," he said. "I cannot expose myself to this sort of chaos. It shall render me vulnerable to a cold, and I do not wish a cold. I hate a cold above everything. For that reason, I shall write to your uncle at once. You have three days to vacate my house."

29

Lucy was awake half the night contemplating her new state. There were spells of control, spells of forgetting. There were options, but thinking of these only led to more crying. She could not hope to control the minds and memories of so many people, and even if she could do it successfully, there was a time when the influencing of people and their minds became more than a strategy, it became evil. This moral position was a luxury she could afford only because she knew that the secret was surely out already. No doubt the servants had told their friends, and the news had spread by now to dozens of houses in London. By this time tomorrow, that number would be tenfold.

"It doesn't matter," she told herself. Over and over again she said it. It did not matter, because an advantageous match and balls and operas and tea gardens — these were not for her. Her task was to rescue her niece, and now she understood she could do so only by destroying an immortal, evil being, though destroying this being meant obliterating its soul, perhaps the most terrible thing she could imagine. That was not hers to consider, however. Hers was to retrieve the pages, and she had begun that endeavor, and she had kept her success hidden from everyone. That was some consolation for her disgrace.

Her disgrace. Best not to dwell on it, she decided. Best not to dwell on her shame or her challenge or any of the difficulties that lay ahead of her. There was but one thing that mattered, and that was the next piece of the *Mutus Liber.* She would have to attempt to discover how to find the next piece, and for that she would have to speak to Mary. She'd said she was returning to Nottinghamshire, and now, apparently, so was Lucy.

In the meantime, she examined the pages she had already. Upon them were chaotic images — bearded men in flowing robes who stood upon cliffs or raised books to the moon. A naked woman lay upon a bed of branches, holding a chalice to her breast. A child flew in the air, soon to land in the arms of a strange creature — part woman, part spider.

It looked like nonsense, and yet, she knew it was not. The pages felt alive to her, vibrant and warm in her hands. If she held one between her thumb and finger, she could feel the thrum of a pulse, and she heard something, a faint whisper of distant words. She thought of how the pages had called to her in Lady Harriett's library in a way the pages had not when Mary had shown her the book with so many false pages. Did the possession of some pages make the discovering and understanding of the rest easier? Would she know how to interpret the pages when she had them all? Would the possession of the entire book give her the terrible knowledge of how to bestow and destroy eternal life?

She had rushed through these pages before, but she knew there was more to be gleaned, more to learn about the mechanisms of persuasion, and given the difficulties in which she now found herself, she would need what advantages she might find. And she found much. When she quieted herself, when she allowed herself to follow the patterns and folds and flow of the images, she saw things in her mind, made connections with the world, opened doors locked within her. She felt as though the pages were hers, that they told her secrets once known but long forgotten, and the secrets were wonderful indeed. What she had, what she believed she could do, would give her new strength, new advantages. Whatever happened, she would be equal to it. She felt near certain.

In the morning she found Mrs. Emmett busy making preparations for their departure. She smiled as she packed, as though she understood nothing of her mistress's disgrace. Lucy said nothing, asked her nothing. Instead, she went down to breakfast, going late that she might avoid the discomfort of sitting with Mr. and Mrs. Gilley. Norah, however, came in to sit with her, and her long, thin mouth was twisted into the most ironic of smiles.

"What a disaster," she said excitedly. "But it is a delicious disaster, you must acknowledge. People are talking everywhere, Lucy. I have taken a stroll about the park this morning, and you would not credit how many inquiries I've received. They say it is Lord Byron. Did you know he has a new book of poetry out this week? It is said to be the most charmingly scandalous thing in the world, and everyone talks of it. They say you ran off with Lord Byron and secretly married him." She leaned in closer. "Or not."

The first volume of his new poem, the book of which he was so proud, was to be put out that week, and yet he had made the time to take Lucy upon her mission. Despite her humiliation, and her fury with Norah, Lucy felt the warm tug of something deeper, something warmer. Byron had done those things for her, placed her quest above his vanity, rescued her from ruin. Oh, he was a terrible man, it was true, but such a good one at the same time. He lived by his own law, and it made her blush to think of it, but in matters other than love, it was clear there was no doubting his honor.

"The rumors could not be more mistaken," Lucy told Norah.

"Then where were you?" Norah demanded. "You must tell me. I shall keep it to myself, I swear it. Only please tell me."

Lucy swallowed. "If you must know, I was held captive by a fairy."

Norah turned around in stage disgust.

Lucy left the house as little as she could in the next two days. She did not want to endure the looks, the whispers, the cruelty. Let them think what they wished, she decided, though there was no choice, really. Soon she would return to Nottinghamshire, and she would be marked there as a whore as well. Her uncle would refuse to give her shelter, and then what? She would have to find the means to live on her own. That ought not to be too difficult, she decided. A cunning woman could always find the means to live, surely. It was not the life she would have chosen for herself, but it was the life she had, and it would surely prove better than most. But these were all worries to trouble her mind after she had defeated Lady Harriett.

When Friday came, and it was time for her to depart, Lucy sought out Norah to say her good-byes. Norah, for her part, was cold. Once it became clear that Lucy would not reveal any secrets, Lucy's worth as a friend had expired. It was one thing if she could provide salacious gossip, but quite another if she was only an outcast slut with nothing to offer the very friend who had brought her the opportunity of becoming an outcast slut.

"I hope," said Norah by way of farewell, "that you acquit yourself with more dignity in Nottingham than you have done here as my guest."

"It is my greatest wish to do so," Lucy said.

She turned and went down the stairs, where she informed the coachman that she was ready to be taken to the inn where she would depart London. The chests had already been loaded, so the serving man gave her a saucy look — one that said he anticipated he knew not what might happen with a young woman of her nature once they were together — and opened the door. Inside, Mrs. Emmett already sat, knitting in her lap. She patted the seat next to her. "This has been quite an adventure," she said absently.

Then Lucy heard someone call her name.

She turned around, and saw Jonas Morrison walking toward her. His cheeks were flushed, and he was out of breath. "Thank God you are well," he said in a panting voice. "Of course, I knew you would be. How could you not be? You are Lucy Derrick, and you can do anything. I know that, and yet I worry."

His manic mode of talking meant nothing. Lucy felt her old anger toward him kindle anew, but even so she was also curious, and she was searching for some respite from her difficulties. Could this man, tricked into believing he loved her, offer what she needed? "Mr. Morrison," she said in a convincingly cheerful voice, "what has happened?"

"The revolution has begun," he said. "I bring terrible news of the prime minister, the leader of my order, Spencer Perceval. He has been murdered."

Lucy was welcomed back into the house only because she was acquainted with a gentleman who brought such shocking news. It was not to be wondered at that a woman such as Miss Derrick would know all sorts of gentlemen, Mr. Gilley observed to his daughter, who returned a smile for his wit. They were now very happy with each other.

"The prime minister has been shot, and he is dead. We know little more than that, but it is suspected that this is the work of the Luddites. Already there is unrest spreading across the city. Anyone of any standing in government is going into hiding now. No one knows who could be next. We fear that this could be the first step toward a bloodbath, much like the revolution in Paris. My people" — and here he looked meaningfully at Lucy, so she would understand he meant the Rosicrucians

— "even now do much to calm the people's mood. I pray it will be enough."

"Surely there is something to be done," said Mr. Gilley. "Cannot the Prince Regent or the army beat back the ruffians?"

"Soldiers now patrol the streets, looking to suppress unrest. The murderer himself is in custody, and I am assured that no means will be spared to discover his name and motivation, but until we learn more, I can only advise that you all keep yourselves safe. I presume you have your own conveyance, sir."

"Of course," said Mr. Gilley.

"Then you must depart at once and bring your daughter and Miss Derrick back to Nottinghamshire."

"I shall take my daughter of course. That young woman shall have to find her own way."

Mr. Morrison stared at him. "I beg your pardon, sir. You would abandon a guest, a helpless young *lady,* in a time of crisis? Did I mistake you for a gentleman?"

Mr. Gilley rose now. "I beg your pardon, sir, but who are you precisely that I must obey your commands or listen to your insults?"

"My name is Jonas Morrison," he said with a bow.

Mr. Gilley's eyes went wide. "Jonas Morrison! Surely not the hero of —"

Mr. Morrison held up his hand. "Sir, your

position with the Navy Office may make you privy to certain state secrets, but they are not to be repeated."

Lucy watched this exchange in wonder. First Mrs. Quince had fled in panic at the mention of Mr. Morrison's name, and now Mr. Gilley could not conceal his astonishment. Who exactly was this man, and what had he done to evoke these responses? Clearly he was more than a cad who liked to toy with the affections of young ladies, though he was certainly that.

"You are quite right," conceded Mr. Gilley. "It is . . . it is just such an honor to meet you. But as you are a man of some import, it behooves me to be direct with you. May I speak to you for a moment in private?"

The two gentlemen went off to a corner for a moment and spoke in quiet tones. They then returned, and Mr. Morrison turned to Lucy. "Miss Derrick, I am sorry to inform you that your host is not nearly the gentleman you thought, and he presumes to judge that which he cannot understand. If your duty required you to travel unexpectedly, even in the company of a scoundrel such as Byron, I applaud your sacrifice. I would never suspect, even for a moment, any improper behavior on your part." He bowed to her.

Though this expression of confidence was no doubt motivated by the spell she had cast upon him, Lucy could not help but be touched by so unexpected a kindness. "Thank you, sir."

"Men will excuse anything in a woman if there is the hope of a sufficient reward," said Mr. Gilley to his daughter.

Norah took her father by his arm. "Let us give them a moment to talk, Papa," she said, and led her father out of the room.

When they were alone, Lucy turned to Mr. Morrison. "Where have you been? While you were off doing I know not what, I was taken prisoner by Lady Harriett and then Mr. Olson, and I had to fire a pistol upon one of the revenants. *That* is where I was." That she had broken into Lady Harriett's estate and stolen three pages of the *Mutus Liber* was beside the point; Lucy was angry now, though some part of her knew she had no business being angry with Mr. Morrison. Nevertheless, she wished to be angry with him. He was supposed to love her (again, her role in this was not relevant at the moment), and he had abandoned her to such misery. She was being irrational, but she wished to take shelter in her own irrationality

"Good God!" he cried out, his distress evident. "Lucy, I did not know. I could not have known. But if I had, I would have moved heaven and earth to come to your aid. I have done everything I can for you. You must believe that. And there is nothing in my power that I would not do."

His reference to what he had already done for her filled her with a new wave of anger. "Fortunately, I had Lord Byron to help."

Mr. Morrison's eyes widened as though slapped. "It is well if you wish to make use of him, but it is only a matter of time before he turns on you."

"He did not turn on me. He rescued me more than once in those two days." She turned to look out the window, affecting an airy disregard for his feelings, but suddenly she turned back to Mr. Morrison. She wanted to look at him. She wanted to be near him, very near him. She stepped back in fright. Was he working some kind of love magic on her?

Then she understood. It was not he who entranced her. It was something he had with him, something strange and familiar and wonderful and intoxicating. She took a tentative step forward, trying to make sense of it, as though trying to identify a flavor she'd tried once, long ago.

He had pages of the book on him. She knew it. She could sense them. Lucy took another step toward him. "Where have you been?" she asked again.

"I could not have known. I have only now returned from Cardiff."

The name of that city summoned an unexpected pang of sadness. Her sister Emily had returned from a sojourn there with friends only weeks before her death. Lucy pushed the memories aside. "Why were you in Wales?"

"Searching for pages of the book, which I found. Two of them."

"Really?" said Lucy, trying to disguise her interest. "Where are they?"

"Upon my person. I was to bring them to Mr. Perceval, but then I heard the news, and I could think of no place safe enough to put them when any part of the metropolis might at any moment burst into flames."

Lucy needed magic, strong, compelling magic, but she had no time to prepare anything. She had no time to fetch herbs and ingredients or make charms and draw out talismans. She needed something now.

Mr. Morrison was already somewhat in her power, and might be subject to her persuasion, but that would not be enough. She needed more than simply to make him do what she wished. And then she recalled that she had just recently learned the very thing she needed.

Much to his surprise, Lucy took Mr. Morrison's hand. She was not entirely certain what she was doing, but she'd done enough, seen enough, to feel that she could manage her way through this on her own, even if she did not follow the instructions precisely. She had a *feel* for the push and pull of magic's energies, and the pages of the *Mutus Liber*

446

had shown her the way. She had wanted to use herbs or talismans or spells. She knew now that she needed only her own hands and her own voice.

"Mr. Morrison," she said, "I want you to look into my eyes. Yes, just like that. And I want you to listen to me. Are you listening to me?"

He nodded slowly.

It all seemed so natural, like following the currents of a river. She did what she thought she ought to do, and it felt proper, correct, easy. "Very good, sir. I want you to listen to my voice, and as you hear my voice, I want your mind to clear itself of everything but my voice. That's right. You are listening, just listening, but thinking of nothing but what I say, awaiting my next command. Are you still listening?"

He nodded once more.

"Are you ready to receive my commands?"

He nodded.

Astonishing. What a remarkably useful tool this was. Of course, Lucy had no illusions. She could not so easily compel Mr. Gilley to listen to her and allow her to stay, for, as she understood these things, he did not really want to listen to her or to let her stay. It was likely she would have had no power over Mr. Morrison if she had not already made him love her. Even so, this new hold she had over him seemed remarkable.

447

"Mr. Morrison, the two pages of the *Mutus Liber.* You have them with you?"

"I do," he said.

"I want you to give them to me."

Mr. Morrison reached into his jacket and retrieved a pocketbook. He opened it, and pulled from it two folded pages, which he gave to her. Lucy quickly concealed them within a hidden pocket in her gown.

"Who else knows you found them?" she asked.

"No one," he said.

"Mr. Morrison," she said, finding her way by intuition and sense. "I want you to forget you found these pages. I want you to forget you ever had them and gave them to me. You will recall only that you went to Wales and met with no success. Do you understand?"

"Yes," he said.

"I shall presently let go of your hand. When I do so, you shall not recall that we have spoken of these pages at all. It shall be to you precisely as it was moments ago."

"Yes, Lucy," he said.

Lucy let his hand drop.

Mr. Morrison blinked. "I am very tired suddenly. I forgot what I spoke of."

"That I must find my own way back to Nottingham. I know not what I shall do then."

"You will still seek the pages of the book, I imagine. Just as I do."

"And you've had no success?" asked Lucy,

testing out her work.

"None," he said, without hesitation. "My visit to Wales was as unsuccessful as our visit to Newstead. Now that Mr. Perceval is dead" — and here he paused, obviously moved by this loss — "there is no one to stop me from seeking out Lady Harriett and searching for the pages in her library. It will be a great risk to do so, but I know not what else to do."

"Do be careful," said Lucy, for despite what he had done to her in the past, she could not let Mr. Morrison venture into Lady Harriett's estate unprotected.

"Have no worries," he said. "We've had dealings with her before."

"Then I shall make my own inquiries," said Lucy. "When I return to Nottingham, I shall speak to my friend, Mary Crawford. I don't know how much I can trust her. She has done things that are . . . well, they are complicated, but I believe she may prove to be of assistance."

Lucy stopped talking because she observed that Mr. Morrison no longer gave any indication of listening to her. Instead, his hands were raised to his face, and he was slouched over slightly. When he, after a moment and some prodding by Lucy, lowered his hands, she observed that his face was red and his eyes were tearing.

"What name did you say?" he asked in a low, rasping sort of voice.

Lucy recalled that she had made it her habit to conceal such things from Mr. Morrison in the past. That she had neglected to do so now ought not to have posed any problems, but surely it did. Was it possible that he, like Byron, knew Mary?

Mr. Morrison took a step forward. "Say her name again!" he demanded, such rage in his voice that Lucy was afraid either to answer or to not answer.

Remaining quiet struck her as the more dangerous of the two options, and so she spoke. She needed to keep him calm at all costs, lest his rage shatter the hold of the love magic she had put upon him. "It is my friend, Mary Crawford."

He put his hands to his face again and turned away. "My God, I could not have believed it. I would not have believed it. Is it truly possible?"

She took a halting step after him. "What is it Mr. Morrison? What has happened? Who is Miss Crawford to you?"

"Then you truly do not know?" he asked.

"I know nothing of her except what she is to me."

Jonas Morrison lowered himself gently into an armchair and sat with his head down, wiping away tears without care to conceal them. When he raised his face to her, he appeared hardly recognizable. The stony, reserved face was now soft and moist and bloated with sadness. "Mary. Miss Crawford, as you style her, was my wife. It was she who was murdered, and she for whom I seek revenge."

There was obviously an error. "I am sorry to have mentioned a name so troubling to you," Lucy said, choosing her words with great care. "Hers cannot be an unusual name."

"It is not a name, it is *she*," moaned Mr. Morrison. "Why did not I see it? You, Lucy Derrick, grown suddenly into a cunning woman. It was your friend who taught you what you know, wasn't it? It was she who put you on this path, on my path, was it not?"

"She encouraged me and she was my teacher. But your wife is dead. You said she is dead."

"She *is* dead," he cried, rising from his chair. "Have you not been listening even to your own words? Do you not understand of what we speak? She is a revenant. She is spirit made flesh. She has come back, in a fragile, immortal form, and it is she whom I seek. She is the one who has set Ludd against the future. Can you not understand the horror of my situation? I loved her and I lost her, and now I must destroy her again, forever. I must destroy her soul."

It was a mistake. It had to be. Mary, dead? Mary, a member of the very race she claimed to fight against? Lucy did not understand it. She could not even make herself think about it. Not now. Not yet. She had to restore some kind of order and meaning to the world.

He turned away from her, but Lucy knew it was her task to comfort him. In the past, he had treated her monstrously, but she had cast a spell so that he would cherish her, and surely in doing so she had inherited some responsibilities. She could not let him suffer like this.

As she approached, however, he spun around. "Dear Lord, how many times must I be humiliated? You cast love magic on me. You have been toying with me since — since Nottingham, the chocolate house. I see it all now."

He gave her no time to answer, which was for the best. There was nothing to say.

"You would use me so? I must endure this as well?" He paused for a moment, wiped his eyes with a handkerchief, and then looked at her, his expression as hard and cold as any she had ever seen of him. "I know you are angry for what you believed passed between us so many years ago. I know you are angry, and I know you are determined, but never did I think you cruel."

He left the room. She heard some forced conversation outside, and then the door shut. Beyond the other horrible feelings that swirled in her mind, Lucy understood that, in a capital on the threshold of revolution, she was now truly all alone without friends or protection. And yet, beyond all this, she thought that she had been exposed to Mr. Morrison, and he still did not recall that he had given her the pages of the book. She now possessed eight of the twelve pages, and to that one triumph she tried to cling, lest she collapse now in tears.

Lucy remained in that room, frightened and ashamed, unable to think of what to say or where to go. Mary was a revenant. She had lied to Lucy from their first meeting. She had tricked and manipulated her into ends Lucy could not now imagine. Lucy, who had felt friendless before, now felt utterly alone and without help.

Her coach to Nottingham had already departed, and she hardly knew what to do. She could arrange for another the next day, but would it be safe for her to travel the streets? What happened upon the streets? Was there violence and murder and riot? She did not know, and she hardly dared to ask her unwilling hosts for intelligence.

After perhaps an hour Mr. Gilley entered the room. Lucy now sat by the window, looking out upon the cool spring day. If Mr. Gilley noticed her distress, he did not trouble himself to acknowledge it.

"I trust we shan't have any more of your gentleman friends trouble us today? All this coming and going brings in chill air, which is very bad for the lungs."

Lucy did not turn her head. "I expect no more visitors."

"You will do me the courtesy of looking upon me while you are in my house."

Lucy turned to him. "I shall endeavor to try. I have missed my coach to Nottingham today. If the streets appear safe, I shall leave tomorrow."

"You shall leave tomorrow regardless," said Mr. Gilley. "I said you had three days to depart this house, and so you shall have."

"And you'll not trouble yourself if I step out into a riot."

"You chose to behave without restraint. I cannot answer for the consequences. I have my daughter to think of, and it cannot be to her benefit to see the parade of rakes you bring through our halls, and it could prove detrimental to my constitution as well." He rose, closed the door, and returned to her, sitting close upon the sofa. "However, as you are now of so generous a disposition as regards the favors of gentlemen, I think it may be possible for me to find a place to stay here in town, provided you are willing to be generous to me."

Mr. Gilley put his hand on Lucy's shoulder and smiled showing his very good teeth.

After all that had happened, Mr. Gilley's proposal filled her with neither fear nor disgust. If anything, she welcomed his blatant expression of desire, his open willingness to state his terms. And what he wanted, what he wished to trade, was of no matter. There were charms she could use to protect her as she walked through the bloody streets. She could make herself safe — she was sure of it. If not, she could alter things otherwise to her liking. Mr. Gilley might desire her now, but it would take relatively little effort to make him love her, and once he did, his demands would be more easily controlled. Or she could make herself invisible to him, or feared by him, or any of a thousand other things. Maybe she was alone and abandoned, but she was not helpless. She had felt helpless her entire life, but she would not feel helpless today.

Lucy looked up at him. "No, I don't believe I shall accept your offer. You may call me disgraced because my responsibilities de-manded I travel from your home without your leave or knowledge, but I have done no wrong. I can assure you, Mr. Gilley, if I could resist Lord Byron's charms, I shall have no difficulty resisting yours. Now, I beg you, remove your hand from my shoulder. You wish me gone by tomorrow, then all shall be as you wish. I shall tend to the coach, and if I must brave riot and mayhem, then so be it."

Her words, direct and calm, horrified him. He took a step back. "You are brazen."

She shook her head. "Shall you tell me so?"

"Perhaps not even another night under my

roof is acceptable," he said.

"As you like," she responded as she rose to her feet. She would give him no satisfaction. She had nothing to fear. His mind was not his own, but hers to use as she wished. She did not love to use magic to alter people's inclinations, but in this case, she would do so quite happily.

Just then came a knock upon the door, and Mr. Gilley's urbane serving man bowed by way of greeting. "Sir, I regret disturbing you, but the young lady has another caller."

"I can hardly affect surprise," said Mr. Gilley. "What manner of debauched devil shall we expect this time?"

"He is a rather plain-looking tradesman sort of fellow," said the servant, "and quite old."

"I do not think Miss Derrick is so discriminating as a young lady ought to be."

"What is the man's name?" Lucy asked.

"He gives his name as Mr. William Blake, an engraver."

Mr. Gilley made it known that he did not care for her welcoming more men into the house, let alone men of this Mr. Blake's sort, and that he had no interest in her turning his house into some sort of bagnio, but Lucy nevertheless prevailed upon him — more through silence than through words — to politely withdraw.

Though she had met him but briefly, and under curious conditions, Lucy was nevertheless delighted to see Mr. Blake once again. He was still little more than a stranger, but his was nevertheless a familiar face and a kindly one, and there were few enough of these in London now.

"We met at Newstead, so I would know you when the time came," Lucy said. "Is this the time?"

"I believe it is," said Mr. Blake with a great deal of good cheer. "It is very exciting."

He settled himself into his chair and looked about the room, but not with the wonder of a poor man in a rich man's abode. No, he gave every impression of watching things that were interesting but not unfamiliar. And his eyes suggested he watched things that moved.

"Miss Derrick, do you know what they are?"

"I beg your pardon, Mr. Blake. Do I know what *what* are?"

"Those creatures that swarm about you. They are unpleasant to look at. I am used to seeing far more beautiful things. There is no shortage of angels in London, you know, and there are other creatures far less grand. But these things are very unusual."

Lucy smiled indulgently. "I do not see them myself."

"No, I suppose not. You give every impression of being a lady who might, otherwise I would not ask. I know others do not see what I see, and I do not expect them to."

"One must be indulgent when your world is larger than that of those around you."

He nodded enthusiastically. "That is exactly right."

"Tell me, Mr. Blake, what can I do for you today? I am told that it is dangerous to travel just now, so something important must have occurred to bring you here. Why is this the time I am to know you?"

"The streets are tense in the wake of the assassination, but my brother Bob assured me I would be safe, and I have come to trust him."

"Is he in a position to know such things?" Lucy asked.

"He is dead, Miss Derrick, and sees with the eyes of the dead."

"Oh," she answered. She had seen too much herself to dismiss anything out of hand, but even so, this man strained her credulity just a little.

"In any event, it is on behalf of the dead that I have come here. There is a very urbane dead gentleman who has been rather insistent that I contact you. Because of my regular congress with Bob, I fear I may have developed a reputation among the dead as a man to whom it is easy to speak. None do so with as much facility as Bob, however, and I have had a hard time understanding what this

458

gentleman wants."

"He is a ghost, then, this dead gentleman, and not some kind of revenant?"

"What a silly question," said Mr. Blake. "If he were one of those revenants then he would hardly need my help in speaking to you."

"You know of them? The revenants?"

"Yes, the fairies. I used to think those little creatures that dance about the flowers were fairies, but it turns out they are a species of angel. The invisible world is very confusing."

"So is the visible one," said Lucy.

"Just so," agreed Mr. Blake. "But, as you say, this gentleman is in the spiritual realm. I do not know if he is a ghost, in the sense that he walks among the living. Rather, he has made his wishes known to me from another place."

"Well," said Lucy, in no mood to answer the commands of yet another pushing gentleman, urbane or not, dead or not. "Who is he and what does he wish?"

"He wishes for us to be friends," said Mr. Blake. "He believes you will need a place to stay, and he wishes that I offer you my modest home. As to who he is, young lady, he tells me his name is Francis Derrick, and that he is your father."

30

There were more questions than she had time to ask, let alone to hear answered. For now, Lucy's chief concern was to vacate Mr. Gilley's house. Though the news that this odd man was in communication with her father came as a surprise, it did not occur to her to doubt it. What struck Lucy above all things was that her father, though three years dead, still looked after her, still cared enough to attempt to help her, though the effort, according to Mr. Blake, of breaking through to our world was a great one.

Mr. Blake, however, conveyed information with an easy familiarity, and while he seemed to understand that most people did not regularly hold congress with the dead, he gave every impression of having grown complacently comfortable with such communication. He explained her father's words not with the deep intoning of a charlatan, but rather with the dull patience of a parent expressing the intentions of a child too shy to speak.

In the Gilleys' parlor, as Mr. Blake told Lucy of his conversations with her father, it became apparent that Mr. Blake considered a third person involved in their conversation. After some minutes, Lucy deduced this presence was the spirit of his brother, of whom Blake was clearly very fond. "Yes, Bob," he snapped. "I won't forget to tell her, but you must wait."

After hearing that her father wished her to accompany the old engraver to his home, Lucy concocted a plausible tale and went out of the room to find Mr. Gilley, who was conveniently nearby, posed as a man who had not been attempting to listen through the door.

"Mr. Blake is my late father's half brother," lied Lucy. "He has offered to provide shelter for me, as doing so for you either is too uncomfortable or comes for me at too high a cost. I would be most grateful if you could have my trunk sent to his address."

"You would be so bold as to walk out of my house?" asked Mr. Gilley.

"You have demanded I leave," answered Lucy.

To this Mr. Gilley had no easy answer, and it was while he stammered in want of a reply that Lucy slipped a talisman into his coat, one meant to make him susceptible to things he most feared. Lucy decided it was high time for Mr. Gilley to catch cold.

Mr. Blake lived on South Molton Street in a less fashionable part of town than where Mr. Gilley resided. The streets there were filthy with rubbish and animal waste, and crowded with workingmen and haggard women, but these were not the desperate streets of the worst parts of the city. These were the laboring poor, people with enough bread, if only just, and so while all was crowded and noisy and dirty, there was also a vibrancy in the air, as though everyone at every time had just been delivered from the terrible fate of being worse off than they were.

Blake's house was above his printing and engraving shop, which appeared a respectable if not entirely profitable enterprise. Lucy had arranged with Mrs. Emmett to arrive later with her things, and so she traveled to the house alone with the old man, a decision she wondered about during the whole of the journey. It ought to have seemed more dangerous and radical than she felt it to be, but the only trepidation and doubt she knew came from her head, not her heart.

When they arrived at his house, Lucy began at once to feel uneasy for Mr. Blake's peace. She had accepted the engraver's offer because she believed he meant her no harm and because he appeared, in all truth, to have been in communication with her father. Only as they arrived at the little house did it occur to her that she would be imposing upon a family.

"Are you married, Mr. Blake? Have you children?"

"My Catherine and I have not been blessed with children," he answered.

"Will your wife not object to your bringing home a stranger to live with you?"

"Should she?"

"No, only I mean, it is an unusual thing, is it not, to bring home a woman because a spirit asked you to do so?"

"Catherine and I have been together for almost thirty years. I hope she is accustomed to me by now."

Lucy need not have worried. Mrs. Blake had not been warned that there would be a houseguest, but nevertheless welcomed Lucy warmly. She was a sweet, plump woman, not at all tall, perhaps once pretty, but now well ravaged by age and the demands of a middling life in London. It took only a minute for Lucy to discern that she was absolutely devoted to her husband, and it would not occur to her to deny him anything. A strange young woman was no burden if it was Mr. Blake who asked that she take a place in their home.

Lucy's accommodations were not nearly what they had been at Mr. Gilley's house.

She had but a garret with a broadly sloping roof — clean, but small and narrow, and inclined to be drafty. Yet, she loved it, and when she sat upon her low, rather lumpy mattress, Lucy let out a breath of relief. The Blakes were not affluent — they appeared almost poor — but here, at last, she was in the company of people with whom she did not have to pretend. She could say anything to them, for nothing would sound so strange as what they said to her.

Within two hours, Mrs. Emmett arrived with her luggage. When Lucy introduced her to Mr. Blake, the engraver examined her with a peculiar expression. "I've never seen one such as you," he said.

"Nor I one such as you," answered Mrs. Emmett.

"We shall have to talk, I think," he said.

"We shall mean to do so," said Mrs. Emmett, "and yet never will."

"Yes," said Mr. Blake. "That *is* true, isn't it?"

And with that, the two peculiar people seemed at ease with each other.

Once Lucy was settled, Mr. Blake invited her for tea alone in his sitting room. She sipped nervously, and took none of the macaroons he offered her, though she was usually very fond of macaroons.

"You must have many questions," said Mr. Blake.

"Tell me about my father," she said.

He nodded, and then nodded to someone invisible. "He is not himself with us. It is only Bob, who has been a helpful intermediary in this matter. The dead are difficult to hear, Miss Derrick, though they hear one another better than we hear them. Your father has tried to speak to you, but he cannot reach you. It is much easier for him to speak to Bob, even though Bob inhabits our realm, not theirs."

Lucy felt the tears build in her eyes. Her father had tried to reach her and she could not hear. She felt as though her heart must break.

"There is no deficiency in you," said Mr. Blake, who appeared to understand her grief. "Do not think so. It is not a matter of will or love or openness. To hear the dead, even those who dwell near us, you must be . . . different. I have always been as I am. When I was a boy, my mother had to keep my father from beating me as a liar after I spoke of seeing angels in the trees. I soon learned to keep such observations to myself, for I understood, even at that age, that the things I saw could not be seen by others."

Lucy nodded. "What does my father tell you?"

"He has almost as much difficulty seeing our world as we have seeing his. There is something you must do, but he cannot yet see what. He wishes you to stay here with me until he can see it. He will then tell me when he can. He also says things of people in your circle. He says one you must trust entirely, another not at all."

"He does not say which is which?"

Mr. Blake shook his head and smiled knowingly. "The dead, even when they mean well, can be rather a pain in the arse."

Within a day it became apparent that there was not going to be any revolution in England and no blood flowing through the streets of the capital. This was certainly good news, but the newspaper Mr. Blake brought home contained its share of troubling news. The assassin was revealed as a madman named John Bellingham. It took Lucy a moment to recognize the name, but then she recalled it was the man she had met at Lady Harriett's house the night she was captured. And Mary had told Lucy that she had taken him away and set him free in London. Mary had, in effect, played a hand in a plot to murder the prime minister.

Lucy could not believe it. Even if her cause was just, how could Mary condone such an act? It was monstrous. On the one side, the Rosicrucians and the revenants and their mills and machines; on the other, the Luddites and the old order — and now murder and treason. There had to be a third way, a better way. If only she could think of it and make Mary see reason. Of course, Lucy did not know if she would ever see Mary again, and now that Mr. Perceval was dead, she did not know that she could have any sway over the Rosicrucians, so even if she could think of a third way, she did not know that there was anything to do with the knowledge.

As for Mr. Bellingham, Lucy believed him to be no more than a madman, manipulated by Mary and her faction. According to what she read, he was angered because of an unjust imprisonment in Russia, for which he believed the British government owed him compensation. Somehow he had been convinced that his best course of action was to kill the prime minister. Justice for Bellingham was swift and terrible, and two days after the murder he was tried at the Old Bailey, where he offered scant explanation for his act but the misery he felt. He was found guilty and sentenced to hang the following Monday.

Mr. Blake, for his part, understood without Lucy telling him that Bellingham had been manipulated by the different invisible factions that now waged their war. Those who are called madmen are much more susceptible to magic, he said, for madness is often nothing more than an openness to the world around them, the world not governed by the cold logic of Bacon and Newton and Locke. These names he spoke with virulent contempt, and it seemed to Lucy that Mr. Blake hated nothing so much as he hated the very idea of reason.

"It is all well and good to apply reason to business plans or a mode of education or a voyage to Italy. One must live in the world after all. But reason, when applied to the universe, to the wonders of nature, to the things hidden from our poor eyes that see not all, but only what the Lord intended that they see — well, that becomes nonsense, doesn't it? To say there are no ghosts because we cannot see them, cannot measure them, cannot weigh them upon scales nor note their reaction to heat in a flask — I hardly see the point of such a mode of inquiry. The world is full of wonders that cannot be measured. That is why they are wonders."

For her first three days at Mr. Blake's house, Lucy was left mostly to herself as she studied the new pages of the *Mutus Liber,* but unlike the earlier pages, these two had no clear content she could divine. She quieted herself and attempted to become lost within the images, and yet she could find nothing of use. While Lucy came away with clear notions of elements — gold, sulfur, and mercury — to what purpose these elements could be put, she had no idea. She presumed it had something to do with the production of the philosopher's stone, but that was mere guesswork. Even so, she thought it best to have such elements upon her in the event the meaning should become clear or subsequent pages tell her what she needed to know. In one of her few excursions out of the house, she visited an apothecary and acquired vials of sulfur and mercury, and she visited a goldsmith, where she purchased a small quantity of gold dust.

She also spent a great deal of time thinking about Byron. He had said she must come to him, and she wanted to. She longed to. She thought about what it had been like to kiss him. Over and over she relived the memory in her mind, recalling every detail, sometimes adding to it something she might have done or he might have said until she could not easily recall what had been real and what her imagination.

She wanted to go to him. Each morning she woke and thought that she would, but by the time she had dressed and eaten, she understood that her desire was but a dreamy absurdity. She had no real home, no protection, and she dared not put herself in his power. If he would but make a proposal of marriage all would be well, but he had not done so.

Instead of running to Byron, she contented herself with conversations with the Blakes, particularly on the subject of what she must do next. Lucy needed to find the remaining pages of the *Mutus Liber* if she was to rescue her niece, but she had no notion at all of where to look. With Mr. Morrison having discovered her treachery, no one could tell her. One evening while they talked of this and drank weak tea, Mr. Blake fell into a reflective quiet for some time. Lucy and Mrs. Blake spoke of other matters for half an hour when Mr. Blake appeared to start awake and interrupted them without ceremony.

"Miss Derrick, your father is of the opinion that you must look to your inheritance."

Lucy felt her entire body tense. She had told the Blakes nothing of that circumstance. She knew she would have to look to it at some point, but now she had more important things with which to concern herself. In any case, Mary had described the matter as hopeless.

Even if, to further her own mysterious ends, Mary had lied, was her inheritance the most important matter at this moment? Why would her father ask her to look to it? Perhaps by proving Mr. Buckles's forgery Lucy could more quickly disrupt Lady Harriett's plans. Was she implicated in the forgery as well? Lucy did not think she would be able to attack Lady Harriett with the laws of the land. For now, she had no choice but to wait and hope to learn more.

So taken was Mr. Blake with Lucy that he

insisted he show her some of his work, so in the bright light of the next morning, he led her down to his shop and began to put into her hands some of his astonishing books — *Songs of Innocence and of Experience, The Marriage of Heaven and Hell, Milton.* Lucy had never seen a book of poetry like this. It was a swirling, vibrant mixture of image and word. Even the text was engraved, and letter and image interwove until one became the other, and she could hardly say where one began and the other ended. It was seamless and elegant and chaotic and maddening.

Yet, as beautiful and eerie and moving as was his art, this is not what struck Lucy most. When she looked at his engravings, Lucy felt as though some unseen hand slid the final piece of a puzzle in place. She felt elation and fear and an insatiable curiosity. "It is time that I show you something, Mr. Blake," she said.

Lucy went upstairs and retrieved her pages from the *Mutus Liber.* She brought them down and then spread them before Mr. Blake without any semblance of ceremony. They were simply there for his inspection.

Blake looked them over, running his fingers along the images, carefully noting the details. He shifted one, held another up to the light. A third he sniffed.

"Remarkable," he said at last.

"They appear very much like your own

work," Lucy said to him.

He nodded. "They do indeed. I would go so far as to say that they are my own work."

Lucy sat down, uncertain how to understand this new information. She had always believed Mary when she said the images dated from the seventeenth century. There was no reason to lie about such a thing, surely. Besides, Mr. Morrison had told her the same thing, had he not? Certainly it was possible that he had received false information, that they both had. Lucy found it easier to believe that Mary would lie than that she would be mistaken, but there was no reason why she could not simply be wrong about something.

"Do you know anything of alchemy?" Lucy asked Mr. Blake.

He shook his head. "Nothing out of the common way."

"Have you ever sought the philosopher's stone, the secret to life immortal?"

He smiled. "I already possess the secret to life immortal, Miss Derrick. It is called Jesus Christ. I need not seek another."

Lucy closed her eyes. If these pages were not part of some mystic book, but merely the clever engravings of an affable if deranged craftsman, then everything she had done was for nothing. Lucy could not believe that. These pages were real. They radiated power and energy and a magnetic force. Lucy felt that these pages were, in some fundamental way, *magic,* whatever that meant. They were, for want of a better way of expressing it, half wedged in that invisible world of wonders that Mr. Blake claimed to know so well.

She turned to him. "When did you engrave these, sir?"

He was still examining them with minute interest. "I don't believe I have."

"But you told me they are yours."

"Oh, they are certainly mine. I know this technique. I know it well, Miss Derrick. Do you know when I learned it? It was shortly after my brother Bob died, and I fell into the deepest and most terrible grief. Of all my brothers, he is the one I have always loved best, and I feared I should never see him again until I left this mortal realm. I was so distraught I did not even attend his funeral. You must think that unfeeling."

Lucy recalled the misery of her father's and sister's funerals. "I think no such thing."

"I could not endure that I should be made to grieve as others expected, that my grief must be a scripted and public spectacle, a stage play as much as an experience. I stayed at home. Then, only a few days later, Bob appeared before me. I had been having many difficulties in my work, unable to figure out a technique for combining text and image in the manner I wished. Bob told me how to do it. He invented this technique I now use. I did not know what to do, and then Bob appeared, explained it, and lo, I knew what to do."

Lucy smiled. "It is the most literal experience of *inspiration* I have ever heard."

Mr. Blake looked at her, as if seeing her for the first time.

"Mr. Blake," she said, "I am confused. You say these are your engravings, and yet you say you have not done them."

"I am confused as well." He appeared more amused than anything else. "I have never made these engravings, and yet they are unmistakably mine. I have no followers in my mode of engraving, and even if I did, no one could imitate my style so well that I would not detect it."

"I was told," she said, attempting to show no emotion, "that these drawings originate from the seventeenth century in La Rochelle."

Blake examined them again. "I see nothing particularly French in them, but the paper is certainly aged. There is nothing in these to say that they are not from such a time and place."

"Mr. Blake, I do not think you are near two hundred years old."

"I thank you."

"How is it, then, that these pages can be?"

"I cannot answer that. I can only surmise that at some point in my future, either I or my work shall be in seventeenth-century France."

"That is nonsense," said Lucy.

"No," he corrected. "We know where the pages come from and we know they are my work. It is not nonsense. It is evident. You say it is nonsense because reason tells us that I cannot ever go to seventeenth-century France, but once again that is the reason of Locke and Bacon and Newton. That is the reason of Satan and hell. You cannot doubt your own experience of the world because your reason tells you that your own experience must be wrong."

Lucy rose and looked out the window of the shop. The day was overcast but not gloomy. She had not yet been outside, and she suddenly felt cramped and constrained, as though she needed fresh air. She turned back to Mr. Blake to announce that she wished to take a walk, but saw that he was very much absorbed in one of the engravings.

"Tell me," he said to her, "who is Mr. Buckles?"

For days Lucy had wanted to go to Byron, but she'd dared not. Now, it seemed, she did not have a choice, for she needed his help. Her father had made it clear to Bob that Lucy must journey to Harrington, her childhood home, for there were pages there. And he had made it clear that she must not travel alone. She would need an escort, and Mrs. Emmett would not do. She required a man who had proved himself, which could only mean Byron.

There was no one else to ask, so Lucy traveled to Byron's house to beg him to take her once more to Kent, this time to the home of Mr. Buckles, where Mr. Blake insisted she might find more pages of the book.

Because her reputation had been damaged, and because she must be vulnerable if she entered his house alone, Mr. Blake agreed to accompany her. They arrived at Byron's London house to discover a string of young ladies loitering on the walk, hoping to capture the baron's attention. It was a beautiful spring day, sunny and bright, with enough of a breeze to offer comfort. There could be no better weather to stand outside a man's home, Lucy supposed, though she could not imagine why they did so. Each of these ladies clutched her copy of an identical volume.

Lucy approached one of the women, a girl with heavy features and sallow skin, but whose eyes shone with bright hope.

"I want to see him," she said to Lucy. "I want only to see him. His work has so moved me, if I may see him and impose upon him to speak to me, I know he will love me."

"What has caused all this fuss?" asked Lucy, astonished.

"You do not know?" This lady seemed as confused by Lucy's surprise as Lucy had been by the lady's ardor. "You have not read it, then?" She held out her book.

Lucy took the book and examined it and discovered it to be the newly published volume of the poem *Childe Harold's Pilgrimage.* "He told me he thought it was remarkable. I see you think so too."

"He *told* you," the young lady repeated. "You know Lord Byron?"

"I know him well," she answered, implying much if saying little.

"He will see you?" the lady asked.

"I believe so," Lucy answered.

"Will you bring me inside with you?"

Lucy smiled indulgently. "It is not for me to invite strangers into his house."

"You are wicked not to share him," she answered.

"Would you share him?"

"I imagine not."

Lucy pushed past the girls and rang the bell. In a moment, a fatigued-looking servant answered.

"Please tell Lord Byron that Miss Lucy Derrick desires a word. I am unlike these other ladies in that he knows me."

The serving man appeared skeptical, but agreed to relay the message. He returned and allowed Lucy and Mr. Blake inside. They had remained in a sitting room for nearly an hour when Lord Byron at last appeared in a dress-ing gown, his hair looking quite wild. In one hand he held a goblet of wine which he swirled carelessly. He took another step, and Lucy observed his movements were stiff and controlled, like that of a drunkard attempting to disguise his impairment.

"Ah, Miss Derrick. You've come to call, and you've brought me an old tradesman. How thoughtful."

Lucy felt shame wash over her. Mr. Blake's expression did not change, but she could not endure that she had brought him here to be so thoughtlessly insulted. Byron was his own man and lived by his own rules, but he had never before been rude to her without cause.

Lucy took a breath to steady herself. Per-haps it was simply her imagination. Perhaps he was not being so cruel as it appeared or his drunkenness only seemed to her like rudeness. "Mr. Blake has been kind enough to attend me. I must ask something of you, Lord Byron."

"Must you now?" he asked. He began to pace leisurely about the room. "You know, since we last spoke, the first portion of my poem has been published. It has proved very popular with the ladies."

"I observed that," Lucy said. The anger began to build inside her. He had no cause to speak to her this way. No cause, and after all the things he had declared. It was unfor-givable.

"Yes, I have two or three of them upstairs just now, and there is an endless stream of new ones at the door. Some prettier than oth-ers, so one must be careful to choose wisely."

Lucy's cheeks burned with indignation. She might have, from time to time, allowed herself to believe that Byron was a more honorable man than her experience suggested. She may have, on occasion, indulged in the fantasy that he would reform and ask her to marry him. She had known these thoughts were flights of the imagination, and yet they had seemed close enough to reality that they had been worth indulging in. But even if she had not deceived herself, and she had never taken Byron for anything but what he so clearly was, this behavior would have been unforgiv-able. "I wish to know why you would speak to me in this fashion. Are you under another curse that makes you act so?"

He laughed theatrically, throwing back his head. "A curse? No. It is but literary success that makes me act as I do. I am free now to treat all as I like and as they deserve, and that includes you, though you would believe you are owed something out of the common way."

"What have I done to deserve this rude-ness?"

Byron coughed out something like a laugh.

"What have you done? I asked you to come to me. I *begged* you, and you did not come. Do you think I beg others? You ignored me when I wanted you because it was not convenient for Lucy Derrick — the great Lucy Derrick — to call upon a mere mortal such as Lord Byron. I saved your life. I took blows for you — blows to the face — but does that impress you? Does that instill in you any sense of obligation? No, you are too busy with your gods and spirits and monsters to trouble yourself with me."

"You must understand the difficulties of a young lady in my circumstances —"

"The devil take your circumstances!" he cried, and flung his goblet against the wall. The glass shattered, and the wine sprayed out like blood. He went to the mantel above the fireplace and swept away all the pottery in a wild, angry thrust, sending a wave of ragged pieces washing across the floor. "The devil take *you.* Do you think the ladies who queue up at my house trouble themselves about their reputations? No, but Lucy Derrick will not be moved by love."

Lucy was too astonished even to speak. Could it be that he really thought this so? Could he really not understand what motivated her? How self-absorbed, how childish he must be to condemn her. It was horribly shameful that this drama must play out before Mr. Blake, and Lucy dared a glance at him, but he only continued to smile blankly.

"I'd thought better of you, Lord Byron," she said quietly.

"Oho! I've disappointed you, have I? Tell me, why did you come here today? Did you wish to see me, to spend time with me, as I begged you to? I think not. Or rather, did you wish to ask me to take you somewhere, accompany you on another of your adventures?"

"That is why I came," said Lucy, her voice betraying her uncertainty.

"That is why you came," he echoed. "You wished more from me. After all I have done, what have I received in return? Nothing!"

"Lord Byron —" Lucy began.

He would not let her speak. "Nothing!" he cried again. "I have done and done and done for you, and you have only trifled with my feelings. Those women who come to my house ask for nothing in return. I cannot imagine why I should not enjoy their company rather than enduring yours."

Lucy's face was now set hard. "Because you claim to care for me. Because a gentleman ought to aid a lady he cares for without demanding she turn whore in compensation."

"It is a convenient arrangement for you, I'll wager."

Lucy turned to Mr. Blake. "Come sir, let us go."

Mr. Blake rose and smiled at Byron, but it

481

was a chilling smile.

They left the house, Lucy tense with rage. Could she have been so wrong about Byron? Had she allowed herself to misunderstand his beauty as goodness? She did not know. She only knew that now, other than Mr. Blake, she was utterly without allies in London.

31

Mr. Blake was a remarkable man. There was no denying that. He saw things and knew things that no ordinary man could see or know, but he was old and eccentric and, Lucy believed, somewhat unpredictable. She would hate to ask a man of his age to accompany her on a dangerous adventure, and all the more so when she could not know if she might rely upon him. All of which meant that she now did not know how to proceed. Mr. Blake said Lucy's father wanted her to seek pages of the *Mutus Liber* at Harrington, her childhood home, but she could not go alone. She had not the money to travel, and she could not ask Mr. Blake, who was poor, to help her in that regard.

That night, after Lucy had picked at her dinner of roast chicken and parsnips, she sat by the fire with Mr. Blake. Mrs. Blake had gone to bed, and now Lucy sat with the engraver opposite her, also with his side to the fire. Across the room, Mrs. Emmett sat with her head slumped, snoring noisily.

Lucy stared at the flames while Mr. Blake told her about the curious mythology that spread throughout his many books. He told her stories that seemed dreamlike and allegorical and yet, strangely not, filled with curious names and a pantheon that evoked classical sources as well as the Bible. Lucy could not keep the names or the struggles clear, but the stories were infused with the themes that preoccupied Mr. Blake: the fight of the human spirit against the oppression of cruel and unnatural law and custom, and the struggle of divine truth against satanic reason. Even if the details eluded her, Lucy took pleasure in the enthusiasm in Mr. Blake's voice, and she admired, even envied, his excitement at his own creation.

It was a testament to Mr. Blake's comforting presence, not a sign of failure as a storyteller, that Lucy found herself drifting toward slumber in the comfortable armchair by the fire. She was not quite asleep, but in a state where Mr. Blake's words took on strange and unpredictable meanings, and she drifted slightly away from herself.

Then Mr. Blake was silent, and Lucy snapped awake. There was another person in the room, sitting in a chair once empty, directly across from Lucy and Mr. Blake, and farthest from the fire. Lucy blinked twice, unable to credit what she saw, for it was Ludd himself. She had not before seen him so clearly or so directly. The room was well lit, and he did not seem to twinkle in and out of existence as he had the previous times she'd gazed upon him, and yet he did not seem to be entirely there either. He was not transparent or insubstantial, the way one might suppose a ghost to look. It was more that looking at him was like looking into a fire. She could not look long, for it strained and clouded her eyes, and she found it was most comfortable to look at him from the corners of her eyes.

Mr. Blake appeared to have no such difficulty. Lucy could see that he stared at him directly, and he blinked in wide-eyed astonishment.

Mrs. Emmett was awake now, and she too had no trouble gazing upon him. "Look at that," she said, as though observing a dog doing a remarkable trick. "How unexpected."

"All depends upon you," Ludd said to Lucy.

"Can you think I don't know it?" she answered. The bitterness of her own voice surprised her.

"I hope you do," Ludd said in his unaccountable, shifting voice. "I hope you comprehend what happens if you fail. I may fail. You may not."

"We do not stand for the same cause," said Lucy. "You arranged for Mr. Perceval's death. You hoped to cause the death of hundreds more in rebellion and unrest."

"We thought it necessary," Ludd said. "We failed. Now your role is even more important."

"What shall happen if Miss Derrick does not stand with you?" asked Mr. Blake.

"Death," said Ludd. "Blood. Machines. Enslavement. An end to everything you love. An end to all that tempers Lady Harriett and her kind. An end to England as any of us have understood it."

"There must be another way," said Lucy. "A way for the machines and the magic to coexist." She did not know how strongly she believed this until she spoke it. "That is my cause. Peace and compromise. That is the third way."

"There can be no peace while Lady Harriett lives," Ludd said. "You must destroy her for there to be peace, and if you compromise, how can you destroy her?"

"Then what do you suggest I do?" asked Lucy.

She asked it to an empty chair.

Lucy was on her feet in an instant, walking about the room as though Ludd might somehow, absurdly, be hiding somewhere.

"Damn them!" Lucy cried, hardly caring how wanton she sounded. Then, after a moment, she said, "Forgive me, Mr. Blake."

"No forgiveness is required," he answered with his customary ease.

"I am so frustrated!" Lucy cried out, feeling like a petulant child. It was the unfairness of it all that drove her mad. "Why can they never speak plainly? Why can they never tell me what must be? Why are they always so opaque and vague and maddening?"

Mr. Blake smiled at her. "You must be patient with them, Lucy. Our world is as difficult for them to see as theirs is for us. That creature did not seek to vex you. It struggled mightily to be clear, but you were just as slippery and evasive to it as it was to you."

This notion startled Lucy, but it also comforted her. It made her feel better to know that at least Ludd was not toying with her.

"I must go to Harrington. I must go to Mr. Buckles's home and take possession of whatever it is he has."

"Yes," Blake said.

"Oh, yes," Mrs. Emmett agreed. "Your father does not wish for you to go alone, so why not ask his brother to accompany you?"

Lucy stared at the woman in surprise. "He had no brother. My Uncle Lowell would never do such a thing for me, and in any case, he is no blood relative, but my mother's sister's husband."

"Not that," she corrected. "Not his brother of blood, but of fellowship. His brother of the Rosy Cross."

Lucy stared at her in wonder and confusion. She felt as though the very floor upon which she stood bucked and twisted wildly. "What do you say, Mrs. Emmett? My father was a Rosicrucian? He was in the same order as Jonas Morrison?"

"Oh, yes," said Mrs. Emmett. "Can you not hear him say so? They were fond of each other. Your father regarded Mr. Morrison as though he were his son."

Lucy sat down heavily in her chair. After all that had happened, after all she had seen, this revelation astonished her more than any of the rest. Everything Lucy knew about her own life, it seemed, was a lie.

Mr. Blake agreed to escort Lucy to Mr. Morrison's house, but he sensed Lucy's somber mood, and rode over in complete silence, his hands in his lap, a sympathetic smile on his lips. Lucy did not wish for him to be there, and she regretted the necessity of an escort. She did not want anyone to witness the confusion and abasement she would be certain to undergo. But there was no helping it. She could not sacrifice her duty for her pride.

Lucy had never before been to Mr. Morrison's town house, had never even seen it, but he was a man of means, and it was never difficult to learn where a rich man lives. She and Mr. Blake called at his house at two in the afternoon and could only hope that he would be home. Whatever Lucy must face, it would be less horrible than her treatment at the hands of Byron. To some degree she knew that Byron had been lashing out, feeling nothing more complicated than frustration. If she had learned anything about him it was that he was childlike in his belief both that his desires ought to be satisfied the moment he felt them, and that he was justified expressing himself in any way he chose. Whatever she had imagined to be her feelings for him now seemed empty and foolish. She had been a fool. She knew that now. Perhaps she had known it all along, and she condemned herself for it.

Lucy was nervous to the point of shaking as she and Mr. Blake were shown into the sitting room. A middle-aged woman of no discernible expression informed them that Mr. Morrison was engaged, but he would be with them when he became available. No doubt he would make Lucy wait longer than necessary. He would wish to punish her, to show that he was not at her disposal, and perhaps even to postpone the unpleasantness of their conversation.

The woman showed them to a pleasant room to endure this waiting. It caught much of the afternoon light, and there were two bookcases filled with innocuous novels, volumes of poetry — mostly of the last century — and some popular history. Upon the walls were paintings of nondescript gentlemen, a landscape of a boy leading a horse across a river, and a ship sailing toward a Mediterranean-looking port. The furnishings were comfortable but unadorned. It was, in short, a room designed to give the impression that Mr. Morrison was a man of mundane taste and an utter lack of imagination.

Mr. Blake took a few moments to examine the contents of one of the bookshelves, and finally settled upon a volume of Milton, which he brought to a chair by the window. He gave every impression of wishing to make himself invisible.

Lucy paced. She attempted to find a book to look at, but as the titles could not hold her attention, she very much doubted an open book would serve as a better distraction. After waiting for half an hour, Lucy heard footsteps outside the door, and when they passed without entering, she breathed a sigh of relief. She would have preferred to wait in that room indefinitely than to start the conversation she came to have. When Mr. Morrison did, after perhaps an hour, enter the room, he appeared flustered and hurried. His hair was messy, as though windblown, and his cravat was soiled, suggesting he had not found time to refresh himself since returning from a journey. Perhaps it was her feelings of guilt for how she had used him, and perhaps it was Mrs. Emmett's revelation that he and her father had been Rosicrucians together, but for the first time since he had appeared at the Nottingham assembly, Lucy did not feel revulsion when she looked at him.

Mr. Blake rose, and Lucy made the necessary introductions between the two men.

"Mr. Blake," said Mr. Morrison. "You are very good to look after Miss Derrick."

"And you, sir," replied Mr. Blake. "Though it is not well known, your service to this country in the matter of —"

Mr. Morrison clapped the old engraver upon his back. "Those sorts of things are not meant to be generally known. Just as the world does not generally know of your particular talents, though they have come to the attention of my order. I hope you will not object if we call upon you from time to time for some small service."

"So long as the service is just," said Mr. Blake.

"Of course. I would not ask otherwise." He now turned to Lucy. "You must tell me what you want," he intoned. His face was stony, his eyes distant.

Lucy had not precisely rehearsed what she was going to say, but she knew what points she wished to make. Now that he was here, she could not think of any of them. She could not remember the logic of her arguments or the turns of phrase that, when uttered in her mind, sounded eloquent and masterful, certainly convincing. She rose, clasped her hands together, and forced herself to speak while trying very hard not to weep.

"Mr. Morrison, I cannot blame you for hating me. I cannot, but I beg you to listen to me, to attempt to hear my words without color or prejudice of the wrong I have done you."

He shook his head. "No, Miss Derrick. You misunderstand me. I mean to say that you must tell me what you want, and I shall do my best for you."

Lucy was too stunned to answer.

"You are a young lady with no money and no influence," Mr. Morrison continued. "You have been drawn into events of national and historical significance against your will, and your sister and her child have been made to suffer. I do not like being used as you used me, and my anger when I first discovered it stemmed in no small part from simple humiliation. Nevertheless, I cannot blame you for using what tools you had at your disposal. This is your war as well as mine, and I admire you for your boldness, though I fell victim to it."

Lucy could have endured his harsh words and held her tears in check, but this was more than she could withstand. The tears fell now freely, and though she removed a handkerchief to wipe them away, she made no other effort to stop them.

Mr. Blake, meanwhile, retreated back to his chair and his volume of Milton. Lucy and Mr. Morrison moved to the far corner of the room. This would have to do for privacy.

"I had not expected such kindness," she said in a very quiet voice.

"I gave you no reason to expect it," he said. "For that I am sorry. Now I shall offer you what assistance I can."

"But why?" Lucy asked. Her tears began to abate, though the effect of his words still reverberated through her. The sense of palpable, overwhelming gratitude was dizzying. "Why would you help me? You must know that we are on different sides of this conflict. I must side with — with Ludd — if I am to save my sister's child."

"No," he said. "Mr. Perceval was a good man, and he led the order as he thought best, but he was wrong in his truce with Lady Harriett. We were prepared to sacrifice too much for expedience, but no longer. The new head of the order believes that there is another way, a compromise position."

"Who is this man?"

"I am he," said Mr. Morrison. "The matter has just now been put to a vote, and I have been elected to this position, for which I am unworthy. It is unusual that one as young as myself would be offered this post, but I have an advantage none of the others could claim."

"And what is that?"

"My friendship with you."

Lucy could not imagine why that should prove an advantage, but even more shocking was his characterization of what stood between them as friendship.

"What do I . . . ?" Lucy did not know how to finish the question.

"You have the pages," he said with a half smile. "You had me turn my own pages over to you. Surely you did not think I would not discover your little mesmeric trick, deft though it was. And, again, I do not blame you. You did what you believed right, and now we believe it right as well."

"I cannot think that your order cares only to save my niece," said Lucy.

"We care whenever there is an innocent in harm's way and we are in a position to save him. But our interests are now aligned, I believe. Ludd and Lady Harriett are poised each to destroy the other, but we believe that an absolute victory of the old way or the new need not happen. We believe that a compromise position that will place a check on the new mechanical developments and allow magic to survive is our best option. And we believe you are the key to that approach."

"In what way?" Lucy asked, not much liking this new burden.

He shook his head. "That is the central mystery, isn't it? I can tell you that since all of this has begun, Lady Harriett, my order,

and" — here he paused — "and Mary Crawford have all understood your centrality. Accordingly, I place myself at your disposal."

"At my disposal how?" asked Lucy, staring
at Mr. Morrison as though he were a stranger
she had never seen before, dressed in some
curious foreign costume.

"At your disposal to go where you wish and
do what you say. I am here to obey your commands, Miss Derrick."

Lucy continued to stare at him for some
minutes, blinking rapidly as she considered
his words. "Then let us go to Kent. I believe
there is a set of pages in the hands of my
sister's husband, Mr. Buckles."

"Then we shall go fetch them," he said.

"There is something else." Lucy looked out
the window as she spoke, unwilling to gaze
upon his expression when he heard what she
had to say. "Was my father, like you, a Rosicrucian? I would know, if you do not mind,
the story of my own life."

Mr. Morrison sat across from her, slumped
forward, his hands dangling between his
knees. He appeared utterly defeated by her
request. He glanced over at Mr. Blake, and
observed that the old engraver sat with the
book on his lap, his mouth open, conveniently
asleep.

Mr. Morrison spoke in quiet tones. "Your
father wished it all kept from you, and after

everything that happened, it never seemed the proper moment to reveal those secrets. I suppose it is the right moment now. Yes, your father was a member of the order. He led the order when I joined. He and I were very close. I thought of him as a father."

Lucy hardly knew how to understand this. "But you chose to corrupt his daughter?"

Mr. Morrison looked away, and then rose, walked to the window, where he adjusted the curtains, and then returned to his seat. "Your father always knew you were special. There were certain card and crystal readings around the time of your birth that alarmed him, and he believed you needed to be sheltered from your own natural talents, which he believed would be too conspicuous. This moment of transition we live in has been long coming, and your father suspected if you were to practice, dark forces would seek you out. That is why he kept you at a distance before Emily died — not because he did not love you, but because he wished to protect you. He wanted that you might live a life free of danger."

"Then why did you attempt to convince me to run off with you?"

Mr. Morrison let out a long sigh. He shook his head and looked away, and then down. "Your father and I had a disagreement. We received intelligence that there would be an attempt upon your life, but he did not believe it, or he did not believe it was something from which he could not protect you. He was not careless with his daughters — you must never think that — but just the opposite. He was so careful, he believed such wards and spells and precautions that he had taken were impregnable. I was less optimistic. I believed there was danger, particularly to you, for Emily could take care of herself."

"What do you mean?" asked Lucy, hearing her voice catch.

"You must know what I mean. Emily practiced. She was very skillful. Your father taught her everything he knew, and she was widely regarded as something of a prodigy, though she lacked the raw talent he believed you to possess."

Lucy could not think of what there was to say. Her father had been a hermeticist, a Rosicrucian, and her sister his apprentice. They had studied magic together, the two of them, locked in his study, as Lucy was later to do — or begin to do. All those books he had her read, the philosophers, the languages, the botany. He had been laying the groundwork for what Lucy would later become. It was all so clear now.

"As the time drew closer," Mr. Morrison continued, "as the hour of danger approached, I became convinced that you would die if you did not leave. I had to get you away, if only for a little while, until the danger passed."

Lucy looked at him. His eyes were cast down, his face was red.

"And so you pretended to love me?"

"I needed you to go with me," he said. "If I told you a tale of magic and spells and curses, you would have laughed at me. I needed you to want to go."

"Then, what you did — you were not being cruel. All this time I have spent hating you, thinking you horrible, and you said nothing. Why did you say nothing?" Lucy felt herself growing angry again. He had let her hate him when she should have regarded him as her friend. She hardly knew where her anger belonged, but it balled up inside her, threatening to explode.

"Your father never forgave himself for being wrong, but he was, and your sister paid the price for it. The curse meant for you found her, and it killed her."

Lucy sat still and silent, hearing nothing but the rushing of blood in her ears. It came on her, wave after wave, grief and rage and anger and loathing for herself. "Emily died, when it should have been me."

"No!" Mr. Morrison jumped to his feet. "No, damn it. Can you not understand? Your father did not want you to know, not because he feared you would blame him. He blamed himself sufficiently that he needed no aid. He never wanted you to know because he feared you would blame yourself. He feared you would see it in that absurd way. You did not know, and you could have done nothing. It should not have been you. It should not have been either of you. She was murdered and it is no one's fault but the murderer's." When Lucy said nothing, he sat down again and took her hands in both of his. "Can you not see that?"

She nodded. "Who was it? Who killed my sister?"

"The leader of the revenants."

It was Lucy's turn to rise to her feet. "Lady Harriett killed my sister, and you struck a deal with her?"

He shook his head. "Lady Harriett was not then leader. She took that post after the death of her husband, Sir Reginald. He had led them for centuries before he died. Before I killed him."

"You?" said Lucy, sitting slowly.

"Out of love for your father, I did what needed doing. They had done the unpardonable, and a message had to be sent. I destroyed him."

"Then you know how to kill them."

"My order has known for a long time, and that knowledge had led to our truce."

"You must tell me," whispered Lucy.

"I cannot. I have taken an oath to guard the secret. It is a simple thing, a mixture of common elements, but the nature of these elements is something I cannot reveal."

Lucy's understanding came into such sharp focus, it was like a slap across her face. "Gold, mercury, and sulfur," she said.

Mr. Morrison's eyes went wide. He said nothing, but he did not have to. His closely guarded secret was now Lucy's.

Lucy kept moving her hands, not quite sure what to do with them, putting them on her knees, winding them together, stroking her chin. There was so much to think about. Mr. Morrison had not been an unrepentant rake all those years ago. He had tried to help her, the only way he could think of. Her father had not suddenly decided he loved her, but he had loved her all along, wanting only to protect her from the terrible dangers posed by her own nature. He had made an error, a terrible, catastrophic error, and Emily had paid the price. So much had gone wrong, and now it was Lucy's lot to set it right. Everything that she had ever done, or that had been done to her, had happened along the path — the crooked, winding, back-turning path — to her destiny.

"And what of Mary Crawford?" asked Lucy, with some trepidation. She did not wish to alarm Mr. Morrison by again mentioning her name, but she had to know. "Is she my friend? Can I depend upon her?"

"No," Mr. Morrison said, his face utterly without expression, his voice entirely flat. "She is dead, and she is no one's friend. She lies. Her kind always lies, Lucy. Never forget it."

"And what has she lied to me about?"

Mr. Morrison sighed. "I hardly know what she told you, so I cannot inventory it all, but if she sent you to look for the pages of the *Mutus Liber,* I suspect she neglected to mention that she, herself, knows the location of two of the remaining pages."

Lucy was on her feet. "What? That cannot be. She would have told me."

"Only if she wished you to know. You think she is helping you? She is using you. No more."

"How can you know that she had them?"

"I can't," he admitted. "Not for certain, but my order had long suspected that two of them were in her hands."

Lucy walked to the window and peered out, taking in none of what she saw. She did not know if Mr. Morrison was right. She supposed it hardly mattered now. There was but one course, and she would follow it.

"My niece awaits," she said. "And so does everything else, I suppose. Mr. Morrison, will you take me to what was once my father's house? Will you take me to Harrington?"

Mr. Morrison rose and bowed. "You need not ask. You need only command. But you must know that Lady Harriett will suspect that Mr. Perceval's death means the end of our agreement. She and her kind will come after us. Are you prepared to face them?"

Lucy thought of her sister Emily, whom she had loved so much. She thought of her niece, the child who bore her sister's name. "Mr. Morrison, I am prepared to kill them."

It was too late to leave that evening, but Lucy and Mrs. Emmett joined Mr. Morrison in his coach at first light. Mr. Blake awoke early to see Lucy out, and he appeared uncommonly pleased that she was going — not because he wished to be rid of her, but because he sensed that she was doing what she must do.

"Your father must be very proud of you," he told her. "I have but known you a little, and I certainly am." He thrust some papers into her hands. "You must take these."

Lucy looked at the pages. They were engravings like the engravings of the *Mutus Liber,* full of similar imagery. Even the pages were old, like the pages of the true book, but these were not true pages. They felt light in Lucy's hand, like dry leaves.

"What are they?"

"They are pages made in the likeness of your own book. I have been practicing against the day that I must make the true pages, even if that day is hundreds of years in the past." He smiled at her. "It is how I live my life."

"Thank you, Mr. Blake."

"They are but a reminder," he told her, "that we are all works in progress. Even at my age, I strive to improve. You must be kind to yourself, my dear girl."

He took her hand and smiled upon her, and then led her to the coach where Mr. Morrison and Mrs. Emmett already awaited them.

When Lucy climbed in, she saw that Mr. Morrison found Mrs. Emmett puzzling. He looked at her and then, realizing he was being rude, looked away, only to sneak glances out of the corner of his eye. As the coach began to roll, he looked at Lucy and, in the dim light, raised his eyebrows questioningly. Lucy answered with a shrug, perhaps not the most reassuring answer as they embarked upon a dangerous mission, accompanied by a curious serving woman.

For much of the morning they rode in silence, Lucy only half awake, watching the landscape pass before her, thinking of everything she'd like to ask Mr. Morrison, but daring to ask none of it. More than anything, she wanted to ask about Mary, but she had seen the look of heartbreak upon his face at the mention of that name, and she would not inflict that upon him. And yet, after everything they'd discussed, one question remained above all else. If he had loved Mary as he said, and if she had loved him, then why were they not together? She had died, but she had come back. What kept them apart?

Lucy continued to dwell on such things

because she did not want to dwell on one thing in particular — that she would be returning to the house where she had grown up and once lived in happiness with her father and her sisters. She had been there since Martha's marriage to Mr. Buckles, but not often, and not since her life had altered so drastically. She did not know what to expect now. She did not know what she would see or how she would feel. She did not want to go there and see her sister and the goblin she believed to be her own baby. Most of all, she did not wish to confront Mr. Buckles in front of Martha.

They had been in the coach not an hour when Lucy turned to Mr. Morrison. "What is this great heroic act that people keep attempting to mention?"

He laughed. "There's always some threat or other, Lucy. I know this must all seem very new to you, but for me this is only one more time I must save the world from destruction."

She looked at him to see if he made sport of her, but she could see no sign that it was so.

They arrived before noon, turning off the main road to enter the grounds, then, onto the circular drive before the old rectangular house, made of dusty and battered red brick. Lucy had thought it grand as a child, but now she saw it was a rather plain house, somewhat tired-looking. Still, it reminded her of Emily and her father, and that was enough to make her love it.

They had sent no word ahead, and Martha came running out of the house to greet them, and Lucy forced herself to stifle a cry when she looked upon her sister. She looked thinner now, and her eyes tired and lined, her skin brittle and dry. She appeared ten years older.

Lucy hugged Martha until she saw she dampened her sister's neck with her tears.

"What has happened?" asked Martha, as she watched Mrs. Emmett and Mr. Morrison emerge from the coach. "For you to come here unannounced, and with — good lord, Mr. Morrison. It is he. I did not think you would really come."

"We have come to see Mr. Buckles," said Mr. Morrison. "Is he at home? We'd just like a quick chat. Nothing terribly violent."

Martha looked to Lucy, but when her sister offered no further comment about the nature of their visit, she turned back to Mr. Morrison. "I expect him later today. I am told you must come in." She cast her eyes down and spoke in a quiet voice. "But you must *not* come in. There are men who wait for you."

"That *is* troubling," said Mr. Morrison, giving every sign of being entirely untroubled. "How many?"

Martha shook her head. "They told me not to say."

"There are three of them," said Mrs. Emmett.

Lucy was about to ask how she could know, but saved herself the trouble. She knew there was no point. Instead she looked at Martha. "We shall have a look."

"You mustn't," said Martha. "These men, they will not be gentle."

"Neither shall I, and we shan't make anything better out here," said Mr. Morrison. "Come, Miss Derrick. Mrs. Emmett, please keep Lucy's sister out of trouble."

Martha turned toward him, and then stopped, instead fixing her tired eyes on Lucy. "Do you know what you are doing?"

"A little," said Lucy.

Mr. Morrison raised his eyebrows and then beckoned Lucy to follow. She had seen him silly and charming and gracious and foolish and in love, but now, Lucy understood, she was seeing him for who he was. She now observed Jonas Morrison fully in his element, with a task to do, unconcerned with the odds or the dangers. This, she understood, was his true nature, and she did not wish to miss seeing it.

They stepped inside the house, and the old front hall filled Lucy with instant melancholy. Things had changed, of course — the paintings upon the walls were different, replaced with new paintings and silhouettes of both Mr. Buckles and Lady Harriett — not one of Martha, Lucy could not but notice. There had been a worn Persian rug in her father's day, but that was gone, replaced by a new rug of garish blue and red. The statue in the corner of the second Charles was replaced by an oriental vase full of bright spring flowers. And yet, for all these changes, it was her old house, her old front hall, and the memories of those years fell upon her, heavy and warm. The wave of nostalgia felt wonderful, but it was soon enough replaced by anger. This house was never to have been hers, of course. It had been entailed to Mr. Buckles, and nothing could have changed that, but so much else had been stolen from her. Here was the house of her happiness, and it had been transformed to the seat of her misery.

Three men approached from the parlor. They looked to Lucy like soldiers or laborers, dressed up like country gentlemen in trousers and plain waistcoats. They were all of them broad in the shoulder and thick in the arms, with bulging necks and the sort of heavy faces that such muscular men often possess.

One of them stepped forward. "Jonas Morrison. They said you'd be foolish enough to come here, and I'm glad you did, for me and the lads was getting restless. Now, let's see your hands up high, so I know you don't mean no tricks."

Lucy took a step back, but Mr. Morrison did nothing other than raise his empty hands to shoulder height and smile amiably at the men. "Nothing in my hands," he said, as though about to perform one of his tricks.

And he was. Lucy understood that only an instant before it happened, and when it did happen, things moved so quickly she could not be sure she saw it all, or could believe what she did see. The brute who had spoken took a quick step toward Mr. Morrison, grinning with pleasure, one fist pulled back, ready to deliver a mighty blow, but he never had the chance. Though Mr. Morrison had demonstrated that his hands were empty, they no longer were so. In his right hand he held a cudgel, heavy and black, of about a foot in length. As the brute swung his fist, Mr. Morrison deftly stepped to one side, and struck the man in the side of his head, quick, hard, decisive. The brute toppled liked a felled tree.

With a quick and easy gesture, Mr. Morrison tossed the cudgel to his left hand, and now in his right hand appeared a piece of chalk, snatched as if from the air itself as the cudgel had been. Finding an exposed spot on the floor, he quickly drew a set of symbols on it — two interlocking triangles inside a square inside a circle, and then whispered something over the symbol. It took but a second, and it was done. He then dropped the chalk and made manifest a second cudgel. He rose to face the two remaining brutes who were now upon him.

One lunged, and Morrison struck him upon either side of the head simultaneously, causing the man to stagger backwards and collapse. The remaining man pulled from his pockets two pistols, which he held in each hand.

"I'll not let you get close enough to use those," he said.

Morrison dropped a cudgel down his sleeve and took Lucy's hand. His skin was cool and dry, as though his efforts had cost him nothing. She felt his pulse in his hand, and it was calm and regular.

"I see we've upset you," said Mr. Morrison. "We'll just be on our way." He began to back up toward the door, pulling Lucy with him.

"You're not going anywhere," said the brute. "Stand still."

"Oh, you won't shoot and risk hitting the lady, will you?" asked Mr. Morrison, continuing his slow retreat.

"If you don't stop moving, I'll shoot the lady first," answered the man as he advanced, just as slowly, clearly unwilling to close distance between them. As he finished speaking, Morrison stopped and so did he.

Morrison smiled and cast his eyes to the floor, where the brute stood upon the symbol he'd drawn in chalk. "Oh, dear," Morrison said. "That's not good."

"What do you mean?" said the brute, though he already began to appear distressed. A trickle of blood began to flow from his nose, and his eyes were so bloodshot as to be almost entirely red. "What do you mean?" he said again, and this time a trickle of blood fell from the corner of his mouth. Then he fell to the floor.

Mr. Morrison let go of Lucy's hand and went to check on the men, feeling the pulses in their necks, lifting their eyelids. "We have two hours, at least."

Martha came into the house and shrieked. Mrs. Emmett took her hand to steady her.

"I do apologize for the mess," said Mr. Morrison. "Let us leave them for your husband to tend to, shall we? In the meantime, your sister and I have business."

"But those men might die here," said Martha.

"Oh, no," said Mrs. Emmett. "Those two right there shall hang within the year, and that one with the fair hair, he shall choke to death upon his own vomit. He drinks to excess, you know."

Martha stood with a hand over her mouth. "What is all this about?" she asked. Her voice was distant and detached. "Why were these men here? Lucy, I do not understand. I don't understand anything, and I am so afraid."

Lucy took her sister's arm. "Martha, you

must trust me. You must have faith that I do what I must and what is right. Now, are father's old books in the library yet?"

"Yes, of course." Martha looked away from the bondmen. "Father's books and many of Mr. Buckles's too."

"May we look through them?"

Martha nodded. "Yes. I suppose. I mean, I cannot say."

Martha gave every sign of swooning, so Lucy took her hands. "I know all of this is strange to you. It is strange to me too. Soon, I think, everything will be different, and better. It is what I hope. For now there is much I must do, and I cannot speak of it. I ask only that you trust me."

Martha began to tear up once more. "You are so altered, Lucy. I hardly know you."

"These years since father died have been hard on all of us. It must change us."

Martha nodded. "Yes, we must all change, but we do not all change for the better. We do not all become stronger. I have diminished and you have become . . . I don't know how to say it. You have become who you were always meant to be."

Lucy hugged her once more, and as they all turned their backs upon the bondmen Lucy, Mr. Morrison, and Mrs. Emmett followed Martha to the library.

When they reached the closed door of the

library, Mr. Morrison put up a hand before Lucy. "A moment," he said. He opened the door, and proceeded to run his hand along the doorjamb, moving slowly, as if feeling for something underneath the wood. He did this several times, his face screwed up in concentration, and then he gave a quick nod to himself.

Reaching into the pocket of his coat, he removed a penknife and began to dig into the wood in a spot at about the height of his shoulder. Martha appeared horrified, and he turned to smile at her, and then went back to his work. Finally, he found something embedded in the wood. It was a small pouch, made of stained white linen, about the size of a grape, and — like Byron's curse — tied with some kind of hair.

Mr. Morrison sniffed at the bag. "Dried spiders, mixed with the ash of unhatched goose egg, if I'm not mistaken. Powerful stuff, designed to interfere with your concentration." He strode into the library and tossed the pouch in the fire. "But that's all behind us. Apologies about the door, Mrs. Buckles."

"How did you know that was there?" Martha asked.

"Lucky guess," he said, smiling quite happily.

Martha looked at the damage to the door, then at Mr. Morrison, then at Lucy. Apparently she decided there was nothing to be gained by further comments. Instead, she offered them refreshment, which they refused.

"We only need some time," Lucy said.

In the distance they heard the shrill wail of an angry infant. At least it would sound like an infant to Martha, and perhaps to Mr. Morrison. She did not know.

"I hardly even hear it any longer," Martha said in response to the unasked question. "I have hired a wet nurse, you know. I hate that I have, but I cannot any longer endure it. My own daughter. I suppose that makes me a horrid mother, but I feared I must lose my mind, but she is so altered."

"You are a wonderful mother," said Lucy. "You can never doubt that."

Martha glanced over at Mrs. Emmett who was standing near the fire, examining the cut pages of a book with her index finger, and humming softly to herself. "Perhaps your woman would care to wait in the servant's quarters."

"No," said Mrs. Emmett. "Not a bit of it. Run along now, girl."

Martha stood with her mouth open.

"She is odd," said Lucy softly, "but harmless. We will keep her here."

Martha nodded and left the library, closing the door behind her.

They were alone. Lucy turned to Mr. Morrison. "How did you do those things — make your cudgels and chalk appear out of nothingness, and that symbol you drew upon the floor? I must know."

He gestured vaguely. "The cudgels and chalk were but a bit of theater, nothing more than the same sort of misdirection I use to pull eggs out of ears or make coins vanish. I have found that combining my technique with a bit of spectacle gives me but one more advantage in combat. And as for the symbol, well, that's very dark magic, soul-blackening stuff. I don't recommend using it, and I only trifle with that sort of thing when the stakes are unusually high."

"And what is at stake here?" asked Lucy.

Mr. Morrison looked at her directly. "You are."

She could not bear to hold his gaze, so she began to walk the room, bright and well lit, looking at the tall shelves of books — thick folios, tiny sixteenmos, and everything in between. She ran her fingers along the spines, thinking that this one or that had been a book she had seen in the hands of her father as he sat in that red velvet chair by the window, his glasses perched on his nose, reading away the long afternoon, oblivious to the commotion in the house around him.

Lucy closed her eyes and quieted herself, trying to feel if there were pages in the room, and at once she felt their closeness. Indeed, they were in the library, she had no doubt of it, but she could not tell where, and she did not know how to sort through all the books to find them.

"Mrs. Emmett," Lucy asked, "can you, by any chance, detect the pages?"

"Me? They are yours, not mine." She continued her strange humming.

Lucy looked at Mr. Morrison. "Were you ever with my father here in this library?"

"Yes, of course. Many times."

"Then you must see what I see," said Lucy. "I did not come in here again after I moved away. When I visited, I avoided the room, for it reminded me too much of him, but here, all around us, is the evidence."

"Yes," said Mr. Morrison, as he walked about the room, looking at the various books. "It was said that he had to sell his library to pay his debts, but here is the library, right before us. Either Mr. Buckles bought it himself or bought it back or . . ." He did not choose to finish.

"He never sold it nor paid for any of it," said Lucy.

"Of course," said Mr. Morrison. "He is in possession of your father's books, but they do not belong to him. This explains why everything comes back to you. Mrs. Emmett — she said as much just a moment ago. I almost didn't hear it, but now I understand why you are at the center of everything."

32

Lucy sat at a writing table, and Mr. Morrison sat next to her. "I've long suspected, but been unable to prove, that Mr. Buckles defrauded you of your inheritance. Of course, I wondered why he would trouble to do so. He was to inherit the house, and after he married Martha he would receive half of your father's wealth. The amount he could gain through fraud could hardly be worth the risk of discovery — not when his future was secure and his patronage from Lady Harriett left him without want."

"He wanted the books," said Lucy, who saw it as well.

"Your dealings with your father changed in that last year. That is why he left you what you see around us — his library. These are your books, Lucy. Mr. Buckles cared nothing of the money he stole from you. Perhaps he took it because he could or because he believed you would be less dangerous if you were even more impoverished, but in the end it was but a distraction. What he wanted was these books."

She could hear Mary's voice in her head. *The* Mutus Liber *is strongest in the hands of the person to whom it belongs.*

"It is mine," said Lucy. "The book was mine all along. They took it from me, and they tore it to pieces, but they dared not destroy it."

"They did not take it apart," said Mr. Morrison. "Your father ordered it done, and I believe he gave the task to the only person he trusted to take the book for herself."

Lucy nodded. "Of course. Emily. She went to Cardiff shortly before she died, and you went there looking for the book. It was Emily who disassembled the book, to keep it safe, and only she knew where the pieces were."

"I believe so," said Mr. Morrison. "But the pages themselves have power. You have discovered that, I think. They contain information for those who know how to read them or are sensitive to them, and so they can be sensed. Some of the pages remain where Emily left them, others have been discovered and changed hands several times."

"All this time, I have been following in my sister's footsteps," said Lucy.

Mr. Morrison nodded. "You see now why Lady Harriett wanted you to marry Mr. Olson. Your property would become his. The book would no longer belong to you. Lady

Harriett wanted desperately for you to marry him before all the pages were recovered, because no one wanted the book reassembled while you still owned it."

"Almost no one," said Lucy very quietly, for Mary dared. She alone dared to urge Lucy to assemble the book that contained the secret of unmaking her.

Mr. Morrison turned away. "Almost no one."

Lucy had to know. She swallowed and forged ahead before she lost the nerve to ask. "If you love her, why does it matter? She left, but she returned, so why are you apart from each other? Why does she not use your name?"

He shook his head. "I will not discuss it."

"I do not mean to cause you pain," she said quietly. "I only wish to understand." It was so odd, she thought as she looked at him. She had spent years hating him, thinking him the most vile of men, but he was never that person. He had only been a kind and loyal man serving Lucy's father — and serving Lucy herself.

To distract herself, she decided it was time to find the pages. Lucy turned slowly about the room, like a sluggish child at absent play. She ran her hand along the shelves as she walked, hoping for some kind of spark or warmth or feeling of nearness. Then, in some noiseless way, she heard its cry. Lucy walked toward a shelf and there she found her father's copy of *Purchas, his Pilgrimage,* just as she had always remembered it, and she opened it up. Inside its pages, folded and neat, were two more sheets from the *Mutus Liber.*

Lucy looked at them. They were as beautiful and strange and inexplicable as the others. On the pages were trees transmuting into vines and into animals, plant and creature alike twirling and twisting upward and down. It was all about transformation and change and melding. It was about the future and the past. It was about insight, Lucy realized, about seeing the truth behind veils of deception and disguise. There was more than that, however. The philosopher's stone was the source of transformation and alteration, and such power required wisdom and judgment and patience, and these too were embedded in these images. Lucy stared for a long time, hoping she might become wise and insightful enough to know what to do next.

And then she did.

She turned to Mr. Morrison and Mrs. Emmett. "I need you to keep my sister away from me. I need you to keep her downstairs no matter what."

"Where do you go?" asked Mr. Morrison.

Lucy swallowed hard, working up the courage to say what would be far more difficult to do. She turned to Mrs. Emmett and straightened herself in a display of determination. "I go to speak to the changeling."

Perhaps she heard someone upon the stairs, for when Lucy reached the baby's room, the wet nurse — a plump and pretty fair-haired woman in her early thirties — emerged. Her eyes were red and heavily bagged, and her posture somewhat slumped. Everything about the woman suggested fatigue and dejection.

"I wish to be alone with the — the infant," said Lucy. "I am the aunt."

"I don't care who you are, mum," the woman said hurrying down the hall. "If you want to be alone with her, she's yours as long as you'll have her."

Lucy stepped into the room. It was dark, with only a small fire burning. This had once been Lucy's own room, but it was unfamiliar now, with pictures of animals upon the wall, a new rug of plain weave, and entirely different furnishings. Near the fireplace rested the baby's crib, but Lucy did not have to approach and peer into it. The creature had already pulled itself up and clutched the railings in its narrow, clawed fingers. Its large, reptilian eyes followed her as she moved into the room, and then, as she drew too close, it hissed in alarm, showing its sharp teeth. Its forked tongue darted out, tasting the air.

Lucy took another step forward. It cocked its head and hissed again. So, it was afraid of her. That was interesting.

"Can you speak?" she asked.

"Can you?" it asked, its voice raspy and low.

"Clearly," said Lucy as she took another step forward.

The thing hissed again and swiped at the air with its claws. "No further, witch."

Lucy stopped, but more as an experiment than out of fear. She was surprised to discover she was not afraid of the creature. She found it vile, but not terrifying, perhaps because it was so clearly afraid of her. "Why do you fear me?"

"You would send me back if you knew how," it said.

"And you do not wish to go back? You enjoy tormenting my sister?"

"I am charged to not let you send me back," it said. "For the baby's sake. It is what my mistress has commanded, and I obey her."

"Your mistress is Mary Crawford?"

"Yes," it hissed.

"How do I find my niece?" Lucy asked.

It opened its mouth, and then only hissed again.

"You were going to tell me," Lucy said. "But you did not. Because you were commanded not to tell me?"

"Yes," it said, evidently unhappy.

"But otherwise you seem inclined to answer my questions honestly. Why?"

The creature turned away from her, rubbing its long hands over the rough skin of its head, as if trying to puzzle something out. It mumbled something Lucy could not understand.

"Speak so I might hear you," Lucy said.

It turned to her and flashed its teeth. "It is the pages of the book. They compel me to tell the truth."

Lucy smiled and approached closer. "Is there anything you can tell me to help me get my niece back?"

"No, you cannot force me to speak of that."

Lucy took a moment to think of what she might ask next. She could not stay here forever. The men downstairs might awaken, or Martha might come in to discover what Lucy did. She needed to hurry. "What must Mary Crawford do to banish you?"

"Even she cannot banish me now, not until certain conditions are fulfilled. Not until your niece is safe."

There must be something it could tell her, Lucy thought. Some truth she could extract that did not directly involve the rescue of her niece but would help effect that rescue. She made another attempt. "Then what of the pages yet missing? Mr. Morrison said that Mary Crawford knew the location of pages. Though why would she not tell me?"

"All she does, she believes is right," the changeling said.

Lucy realized it had answered part of her

question, but not all of it, so she tried again, asking more precisely this time. "Do you know where I will find the last pages of the book?"

The creature backed up in the crib. It looked this way and that and appeared so desperate that Lucy almost felt sorry for it. But she pressed her case and pointed at the changeling. "Tell me."

And it did.

Downstairs Mr. Morrison rushed toward her, evidently concerned. "Is all well?"

"No," said Lucy. "It seems you were right about Mary. She did deceive me. She had pages hidden away all along, and now, unfortunately, I know where."

"Why is that unfortunate?" he demanded.

Lucy turned to study his face carefully, hoping for some clues, some explanations. "Because it seems we were all along deceived, Mr. Morrison. The remaining pages are to be found where we first looked. They are within Newstead Abbey."

They found Martha sitting near the fire in the sitting room. She held some sewing, but did not appear to have done much of anything with it.

Lucy approached her and took her hands. "I am sorry, Martha, but we must go at once."

"What shall I tell my husband when he

returns?" asked Martha, now sounding alarmed.

"Tell him the truth," said Mr. Morrison. "With any luck, it shall not matter."

Lucy gathered at once that Martha feared Mr. Buckles. "I would take you with me if I could, Martha, but where I go is far more dangerous than here. When . . . when all this is finished, I shall take you then, if you like. I shall save you."

Martha laughed. It was a bitter, barking sound. "Save me. How shall you do so? You have no money, Lucy."

"I have other resources."

"If you want shelter," said Mr. Morrison, "or if you want money to go where none may find you, then you need but ask. I shall never again neglect to be a friend of your family."

Martha stared at them. "You have set yourself against Mr. Buckles, haven't you?"

"Lady Harriett has made herself my enemy," answered Lucy. "She has, in ways I cannot begin to explain, inflicted terrible harm upon both of us, and she has used Mr. Buckles as her instrument. I am sorry to say this. I do not wish to speak ill of your husband, but it is so. I have not set myself against him, but he has chosen to follow a mistress who has declared me her enemy. I hope you will recollect that I act not against him, but to defend myself. To defend all of us."

Martha shook her head. "I wish you would

say what you mean, what you really mean, instead of speaking in riddles all the time."

Lucy smiled. "When there is more time, I shall tell you all."

Martha turned away. "I have this terrible idea in my head that Mr. Buckles will not survive what is coming. Am I all but a widow?"

"Is the wife of the condemned man a widow before he hangs?" asked Mrs. Emmett.

Martha let out a gasp.

Lucy gave a harsh glance at Mrs. Emmett, who only smiled in return. She turned back to her sister. "I do not know what is going to happen. I know only that everything I've done, everything I will do, is for you and your child. I beg you to believe that."

Martha rose and hugged Lucy. "I am afraid."

Lucy returned the hug and stepped back. "For yourself, you have nothing to fear." She did not know that it was true. But it would all be over soon. Lucy would find those final pages, and then all would be set right.

"You sound so sure of yourself," Martha said. "What do you have to fear?"

Lucy forced a smile. "Everything."

It was to be a long and awkward ride to Nottinghamshire. They would necessarily have to travel slowly once it grew dark, and so be vulnerable to highwaymen, but they dared not stop until morning. There was too much at risk. Both Mr. Morrison and the coachman primed pistols, and they began their long and slow trek that would probably not bring them to their destination until after dark the next day.

They were silent for some time. As was her habit in the coach, Mrs. Emmett fell into a deep sleep at once, snoring in a loud, rasping manner. Lucy did not believe she would be able to sleep so easily. She lay awake and still and frightened she knew not how long. She had presumed Mr. Morrison to be asleep when he, at last, spoke.

"They change," he said.

"I beg your pardon." It came out too clipped and formal, for he had surprised her.

"The revenants. They are not what they once were. They are not the people they were before their alteration. It is why I cannot love her, nor she love me. That part of us is lost."

"I am sorry," Lucy said. She recalled what Mary had told her about the revenants — that mortality is a fundamental part of humanity. Lucy had no notion at the time that Mary had been speaking of herself.

"What is she like now?" asked Mr. Morrison. The strange flatness of his voice betrayed a pain Lucy could not contemplate.

"She was lovely to me — kind and patient and understanding. She always said what I most needed to hear. Even now, when I consider all I have seen and done, the places I have gone, the enemies and dangers I have encountered, I know that I could have done none of it had she not prepared me."

"Then you trusted her? You trust her yet, though you know she deceived you?"

"I do not know," said Lucy. "Perhaps she had her reasons, but I have come to see that, for all her goodness to me, she is cold and calculating and ruthless. She is, in some ways, unknowable."

"I understand you," he said. "We spoke once, you know. After she returned."

"Mr. Morrison, you do not need to tell me these things. I can hear in your voice that it is painful for you. I thank you for your consideration, but you owe me no candor in this manner."

He laughed. "You are a sweet girl. I cannot imagine how you have come so far and remained so innocent. I do not tell you these things because I wish to unburden my heart. I tell you what you may need to know if you are to survive what comes. You can have no illusions about Mary Crawford, as she now styles herself. It may come to pass that we must destroy her."

"I will not destroy her," said Lucy. "Though she lied to me, she is my friend."

"She has been good to you, and she may even, in her own way, care for you, but she will not be your friend if it is not in her interest. She knows better than all of us that death is not the end, and she will not hesitate to send you on your journey should she believe the situation requires it. Some part of her hates you for your mortality, that you can move on and she cannot."

"I don't know that I believe you."

"I think you had better learn to believe me," he said. "I cannot go in with you if you are not willing to destroy her if you must."

For a long time, he said nothing more. In the dark she heard him stir, as if trying to grow more comfortable. He coughed softly, the sound muffled by a handkerchief. Somewhere outside the cart they heard the lonely howl of a dog.

"You cannot know how I loved her," he said. "At first what I felt for her was more moderate. It was time for me to marry, and she was suitable in so many ways, and I suppose what I felt for her was love, after a species. She loved me, and I hoped that would be enough."

"She told me of her husband, though she was certainly vague. But she said that he'd been in love with someone else."

Mr. Morrison said nothing for a moment. "When I met her, I thought I would never love again. I was heartbroken, but I came to love her more than I can say. She was clever and witty, and she understood me better than anyone I had known. And she loved me. Only someone utterly coldhearted could be so adored and unmoved by it. And, of course, she was beautiful. Now she is even more beautiful than she was. Her hair, her eyes, her complexion — they are different, as I am told sometimes happens. Her new nature fairly radiates something so compelling that when we were reunited I was all but lost in an instant, but she did not want me to be lost. When she spoke to me — I know not how to describe it. For all that she resembled my Mary, for all she retained her beauty, and that beauty had grown, it was as though I spoke to the dead. She is not soulless, but the soul is no longer human. I saw in her eyes that she felt nothing for me, that she could hardly remember having felt anything for me. And I knew that my feelings were for someone who was gone forever."

"How did she come to be what she is?" Lucy asked. "One does not simply . . . return."

"No," he said. "The tale is strange and terrible. It is hard for me to speak of it, so you will forgive me if I pause from time to time to collect myself. I would rather not say any of these things, but I have already withheld too much for too long. You must know everything."

Mary Crawford had come from Northamptonshire with her brother Henry. They had been before in London, but circumstances had required a move, and there Mary had, if not quite fallen in love with a neighboring gentleman, at least imagined she was in love for a while. Then that gentleman had thrown her over for his penniless cousin, something of a simpleton, and Mary's brother had become involved in a scandalous affair. The whole business was unpleasant, and at times sordid, and when it reached its conclusion Mary found herself unhappy and vulnerable.

It was then that she met Mr. Morrison, who was also unhappy and vulnerable in his own way, and at once she fell in love. They had met at a mutual friend's house in London and, before they had parted ways on that first occasion, Mr. Morrison believed he wished to marry her. He saw something in her, in her soul, perhaps.

Soon enough they had married, and relocated to Mr. Morrison's estate in Derbyshire, though they returned to London for the season, and it was there that the trouble began. Mr. Morrison and his wife came to be acquainted with a young nobleman who mistook Mary's social graces for an interest greater than what she entertained. He began to press his case to her, and when she flatly refused an improper relationship, he chose not to accept defeat. He appeared in her way often, speculating upon whom she might visit, what events she might attend, even what paths she might walk. He would attempt to visit her at her house when he knew Mr. Morrison was away. In short, this man would not be discouraged.

Mr. Morrison visited him and warned him that he must stay away, but the young nobleman laughed in his face. He would not duel. He would not stoop to take Mr. Morrison's complaint seriously.

Before events could unfold in this way, the nobleman took a more drastic course. He assaulted Mary's coachman one afternoon, knocking him quite insensible. He then threatened Mary with his ferocious dog, and forced Mary to drink a tincture of opium, which put her into a deep sleep. With his beloved in the back of the coach, he drove her far outside London to his country estate. The nobleman had convinced himself that, once she awoke there, away from London and her unworthy husband, she would not only accept her fate, but embrace it. She would recognize that she wanted to remain there and be happy.

It did not happen that way. Mary was angry and outraged and terrified. She feared for her life and her virtue, and attempted to run away and seek help. She broke free, escaped her prison, even killed the man's dog. But the villain, now that he had her, could not let her go. He caught up with her and a struggle ensued. Perhaps he never meant to hurt her, and perhaps, in the passions of the moment, he lashed out, but either way he struck Mary's head against the ancient stone of his hall, and she fell to the ground, dead.

Lucy sat listening in silence. It was a horrible story — chilling and terrifying — but only now did she believe, truly believe, that the woman whom she had called her friend those many months in Nottingham had been dead, a revenant, something inhuman. Before it had been an idea, a notion; now she felt the truth of it. She saw the truth of it on Mr. Morrison's face.

"This man," said Lucy. "What has happened to him?"

"You know him," said Mr. Morrison in the dark.

Lucy felt at once unbearably cold. It seemed that the carriage had disassembled all around her and she was floating unmoored through space. "No," she whispered. "It can't be."

"It was Byron who killed my Mary. On looking upon what he had done, he was filled with — I cannot even guess how his mind functions — remorse, terror, disgust, grief? I shall not trouble myself to speculate. But he wished, as so many in his place have wished throughout time, that he could undo what cannot be undone."

"Except he could."

"No, not he. His mind may be able to

conjure up silly rhymes, but he does not have the capacity to decipher the *Mutus Liber,* let alone construct the philosopher's stone through some other means. Instead, he brought Mary's body to someone he believed could do these things: Lady Harriett Dyer."

"How did he know her or know what she was?"

"It has always been so on this island, Lucy. Their kind infuse the nobility, and those mortals who hold titles learn the secret. According to what we have learned, Lady Harriett had already sought out Byron, detecting in him a weakness and self-love that could be exploited by her kind. She even sent him on a mission to Greece on behalf of the revenants' interests."

"But why should Lady Harriett agree to help him in this? I can only imagine that others with power and influence have asked for this favor. I know that they do not make these transformations lightly, so why do this for Byron?"

Mr. Morrison laughed a quiet and bitter laugh. "Byron is not like other men. You've seen how women respond to him — as men do toward beautiful women."

"Do you mean to say that Lady Harriett is in love with him?"

"No, of course not, but she understood that a man like that, with the power to enchant, would be an asset. So she did something for him that would put him forever in her power."

So here was something yet more astonishing, something that defied imagination. Byron was the man who had killed Morrison's wife, had turned her immortal soul into a twisted, fragile, vulnerable distortion of the true Mary. A man might console himself with the dream of reuniting with his wife in heaven, but not Mr. Morrison. His beloved Mary was damned forever to this terrestrial sphere because Byron had struck, and then struck again.

"You told me once," she said softly, "that what you cared about was revenge. And yet, since these events began, you have been in Byron's presence. But you did not act."

"I have accepted a responsibility far greater than my own desire for revenge," he answered. His voice was quavering, and Lucy had no doubt that, in the dark, the tears fell freely. "I promised I would not seek revenge until I had settled the matter with Ludd. I promised I would not put my desire to destroy Byron above my duty to my nation. You cannot imagine how I've wanted to strangle him each time I have been near him, but I have restrained myself, thinking that the day must come soon."

Lucy parted the curtain to look out at the passing blackness. She wished she knew what to say to Mr. Morrison, what response was appropriate to this story of love lost and murder and delayed vengeance. She could think of nothing, so she said, "If I may ask, who was the woman whom you loved before Mary?" Then, at once, she regretted it. She had caused him enough pain, made him recount enough of his losses, so she quickly spoke up again. "I am sorry. I should not have asked that. It is none of my concern."

"Of course it is your concern," he answered. "Can it be that you truly do not know? But I suppose that is what makes you who you are. After Emily died, your father made me promise never to tell you the truth of the circumstances, for your sake, and I agreed. I would have kept that promise until the day I died had not it been necessary to reveal the truth."

"But what has that to do with this woman?" asked Lucy, but as soon as she asked the question, understanding dawned on her, and she felt her face burn with embarrassment and her heart flutter with surprise.

"It has everything to do with her," said Mr. Morrison, his voice heavy and thick. "The woman I was in love with, with whom I could never be, is you."

Lucy could not consider, truly consider, what he said, and what his words meant or how they made her feel. She dared not ask herself the most pressing question of all — had Mary known, when they first met, that Lucy was the woman her own husband had once loved? She would not torture herself with a question to which she could find no answer. She could only think that here was a man who had lost everything, had sacrificed his heart for duty and service and loyalty. Everything Lucy had ever known or thought about Mr. Morrison was wrong. Never in her life had she misjudged anyone to so great a degree, and she could hardly comprehend what this new information meant to her, but even in her numbness she could no longer deny that her feelings for him had undergone the most profound of alterations.

33

In the morning, they stopped at an inn to breakfast and refresh themselves. Hardly a word passed between them, for Lucy feared anything she might say would be wrong. Mr. Morrison, for his part, showed no sign of regretting what he had confessed, but he appeared interested in giving Lucy the quiet she desired. Sensing their mood, Mrs. Emmett also kept quiet. She amused herself by humming and playing some sort of counting game on her fingers, while Lucy kept her eyes down in embarrassment.

Finally she could take it no longer. "If what you said was true," she began, not willing to speak of his supposed love for her aloud, "why did you not search for me after my father died?"

"I promised him I would not trouble you. He wanted to protect you from the memory of what happened to Emily, and he was a man, and all men are weak. I think he wanted to protect himself. But he made me give my word, and then I'd heard you had gone to live with a wealthy uncle in Nottingham, and I presumed you were well."

"If you'd known I was miserable?" she asked.

"Then I would have broken my promise to your father for your sake, not because I hold my promises cheap, but because the substance of the vow was to protect you, and I know your father would have preferred anything to your suffering."

Jonas Morrison, the man who had taught her that love was a lie meant to turn young women into whores, was showing himself to be the opposite of what she had so long supposed. He was a good man and honorable and romantical.

Later that morning, as they continued their journey, Lucy said, "When this is over, what will you do to Byron?"

Mr. Morrison watched her closely for a moment, and then turned slightly away. "Let us see if I am still alive. I don't know how likely that is. But revenge is a strange thing, Lucy. For so long I have longed to kill Byron, to run him through and be done with it, but part of me fears doing so. Once I have my revenge, what will there be for me? What reason will I have to live?"

"Your duty?"

"Let someone else take upon his shoulders the next task. I have done enough."

Lucy decided to speak without censoring herself. "If you allow yourself to be killed in some foolish, noble sacrifice, I shall never forgive you."

"What a terrifying fate," he said. "Never to be forgiven by Lucy Derrick."

"You and I are in this until the end. I am risking my life as well, and I shall not be happy if you leave me to fend for myself."

He laughed. "You are coming to protect me, not the other way around."

"Just promise me you will not be reckless," she said.

"I am surprised you would not push me off that precipice yourself. Have you come to hate me less?"

"Yes," said Lucy, managing to smile. "I have come to hate you very much less indeed."

As they arrived in Nottinghamshire, the sun was setting. It had been temperate during the day, and did not much cool off after dusk as dark clouds domed the sky. At the outskirts of town, Mr. Morrison dismissed the driver with compensatory pay for having to find his own way back to London. He did not want any others to face what he, Lucy, and Mrs. Emmett must, and so he prepared to take the reins himself for the final miles.

"I hate to enter the abbey at night," he said as he climbed up to take the reins, "but we cannot wait for morning."

Though terrified, Lucy affected good cheer. "Whatever we find at Newstead might be less frightening in the light of day, but likely no less dangerous."

Mr. Morrison grinned. "Though possibly harder to see."

And so they rode on to Newstead. This night was far less well lit than the last time they had come, but the weather was warmer, and without the chill breeze in the air, the place struck Lucy as less menacing. That was a mistake, of course. She must not let down her guard.

There was nothing to be gained from secrecy. They could not slip into the abbey unobserved if anyone was there to guard against them, and so Mr. Morrison drove the carriage through the gates toward the main building. It was dark and cool, and not a light shone within.

Lucy began to collect the trinkets she needed from her bag. She put on her various charms and talismans and herbs of protection. She handed similar items to Mr. Morrison.

"Our goal," he said, "is simple. We enter, we find the pages as quickly as we can, and then we flee. If we can do this without conflict or encounter, I shall be very happy."

"And then what?" asked Lucy.

"Once we have secured the pages, we can move against Lady Harriett. After she is destroyed, your sister will have her child returned to her."

"You have loftier goals than returning my sister's child," Lucy said.

"I am here to save lives, Miss Derrick. With your niece safely returned, I will depend upon your help to move against Ludd. He and his followers must be restrained. If necessary, we will act against Mary, though I should hate to do so."

"And if Lady Harriett tries to stop us before we have the pages?"

"Then we shall deal with her."

Lucy felt a strange thrill. The two of them, working together, she with this new Jonas Morrison, this man who had never been vile, never been evil, but had always been tender and caring and witty and protective. It was strange how quickly she found herself adjusting to this new understanding of a man she had hated for so long.

Lucy, Mr. Morrison, and Mrs. Emmett disembarked from the coach, and Mr. Morrison began to assemble his things. He brought a heavy leather bag, which he slung over his shoulder. He placed pistols in his pockets, and strapped to his back two shotguns. He looked like a man preparing to attempt a prison break.

Lucy tended to her own preparations, making certain she had what she needed and could reach her various talismans and ingredients when she needed them. She had so much upon her — herbs and dried flowers and other elements. She had talismans she'd made so long ago, and some she'd made recently. She was as prepared as she could be, but she did not feel nearly prepared enough.

After checking the contents of his bag one last time, Mr. Morrison looked up at Lucy and grinned. "Let us go make our enemies hate us more, shall we?"

They began to walk toward the main building. Despite her pelisse and the relative warmth of the night, Lucy felt cold, and she wrapped her arms together across her chest. Her heart bounded, and her breath came deep and heavy. To one side stood Mr. Morrison, his grim expression visible in the near perfect darkness. On the other stood Mrs. Emmett, her hair and bonnet nearly to her eyes, smiling with her usual lack of concern. This is real, Lucy thought. This was her life and it was happening, and they were about to do something likely dangerous and possibly fantastic. Whatever it was, there was no turning back.

From the shrubbery off to the left of the main door they heard a rustle of leaves and then soft footsteps. Mr. Morrison reached into his coat for one of his pistols, but did not pull it out. It might have been an animal or a person or some terrible creature none of them could imagine, but the form soon took shape as a woman — slight and unthreatening. It was the deaf girl, Sophie Hyatt.

Lucy let out a breath in relief. Mr. Morrison let go of his pistol. For her part, Sophie began to scratch out some words on her slate, and Mr. Morrison took out the lantern from the coach. Sophie showed the slate to Lucy.

Go back. Something is here.

"What is here, Sophie?" Lucy asked.

Something bad.

"Is it Byron?" Mr. Morrison asked.

Was here. Came, took some things, left. Then something else came. I am frightened.

"He knows I am after the pages," said Lucy. "He has attempted to please both me and Lady Harriett for too long. Now that we are down to the end of it, he has made his choice."

"Damn it!" Mr. Morrison cried. "If that is so, then there is no guessing where the pages could be now."

"No," said Mrs. Emmett in a tone unusually forceful. "You are meant to be here. Maybe the pages are here and maybe they are not, but you must go inside."

Lucy closed her eyes and reached out, feeling the pages that were upon them, wanting to sense their link to their brothers. They were hers. They belonged to her, they belonged to each other, and they wanted to be found by their owner, they wanted to be reunited. If she could but feel their yearning, Lucy would surely be able to sense, if nothing else, at least a direction.

Then it seemed the ground opened up under her, and she grabbed on to Mr. Morrison's arm lest she fall. "Whatever he took, is wasn't the pages," she said. "They are still inside the house."

Mr. Morrison smiled without humor. "That is two pieces of good news. The pages are here, and Byron is not. Perhaps this will be easier than we imagined."

"Yes, so long as we are polite to the dark things, all will be well." Lucy turned to Sophie and held the girl's shoulders so her lips would be easier to read. "Go home, Sophie. Mr. Morrison and I must do this, but I would have you safe. Will you go and be safe?"

She nodded.

Lucy turned to Mr. Morrison. "Then let us find the pages."

They made it only halfway to the front entrance of the abbey before Lucy halted in her tracks. She could feel it, the dark thing Sophie had spoken of. She was not overwhelmed by fear, but there was an energy here, a force of something building, the way the air crackles with electricity before a storm.

"Oh, my dear," said Mrs. Emmett. "I am so sorry."

"Sorry for what?" asked Lucy.

Mrs. Emmett shook her head.

Mr. Morrison turned to her. "I must say, I grow weary of your opaque observations. If you know something, tell us."

"I know only that I wish I had played no part in Miss Derrick's being here. Better I should never have come to be than lead her to this, and yet she must go on."

Mr. Morrison held the lantern up to her heavy face. She seemed not to react at all to the light. She stared at it, her eyes wide below the heavy curls upon her forehead.

"What will happen in there? Is Miss Derrick in danger?"

"I don't know what will happen, but Miss Derrick has always been in danger. You know that, Mr. Morrison. There is nowhere to go where the danger shan't find her. There is nothing to do but forge ahead. I don't know very much, sir, but I can tell you this: There shall never be a better time to strike. This is the moment, danger or no, that she must act."

Mr. Morrison nodded. "That may be, but things have been stirred up. We will be made to earn those pages."

"Then you feel it too," Lucy said in a whisper, for as soon as he spoke the words, Lucy knew it was true.

He shook his head. "No, I am not so sensitive as you, but if things were not stirred up, we would not see something like that quite

545

so clearly." He gestured with his hand slowly, as though afraid to disturb the air with his movements.

Sitting upon the steps leading to the entrance of Newstead Abbey, white and milky and translucent, was the spectral image of a Newfoundland dog. It seemed not to notice them, but instead pointed its muzzle to something far off in the distance.

"I think it's Boatswain," said Mr. Morrison. "Byron loved that dog."

"Only Byron would have a ghost dog," muttered Lucy. "What do we do about it?"

"We ignore it," said Mr. Morrison. "We have amethysts upon us. I am surprised it even manifested before us while we are so protected, but it certainly will not approach us. Likely it will not notice us."

They took another few steps toward the door, and the dog's head turned sharply toward them. It began to bark, distant and hollow, as though they had plugged their ears with wax.

"It's noticing us," said Lucy.

"Yes," said Mr. Morrison, clearly irritated. "We may have a problem."

"I don't think the ghost dog can actually bite us."

"The dog will not harm us," he said, "but it should not be here at all. All our charms and protections and wards ought to keep such things at a distance, but they are not doing so."

"What does that mean?"

"It means many of the charms and wards shan't work," said Mrs. Emmett. "It means that the defenses you have been depending upon will fail."

"And what do we do?" asked Lucy.

Mr. Morrison adjusted the bag upon his shoulder and took hold of the coach lantern. "We go and have a look."

The dog, as he predicted, was no danger. They walked past it, and the creature offered nothing more than a ghostly bark or two, and then they were inside the cold and cryptlike entrance to the abbey.

"Have you a sense of where the pages are?" Mr. Morrison asked, keeping his voice low.

Lucy closed her eyes and reached out, as she had done before. Immediately she gasped and staggered backwards. There was something there, blocking her. It was dark and ugly and forbidding — alive. It was like the creature she had seen surrounding Byron when they first met, a creature of void and vastness, featureless and yet grotesque in its features.

"What is it?" Mr. Morrison asked, taking her arm.

"There is something there, in my path. It is . . . terrible."

"It is well we are terrible too," said Mr. Morrison.

Lucy looked at him. "Mr. Morrison, you appear extraordinarily cheerful under the circumstances. Do you know some advantage offered to us with which I am unfamiliar?"

"Let us say that I have confidence in the both of us."

Lucy would have responded, no doubt saying something cautious and uncertain, but the words never left her lips because that was when Mr. Morrison was struck down by a tortoise.

Newstead Abbey offered many dangers, but among the things Lucy feared most were the animals that Byron, in his lordly indulgence, allowed to roam the grounds. Most frightening among these were the wolf, which they had already once faced, and the bear, which might have been only local myth. That Lord Byron included a tortoise in his menagerie was well known, but it had never occurred to Lucy to fear it. She had been shortsighted in this regard.

It came down the hallway at a gallop, as fast as any horse, and then leapt into the air, its thick and stunted front legs stretched out, clublike. Mr. Morrison attempted to push Lucy out of the way, but it was intent on her, and appeared to change its direction in mid leap. It was as large as a pig, and almost as broad as it was long. And its shell made it heavy, so heavy it ought not to have been able to leap at all, but then it opened its mouth and snapped at him with its birdlike beak, and saliva flew from its jaws.

Lucy was on the ground, landing so hard that for a moment she could not breathe. Both of her hands pushed on the bottom of the tortoise's shell while it stretched around its thick, leathery neck, trying to bite her, and though its teeth were small and blunt, its power and rage made the creature ferocious. Gaining no ground in its efforts to reach her neck, it attempted to peck at Lucy's eyes with its pointed beak. She heard it snort, felt its hot reptilian breath upon her face, clogging her nostrils with its thick mustiness. She turned her head aside, but not in time to avoid the creature entirely, and she felt the heat of tearing flesh across her cheek, dripping salty blood into her eye. Smelling this blood, the tortoise hissed and wheezed, then tasted the air with its tongue, and jabbed at Lucy's face once more.

All of this happened in a matter of seconds. From behind the tortoise, Mr. Morrison grabbed the creature's head, clamping its jaws together in his hands. Lucy watched in amazement as he pulled the animal's head backwards until it began to bend toward him. The creature could not open its mouth, but it made a mewling sound between its clamped jaws and let out a series of rapid snorts from its flaring nostrils. With a sharp jerk, he pulled outward and upward, and ripped the tortoise's head from its body. Lucy managed to roll away in time to avoid a spray of blood as the beast collapsed. Mr. Morrison dropped the head near the body and took a step backwards.

Lucy crabbed her way backwards and then scrambled to her feet. She panted hard as she wiped at the blood on her face, and then dusted herself off as though wishing to remove any taint of indignity that comes with having been assaulted by a great turtle.

Mr. Morrison took her chin in one hand and dabbed at her cut with his handkerchief with the other. "Not so bad," he said. "I've seen worse results from a turtle attack."

"It is my own fault. I neglected to bring my turtle bane," Lucy said. She did not know how necessary were Mr. Morrison's ministrations, but she was in no hurry for them to end.

Mr. Morrison smiled. "Lesson learned, eh, Miss Derrick? Do you need a moment?"

"She needs no time," said Mrs. Emmett. "The beast is dead. We must move forward."

"Keeping us upon our toes?" Mr. Morrison let go of Lucy, put away his handkerchief, and gestured down the corridor. "I suggest we make our way back to the drawing room. It is, in its barbaric way, the most habitable portion of the estate."

Mr. Morrison took hold of the lantern once more, and they ascended the stairs that would take them to the dining room. Lucy felt her breaths come short and gasping. Behind her, the flickering light flashed on Mrs. Emmett's pacific expression. They made their way along the darkened abbey, hearing the vague and distant sounds of movement, but seeing nothing. Then, past the dining hall, they climbed the brief stairway and entered the drawing room, where they had encountered Byron during their previous visit.

At the center of the room she saw a dark figure, alone and unmoving. Mr. Morrison walked closer, moving slowly, and she saw that it was someone in a chair. Another few steps and they saw the person's back was toward them and that his hands were tied behind his back. He wore no hat, but it was upon the ground near the chair. There was a string of cloth tied across the back of his head, and Lucy realized the man was gagged.

Lucy started to move forward, but Mr. Morrison held her back. "No," he said softly. "We go slowly."

At a great distance they circled around him, not wishing to approach until they saw everything that lay between them and him. When they reached the far side of the circumference, and believed the approach unhindered, they took a few steps forward. Mr.

Morrison held the lantern out as far before him as he could manage. In the dim light of the room they saw that sitting in the chair in the center of the great hall, bound and gagged, was the owner of the estate, Byron. And upon his lap were two sheets of paper that, even at this great distance, Lucy recognized as the final two pages of the *Mutus Liber.*

This would have struck her as good news had the whole thing not been so very convenient, and had not Byron's eyes been so wide with terror.

34

Lucy moved forward, but Mr. Morrison, once more, stopped her by putting a hand on her shoulder. His touch was gentle and hesitant, and even in these terrible circumstances, it had a tentative shyness that thrilled her.

"Wait," he said. "Let us not do anything hastily."

"We can't leave him bound like that," Lucy said.

"Can you explain why not?" Mr. Morrison asked.

It seemed a good question. Lucy had no wish to set Byron free, not after the way he had treated her, but letting him suffer because he was a scoundrel hardly seemed right. "Because as vile a man as Lord Byron is, he is not our enemy right now, and I should very much like to know who put him there and set out those pages for us."

"Hold the lantern," Mr. Morrison said, thrusting it out to Mrs. Emmett. "I want to make certain there is not some trap upon the pages. Then we shall see to Byron."

While Mrs. Emmett held the lantern aloft, Mr. Morrison carefully approached the baron. Byron's eyes were wide and wet. He rocked back and forth in his chair, and he mumbled under the gag. Perhaps he feared Mr. Morrison would harm him, but somehow Lucy did not think that would happen. Mr. Morrison had been tempted before and resisted, and he was not the sort of man who would take pleasure in revenge against so helpless an enemy. It was possible that Byron would not recognize that, being the sort of man who would take revenge against a helpless enemy.

Mr. Morrison approached, examined with his eyes the pages upon Byron's lap as best he could, and then snatched them up in a rapid gesture. Nothing happened. No monsters attacked and no trapdoor opened. He walked back to Lucy and handed her the pages. She did not even need to look at them to know that they were real. She felt their harmony with the ones in her bag, and she put them in to join their brothers. She saw the familiar images now, which she associated with Mr. Blake — the men at work, struggling against bonds or busy at their labors. One man, nearly naked, held a great boulder upon his back. A woman lay upon her side, suckling wolves. A divine arm extended from the heavens, giving something to the people below, or perhaps unleashing punishment.

As she held them, she felt an energy course through her, but their message was harder to understand than that of the other pages — not because it was less significant, but because it was more complex. Deciphering these pages, let alone the entire book once assembled, would not be the work of hours, but days or weeks. She knew that at once, but she did not know if she would have such time.

"I am going to untie him," Lucy said.

"For what reason?"

"So we know how he got there. Do you not think it important?"

"No," said Mr. Morrison. "We have the pages. We should go."

She shook her head. "I cannot believe it will be that easy, that we will be permitted simply to walk away. Someone has orchestrated this for their benefit, and I would know who."

"Then for God's sake ungag him, but do not let him go."

Lucy walked over to Byron and grabbed the gag from behind his head. He grunted as she tried to pull it off. Clearly it hurt him, but Lucy could see no alternative.

She found the slack and pulled it off. Byron gasped and spat and swallowed and then gulped down the air. He breathed hard, but grinned wildly. "Thank you, Lucy. I knew I could depend upon your goodness."

"I have very little goodness left for you. How did you get here? Who tied you thus?"

"Oh, I cannot recall," he said. "Perhaps my memory will return when you free me."

"Perhaps if I cut off his nose he will recall," Mr. Morrison said drily.

Lucy went to her bag and retrieved a knife. "If I cut him free and he refuses to help us, you may cut off as many pieces of him as you like. For now I will depend upon his humanity."

"That is a poor prospect," Mr. Morrison said.

Lucy cut free his hands and then his feet. Byron rubbed his hands together and raised and lowered his legs as he attempted to restore circulation.

"Ah," he said. "That is the most gratifying thing you have ever done for me, Lucy. There is some hope for you yet."

"Shut your mouth," Mr. Morrison snapped. "Tell us what we want to know. How did you get in this state?"

" 'Shut your mouth'?" Byron repeated. " 'Tell us what we want to know'? Once again, Morrison, you are an intruder in my house, and it seems to me you have no business ordering me to do anything."

"Lord Byron, please," said Lucy. "I know you have done terrible things, and there must be a reckoning, but I have also seen you be brave and selfless. Set aside what you feel for one moment, and do what is right. Tell us."

He sighed. "Only because you are so much kinder than this dullard. Alas, I can tell you almost nothing. I do not know who brought me here. I came from London in search of some personal effects. Once I left, I was upon the road and then abducted. A bag was placed over my head, and I saw nothing of my attackers. They brought me here and kept themselves hidden from me. I have been waiting in that chair since this morning, and, if I may be so bold, I must piss at once or I shall die. Will you excuse me?"

"The quality of this meeting, much to my surprise, continues to deteriorate," said Mr. Morrison. "And that is keeping in mind how basely it began. Let us go, Lucy."

Then came the voice from behind them. "I packaged him for you like a present, and you let him go. I am disappointed, Jonas."

They turned to see Mary Crawford.

She seemed to glow in the near darkness. Her skin was like ivory, her hair almost white, and her gown as white as her hair, but she was not a figure of loveliness. Like her widower, Mary was prepared for war, and she bore two shotguns upon her back in the precise manner Mr. Morrison did. It occurred to Lucy that she knew almost nothing of their lives together. Had they gone on adventures, faced magic and monsters? What had passed between them had been real and true and lived, not like the silly infatuation she had felt for Mr. Morrison when she was sixteen or the foolish attraction she'd felt for Byron. Theirs had been a true love, forged and built and earned. She could see that in Mr. Morrison's eyes as he gazed upon her. He swallowed hard, and appeared to look away, but then turned back, determination in his eyes. He would be telling himself that this was not his wife, not his Mary, Lucy thought. She could not imagine the suffering.

She would have imagined Mrs. Emmett would have reacted more strongly to seeing her old mistress, but she only stood, gazing almost stupidly, awaiting the next situation that would require her attention. This one, evidently, did not.

"I'll not murder him in cold blood," said Mr. Morrison. "Not like that."

"He deserves no better," said Mary.

Mr. Morrison gritted his teeth, and then took a deep intake of breath. "Perhaps not, but I shall have to live with what I do, and I cannot be so base as he. But you don't need me. You could do what you like for yourself."

She shook her head. "I have no fear of consequences. No fear of God or damnation or my immortal soul. I *am* my immortal soul, and if I kill, even once, then why shall I not do so again when it is convenient or when I am angry or looking to amuse myself? I will save this world if I can do so, but I will not take a life except to save another."

"Perhaps you are more like what you once were than I credit," Mr. Morrison said in a quiet voice.

"No," she answered. "If it were you to whom he had done this, my old self would have slit his throat in that chair and never regretted it."

"You killed Spencer Perceval," said Lucy. "You have murdered already."

"I merely put his murderer in Perceval's way," she said. "It is not the same."

"Ahh," said Byron, who had gone off to a corner to make use of a necessary pot. Lucy tried to ignore the sound of splashing. "That is just the thing. Almost better than deflowering a virgin."

"And so you thought to deliver to us Byron and the last two pages," said Lucy.

Mary laughed. "Lucy, you are so sweet. You must understand that those were the only pages I had the means to find, that I ever had the means to find. I did not give the last two pages to you. You have brought the first ten pages to me. Now I must ask you to make them mine, so I can best use them."

Lucy felt her face burn. She felt dizzy, as though the floor had vanished beneath her and she tumbled through space. She thought about the will she had written, leaving the book to Mary. Had this been her strategy all along? Did she mean to kill Lucy now? Lucy had some notion of how to kill revenants, and she had the means upon her, but Mary was strong and quick and clever, and she did not believe she could defeat her in a fight.

"All along, you lied to me," Lucy said quietly. "You used me. You are no better than Buckles or my uncle or Lady Harriett."

"Do not say it, Lucy. I have withheld information I did not think you ready to hear, but it was always with your interests in mind. And in this matter, I have been truthful. It was your destiny to gather the leaves. It was your duty to fight this war by my side. I have always said it, but I will not ask you to do what comes next. I do not wish to trick you, but to fight for you. If you will give me the pages and let me do what needs to be done, I will not take human life, but I will grind Lady Harriett and her kind into the dust. I would fight on behalf of those who labor with their hands, not those who would own that labor and crush those hands. Tell me I am wrong, Lucy, that what I do is in error, and mean it, but if you cannot say it, and have not the will to fight by my side, I do not judge you. I only ask that you step away."

"You may ask," said Mrs. Emmett, "but you may not command."

Mary smiled at the serving woman. "I have

instructed you well, I see. You are Lucy's now, as I wished. But Lucy, you will have to act decisively, and you cannot hesitate. You cannot show compassion for Lady Harriett. You cannot think to spare her or hope she reforms herself. You must have the strength to kill her."

Lucy understood that Mary was right, but she did not like the implications. There were many revenants after all. "It will not end there, will it? Those others, the strange men and women I saw at her estate, they are like you, are they not? If you destroy them, you destroy them forever."

"There is no other way," said Mary. "This is the time of reckoning. Now, Lucy. Tonight. We shall not do things by half measures. We shall not simply destroy Lady Harriett and hope that magic and machines can find some balance. No, Lady Harriett and her kind will fall. Those who have been her toad eaters, like that monster there, with his foolish grin" — she pointed, of course, to Byron — "shall fall with them."

"With you as the new ruler?" asked Mr. Morrison.

"Do you know nothing of me?" she asked. "I know I am not what I was, that I cannot feel as I felt, but am I so alien to you that you think I seek only power? I want only to live in a world worth living in. I will fade into obscurity when this work is done."

"Nevertheless, you've indulged your power, haven't you?" said Byron from across the room. "Someone sent me to warn little Lucy off marrying her intended. Someone made me believe I had feelings for her. That tenderness could not have been mine."

Lucy turned to her. "Is it true? Did you use me so?"

Mary looked down. "I did not use you. I used Byron, and I shall not repent of it. I put him in your way because you needed your world to change. Though I despise him, I knew Byron's appearance and his clumsy affections would have that effect. There was never any real risk to your heart, Lucy, and I cast no love magic upon him. That was you, Lucy. It was your charm, your own magic. You brought out in him what was best even in so base a creature."

Mary's reasoning was cold and logical. She had toyed with Lucy's feelings to effect the end she wanted. It frustrated her because, as terrible as Mary's actions were, they were not so different from what she herself had done to Mr. Morrison.

None of this was about her or her pride, however. She would examine her resentment more closely another time. "And Ludd, whom you have summoned into this world?" she asked. "What does he care for?"

"This island," answered Mary. "This land. The people in it. Nothing more. He cares not for power, nor for empire, or dominion over nations — which has been the care of your little band of Rosicrucians, has it not, Jonas? We have no care if England is the weakest or the strongest nation in the world so long as its people have bread and their share of happiness."

"The *Mutus Liber* is strongest in the hands of the person to whom it belongs," Lucy said. "You want me to gift you the book because you do not think I will do what must be done."

"I would spare you from doing it," Mary said.

"Spare me nothing," said Lucy. "This is my task, and I shall endure it, I hope with your help. But for now, let us take the book and go while we still can."

"Hold," said Mr. Morrison. "If her intentions are no more than she says, then why did she send her monster to attack us?"

"What monster?" asked Mary, her eyes suddenly narrowing.

"Byron's tortoise," Lucy said. "It was transformed into a raging beast and set upon us."

Mary's expression darkened. "Lucy, for the love of God, we must leave at once."

"What is it?" Mr. Morrison asked.

"If what you say is true, then Lady Harriett is here, upon these grounds."

■ ■ ■ ■

In a swift motion, Mary removed one of her shotguns and held it in her hands. It looked absurdly incongruous — she, the pale, ethereal beauty, taking hold of the weapon.

Mr. Morrison watched her for a moment then took one of his own weapons. "They're here?"

She nodded. "I can feel them. I've loaded my gun against their kind, but my little trick won't work on Lady Harriett, you know. She is too powerful."

"I know," he said. "After I killed her late husband, she found a way to indemnify herself against it, but not the others."

"Have you discovered what will work on her?" asked Mary.

"Not yet," he said.

Mary turned to Byron. "Why would she choose to come here? Have you made any arrangements with Lady Harriett? Have you leased her any land? Is anything here *hers?*"

Lucy understood. At Lady Harriett's estate, Lucy's charms had been ineffective because there had been wards against them, wards that only the rightful owner of a property could employ. Newstead ought to be neutral, but if Lady Harriett had legally acquired the rights to part of it, that part might be protected.

"Oh, put the shotgun away, Mary," said Byron. "It is unbecoming. Yes, I leased her some land. She wished to use part of my property to establish a hosiery mill, of all things."

Mr. Olson's new mill. It came full circle. "So much for your speech in defense of the Luddites in the House of Lords," Lucy said.

"Oh, I never really believed most of that. It sounded quite right, of course, but there is politics and there is money, and I know which I value more, so when Lady Harriett made her offer, my lukewarm sympathy for the Luddites cooled entire. In any case, I owed her a debt, and Lady Harriett is not someone to refuse."

"There must be something in the contract that grants her power here," Mr. Morrison said to Lucy. "She will first try to make you give her the pages. She will want to take them from you by force, but her first choice will be to own them. Lucy, you cannot let her have them. Better to destroy the book than to let her have it."

Lucy clutched the pages to her chest. "If we destroy the book, we will have no weapon against her. If I cannot defeat her, I cannot safely return my niece to her mother. We must get away until I've had a chance to learn what the book will teach me."

Mary smiled at Lucy. "I admire your courage, Lucy, and applaud your sentiments. I shall lead the way. In the meantime, I suggest we do something about Byron. He is a menace and unpredictable."

The latter part of her assessment certainly proved correct, for when they looked around, Byron was nowhere to be found. After a brief discussion it was agreed that he could not easily be discovered if he wished to hide in his own ruined abbey, and that he possessed little that could harm them and nothing they needed. While he might have run off to alert Lady Harriett to their presence, taking the time to search for him would be a self-defeating effort. In short, their first priority was flight. Byron was a problem that would wait for a more opportune moment.

Lucy held out her hand to Mary. "We might be separated. I must have what is mine."

With no more hesitation than a few rapid blinks, Mary handed the final pages to Lucy. They felt as heavy as iron in her hands, as alive as a beating heart, as vital as a bolt of lightning. She did not even look at them except long enough to see the telltale signs of Mr. Blake's designs. They felt so powerful, they frightened her, and they seemed to be gathering power, quickening in her grasp, urging her to action. The pages wanted to be looked at, to be understood and deciphered.

She closed her mind to them. New ideas would only confuse and distract. There would be time enough for that when she was alone.

Instead she took the pages and placed them with the others. She rolled them up into a tube and placed them into the secret folds of her frock, where she kept her herbs and charms and tokens. The secret pockets were getting heavy with old and discarded tokens of her adventure that she dared not throw away, for she could not know what she would need to survive.

Mary led them out of the hall toward the main entrance. The body of the horrible tortoise lay there, already covered with an impossibly thick halo of flies. More flies crawled upon it, countless flies, an impossible number, so that the body appeared a living, writhing, buzzing mass. It turned Lucy's stomach, and she hesitated to approach, and in that moment of hesitation she saw movement in the darkness. Four figures, cloaked in shadow, and yet vaguely familiar. In the flickering light of Mrs. Emmett's lantern, Lucy recognized the revenants she had seen in Lady Harriett's house, led by the gray-haired Mr. Whitestone.

"Oh, dear," said Mr. Whitestone, stepping forward. "Lady Harriett says we are to take your book, young lady. Please hand it to me."

At that instant, Mr. Morrison and Mary raised their shotguns.

Mr. Whitestone managed a nervous smile. The other three revenants looked at them and then at Mr. Whitestone, then at the ground. They seemed dazed and disoriented, and Lucy understood they were so impossibly old that their sense of self had in some manner altered. They had been in the world so long, they were no longer of this world.

"You cannot harm us," said Mr. Whitestone. "There is no point in resisting."

"If we cannot harm you," said Mr. Morrison, "why did Lady Harriett not come herself?"

"We *can* harm you, and we will," said Mary.

"No," answered Mr. Whitestone. "You would not use our own secrets against your own kind. You have never wished to be one of us, but you cannot be so lost as that, Miss Crawford."

He stepped forward, reaching out as if to take Mary's weapon away from her. She fired. The heavy scent of rotten eggs filled the air, and Mr. Whitestone staggered backwards, a massive wound open in his chest. Shot had scattered among the other revenants, but their wounds were smaller, less brutal. They bled all the same.

"This feels odd," said Mr. Whitestone, looking down at his wound. "It does not close."

They had filled their shotguns with sulfur, mercury, and gold, allowing the shot to penetrate and preventing the wounds from closing. The same understanding crossed Mr. Whitestone's pale face. He staggered forward and fell to his knees. He looked up at Lucy, as though she were the one who had fired upon him. "All along," he said, "it was you. And here is the other secret." But he said no more. He pitched forward, face-first onto the cold stone.

The three remaining revenants looked at one another, then looked down at the body, then looked at Mr. Morrison and Mary, who was in the process of discarding her spent weapon for the fresh one. Perhaps the creatures were so outraged that one of their own had been, impossibly, killed, but Lucy did not think so. Even at that moment she could not help but believe they wanted to die, to end their existence, these creatures who had walked the earth for so many centuries that they could no longer remember who or what they were. They leapt forward and Mary and Mr. Morrison discharged their weapons nearly simultaneously. Mr. Morrison then cast his spent gun aside and took the fresh one, and fired it into the mass moving toward him.

Smoke engulfed Lucy and her party. Neither Mr. Morrison nor Mary made an effort to reload their weapons, and Lucy suspected the process was too complicated to do in the midst of a conflict. She had no idea what they intended to do if the revenants were not all down, but as soon as the smoke began to clear, she saw that they posed no further threat. Two of them were still, and one — a woman with thick white hair — lay on her back, her gown covered with blood, her fingers twitching like a dying beetle. It sickened Lucy to look at it, but in a moment the creature stopped all motion. It lay still, eyes impossibly wide.

Lucy looked at Mary to see her reaction, to see if killing her own kind had taken a toll, but on her face was only grim satisfaction. "Let us reload and continue," she said.

"Mary —" began Mr. Morrison.

"You cannot understand, so there is nothing to say," she said, not unkindly. "This is why I am here. Not to talk, not to negotiate, and not to capitulate. I am here to end them. Now reload." She tossed one of her weapons to Mrs. Emmett, who caught it easily with one hand. "You know what to do?"

"I've always known," said Mrs. Emmett.

Mary smiled. "In case you needed to protect Lucy from me."

Mrs. Emmett betrayed neither pleasure nor pride. "I did not think it likely, but I thought it best to be prepared."

Some ten minutes later, after a lengthy process of mixing shot, gold dust, sulfur, and mercury into their weapons, they were ready to proceed. Lucy was frightened and determined, but she also felt strangely useless. She might have owned the book, but this was Mr. Morrison and Mary's adventure. She was merely the person who needed protecting. They were a team. She hated the feeling of being left out, and she realized, much to her own surprise, that what she wanted was to impress them — to impress Mary, to be sure, but to impress Mr. Morrison most of all. She wanted to be worthy of him, to be as useful as Mary made herself, but even after all she had learned and done, she was still weak and ignorant and helpless.

"Will there be more?" asked Lucy.

"That depends on how much they want to die," answered Mary.

They walked out the front door, and Boatswain, the ghost dog, remained there, but it flared its ghostly nostrils in Mary's direction, let out a hollow bark, then a whimper, and fled.

They took only a few steps before Lucy realized the coach in which they had arrived was no longer there.

"Very well," said Mr. Morrison. "It does seem rather hopeless, but it's not. Not entirely. Here is what we are going to do."

He never had a chance to explain his plan, however, because right then men emerged from the woods. There must have been a dozen of them, their long rifles raised to their eyes as they advanced like soldiers upon a battlefield. These were not revenants, but mortal men.

"They cannot harm me," Mary said quietly,

"but I cannot disarm them all before they fire their weapons. The chance of harm coming to you or Mr. Morrison is too great."

"What do we do?" asked Lucy.

"You may have to confront Lady Harriett now. Tonight."

"I am not ready," Lucy said. She felt lightheaded and terrified. She was not ready for this. The confrontation could not come now. "I don't know what to do. You and Mr. Morrison know what you are doing, but I do not."

"You will have to be ready," Mary said. "The book is yours. Be worthy. Take what the book offers. Remember what I told you. Twelve pages and twelve enchantments. Power and luck. Do not depend upon them, but know that the pages want you to succeed."

"You *are* ready," said Mr. Morrison. "You know more than you allow yourself to believe."

His voice cut through the buzzing in her head, the cold grip of fear. There was something else. A warm feeling she hardly understood until she realized that he held her hand firmly in his own. He smiled at her, and Lucy managed a smile in return. She would be ready. She had to be.

One of the men stepped forward to collect their weapons. They took Mr. Morrison's guns and bag, and they took Mary's guns, but they did not search her or Lucy other than to ask them to remove their pelisses to make certain they contained no weapons. Lucy still had the pages of her book and many more things besides hidden in the folds of her frock. She did not know that she would be able to put what she had to use, but it made her feel better to have at least something.

Half the men moved behind them, with two at each side, and two in front. They were then marched along a path around the back of the estate. Lucy huddled close to Mary, and Mr. Morrison walked behind the two of them, trailed by Mrs. Emmett, who hummed softly to herself.

The men led them through a narrow path that bisected a thick wood. Off in the distance they saw glowing lights through the trees, and Lucy perceived that they were coming upon some sort of habitation. In another moment or two she began to hear a repetitive and discordant clicking noise, one she had heard before. It took her a moment to recognize it as the beat of stocking frames. They were hard by the newly built mill. It was low and flat and wooden. Despite the late hour, it was in full operation.

The path took a sharp turn around a thick and ancient copse that had been obscuring their vision, but when they came out into a clearing the mill was revealed, larger than Mr. Olson's old mill, nearly twice as large.

Though it had few windows, the light blasted out of them as though the building were on fire. It was also guarded. Here was a mill that would stand against the Luddites. Armed men stalked the perimeter, and there was even a tower from which one man stood with a long rifle. The guards showed no alarm at their arrival, however. Near the door, a burly man with a few days of beard raised his upper lip in a sneer.

"Got them, did you?"

"Likely so," said one of the armed men.

"We was told to expect only three women."

Lucy looked around, not knowing what he meant, but walking alongside was Sophie Hyatt. How long she had been with them, and how had she joined them without the armed men knowing or objecting? Lucy turned to her. "What do you do here, Sophie? It isn't safe."

She shrugged. Whatever her reasons, she was unwilling to write it upon her slate.

These men would hardly let Sophie go, but Lucy wished to try something.

She could not simply react to whatever circumstance Lady Harriett presented. She would need to plan ahead, form her strategy, anticipate her enemy's actions. While the armed men talked among themselves, Lucy took the deaf girl aside. The others watched as the girl wrote a few things on her slate. Lucy nodded, and Sophie wiped away her words with her palm. And though she hated to take the risk, Lucy did what she had to. She put herself at risk, she put Sophie at risk, and worst of all, she put Emily at risk, but to not take that chance would be to condemn them all.

"You will not betray me?" Lucy asked.

Sophie shook her head. *Never,* she wrote on her slate.

It would have to be good enough. Lucy prayed it would be.

At last the guards opened the door for them, and the armed men gestured for them to go inside. They did not follow. Lucy stepped inside and saw a mill much like Mr. Olson's previous establishment, though better lit for the nighttime work, and far, far bigger. There was row upon row of women and children and the elderly, working their stocking frames as overseers walked the space between them, cudgels at the ready. It was an almost deafening tumult from the machines as they churned out their hosiery, and the noise was interrupted only by the occasional thwack of a cudgel or the cry of a stricken worker.

Mr. Olson now came up to them, hobbling upon a cane, one leg bulky under his trousers where it was no doubt wrapped in bandages. He was red in the face, and his eyes were sunken and ringed with alarming blackness, and yet there was a look of contentment, almost childlike happiness, on his face. Lucy had never seen him so happy, and she could not help but see his mood as a dark sign.

"Ah, Miss Derrick," said Mr. Olson, waving his hand in a vestigial hint at a bow. "Reunited at last. And I am told Mr. Buckles is on his way, too."

Lucy snorted. "You cannot still think to force me to marry you."

"We are past that, I fear," he said. "What happens now is all in Lady Harriett's hands. She wishes for you to meet her in her chamber. Follow me, though we shall not move too quickly, I fear. I'm not so limber as I once was." This last was said without bitterness. Indeed, he barked a little laugh.

"I think we are all quite comfortable here," said Mr. Morrison. "Well, perhaps comfortable is overstating it a bit, but we are as comfortable as we should hope to be. I think if Lady Harriett wishes a word with us, she ought to come out here."

"I beg your pardon, sir," said Mr. Olson, leaning heavily upon his cane. "You have been rude to me in the past, and I am grieved to see you would continue this infamous tradition."

"You may call it rudeness if you like, but I am determined. Now run along and fetch her. We are waiting patiently."

"It is too loud," said Mr. Olson. "The noise will distress Lady Harriett's ears. She has condescended to speak with you, and it is wrong to reject her generosity."

There was something in his tone that seemed familiar to Lucy. It took her a moment, but then it occurred to her that he was acting and speaking like Mr. Buckles. Could it be that Lady Harriett had worked some sort of enchantment upon him, and she now worked it upon Mr. Olson?

"No doubt this entire building is well warded," said Mr. Morrison, "but she will have particular protections in her chamber. I don't think that suits us. As for the noise, if she doesn't care for it, send your workers home."

The expression of good humor dropped from Mr. Olson's face. "Have you any idea what a night's labors is worth?"

"No," said Mr. Morrison. "Nor do I care. But I believe I understand what Lady Harriett's patronage is worth to you."

Mr. Olson stared at him, and then turned to limp off to the far end of the mill. In a few moments the overseers removed whistles, and began to let out a series of sharp tones. The workers looked about in surprise, but were soon setting down their hose and exiting the building. It took perhaps a quarter hour for them all to depart, and soon the five of them found themselves standing alone in a cavernous and deserted building. Without the workers and their sounds, the space seemed larger and even more forlorn. The overseers were gone, and strange though it was, Lucy would have felt comforted by their presence. Perhaps they might have acted as a restraint upon Lady Harriett.

"What now?" asked Lucy.

"She'll come," said Mary. "You should be in no great hurry."

"I've faced her before," said Lucy, attempting to summon her courage. She had seen Lady Harriett toss Byron across the room as though he were an unwanted pillow. What could they do to stop her now?

"You have not faced her when she is desperate," said Mary. "She will do anything to get that book from you. You must know it. She will want you to gift it to her. It is not too late to gift the book to me, Lucy. I can protect it better than you."

"Leave her be about the damn book!" said Mrs. Emmett, her voice sharp.

Everyone stared at her. Lucy had never heard her speak so, and it seemed to her, as it must seem to everyone, that this strange, meek woman, with her hair perpetually in her eyes, must be incapable of such passion.

Mary recoiled as though slapped. "I want only to help."

"I know you do," Mrs. Emmett answered. "You want to bear the burden for her, but you cannot. It has always been Miss Derrick. You must accept that. You resist it because you love her, but you must not permit her to doubt herself."

They heard a door open and footsteps. They could not see across the mill, for the stocking frames obscured their vision, and in silent assent they agreed not to move. Soon Lady Harriett appeared, flanked on one side by Mrs. Quince, on the other by Mr. Buckles. So, Mrs. Quince had, all that time, been in Lady Harriett's employ. Lucy should not have been surprised. Indeed, it all made sense, and she would have felt more indignation had not her attention been arrested by a far more urgent matter. Mr. Buckles held in his arms a baby, and Lucy knew it at once to be Emily. The real Emily, small and pink and sleeping sweetly in the arms of her father, who was so eager to sacrifice her to his mistress. Yet, she appeared calm and healthy and unharmed for the moment. Lady Harriett would use Emily's life to bargain for the book. Of that there could be no doubt, and Lucy did not know that she would have the strength to resist. And yet she would have to, for Emily's sake, for everyone's sake.

The urge to step forward and grab the child was overwhelming. It roared in her ears and spots manifested before her eyes. She wanted that baby, wanted to protect her from her father and Lady Harriett, but she knew that was not the way. Attempting to take Emily by force would only endanger her. She would protect her niece, but she would have to be clever. Lady Harriett would try to force Lucy to choose between the child and the book, but Lucy could not. She would be worthy of the burdens placed upon her and find a way to leave with both.

Lucy looked over at Mr. Morrison, and he inclined his head in the most imperceptible of nods. He seemed to have deduced her reasoning, and agreed with it. Do not rush. Do nothing to put the child in danger. Wait for the moment.

Mary was less calm. "Dear Lord. She's found Emily. I would not have thought it possible."

Lucy had been so absorbed by her niece that she had hardly given Mr. Buckles a second glance, but now she observed that he was greatly altered. His skin appeared less sallow and more pale. His hair had turned far lighter, and his eyes were a peculiar blue. Gone was his expression of simpering foolishness. He looked at Lucy, and his countenance held nothing but cold cruelty. He was not what he had been before. Mr. Buckles had died and returned. He was now a revenant, and that meant none of them, not even Mary, could hope to be fast or strong enough to rescue the child by force.

Lady Harriett and her retinue stopped perhaps ten feet from them. "So, it comes to this," she said. "All will be resolved tonight."

"Lady Harriett," said Mr. Morrison. "You look well. No, that's not it precisely. Not well. Awful. That is what I meant. You look awful. Like the dead warmed over, so to speak."

"Silence, Morrison," said Lady Harriett. "You and your kind disgust me. You cannot hope I shall let you live."

"What makes you think I shall let *you* live?" answered Mr. Morrison.

"Your shotgun shall not work on me. You must know that. I have ordered it so the revenant who leads is imbued with a special strength, and so resistant to those elements."

Mr. Morrison scratched his head, as though genuinely confused. "I do recall hearing something about that, yes. On the other hand, I was told that your late husband would be impossible to kill, and I made short work of him. Or perhaps you did not know that was I."

It seemed to Lucy Lady Harriett had not known that Mr. Morrison was responsible for the destruction of her beloved Sir Reginald. She blinked at this intelligence, and then glanced at Mr. Buckles. "Give them a taste of things to come," she said.

Moving forward quickly, impossibly quickly, Mr. Buckles was no longer ten feet away, but directly before Mrs. Emmett. Mrs. Quince now held Emily, and Mr. Buckles, with his lips pulled back in a vicious sneer, grabbed the serving woman by the hair, and, gather-

581

ing it all in his left hand, he lifted her off the ground. Mrs. Emmett's eyes went wide, and her mouth opened, but no noise came out. Below her skirts, her legs kicked, and her arms flapped like a drowning woman's. Below Mr. Buckles's clenched fist Lucy could see, for the first time, Mrs. Emmett's forehead, and she now understood she had kept her hair and bonnet low in order to conceal her flesh. Inscribed, just above her thin eyebrows, written seemingly in thick black ash, were three Hebrew letters: אמת. Lucy struggled with what little she knew of Hebrew, and realized, once she remembered to read the letters from right to left, that the word spelled *emmet.*

Lucy searched her memory — for it was so familiar — and then it came to her. The Jewish story of the golem. She'd read of it in more than one of the books she'd had from Mary. In the legend, Jewish magicians were able to create a man out of mud, and upon its forehead was inscribed the word אמת — *emmet* — meaning "truth." To destroy the golem, the first letter was erased leaving only מת: *met.* "Dead."

Mr. Buckles smiled, as though he saw that Lucy now understood. He raised his free hand and allowed it to hover over the א.

"No," said Lucy.

"It is mindless thing," said Lady Harriett. "It has no soul. It is an abomination, but I

582

know it is of some value to you, so I shall give you one opportunity to save it. Give me the book now, or I shall have Buckles destroy it."

Mrs. Emmett's eyes went wide. "I shall not be used against Miss Derrick. I could never allow it. The sacrifice I make, I make for her." So saying she reached up and, shoving Mr. Buckles's hand out of the way, wiped away the ℵ. from her forehead in a clean and simple stroke.

It happened faster than the eye could register. Mr. Buckles held nothing in his hand. At his feet fell a tangle of wet, watery mud and clothing. It landed with a solid splash, heavy and sickening. Mrs. Emmett was gone.

Unspeakable sadness shot through Lucy. She felt Mary take her hand, and she squeezed it hard for a terrible moment, as though her friend's cold touch was the only thing that prevented her from collapsing. She stood that way, like the victim of a lightning strike, absorbing electricity, and then it passed. She let go, for though the sadness was not diminished, it had receded. Anger took its place.

That anger was real and solid and heavy, but it was not all she felt. Lucy felt alive and strong, coursing with a new vitality. It was Mrs. Emmett's words. She knew that. She had made a *sacrifice* of herself, and Lucy had gained something. She knew not what, but it was powerful, and it wanted to strike.

Mr. Buckles lifted his lips in a lupine approximation of a smile as he retreated to stand by Lady Harriett. He brazenly put a hand upon her shoulder, a gesture of startling intimacy.

"It is remarkable," said Mrs. Quince. "I tried to make such a thing once. Jewish magic was always too devious for an honest Englishwoman like myself."

"I shall teach you," said Lady Harriett. "It is no difficult thing, even for a weak-minded woman like you, Quince. Though Mary made a particularly clever one. Still, even the cleverest of tricks can be undone, as we have witnessed. And what of the infant? Is not that baby but another trick, an ugly illusion of copulation and generation. It sickens me."

"It was as vile in the making as it is now," said Mr. Buckles.

"Dear God," Lucy said. "I hate you for daring to touch my sister."

"Oh, don't be so sanctimonious," said Lady Harriett. "You cared for that lifeless bit of clay, so what do your feelings for your sister or her wretched child signify? You will give your pathetic heart to anything who looks upon you. It is what has undone you, you know. Your compassion."

Lucy felt black rage course through her. She had known people who were small and petty and selfish and vile, but never had she encountered pure evil. Whatever reservations she had had about destroying Lady Harriett, destroying her forever, were gone. She would do what she must. "My compassion does not extend to you," she said.

"I do not fear you," said Lady Harriett. "How could I, when your loyalties are so easily manipulated? Now, here is what happens next. You shall give me the pages of the *Mutus Liber,* and I shall give you your niece. If you do not, I shall make you watch while Mr. Buckles kills her. None of your spells will work here, girl. This building, like my home, is warded. You can give me the pages in fair trade, or I can take them by force, and you would not like that."

Lucy had defeated wards before, but she did not think she could depend upon doing so. "How can I know you will give me Emily?"

"What care I for the baby?" asked Lady Harriett. "It was only ever of interest because it was important to you. But I am serious in my threat. Mr. Buckles, take the child, and be ready to strangle it when I command."

Buckles took the baby from Mrs. Quince's arms. He held it in the crook of his arm, but there was no tenderness in him. He might have been holding a log.

"You must not believe her," Mr. Morrison told Lucy. "Do nothing on her terms."

"I cannot see that I have a choice," she answered. She turned back to Lady Harriett. "What will you do with the pages besides cast away Ludd?"

"That is my concern, not yours."

Lucy stood still for a long moment, neither moving nor blinking. She then reached into the folds of her gown and pulled out a rolled tube of papers. Tentatively, she held them out while Lady Harriett stepped forward and snatched them from her hand, as though fearful that Lucy was a serpent ready to strike.

"No!" Mary and Mr. Morrison cried out at once, but the act was already finished. Lady Harriett had the pages.

Lady Harriett retreated back to her own people and examined the pages. "They are remarkable," she said, leafing through them. Her chest heaved with her breathing, and her face colored. "You give them to me? These are mine?"

"Lucy," Mary cautioned.

"Yes, I give them to you," said Lucy. "They are yours for so long as you want them. Now give me my niece."

Lady Harriett smiled at her. "No. I don't think I will."

"Why do you want her?" said Lucy. Her voice was shrill, even to her own ears. "You said she means nothing to you."

"I want her for spite," said Lady Harriett. "Perhaps it is because of your friend Mr.

Morrison, and the debt I owe him for striking down Sir Reginald. Perhaps it is because I hate you enough for your own sake. Perhaps I want to keep her to punish you for standing in my way, and to mock you for agreeing so foolishly to trust me. Having her gives me pleasure in direct proportion to your pain, and it allows me to show you how poorly you played your hand. I now have everything, and you nothing. With this book I can destroy all of you, and there is nothing you can do. You have made a great blunder."

Lucy could not help but smile. She did not think of herself as a vengeful person, as one who took pleasure in the suffering of others, but this was different. Here was Lady Harriett who had lost all shred of her humanity, who was evil beyond reckoning. She thought herself superior to everyone, but she was not superior to Lucy Derrick.

"I would have blundered indeed," said Lucy, "had I given you the true pages."

Lady Harriett looked through them again. "You lie. I have seen the false pages, and these are not the same, but they are of the same hand."

"I had them of the artist who drew the true pages," said Lucy. "They were a parting gift from a very wise man. I believe this is what Mr. Morrison would call sleight of hand."

From the corner of her eye, she saw Mr. Morrison gazing at her with open admiration. She suspected that if she took the time to think about it, she would very much like the feeling.

Lady Harriett looked at the false pages. She stared at them and then sniffed them like a dog and rubbed them against her face. The truth of Lucy's claim made itself known to her, and she tossed Mr. Blake's drawings down in disgust.

"Very clever," said Lady Harriett. "But I do not make idle threats. A father sacrificing a child on my behalf — a sacrifice on that order shall give me the power I need to force you to gift me the book. Kill the child, Buckles."

"He shall not!" cried Mary. "Lucy, be prepared to take the baby."

Lucy turned and saw that, while their attention had been on Emily, Mary had surrounded herself with something upon the floor, a circle that glinted and sparkled in the dim light. Lucy understood at once what it was — Mary had encircled herself in gold.

Casting her gaze to Mr. Buckles, she saw him standing in mute horror, the baby still cradled in his arm, but he appeared to have forgotten it. He made no effort to harm it. He merely stared in disbelief.

"No," said Lucy, her voice cracking. She remembered the story Mary had told her, and she knew what the circle meant. "There must be another way."

Mary shook her head. "No, my dear Lucy.

588

There is but one way."

Lady Harriett had her eyes fixed upon Mr. Buckles, and seemed not to have noticed the circle upon the floor. "Buckles, why is that child still alive? Sacrifice it to me."

"Look at the Crawford woman," he snapped back. "She's drawn a circle."

"Don't be an idiot," said Lady Harriett. "Spells won't work here."

"Not a spell circle," hissed Buckles. "One of *our* circles."

"It is far more elemental than a spell," said Mary. "You should know that. It is the flow of the universe itself, and your wards will no more hold it than you could hold back the wind with a basket."

Lady Harriett turned toward Mary, and seeing the thin line of gold upon the ground, she set her jaw hard, perhaps in defiance, perhaps in disdain. "You'll not sacrifice yourself for that infant."

"I cannot let you have the book. If you take possession of it, the age of the machine will be ushered in, and nothing will stop it."

"No," said Buckles, his eyes wide with understanding. He understood what Mary did, what it meant. "I won't harm the child. Here, Quince, take it."

Mrs. Quince shrank back. She wanted no part of the child either, and so, desperate, Mr. Buckles rushed forward and handed his daughter to Lucy. "Take it! Take it, and see that I do not harm it. Now stop your friend."

"You blockhead!" cried Lady Harriet.

"Get behind me!" shouted Mr. Morrison, raising his shotgun. "This may not kill you, Lady Harriett, but I'll wager it will sting."

Lucy retreated behind Mr. Morrison. Emily was deep in infant sleep, but healthy and unharmed. It was her niece. She hugged her to her chest, feeling her warmth, listening to the low rumble of her breathing, smelled the yeasty odor of milk about her mouth. It was truly her niece in her arms, safe at last.

Lady Harriett stepped forward, but Mr. Morrison put his finger on the trigger, and she stopped.

"That's right," he said. "It's hard to retrieve a baby when you are writhing upon the floor in pain. I recall that is how it was with your husband. The first blast did not kill him, but it made him much easier to manage."

Lady Harriett balled her fists in rage. Her face turned red, and she whirled on Mrs. Quince. "Do something!"

"I don't know what to do!" Mrs. Quince cried out.

Mr. Buckles was in full panic. "She hasn't stopped. Why hasn't she stopped? I've returned the child. One of you must stop her."

Mary looked up, and her eyes were moist. Her hands trembled as she poured a sprinkling of sulfur atop the gold, but there was a smile upon her lips. "I cannot let you live while you are willing to destroy what Lucy loves best. You would harm your own daughter simply to gratify your mistress, and so that is why I have already done it. Can you not see that? I have contained myself in the circle. I cannot turn back."

"Please," said Mr. Buckles. "Miss Derrick, you have the child. Tell her to spare me."

"Mary," Lucy said softly, beginning to understand what her friend intended. "You may stop."

"It is too late to stop."

Lucy clutched her niece even more tightly, as if her hold on this infant could steady her while her world appeared to whirl around her. "Mary, you cannot. I have Emily. I have the pages. With your help, we can escape and defeat Lady Harriett another day."

"It cannot be undone," said Mary. "Gold and sulfur have been set down, and I have made this sacrifice. Like Mrs. Emmett, I make the sacrifice for you."

Mr. Morrison turned to her. "No, Mary, you cannot."

"Oh, Jonas, I am sorry you must see," she said. "I tried to love you — to remember what it was to love you, but that part of me died with my flesh. Even so, I feel compassion for you, and I beg you not let the past stop you. And Lucy, you have been my friend. I have loved you, and I do this for you."

"Oh, Mary," said Lucy, "please don't."

Mary smiled at her. "It is better to be nothing than to become like one of them." She looked at Lady Harriett and Buckles. "How long until I forget what I was, and care nothing but for my own pleasures? How long until, like her, I am willing to murder an infant for some strategic advantage or the pleasure of shocking my own sensibilities, to destroy a world if it will better suit my needs? How long until I become like those wraiths she shepherds, existing but hardly alive? If I can end my existence in an act of love, then how much better for me to face oblivion as some reflection of my true self, than eternity as a perversion of what I once was." She took out a vial, this one containing mercury, and she began to pour it in a circle around her. "Thank you, Lucy," she said.

And then she was gone.

There was no flash, no cry, nothing to mark her passage. She simply dissolved out of existence, as though the air folded over her. At the same instant Mr. Buckles was gone. He was no longer in the room with them, and Lady Harriett stood in mute astonishment.

Lucy set down the child behind Mr. Morrison, who kept his gun trained on Lady Harriett. She needed her hands free. Reaching into the hidden pocket of her frock for her little pouch and fishing out the talisman she needed, finding it by touch even as she worked herself into a sprint, Lucy ran directly at Lady Harriett. Perhaps she was about to die, but she would not let anyone else die for her. There had been sacrifice enough, and Lucy would rather die than let Mrs. Emmett and Mary destroy themselves for nothing.

With the talisman in her hand, she leapt at Lady Harriett, shoving it deep into the revenant's black gown. It was the talisman to vulnerability, the one she had made in Lady Harriett's house after seeing Byron tossed across the room. The wards should have rendered it useless, but Lucy remembered Mary's words the day she had first told her about the *Mutus Liber.* The most powerful sacrifices could nullify the most powerful of wards, she'd said, and the most powerful sacrifices are those that friends make out of love. Two of Lucy's friends had obliterated themselves from the universe out of love for her.

Lady Harriett toppled under her. Lucy saw the look of surprise on her face as the two of them struck the earth of the mill. Lady Harriett tried to rise, tried to push her off, but her arms had no strength, and Lucy saw the panic in her ancient eyes.

Straddling Lady Harriett, holding her still with the weight of her body and her left arm, Lucy fished in her bag until she found her tiny vials of gold, sulfur, and mercury. Placing them between her fingers, pressed near her knuckles, she removed the cork stoppers with her teeth. She then gripped all three vials in her tight fist, and glared hard at Lady Harriett.

"You are a fool if you don't know that I am immune," said Lady Harriett.

"Oh, I know," answered Lucy.

"Then what do you mean to do with your elements?"

"I mean to make you eat them."

She pressed her free hand to Lady Harriett's jaw and forced it open, as one would with an animal, and poured in the contents of all three vials. Lucy shifted hands, using her left to hold Lady Harriett's head still. The revenant's eyes bulged. Her body bucked weakly, and her arms flailed ineffectually at Lucy's sides. She might have been immune to the elements, but surely they were unpleasant. Beneath her shut mouth, Lady Harriett appeared to retch.

Maybe her efforts would amount to nothing, and maybe all her friends had given would be in vain, but what Lucy intended *seemed* possible. She *might* suceed, and so Lucy intended that she *must* succeed. The pages would want that. Twelve pages and twelve enchantments. By itself that meant little, but with everything Lucy knew and did, with everything Mary and Mrs. Emmett had given, perhaps those twelve enchantments would mean everything.

"Mr. Morrison," called Lucy. "As we have

been disarmed, be so good as to find a knife for me as quickly as you might."

Mr. Morrison, with his free hand, drew one from inside his waistcoat and handed it to Lucy. "Sleight of hand," he said. "But what do you mean to do, Lucy? The power of those sacrifices must wear off soon, and the elements may make her unhappy, but they shan't kill her."

"Let's see about that," said Lucy. She took the knife and began to carve into Lady Harriett's forehead. She would have to act quickly because she knew that the revenants healed with remarkable speed, but she believed she could effect it in time. That she was straddling this woman, carving into her flesh, she was distantly aware of, but she was too focused on the act, on the necessity of what she did to dwell on its strangeness and barbarity. First she drew a square of tolerable symmetry, and then, within it, a triangle. Below her, Lady Harriett struggled against the power of the symbol, and she understood its meaning. She redoubled her efforts to throw Lucy off, and Lucy detected a new strength. Perhaps it was her will to save herself, or the power of the sacrifice was already fading. Either way, Lucy was almost finished. It was the same symbol Lucy had left upon Mr. Gilley, who was so afraid of catching cold — the talisman to make its victim susceptible to what he most feared.

With one last quick stroke, Lucy made an X inside the triangle, completing the charm by speaking Lady Harriett's name. Briefly Lucy wondered how she would know if it worked, but it was but an instant, for Lady Harriett was gone, vanished as if she had never been there. Lucy knelt over the empty earth, knife in her hand, and even its tip was clean of blood.

Lucy rose, letting the blade fall to the earth. She scooped Emily off the floor and cradled the cooing child to her breast. She had done it. She had done it all. She had rescued her niece, saved the book, and destroyed the most powerful and dangerous creature to walk the earth. It had cost her Mrs. Emmett, and it had cost her Mary, and Lucy could take no joy in what she had done. She must settle for relief.

Lucy wanted to cry for her friend and for herself and for her loss, but she would not. She would cry later. "Have we won?" she asked Mr. Morrison. "Is there more to do, or have we won?"

Mr. Morrison stared at the spot where Mary had stood, he looked at the empty circle. "Yes," he said. "You have done it."

Lucy clutched the baby tighter. How she resembled Martha, and also her namesake, Emily. There was nothing of Mr. Buckles in the baby, though perhaps that was wishful thinking. What mattered was that the child was safe. Lucy had the sweet, sleeping child in her arms. Their struggles were over. Mr. Morrison had said so.

She turned to him to say something to comfort him, to let him know that he was not alone in his grief. She was about to speak, but no sound came out for she watched as his chest exploded with blood.

Lord Byron strode into the room, tossing aside the freshly fired pistol. In his other hand he held a torch, and with his newly free hand he removed another pistol from his pocket "That was so we know that I'm serious. Also, I've always hated him. Now, Lucy, give me the book, and give me the baby. The baby you shall get back. It is merely a means by which I can get away unharmed. You'll not curse me or bring down any dark magic upon me if the baby is in my care. When I am somewhere safe, I shall send you the child."

With Emily clutched to her breast, Lucy bent over Mr. Morrison. He was breathing, but his breaths came shallow, and there was blood in his mouth. She needed to work magic upon him, but she could not do it in the mill, not with all the wards set upon it.

"You have not much time to act," said Byron, tossing his torch onto a pile of hose. It went up at once, and the flames began to catch, spreading over the stocking frame, and then catching to the next. "Hand me the pages, Lucy. And the child. If you do not, I shall shoot you and take the pages off you myself. How shall your niece fare then?"

The building would burn in ten minutes, but Mr. Morrison had not that much time. The moment had come. She saw it with perfect clarity. She had been carrying the piece of paper upon her for weeks, for Mrs. Emmett had said she must. Mrs. Emmett had known this time would come. Lucy's fingers trembled as she reached into her sack. Doing this was against everything she believed, and yet she could not let Mr. Morrison die. Not when she had discovered that she loved him.

She took out the paper, the magic circle she had botched, the one Mrs. Emmett had saved her from using because it contained a flaw, a flaw that would set the demon free and have it assault the most arrogant living thing in the room. Here and now, that must be Byron. It had to be.

She balanced the sleeping baby in the crook of her arm while taking the circle between her fingers. Using her thumbnail, she dug savagely into her own finger until she succeeded in making a cut. It was small, but it was enough, and she let a drop of blood form upon the circle.

"What are you doing?" asked Byron. "Your spells won't work here."

"The spell was cast long ago," said Lucy. "I

merely awaken it."

It happened too quickly to see. It was like a wall of wind, dark and terrifying in its shapelessness and void. It was without form, and yet that form had a face and eyes and teeth in its nothingness. It was like the creature she had seen those months ago when she had freed Byron of his curse, but more so — blacker and more shapeless and more horrifying. It was invisible to the eye, and yet it blotted out all light. It was terror itself, and Lucy's mind reeled at the thought of what place such a being must come from.

She staggered back, remembering to hold the baby, concentrating, for she knew if she did not, she would let go. She would let go of everything — the child, her sense of self, her sanity. She had unleashed this thing upon the world, and she had to hope it did not destroy her.

The terrible, empty void lifted Byron and tossed him across the room. He hit a wall and landed upon the floor. His body rocked with spasms, and blood flowed freely from his mouth. Then he was still, his eyes wide and unblinking. Whatever manner of creature had killed him had gone back to whence it had come. It had been in the mill for but a few seconds, but Lucy believed she was lucky to have escaped with her sanity intact. Lord Byron was not so lucky. The poet lay amid the growing flames with his neck twisted into an impossible, grotesque angle. Blood poured from his nose and open mouth. Lord Byron was dead.

There was no time to regret what she had done. The fire was spreading quickly, and smoke was already choking the mill. Mrs. Quince had already fled the building. Sophie ran over to Byron's broken body, weeping silent tears.

"There is no time," Lucy cried. "He is dead. Get out before the whole place burns."

Sophie could not hear her. Had she the power to hear, she still would not have comprehended the words. She was lost in grief.

Holding Emily in one arm, Lucy put her other around Mr. Morrison's chest and began to drag him to the door. He was so heavy, and her exertion strained her every muscle, yet she would not relent. Out of the corner of her eye, she saw Sophie doing the same with Byron. She was making great progress as well. Good for her, Lucy thought. Let us see what she could do with a baby in one arm.

Emily began to cry, perhaps from the movement, perhaps from the growing heat. Lucy could spare nothing even to soothe her. She pulled and pulled, gaining ground by inches, until she managed to get Mr. Morrison out of the building and ten feet away. She dropped him, heaving, panting for breath.

Emily was wailing. Lucy saw a crowd of workingmen, of machine breakers, of Luddites. She recognized one from the crowd who had, so long ago, accosted her outside Norah Gilley's party.

"Don't worry, miss," he said. "We won't keep the mill from burning, but we'll make sure it don't spread. And we already took care of Lady Harriett's men and her woman Quince too. You do what you've got to, while we put out the fire and then destroy every frame in there." In the crowd she thought she saw a familiar form, stooped and ragged and visible only out of the corner of her eye. It was Ludd. Only it was not Ludd any longer. He was diminished — perhaps by Mary's death. Lucy could not know. Now he was but a man, a strong, healthy, and vibrant man, but no longer magnificent and unknowable

Lucy set down the baby, who continued to wail loudly, but out of fear, not pain. For now Mr. Morrison needed her. She took out her bag, and began to reach for her healing herbs. She tore open his shirt to reveal the wound, above the heart and to the right. It bled copiously. It would be fatal, she was sure, without her help, but she would keep him alive. She would save him. He would still need a surgeon to remove the bullet, but she would keep him alive until one was found.

Lucy applied her herbs. She wrote out a healing charm in the dirt around him, and gathered dirt and put it in his pocket. She placed a bloodstone and a piece of quartz in his pockets.

His breathing came more easily. He turned to her. "Byron?" he asked.

"Dead," she said.

"And me?"

"Not dead." She forced herself to smile. "I mean to keep you that way."

"If I do not live, you must not use the book on my behalf. I do not want that."

"I could not if I wished it," said Lucy. "Sophie had the book all along. I could not risk Lady Harriett finding it upon me."

Mr. Morrison tried to rise but fell back again. "You must get the pages away from her. She has knowledge of the craft."

"But what could she . . . ?" Lucy began to say, and then she saw what Mr. Morrison meant. She knew what Sophie could do with it. Holding the crying child close to her breast, she darted up to where she had last seen Sophie, but the girl was gone, as was the body of Byron. In the soft earth, two sets of footprints led away, and remaining, pressed to the earth with a stone, were only the pages of the *Mutus Liber* fluttering gently in the soft breeze as though they were not mere paper, but living things.

35

Summer was now come to the house called Harrington in Kent, and it was thus far a mild summer, pleasant but not cool enough to worry the farmers who longed for a good harvest. The days were bright and green, and Lucy could not remember ever seeing her sister, Martha, so happy. Little Emily showed no ill effects of her abduction in the spring. She was, as before, a cheerful and robust child, prone to inexplicable bouts of irritation and sadness, as were all babies, but easily soothed by her mother's kiss or a happy diversion. She was a precocious thing, not yet ten months, already spewing a babble of noises in imitation of words, crawling quite skillfully and making the occasional, if unsuccessful, attempt to walk upon her plump legs.

Lucy was gone from her Uncle Lowell's house, with no intention ever to return. She was in her old home, and she could not be happier, though her stay there was but temporary. Upon Mr. Buckles's death, Harrington reverted to an even more distant cousin, a naval captain of no small heroic reputation. He had written a long and blustery letter to Martha, proclaiming that he was in no hurry to take possession of the estate, not when there were so many French prizes yet to be had, and left the house in her care until such time as the war ended and he had the leisure to see to mundane affairs such as farming and household management. She and Martha would have to vacate sometime, but Lucy was grateful for this period of gentle transition.

She went to town but seldom, and only when necessary. Rumor of her shame at the hands of the rake poet Byron had spread quite rapidly to Kent, and Lucy could not appear in public without exposing herself to the upturned noses of women or the lecherous stares of men. The world believed Lucy would lift her skirts without hesitation, and while this infamy saddened her, she could not regret it. Her reputation was a small sacrifice to preserve the people she loved — small indeed in comparison to what Mrs. Emmett and Mary had given.

Mary had given everything to preserve England, to save Lucy and her niece, and to make certain the *Mutus Liber* did not fall into the wrong hands. Now the book was back with its true owner, and every day Lucy dedicated long hours to decoding the confusing and obscure elements of alchemy. Slowly she came to understand its symbols and how to apply them. Alchemy was change, and change was but an alteration of what was into another shape. Lead into gold, aging into immortality — these were but the low-hanging fruit that had tempted generations of alchemists, but the art was so much more than that, so much more subtle, and Lucy regularly sat up long into the night, her eyes straining by the candlelight, to grasp what was, by its nature, almost too slippery to be contained.

More than once she had almost quit the endeavor and thrown the book aside as incomprehensible madness. Or, if not that, at least too complicated for her mind. Perhaps others might make sense of it, but Lucy would entrust it to no one. In those dark moments she told herself that she need not master the book. Perhaps it was best that she not master it, and enough that she keep the book out of other hands. These moments of despair did not last long, and soon enough, feeling ashamed of her weak will, Lucy returned to the task. Mary had allowed herself to be erased from existence so that Lucy might retain control of the book. Lucy would make certain she honored Mary's sacrifice.

Lucy could not think of Mary without being struck by melancholy. She had chosen annihilation and oblivion, had elected to be blasted out of existence, with no hope of continuation or resurrection.

Or, Lucy thought, one morning a month or so after the decisive encounter at Newstead, it was what she *believed* she had done. Could Mary know, truly know, what she would face after her earthly demise? Was she not as ignorant as men are of their own fate? That something lay beyond this life was now a certainty to Lucy. She had seen far too much evidence to doubt it, but Mary could not know that she was barred from such a continuation. It soothed Lucy to think that somewhere, in some state, her friend continued.

It also comforted her to look upon those who had benefited from Mary's sacrifice. Emily thrived, as did Martha. The loss of her husband had initially been a terrible blow. Lucy had not told her sister the truth, not at first, for there was so much to absorb, but in time Lucy chose to sit Martha down and tell her everything. First she told her about the magic, proved it to her with a dozen demonstrations before Martha could bring herself to anything like belief. Then she unveiled to Martha the truth about Mr. Buckles, and all that had passed between them. It had been a difficult evening, full of tears and horror, but it had been necessary. She would not say it, but Lucy knew that Martha had accepted that if ever a creature deserved destruction, it was Mr. Buckles, a man willing to sacrifice his own child at his mistress's whim.

Martha's life was made easier by not wanting for money. Martha immediately gave Lucy the five thousand pounds that should have come to her upon the death of their father. The money itself meant not so much to Lucy, now that she was free of her uncle's tyranny, as well as any threats of unwanted marriage. She also felt certain she could use her talents to meet any needs. What mattered to her was that her father's wishes had, at last, been fulfilled, and that somewhere he knew that. Other than the safe return of her niece, nothing she had done in her life gave her more satisfaction.

Lucy had exchanged several letters with Mr. Blake, who accepted her recounting of the events at Newstead without question, finding nothing strange or improbable in anything. He had sent to Lucy copies of his handcrafted books, which were strange and perplexing things, but Lucy treasured them, and believed they might contain important information if only she could figure out how to make sense of them.

As for Mr. Morrison, little was heard of him in the many weeks subsequent to the incident at Newstead. The ball from Byron's pistol had not done serious harm to his heart or his lungs, but it had shattered a portion of his collarbone, and his recovery had been both long and painful. Lucy had done what she could in those early days when he was too fragile to move and was confined to his room at a Nottingham inn. She showered him with talismans and herbs and poultices. She spent hours each day leafing through her books for formulas and secrets that might speed his recovery. That she did much good was beyond question, for his surgeon, who feared for his life, was amazed at how quickly Mr. Morrison recovered despite the severity of the injury.

Nevertheless, the wound required a long convalescence, and as soon as he was well enough to travel, he took his leave and departed for his family estate in Derbyshire. Lucy had received a few letters from him, in which he discussed very little but his health. He thanked her for all she had done on his behalf and that of the country.

In response, Lucy wrote him long and chatty letters, informing him of the circumstances of her family, whose happiness owed much to his efforts and sacrifices. In one letter she spoke of her opinion about Mary's fate, about how no one could truly know her ultimate destiny. To this note she had received no answer, and Lucy feared she had overstepped her bounds. It seemed to her that she might never hear from him again.

Then, in midsummer, she received notice from Mr. Morrison that he was much recovered and was now traveling. He wished to call upon Lucy and her sister. He did so, without any further warning, some weeks later.

Lucy watched from the window as he exited his carriage, and the delight she felt upon seeing him took her by surprise. She wanted to see him. She knew that. She had been anticipating his visit each day, feeling disappointed when there was no word from him. And yet, despite all that, she had not expected to feel as though the breath had been struck from her lungs. She had not expected her heart to thunder so alarmingly or her hands to shake. She had begun to suspect that the feelings for him that had come upon her in those dark days were an illusion brought about by the danger of their adventures, but now, seeing him healthy and recovered, she realized that it was far more than that. She knew that she had been living for this moment.

Martha rushed to the door and ushered Mr. Morrison within. Lucy marveled to see him so strong and healthy. A little thinner and more drawn in the face, but his color was good, and he appeared quite cheerful. He wore a handsome light brown suit, and looked so . . . so, Lucy did not know what. Remarkable, she supposed. He appeared healthy and confident and comfortable. He appeared every bit the man who had so fascinated her four years ago, and every bit the man she had fallen in love with only months past.

When he set eyes upon Lucy, he colored considerably, and rose from his chair in the sitting room to bow to her. Lucy felt herself break into a great smile, and it was all she could to do keep herself from embracing him.

After much fussing about tea and cakes and fruit, the three of them sat together for well over an hour, and little of moment was discussed beyond Mr. Morrison's health, which he claimed was as good as could be expected. He still experienced some pain and limitations in movement — a result of the ball remaining lodged in his flesh — but his recovery had far exceeded even the most optimistic hopes of the medical men, and he could complain but little.

After a sufficient time had passed, Mr. Morrison cleared his throat and inquired if anyone would care to walk outside on so beautiful a day. Lucy at once expressed her enthusiasm for the notion, but Martha had the good sense to decline. And so it was that the two of them went outside to stroll down the country lane in the general vicinity of town.

"The Luddites continue their insurrection," said Lucy after a prolonged silence. "I read that they make inroads into Lancashire and Yorkshire."

"And my own Derbyshire as well," said Mr. Morrison. His voice was easy and neutral. "Ludd's power is now one of influence and inclination. He can lead men to destroy what he hates, but little more. They make their statement, and perhaps it is even a statement that needs to be made, but I do not think their insurrection will amount to much."

"So I failed?"

Mr. Morrison laughed. "*They* failed to end the world as we know it, certainly, but I do not consider your efforts a failure. Ludd's vision was as flawed and dangerous as Lady Harriett's. Neither side has won, and we will find a balance in the end. The world found its third way and did so because of your actions."

Lucy blushed, but she also smiled.

"I appreciated your words regarding Mary," he added. "I can hope she still continues somewhere, but I cannot know, and in that I suppose I am like any widower. Perhaps that is some comfort. I loved her excessively, you know."

"I know you did," said Lucy, her eyes cast down.

"But that was long ago. You must know I told you the truth when I said I had no pretensions that the woman you knew as Mary Crawford was the woman I loved as Mary Morrison. What she did, destroying herself, was courageous beyond anything I have witnessed. She was a heroine of the first order, but Mary, my Mary, would not have done that. My Mary would not have abandoned hope. This was not a better person, but a different one. I shall honor her sacrifice forever, but I did not lose my wife a second time."

"I wish I could say I understand," said Lucy. "I believe you, but it is so hard to comprehend how you can differentiate them so."

"The rest of the world saw your niece as what she had always been, but you saw a monster."

"I saw what it truly was."

"Yes," said Mr. Morrison.

They were silent for a long time. Then Lucy said, "Will you kill Byron?"

Mr. Morrison laughed and shook his head. "I do value your directness, Lucy. I shall be direct too. I do not know what I shall do. He is revived but much altered, and so not the same man who shot me or killed Mary. I don't see how I can take my revenge upon him."

"He is certainly living the life of a libertine poet still," said Lucy. "The papers are filled with his exploits."

"Yes, but I shan't kill him for his libertinism. Or for his poetry, for that matter."

Lucy could not think of a fitting response. It was not for her to say what Mr. Morrison should do with this new incarnation of Byron. She did not know what Byron was now, but she could not help but think that an immortal Byron — one with unthinkable strength and one free to live outside the laws of men — must be worse than the old one. When she thought of what he had been, Lucy felt nothing but contempt for him and disgust for herself for having been deceived. She could not say if the revived Byron deserved the punishment of his mortal self, but she hoped never again to have to look upon him.

"I am curious," said Mr. Morrison. "I long to know what you have learned from the *Mutus Liber.* What shall you do with your new knowledge and power? Do you have plans?"

"Do you ask this on behalf of the Rosicrucians?"

"No, on behalf of myself."

"I have hardly even begun to decipher its mysteries," she said, "but what I have learned so far is beyond wonder and astonishment. What I have been able to do staggers the imagination. As to what I shall do next, I should like to end the war with France."

He studied her. "You believe you can do that?"

Lucy nodded. "I know I can, though it may take some time, and I may require the resources of an organization such as yours."

"It is at your disposal," he said, reaching into his coat. He handed Lucy a sealed envelope, thick with documents. "As is much else. I know you need not fear for your sister's generosity, but it is good to be independent as well. Before she died, Mary Crawford initiated a series of costly legal investigations on your behalf. Apparently she also instructed her solicitor that if anything were to happen to her, I was to take up the cause. Perhaps she feared more funds would be required and knew I would be willing to pay. In any event, the matter has been brought to a close more speedily than anyone had expected, I believe because of documents that have surfaced following Mr. Buckles's death."

Lucy took the documents. "What is this?"

"Information relating to your father's will, and proof that you were cheated. Your father's library, and your share of your inheritance, is now yours. There will be some trips to London required to sort it all out officially, but the work is largely done."

"I am so grateful to you," she said.

He shook his head. "I am but the messenger, though I am happy to deliver such happy intelligence."

They walked another few moments in silence, and then Mr. Morrison stopped. He took Lucy's hand in his and gazed directly upon her. "Do you remember Mary's last words to me, Lucy?"

Lucy nodded. "She said that you must not let the past stop you. I believe she was trying to tell you something important, though I did not understand the message."

"I understood her, for even in her altered state she knew me well. I required time to recover in body and in spirit. I have done both, and find myself compelled to ask you, Lucy, if you could ever forgive me for what happened between us those years ago? I know deceiving you was inexcusable. I know I made you miserable and you had every right to hate me, but I hope — I have dared to hope — that you might see things differently now."

Her face felt as though it were on fire. "You withheld the truth from me out of loyalty to my father and because you believed it was best for me to do so. You deprived yourself for my sake. I cannot blame you for doing what you thought was right."

He fixed her hard with his eyes, as though attempting to take in every detail of her face. "You said shortly before we arrived in Newstead that you had come to hate me less than you had. I have dared to hope, Lucy, that your feelings were something more than a diminished hatred — that they had turned in an entirely new direction."

She wanted to look away, to dissemble, to pretend that she did not understand him, but that was no longer who she was. She did not play such games. She looked at him and nodded. "They have."

"I had convinced myself my love for you

was gone, something never to be recovered. It was a lie, I told myself, because I could not endure the truth. But your courage and cleverness and beauty and spirit have awoken in me what I have tried so hard to keep dormant. Should you reject me, I must still always be in your debt for rekindling in me a sense of hope and wonder I never again thought I would feel. I pray you will not reject me, however. You are your own woman now and must depend upon no one. You are free to make your own choices without fear of want, and so I may ask you now what I have so wanted to ask, and know your answer will be dictated only by your heart. Lucy, I pray you will agree to be my wife."

Lucy let go of his hand and stepped away from him. "Perhaps you don't understand, but as a result of my actions in London, my reputation has suffered, and I could not ask —"

"I don't give a damn about your reputation. You speak of ending the war with France, and yet you worry what the grocer whispers to the fishmonger? Or worse. You think *I* might care what gossips say! I care only for you and who you are and what I know you to be. I care for what I have seen with my own eyes and loved with my own heart, and I ask you again if you will marry me."

Lucy stepped back toward him and took

both his hands in her own. "Dear Lord, yes. I love you, and I will marry you."

He leaned forward and kissed her. It was soft and sweet and tentative, as though he was afraid he might break her, and she loved him even more for his gentleness.

"We must marry soon," he said.

"Very soon," she agreed.

A tear formed in Mr. Morrison's eye, and he turned away, gently released her hand, and then began to walk. However, he stopped at once and moved his neck back and forth in a curious fashion.

"Is something wrong?" asked Lucy, hardly able to conceal a smile.

He continued to move his neck, to twist his shoulders. "It is the ball from Byron's pistol. The surgeon could not remove it, and I feel it always when I move, but I do not feel it now."

"No," said Lucy, grinning quite freely. "I don't suppose you do." She held out her fist and then opened it, palm upward, to show Mr. Morrison a compressed piece of metal, a flattened and blasted ball, glittering in the summer sun.

Mr. Morrison stared at it. "But how? How can it be possible?"

She could not suppress a grin. "The *Mutus Liber* has changed my notion of what is possible and what is not."

Mr. Morrison opened his mouth to speak,

closed it, and then tried again. "But how did you do it? How can it be?"

Lucy began to walk back toward the house. After a moment, she turned around to glance at the still motionless Mr. Morrison. Everything felt right to her, as right as it had in a very long time, and that unfamiliar sensation that washed over her was happiness, and something more. It was the feeling of living a life that was hers, of being herself, of being home. Things felt *right,* and she liked the sensation very much indeed.

Lucy laughed and then indulged herself a coquettish shrug, before turning away to walk, knowing that it mattered not where she went, for he would follow. "How?" she repeated over her shoulder. "Surely, you know the answer to your own question, Mr. Morrison. It is magic."

ABOUT THE AUTHOR

David Liss is the author of *The Whiskey Rebels, The Ethical Assassin, A Spectacle of Corruption, The Coffee Trader,* and *A Conspiracy of Paper,* winner of the 2000 Edgar Award for Best First Novel. He lives in San Antonio with his wife and children.

The employees of Thorndike Press hope you have enjoyed this Large Print book. All our Thorndike, Wheeler, and Kennebec Large Print titles are designed for easy reading, and all our books are made to last. Other Thorndike Press Large Print books are available at your library, through selected bookstores, or directly from us.

For information about titles, please call:

(800) 223-1244

or visit our Web site at:

http://gale.cengage.com/thorndike

To share your comments, please write:

Publisher
Thorndike Press
10 Water St., Suite 310
Waterville, ME 04901